Chapter 4: Garuda of Fire

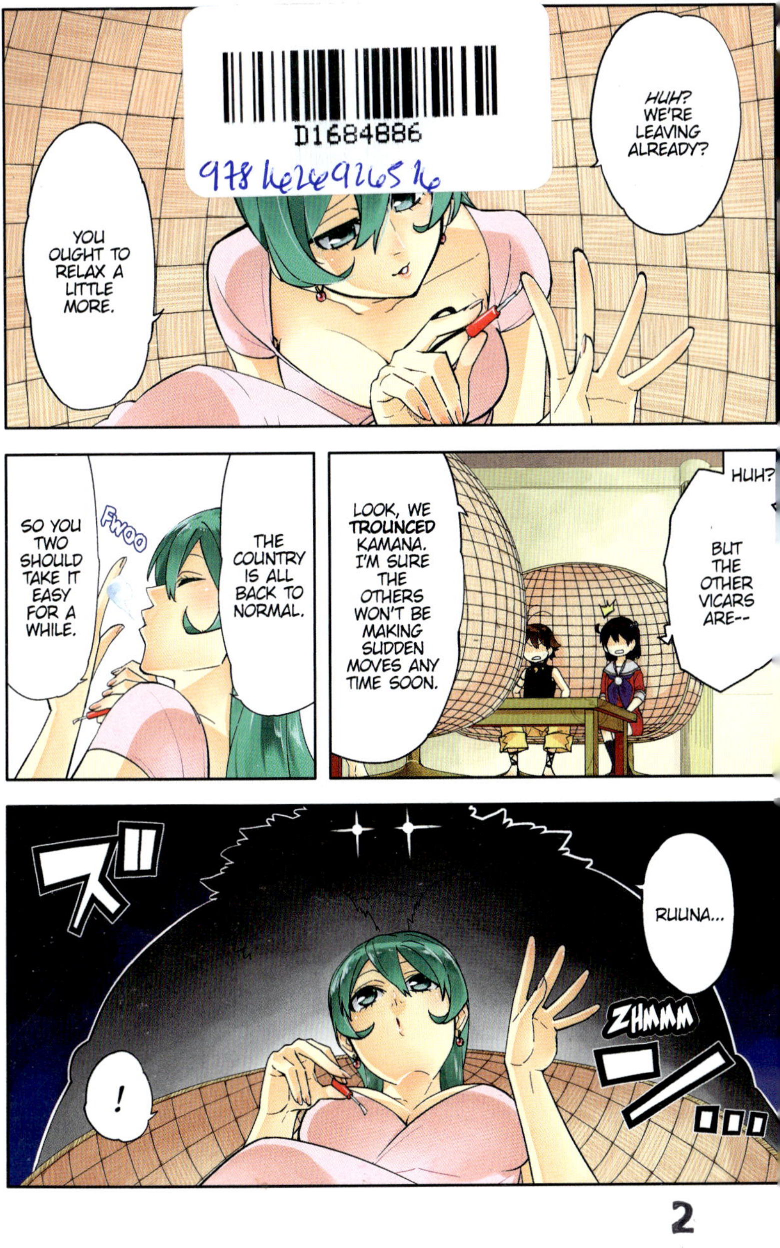
HUH? WE'RE LEAVING ALREADY?
YOU OUGHT TO RELAX A LITTLE MORE.
HUH?
BUT THE OTHER VICARS ARE--
LOOK, WE **TROUNCED** KAMANA. I'M SURE THE OTHERS WON'T BE MAKING SUDDEN MOVES ANY TIME SOON.
THE COUNTRY IS ALL BACK TO NORMAL.
FWOO
SO YOU TWO SHOULD TAKE IT EASY FOR A WHILE.
RUUNA...
ZHMMM
ズ
!

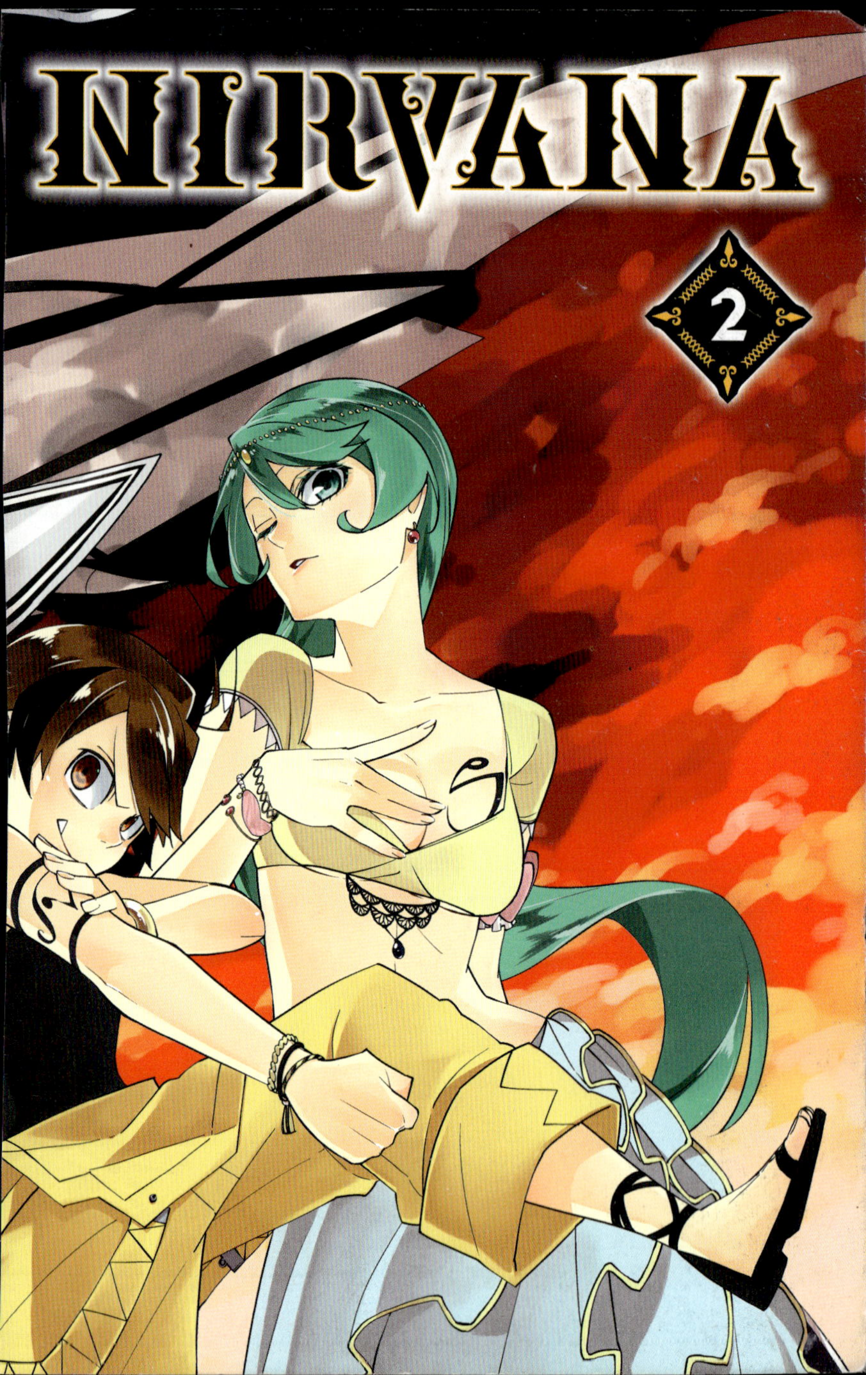
NIRVANA
2

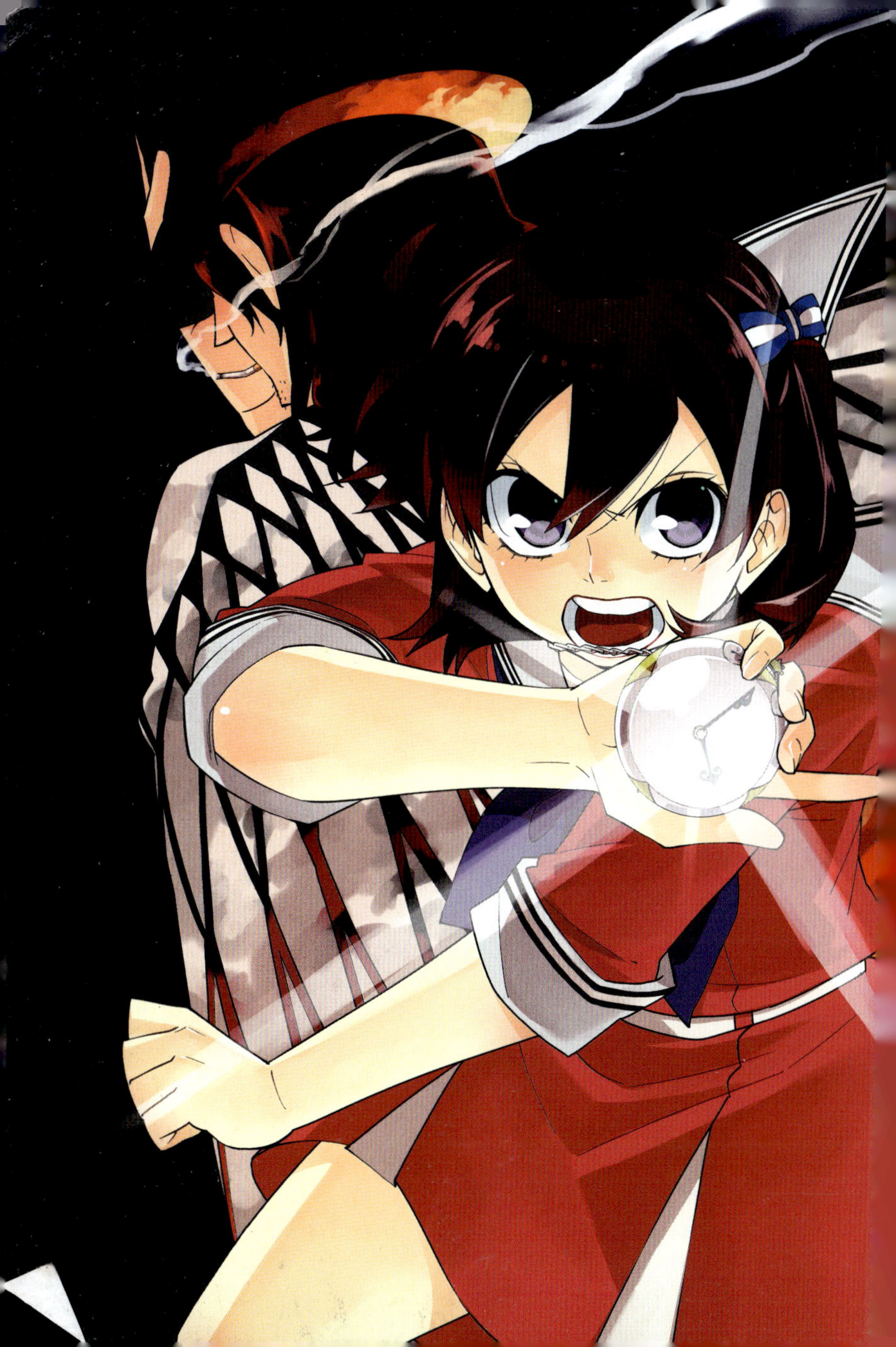

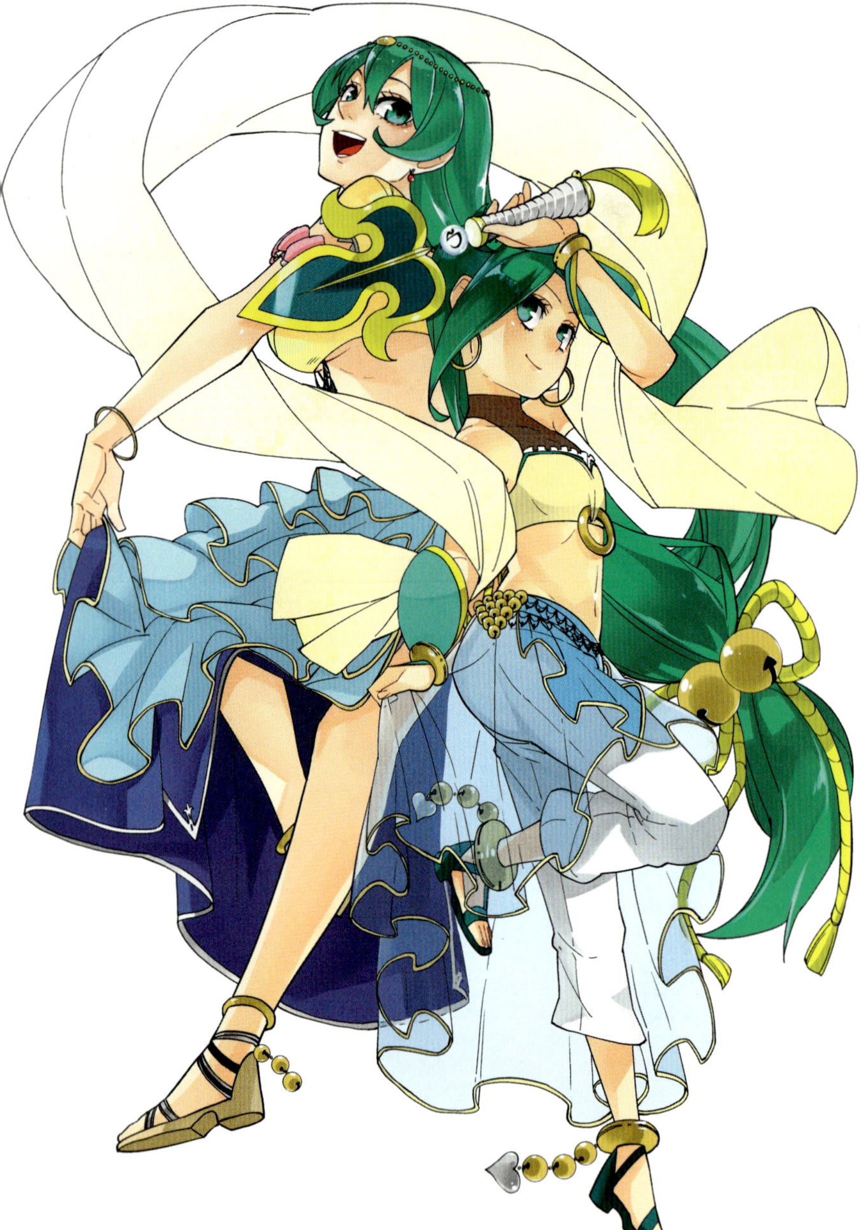

CHARACTERS

Jin & Sayuki
Present
NIRVANA Vol.2

Maru Barah

The "boar" of the Twelve, he possesses the Nidana of Earth. To fulfill his older brother's wishes, he decided to follow Yachiyo.

Ruuna Sarubaaj

The princess of Mahar. She is the "monkey" of the Twelve and carries the Nidana of Wind. Bewitched to appear as an old lady, she was saved by Yachiyo.

Yachiyo Hitotose

A girl called the "modern-day Florence Nightingale" by others. She can use the legendary power of "Nirvana."

Tenka

A boy who peered at Yachiyo and the others in the Country of the Monkey.

STORY

Yachiyo awakens as the reincarnation of the goddess Sakuya in a foreign world called Gulgraf. Upon witnessing the suffering caused by the blau, she stands up to save the world. In order to defeat the Vicars, Yachiyo and Maru depart on a journey to search for the other Twelve, who each hold the power of Nidana. They first arrive in the Country of the Monkey, Mahar, but immediately get captured by the Vicar Kamana of Lies, who was impersonating the king. Yachiyo manages to escape certain death by activating Nirvana with help from the true "monkey" of the Twelve, the princess Ruuna. Yet a mysterious boy stands in the distance, observing Yachiyo and the others...

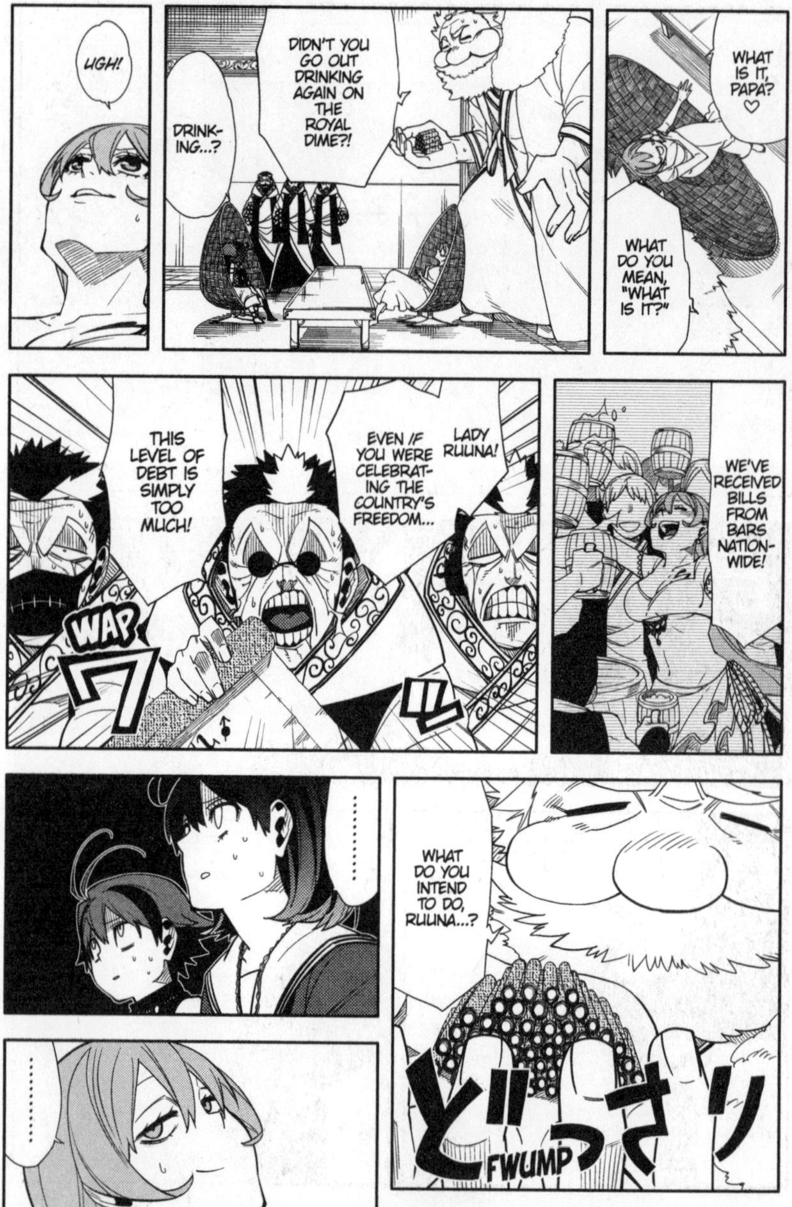
WHAT IS IT, PAPA? ♡
WHAT DO YOU MEAN, "WHAT IS IT?"
DIDN'T YOU GO OUT DRINKING AGAIN ON THE ROYAL DIME?!
DRINK-ING...?
UGH!
WE'VE RECEIVED BILLS FROM BARS NATION-WIDE!
LADY RUUNA!
EVEN IF YOU WERE CELEBRAT-ING THE COUNTRY'S FREEDOM...
THIS LEVEL OF DEBT IS SIMPLY TOO MUCH!
WAP
WHAT DO YOU INTEND TO DO, RUUNA...?
どっさり
FWUMP
......
......

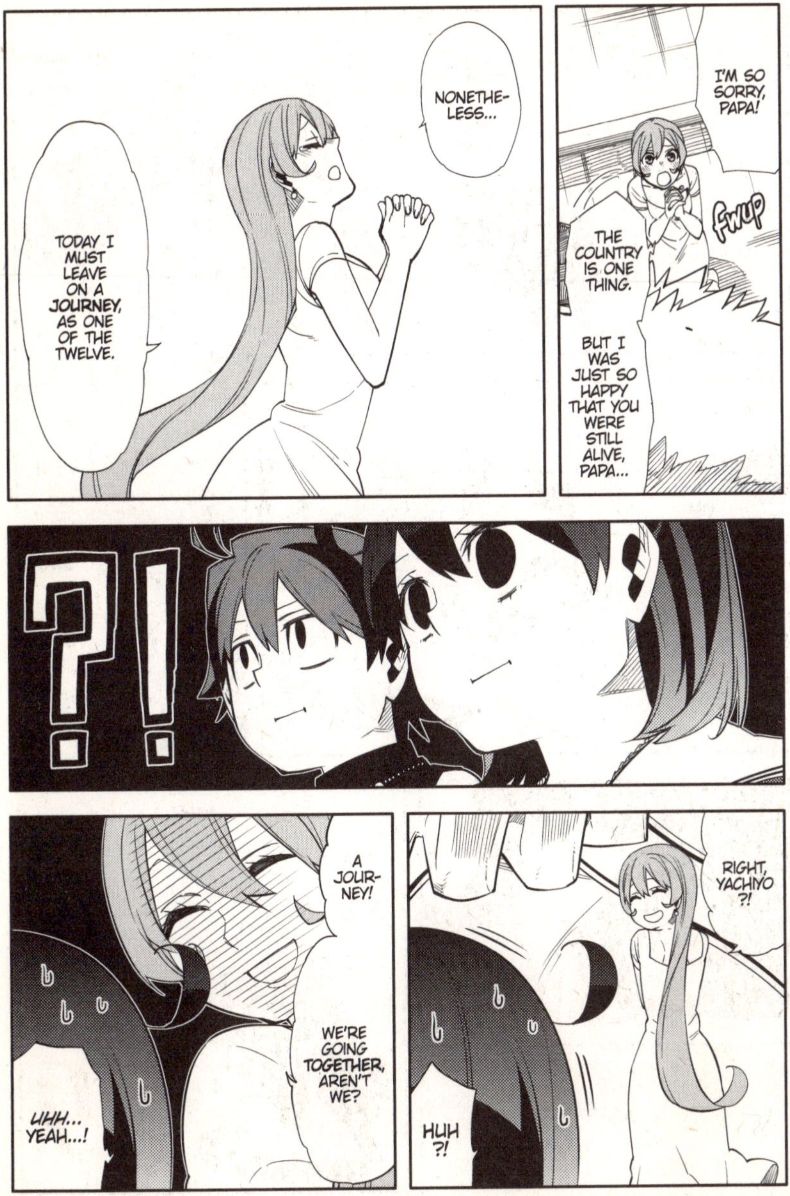
I'M SO SORRY, PAPA!
FWUP
THE COUNTRY IS ONE THING.
BUT I WAS JUST SO HAPPY THAT YOU WERE STILL ALIVE, PAPA...
NONETHE-LESS...
TODAY I MUST LEAVE ON A JOURNEY, AS ONE OF THE TWELVE.
?!
RIGHT, YACHIYO ?!
HUH ?!
A JOUR-NEY!
WE'RE GOING TOGETHER, AREN'T WE?
UHH... YEAH...!

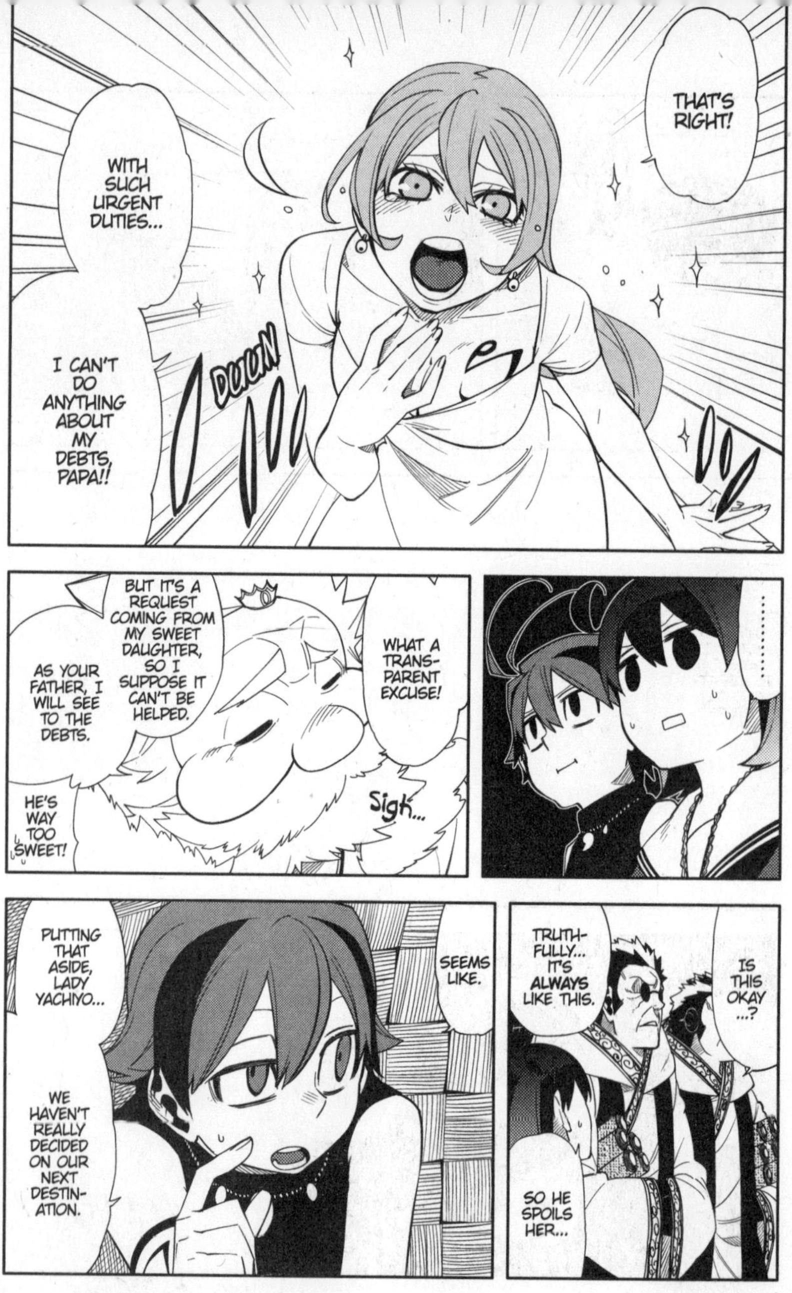
THAT'S RIGHT!
WITH SUCH URGENT DUTIES...
DUUN
I CAN'T DO ANYTHING ABOUT MY DEBTS, PAPA!!
......
WHAT A TRANSPARENT EXCUSE!
BUT IT'S A REQUEST COMING FROM MY SWEET DAUGHTER, SO I SUPPOSE IT CAN'T BE HELPED.
AS YOUR FATHER, I WILL SEE TO THE DEBTS.
Sigh...
HE'S WAY TOO SWEET!
IS THIS OKAY...?
TRUTHFULLY... IT'S ALWAYS LIKE THIS.
SO HE SPOILS HER...
SEEMS LIKE.
PUTTING THAT ASIDE, LADY YACHIYO...
WE HAVEN'T REALLY DECIDED ON OUR NEXT DESTINATION.

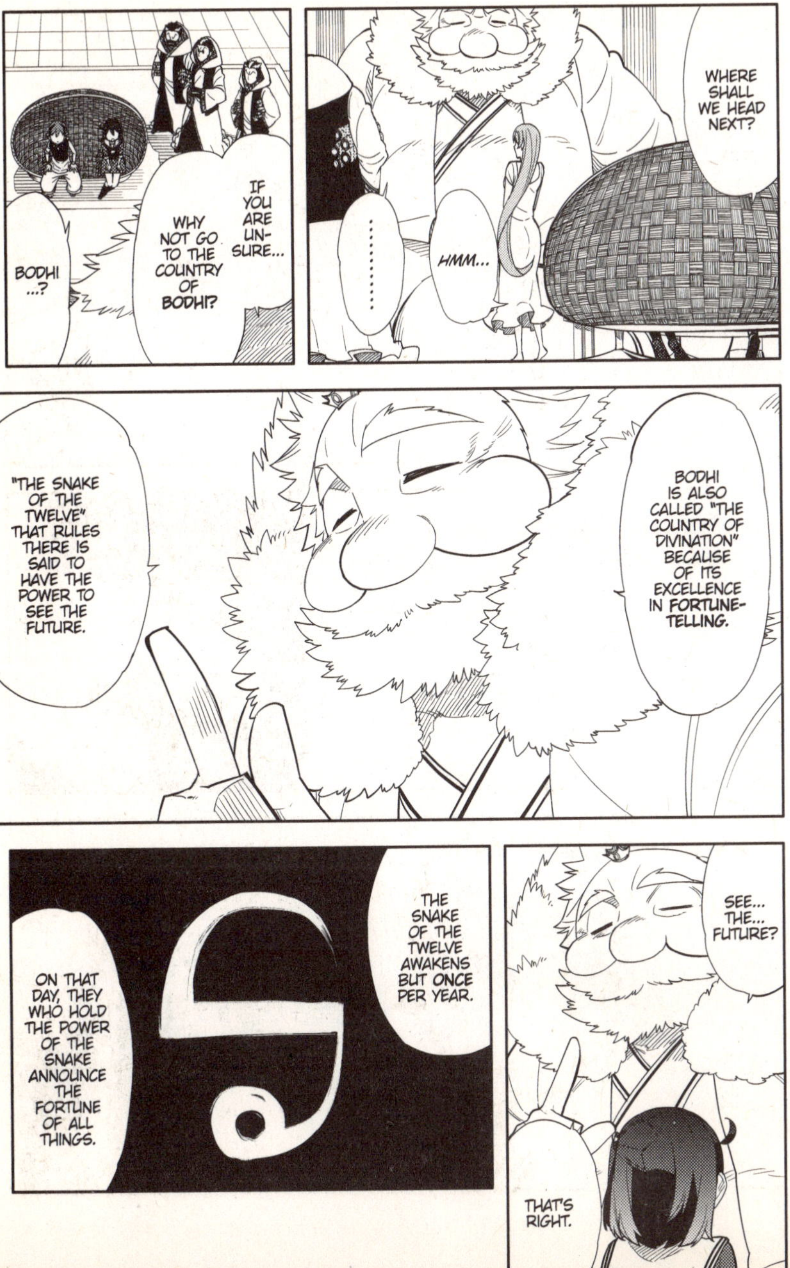
WHERE SHALL WE HEAD NEXT?
HMM...
....
IF YOU ARE UN-SURE...
WHY NOT GO TO THE COUNTRY OF BODHI?
BODHI ...?
BODHI IS ALSO CALLED "THE COUNTRY OF DIVINATION" BECAUSE OF ITS EXCELLENCE IN **FORTUNE-TELLING.**
"THE SNAKE OF THE TWELVE" THAT RULES THERE IS SAID TO HAVE THE POWER TO SEE THE FUTURE.
SEE... THE... FUTURE?
THAT'S RIGHT.
THE SNAKE OF THE TWELVE AWAKENS BUT **ONCE** PER YEAR.
ON THAT DAY, THEY WHO HOLD THE POWER OF THE SNAKE ANNOUNCE THE FORTUNE OF ALL THINGS.

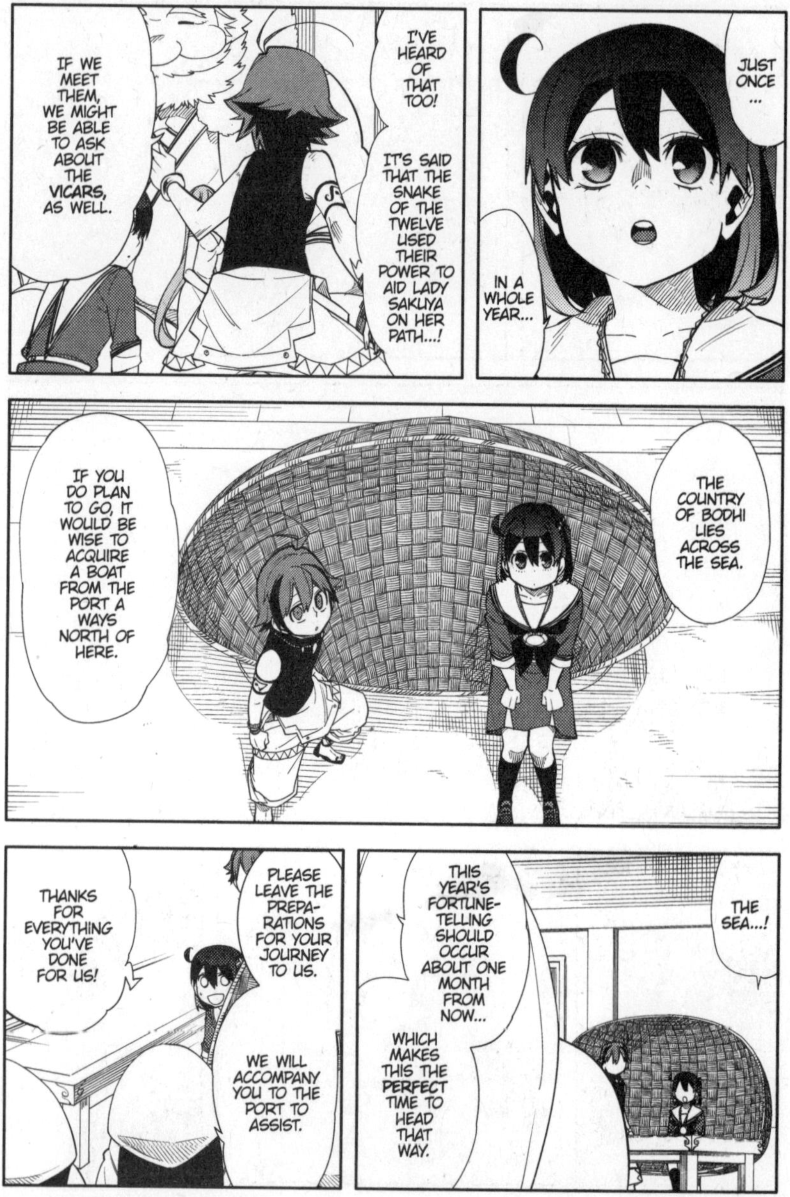
JUST ONCE ...
IN A WHOLE YEAR...
I'VE HEARD OF THAT TOO!
IT'S SAID THAT THE SNAKE OF THE TWELVE USED THEIR POWER TO AID LADY SAKUYA ON HER PATH...!
IF WE MEET THEM, WE MIGHT BE ABLE TO ASK ABOUT THE VICARS, AS WELL.
THE COUNTRY OF BODHI LIES ACROSS THE SEA.
IF YOU DO PLAN TO GO, IT WOULD BE WISE TO ACQUIRE A BOAT FROM THE PORT A WAYS NORTH OF HERE.
THE SEA...!
THIS YEAR'S FORTUNE-TELLING SHOULD OCCUR ABOUT ONE MONTH FROM NOW...
WHICH MAKES THIS THE PERFECT TIME TO HEAD THAT WAY.
PLEASE LEAVE THE PREPA-RATIONS FOR YOUR JOURNEY TO US.
WE WILL ACCOMPANY YOU TO THE PORT TO ASSIST.
THANKS FOR EVERYTHING YOU'VE DONE FOR US!

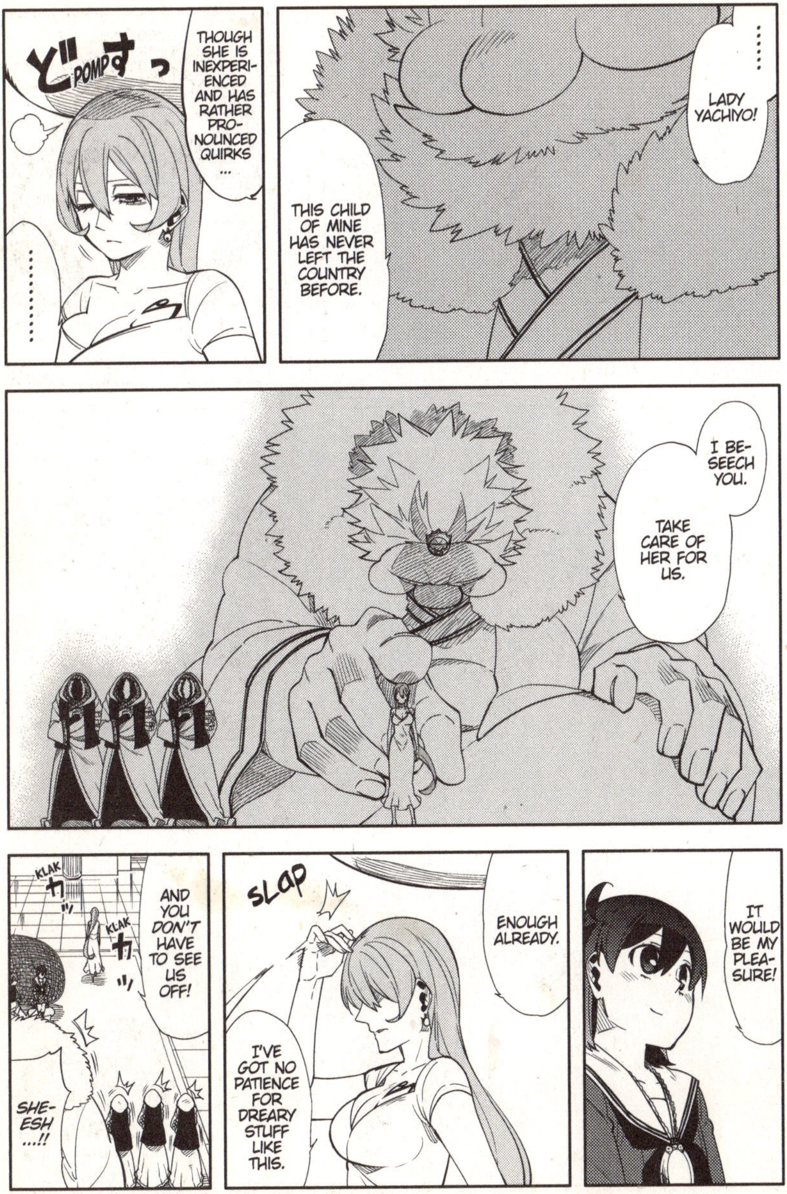
......
LADY YACHIYO!
THIS CHILD OF MINE HAS NEVER LEFT THE COUNTRY BEFORE.
THOUGH SHE IS INEXPERIENCED AND HAS RATHER PRONOUNCED QUIRKS ...
どすっ POMP
......
I BESEECH YOU.
TAKE CARE OF HER FOR US.
IT WOULD BE MY PLEASURE!
ENOUGH ALREADY.
SLAP
I'VE GOT NO PATIENCE FOR DREARY STUFF LIKE THIS.
AND YOU DON'T HAVE TO SEE US OFF!
KLAK カッ
KLAK カッ
SHEESH ....!!

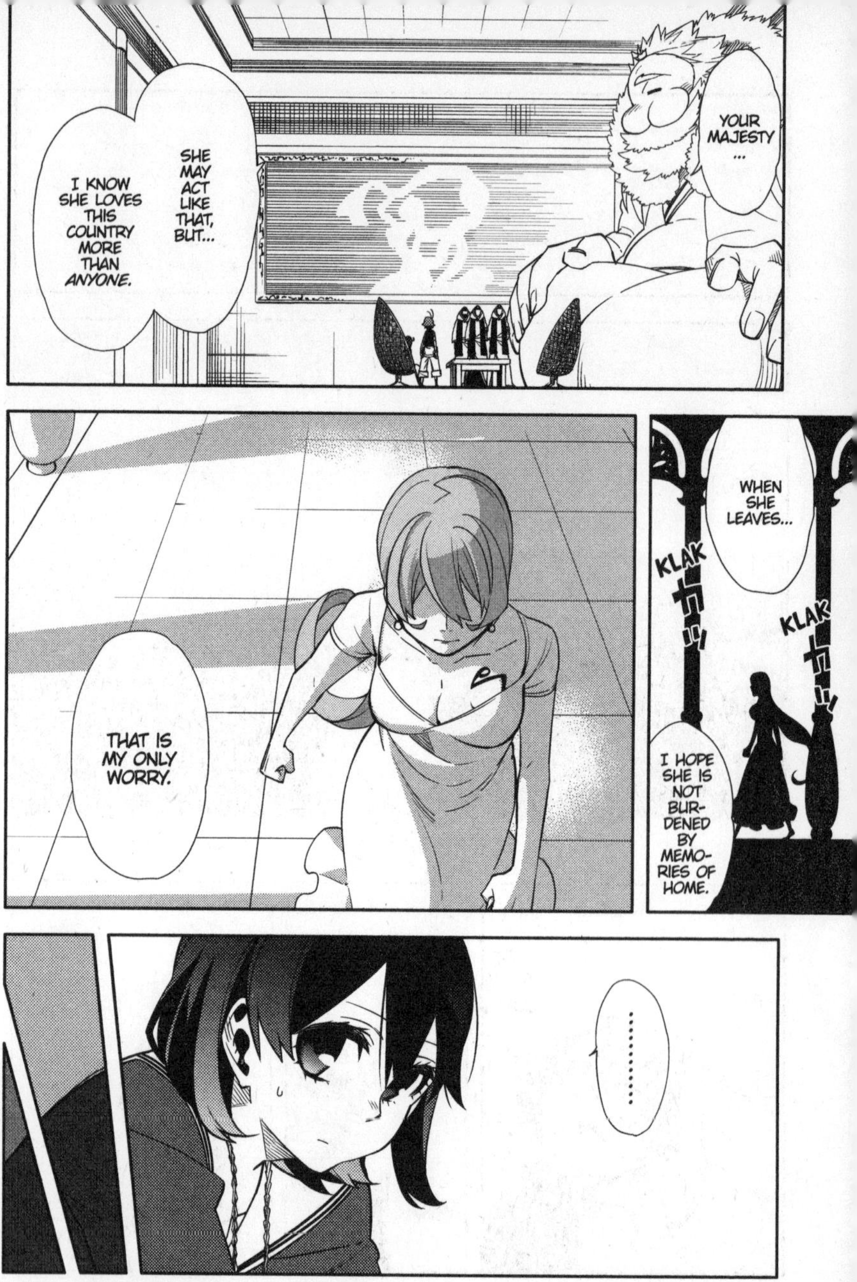
YOUR MAJESTY ...
SHE MAY ACT LIKE THAT, BUT...
I KNOW SHE LOVES THIS COUNTRY MORE THAN ANYONE.
WHEN SHE LEAVES...
KLAK
KLAK
I HOPE SHE IS NOT BURDENED BY MEMORIES OF HOME.
THAT IS MY ONLY WORRY.
....

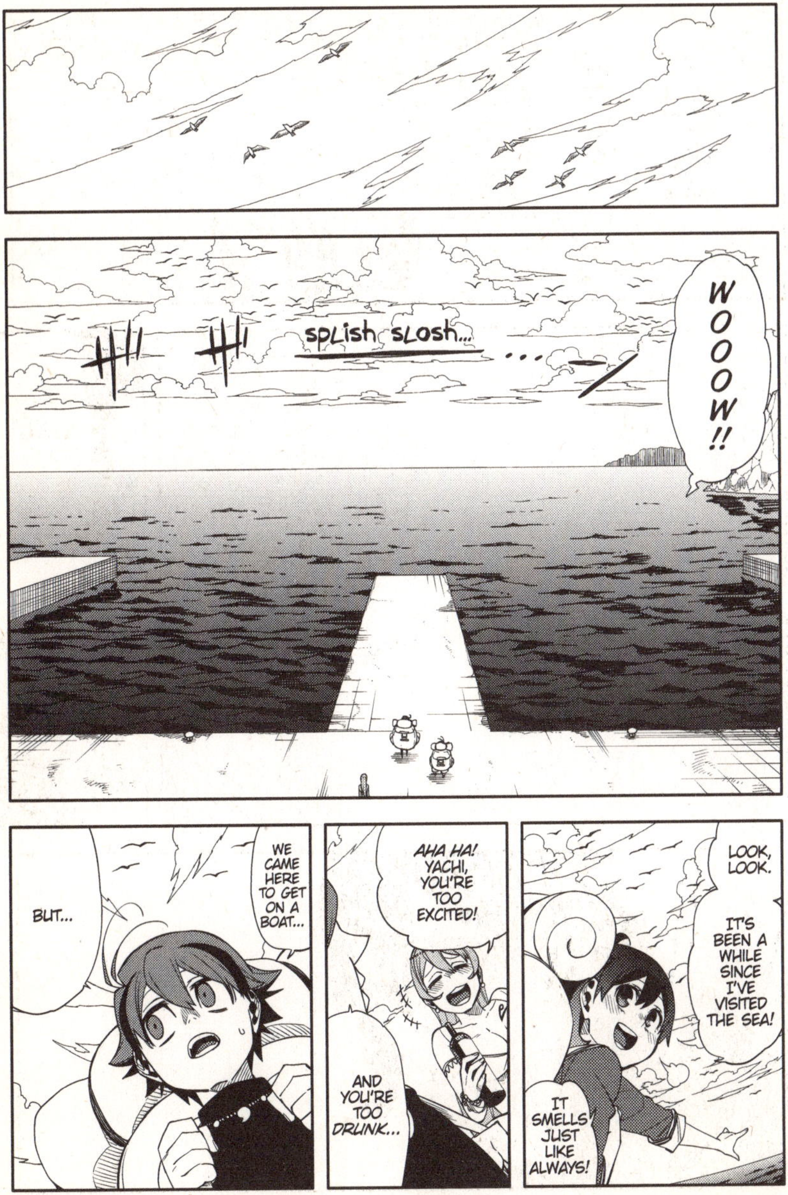
WOOOOW!!
splish slosh...
LOOK, LOOK.
IT'S BEEN A WHILE SINCE I'VE VISITED THE SEA!
IT SMELLS JUST LIKE ALWAYS!
AHA HA! YACHI, YOU'RE TOO EXCITED!
AND YOU'RE TOO DRUNK...
WE CAME HERE TO GET ON A BOAT...
BUT...

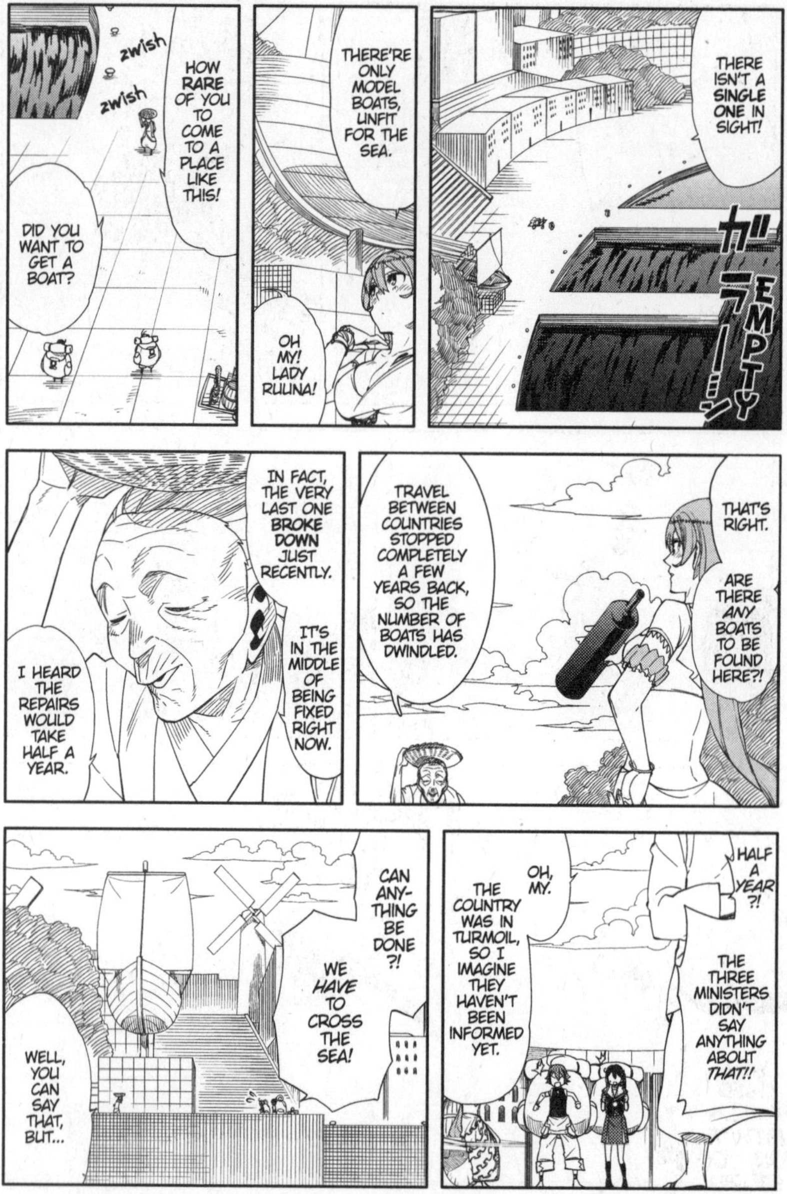
THERE ISN'T A SINGLE ONE IN SIGHT!
ガラーン
EMPTY
THERE'RE ONLY MODEL BOATS, UNFIT FOR THE SEA.
OH MY! LADY RUUNA!
HOW RARE OF YOU TO COME TO A PLACE LIKE THIS!
zwish
zwish
DID YOU WANT TO GET A BOAT?
THAT'S RIGHT.
ARE THERE *ANY* BOATS TO BE FOUND HERE?!
TRAVEL BETWEEN COUNTRIES STOPPED COMPLETELY A FEW YEARS BACK, SO THE NUMBER OF BOATS HAS DWINDLED.
IN FACT, THE VERY LAST ONE **BROKE DOWN** JUST RECENTLY.
IT'S IN THE MIDDLE OF BEING FIXED RIGHT NOW.
I HEARD THE REPAIRS WOULD TAKE HALF A YEAR.
HALF A *YEAR*?!
THE THREE MINISTERS DIDN'T SAY ANYTHING ABOUT *THAT*!!
OH, MY.
THE COUNTRY WAS IN TURMOIL, SO I IMAGINE THEY HAVEN'T BEEN INFORMED YET.
CAN ANYTHING BE DONE?!
WE *HAVE* TO CROSS THE SEA!
WELL, YOU CAN SAY THAT, BUT...

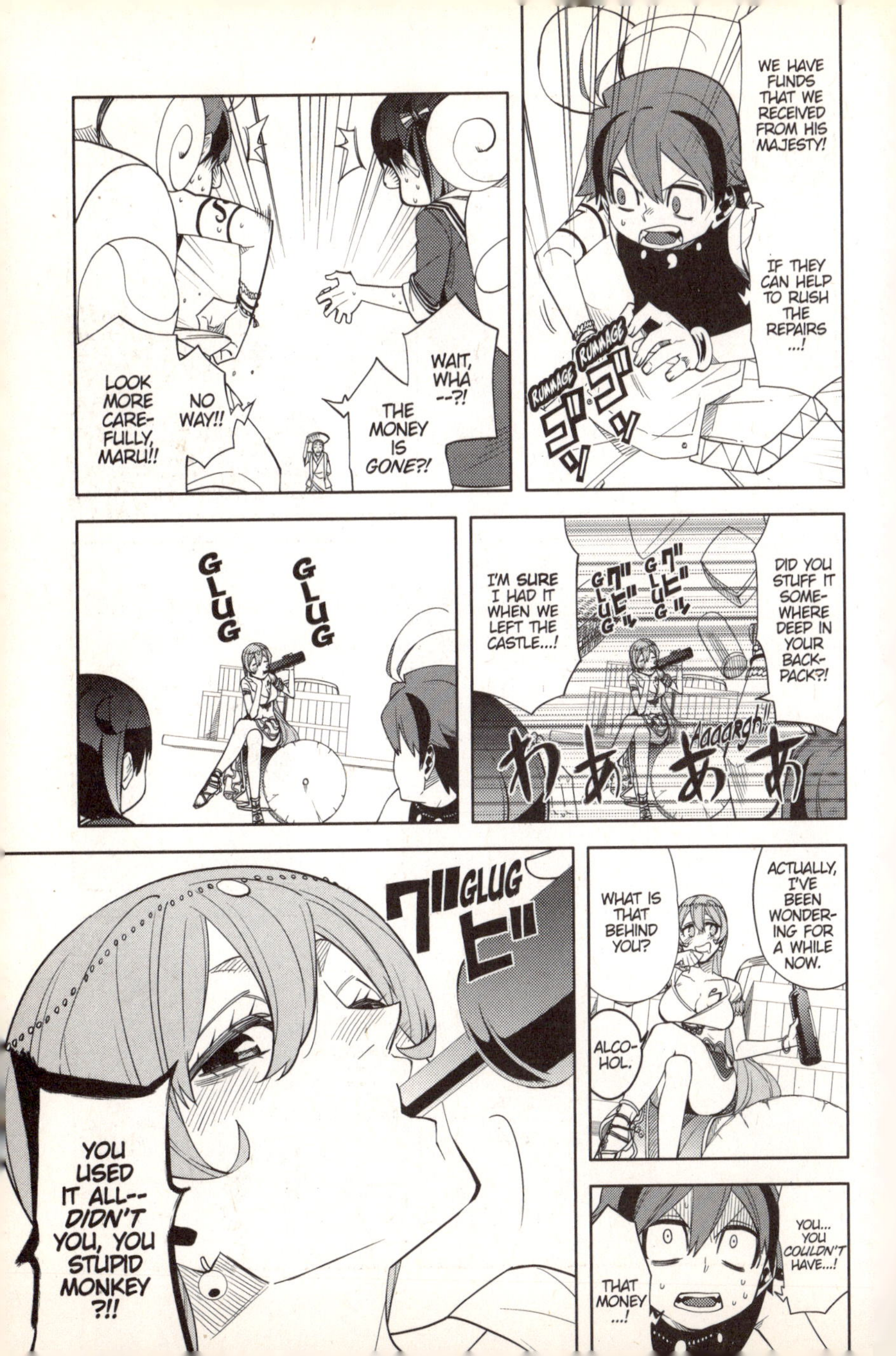
WE HAVE FUNDS THAT WE RECEIVED FROM HIS MAJESTY!
IF THEY CAN HELP TO RUSH THE REPAIRS ...!
RUMMAGE RUMMAGE
WAIT, WHA --?!
THE MONEY IS GONE?!
NO WAY!!
LOOK MORE CARE-FULLY, MARU!!
DID YOU STUFF IT SOME-WHERE DEEP IN YOUR BACK-PACK?!
I'M SURE I HAD IT WHEN WE LEFT THE CASTLE...!
GLUG GLUG
Aaaargh!!
わあああ
GLUG GLUG
ACTUALLY, I'VE BEEN WONDER-ING FOR A WHILE NOW.
WHAT IS THAT BEHIND YOU?
ALCO-HOL.
YOU... YOU COULDN'T HAVE...!
THAT MONEY ...!
GLUG
YOU USED IT ALL-- DIDN'T YOU, YOU STUPID MONKEY ?!!

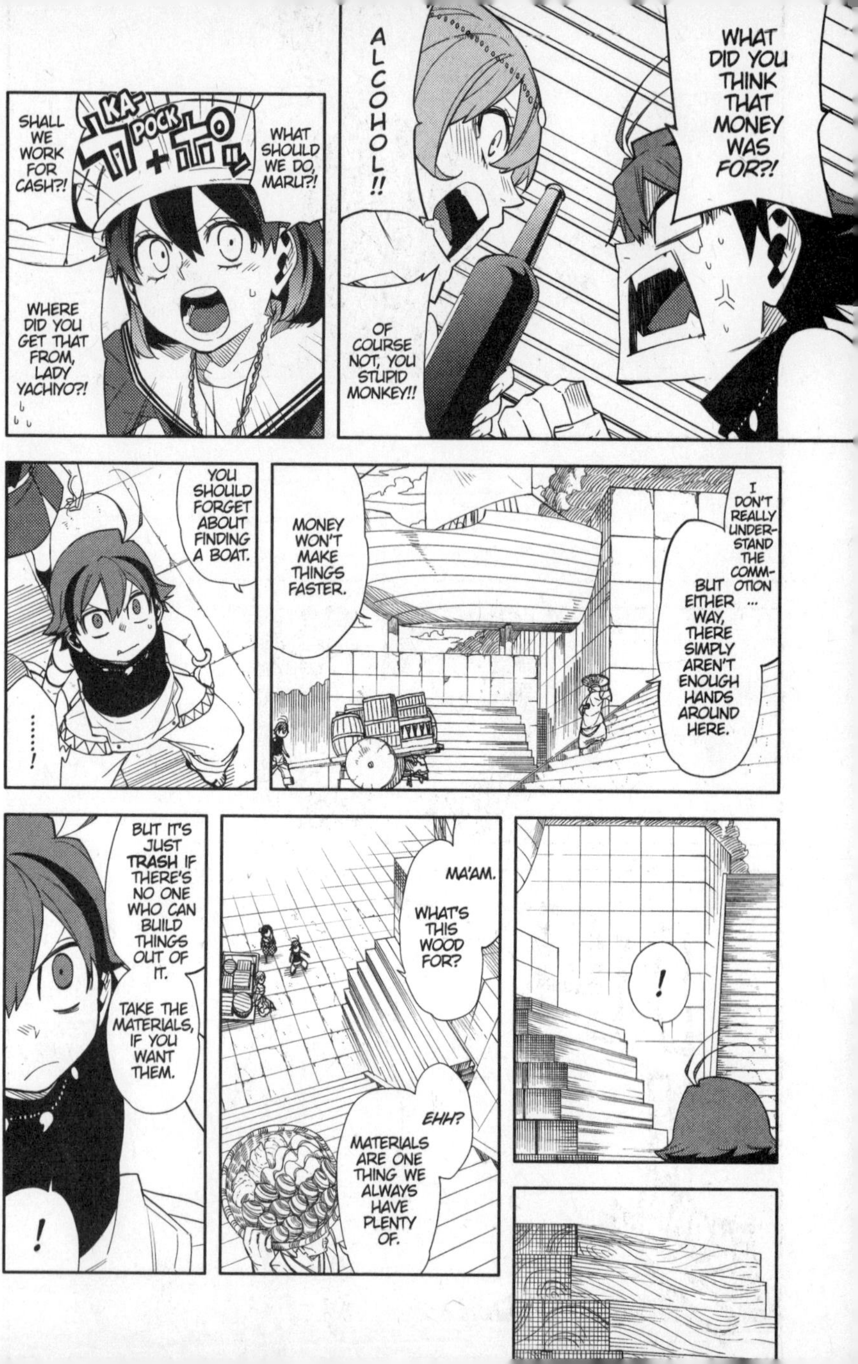
WHAT DID YOU THINK THAT MONEY WAS FOR?!
ALCOHOL!!
OF COURSE NOT, YOU STUPID MONKEY!!
WHAT SHOULD WE DO, MARU?!
SHALL WE WORK FOR CASH?!
KA-POCK
WHERE DID YOU GET THAT FROM, LADY YACHIYO?!
I DON'T REALLY UNDERSTAND THE COMMOTION ...
BUT EITHER WAY, THERE SIMPLY AREN'T ENOUGH HANDS AROUND HERE.
MONEY WON'T MAKE THINGS FASTER.
YOU SHOULD FORGET ABOUT FINDING A BOAT.
......!
!
MA'AM.
WHAT'S THIS WOOD FOR?
EHH?
MATERIALS ARE ONE THING WE ALWAYS HAVE PLENTY OF.
BUT IT'S JUST TRASH IF THERE'S NO ONE WHO CAN BUILD THINGS OUT OF IT.
TAKE THE MATERIALS, IF YOU WANT THEM.
!

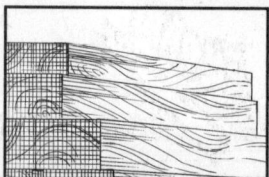

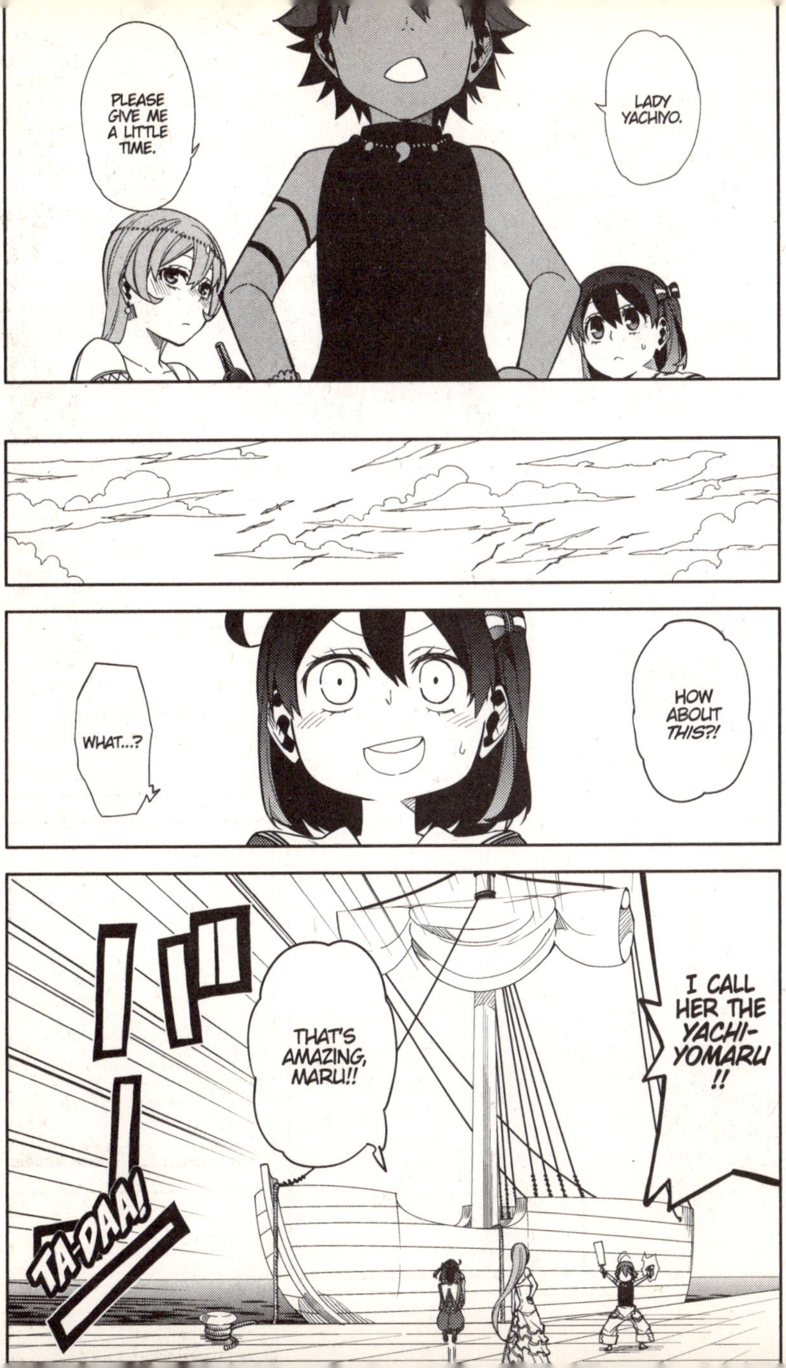
LADY YACHIYO.
PLEASE GIVE ME A LITTLE TIME.
HOW ABOUT *THIS?!*
WHAT...?
I CALL HER THE *YACHI-YOMARU* !!
THAT'S AMAZING, MARU!!
TA-DAA!

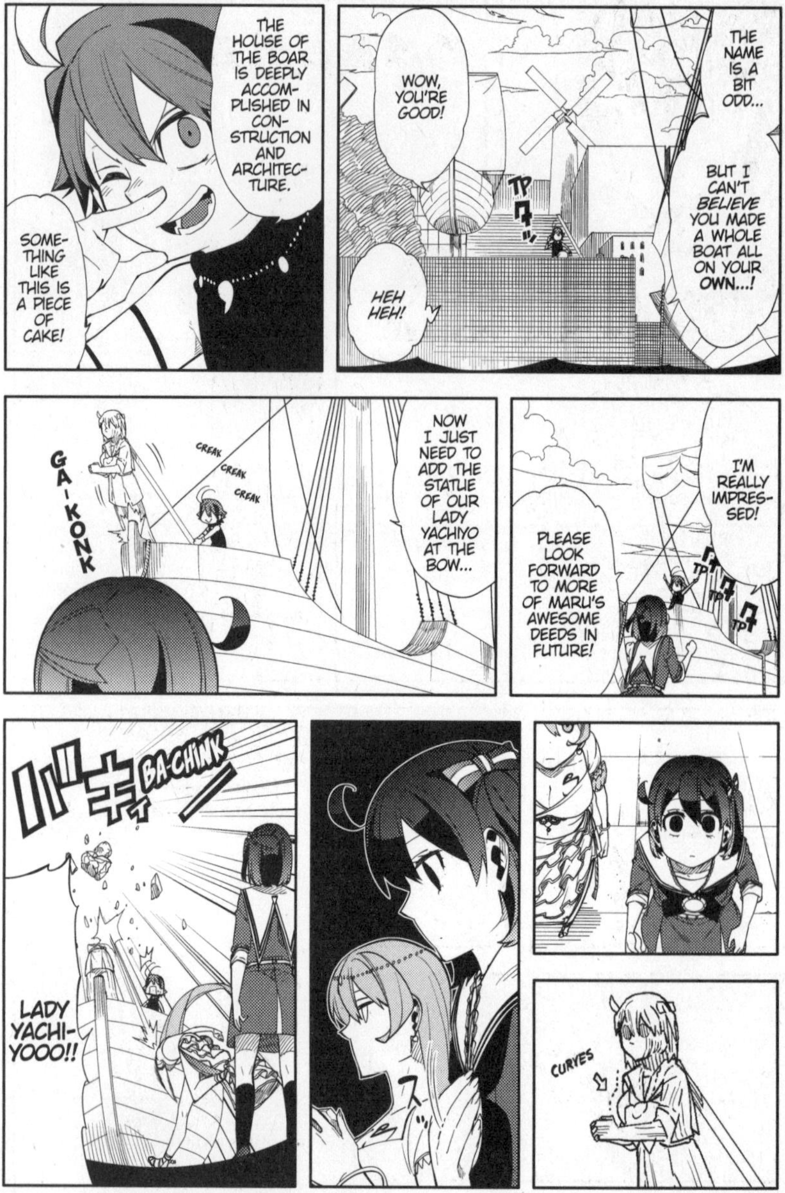
THE NAME IS A BIT ODD...
BUT I CAN'T *BELIEVE* YOU MADE A WHOLE BOAT ALL ON YOUR OWN...!
WOW, YOU'RE GOOD!
TP
HEH HEH!
THE HOUSE OF THE BOAR IS DEEPLY ACCOMPLISHED IN CONSTRUCTION AND ARCHITECTURE.
SOMETHING LIKE THIS IS A PIECE OF CAKE!
I'M REALLY IMPRESSED!
TP TP TP
PLEASE LOOK FORWARD TO MORE OF MARU'S AWESOME DEEDS IN FUTURE!
NOW I JUST NEED TO ADD THE STATUE OF OUR LADY YACHIYO AT THE BOW...
CREAK
CREAK
CREAK
GA-KONK
CURVES
BA-CHINK
LADY YACHI-YOOO!!

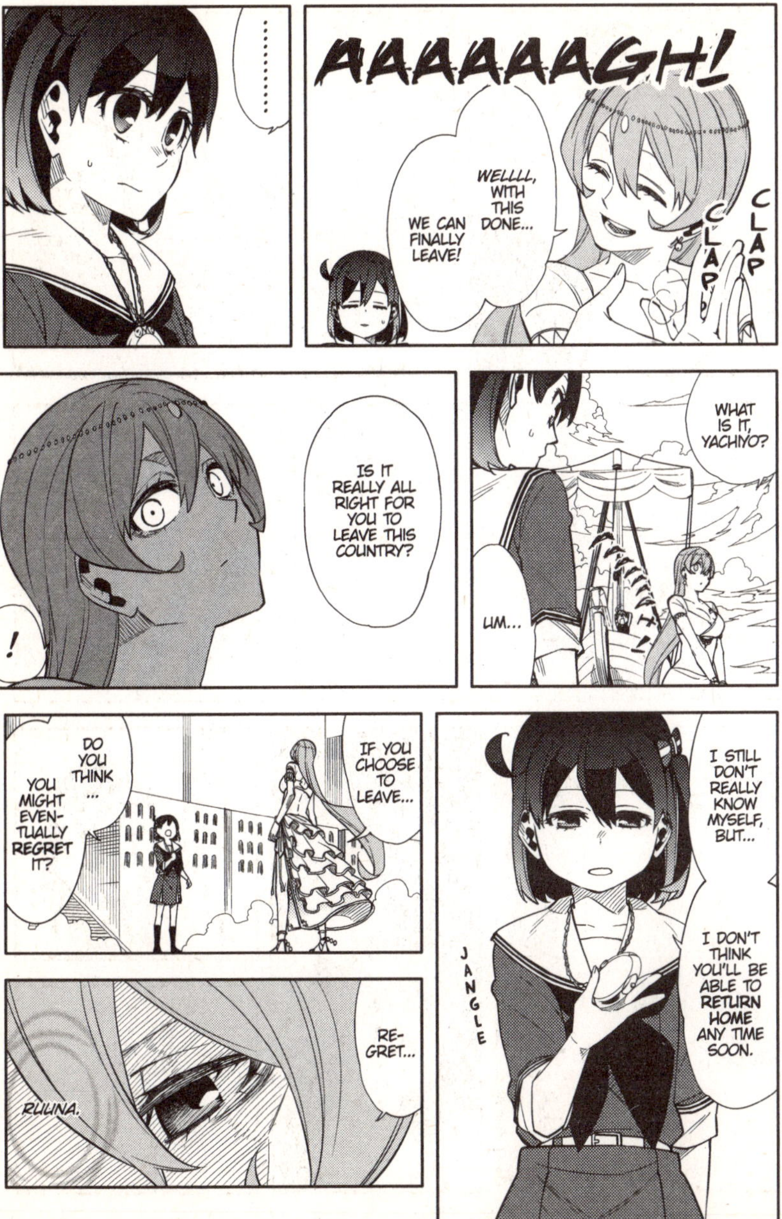
AAAAAAAGH!
CLAP
WELLLL, WITH THIS DONE...
WE CAN FINALLY LEAVE!
CLAP
......
WHAT IS IT, YACHIYO?
UM...
IS IT REALLY ALL RIGHT FOR YOU TO LEAVE THIS COUNTRY?
!
I STILL DON'T REALLY KNOW MYSELF, BUT...
I DON'T THINK YOU'LL BE ABLE TO RETURN HOME ANY TIME SOON.
JANGLE
IF YOU CHOOSE TO LEAVE...
DO YOU THINK...
YOU MIGHT EVENTUALLY REGRET IT?
RE-GRET...
RUUNA.

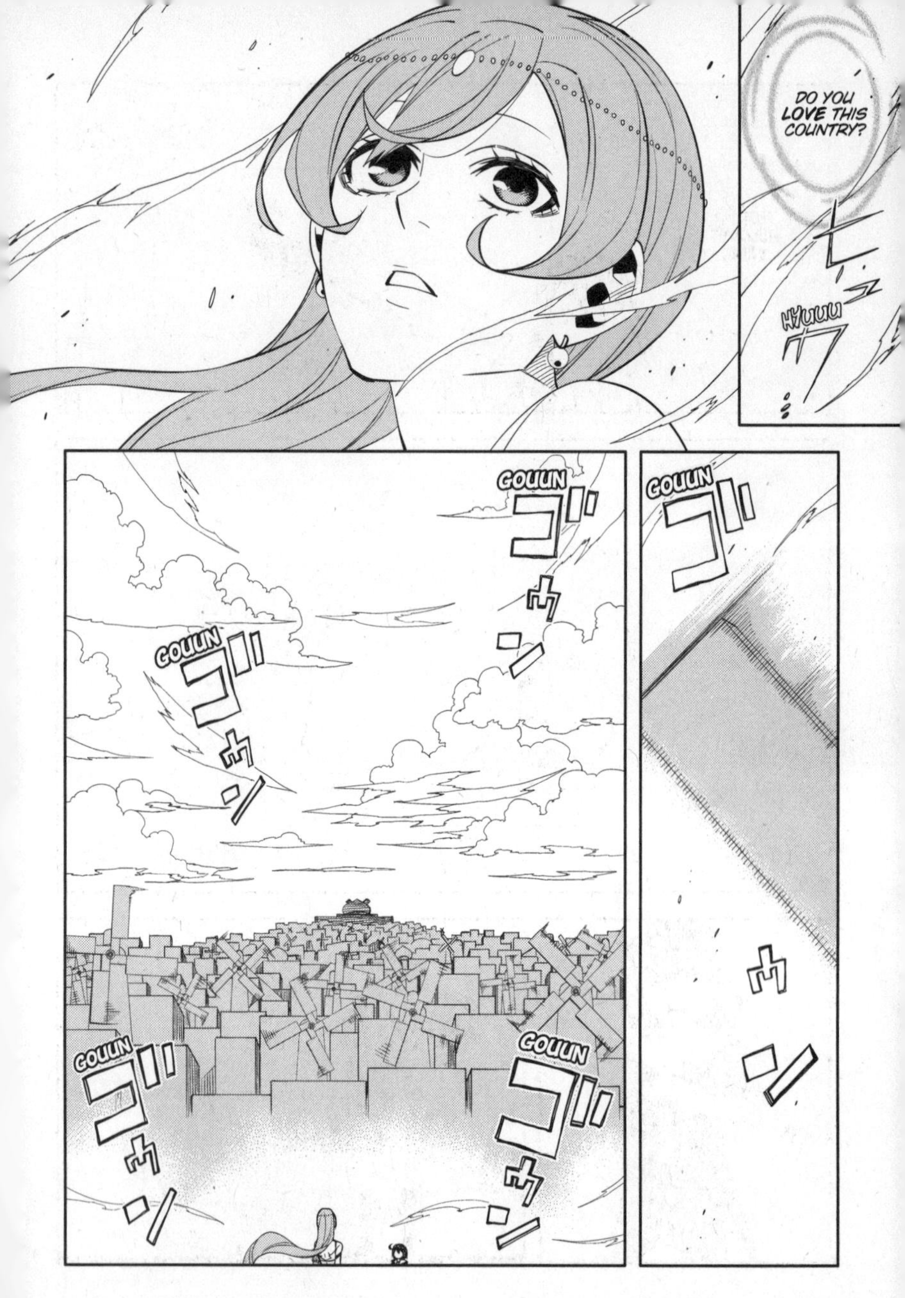
DO YOU LOVE THIS COUNTRY?
HYUUU
GOUUN
GOUUN
GOUUN
GOUUN
GOUUN

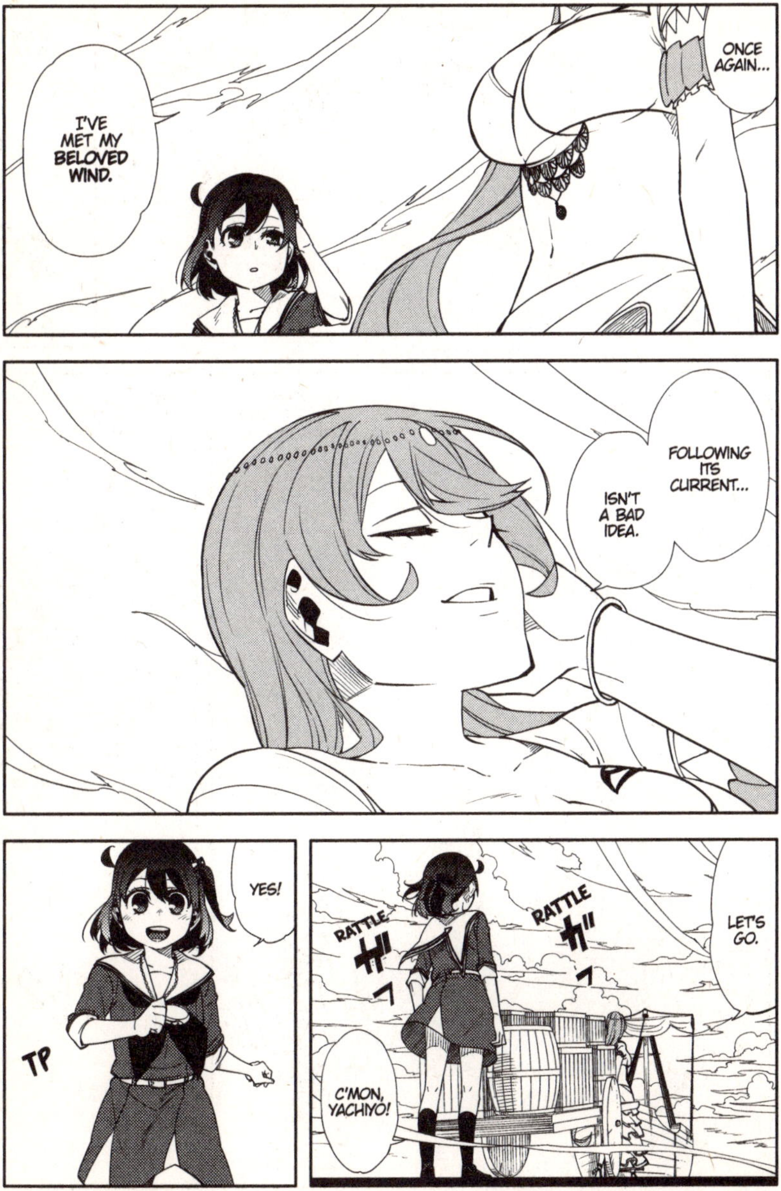
ONCE AGAIN...
I'VE MET MY BELOVED WIND.
FOLLOWING ITS CURRENT...
ISN'T A BAD IDEA.
LET'S GO.
RATTLE
ガッ
RATTLE
ガッ
C'MON, YACHIYO!
YES!
TP

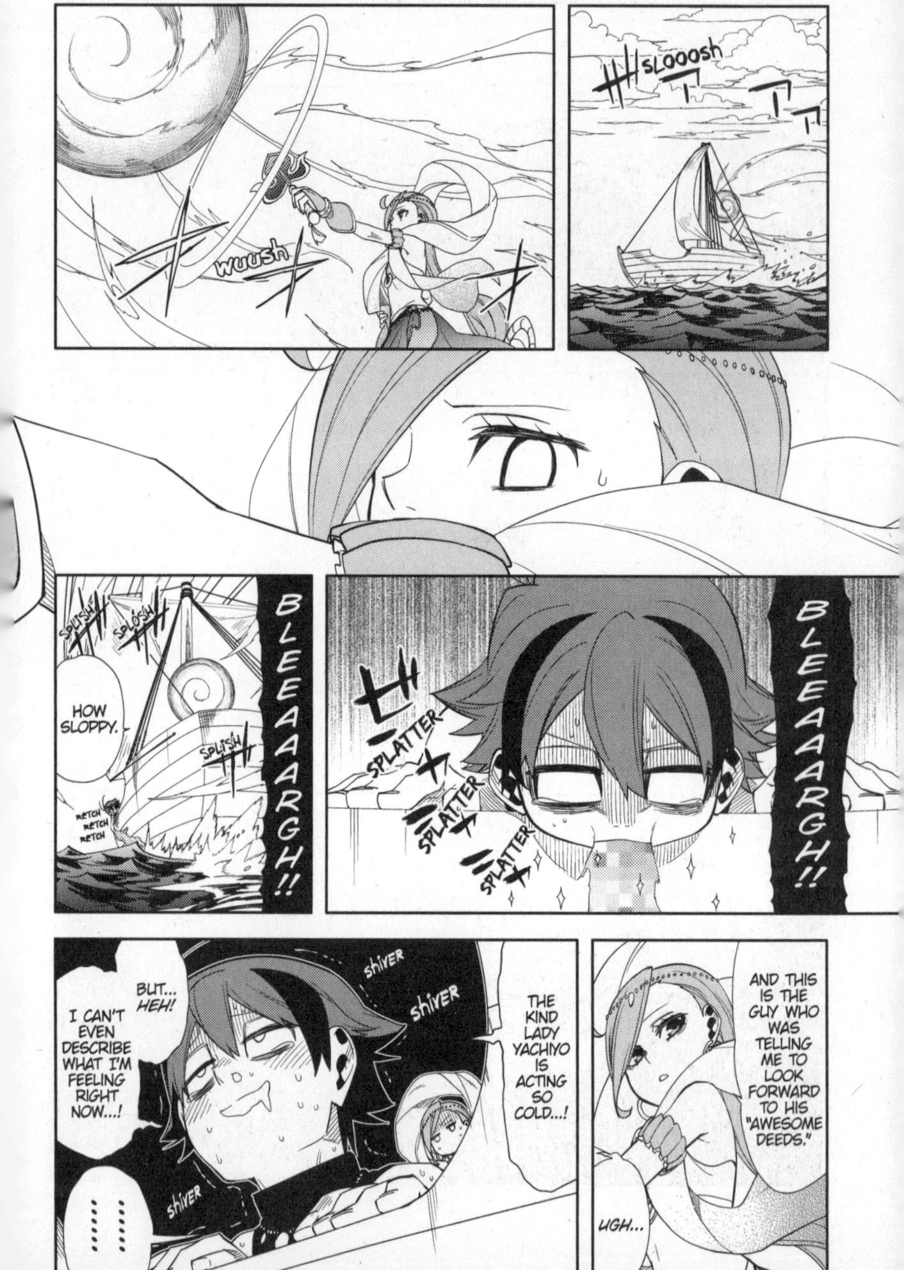
SLOOOSH
wuush
BLEEAAAARGH!!
SPLATTER
SPLATTER
SPLATTER
BLEEAAAARGH!!
SPLISH
SPLOSH
HOW SLOPPY.
SPLISH
RETCH RETCH RETCH
AND THIS IS THE GUY WHO WAS TELLING ME TO LOOK FORWARD TO HIS "AWESOME DEEDS."
UGH...
THE KIND LADY YACHIYO IS ACTING SO COLD...!
shiver
shiver
BUT... HEH!
I CAN'T EVEN DESCRIBE WHAT I'M FEELING RIGHT NOW...!
shiver
......

HM ...?!
SLOSH
SLOSH
THAT'S ...
SLOOOSH
LADY YACHIYO! THERE'S SOMEONE ON THE WATER...!
?!
FWUP
SLOSH
SPLOSH

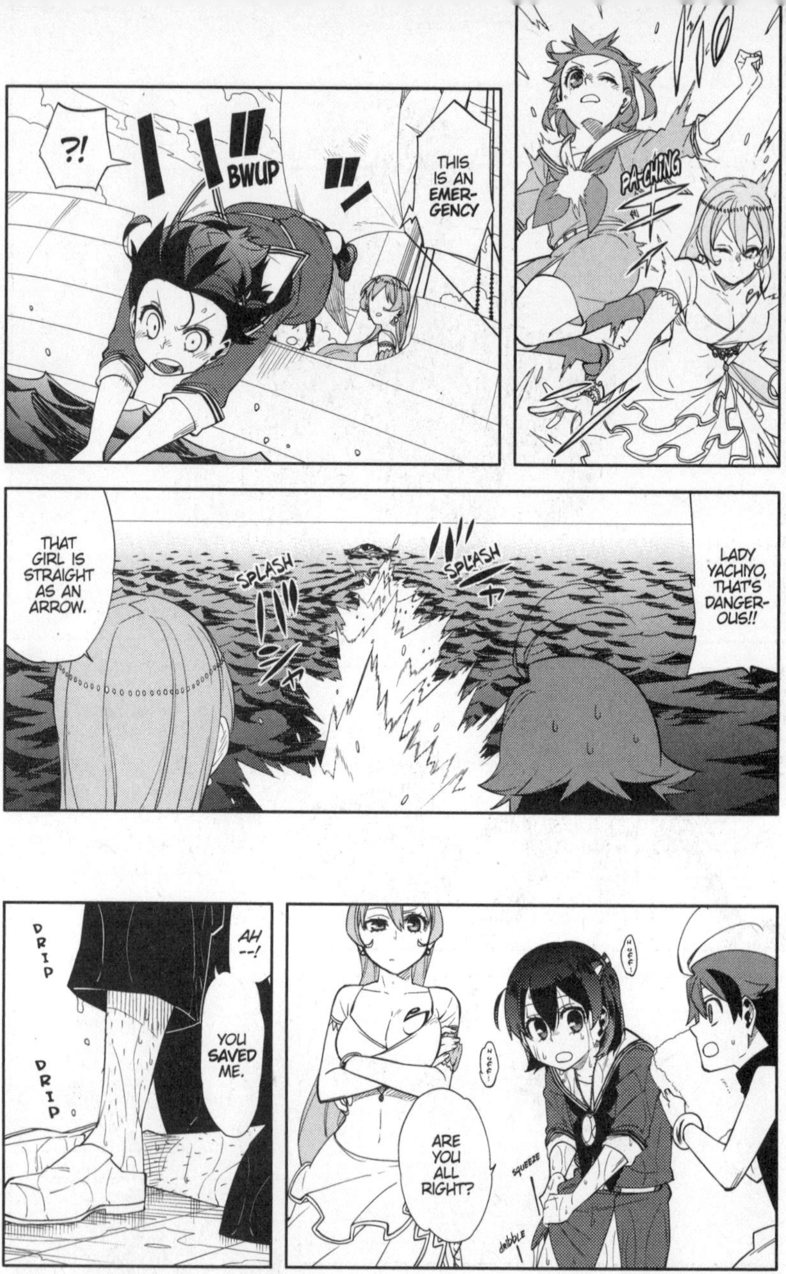
PA-CHING
?!
BWUP
THIS IS AN EMERGENCY
LADY YACHIYO, THAT'S DANGEROUS!!
SPLASH
SPLASH
THAT GIRL IS STRAIGHT AS AN ARROW.
ARE YOU ALL RIGHT?
SQUEEZE
dribble
AH--!
YOU SAVED ME.
DRIP
DRIP

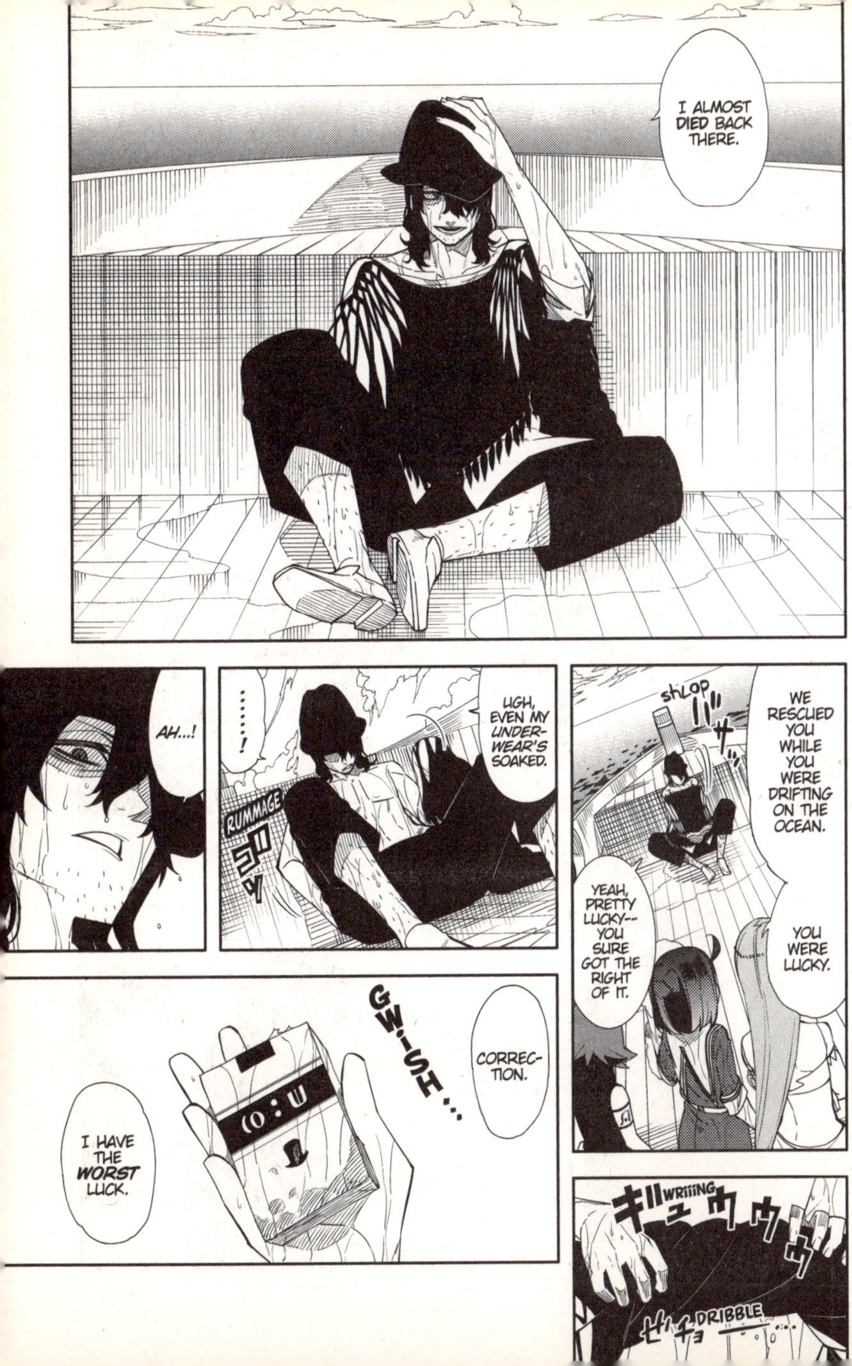
I ALMOST DIED BACK THERE.
shLOP
WE RESCUED YOU WHILE YOU WERE DRIFTING ON THE OCEAN.
YOU WERE LUCKY.
YEAH, PRETTY LUCKY-- YOU SURE GOT THE RIGHT OF IT.
WRiiiNG
DRIBBLE
UGH, EVEN MY UNDER-WEAR'S SOAKED.
......!
RUMMAGE
AH...!
GWISH...
CORREC-TION.
I HAVE THE WORST LUCK.

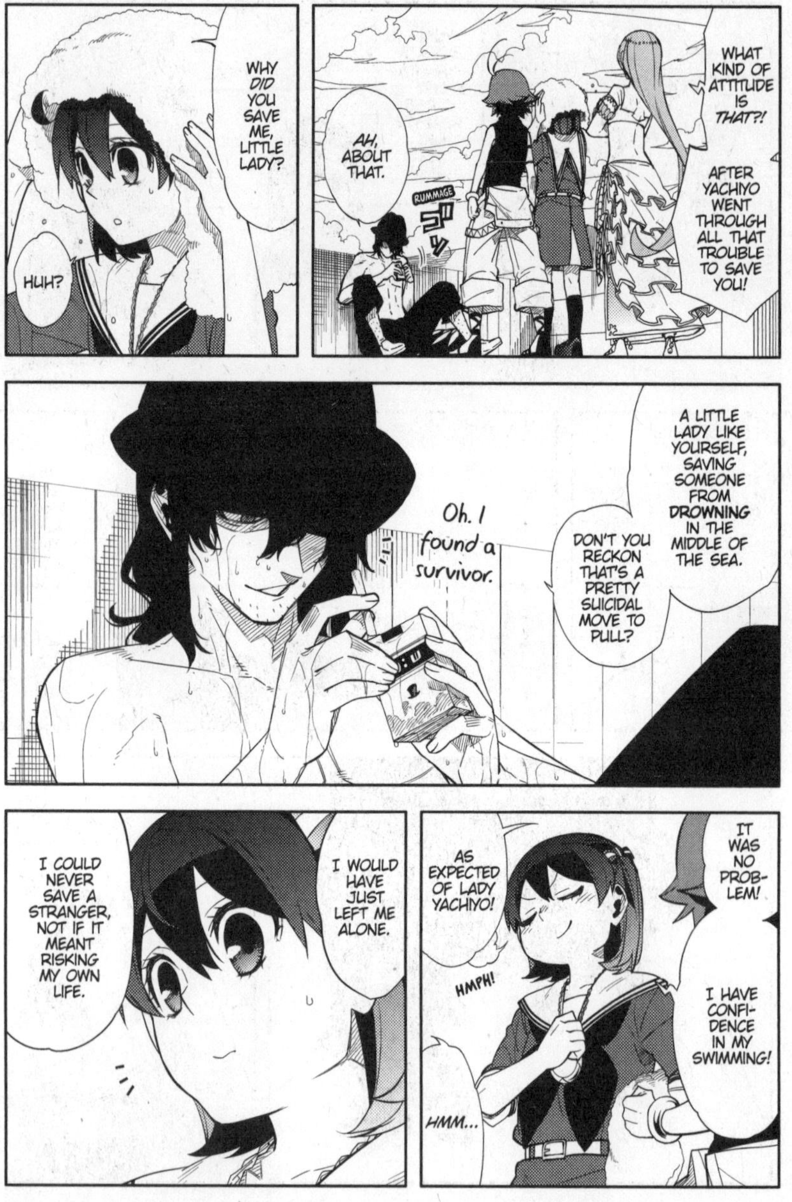
WHAT KIND OF ATTITUDE IS *THAT?!*
AFTER YACHIYO WENT THROUGH ALL THAT TROUBLE TO SAVE YOU!
AH, ABOUT THAT.
RUMMAGE
WHY *DID* YOU SAVE ME, LITTLE LADY?
HUH?
A LITTLE LADY LIKE YOURSELF, SAVING SOMEONE FROM **DROWNING** IN THE MIDDLE OF THE SEA.
DON'T YOU RECKON THAT'S A PRETTY SUICIDAL MOVE TO PULL?
Oh. I found a survivor.
IT WAS NO PROBLEM!
I HAVE CONFIDENCE IN MY SWIMMING!
AS EXPECTED OF LADY YACHIYO!
HMPH!
HMM...
I WOULD HAVE JUST LEFT ME ALONE.
I COULD NEVER SAVE A STRANGER, NOT IF IT MEANT RISKING MY OWN LIFE.

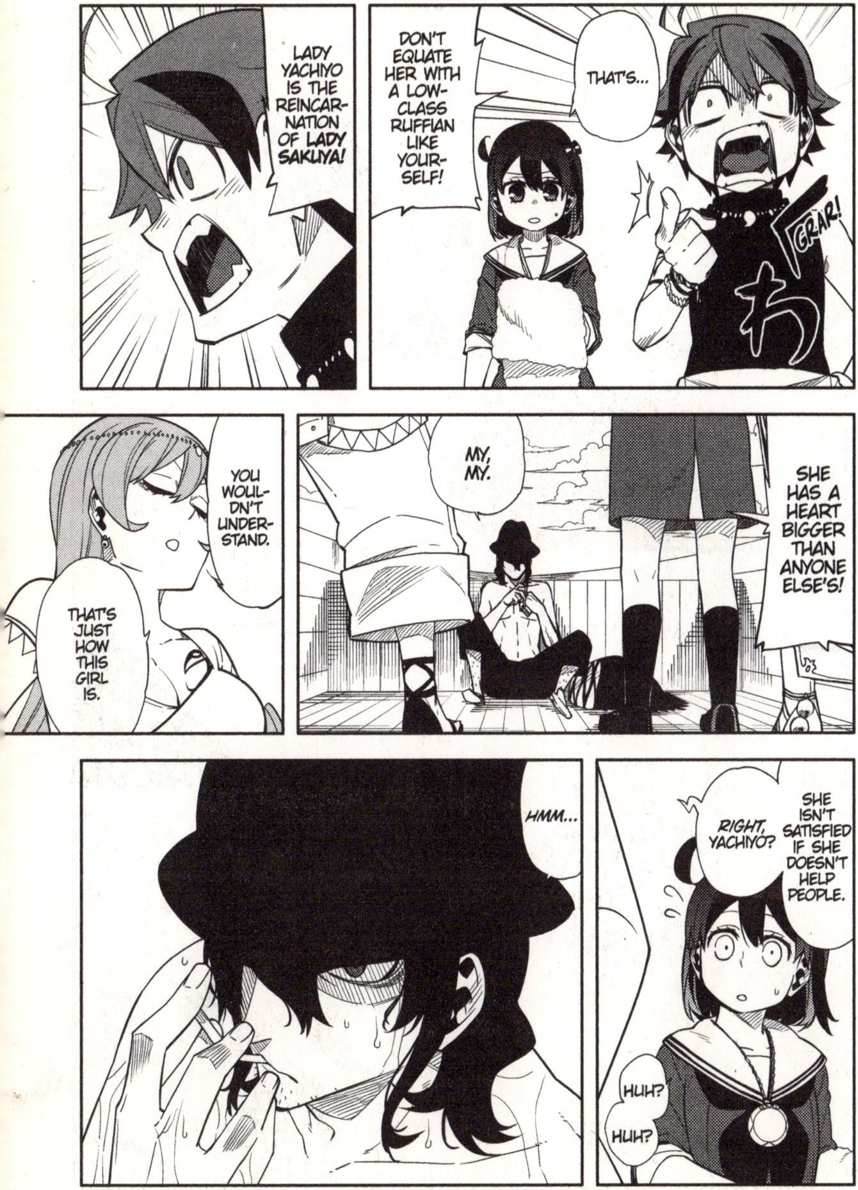
THAT'S...
DON'T EQUATE HER WITH A LOW-CLASS RUFFIAN LIKE YOURSELF!
GRAR!
LADY YACHIYO IS THE REINCARNATION OF LADY SAKUYA!
SHE HAS A HEART BIGGER THAN ANYONE ELSE'S!
MY, MY.
YOU WOULDN'T UNDERSTAND.
THAT'S JUST HOW THIS GIRL IS.
SHE ISN'T SATISFIED IF SHE DOESN'T HELP PEOPLE.
RIGHT, YACHIYO?
HUH?
HUH?
HMM...

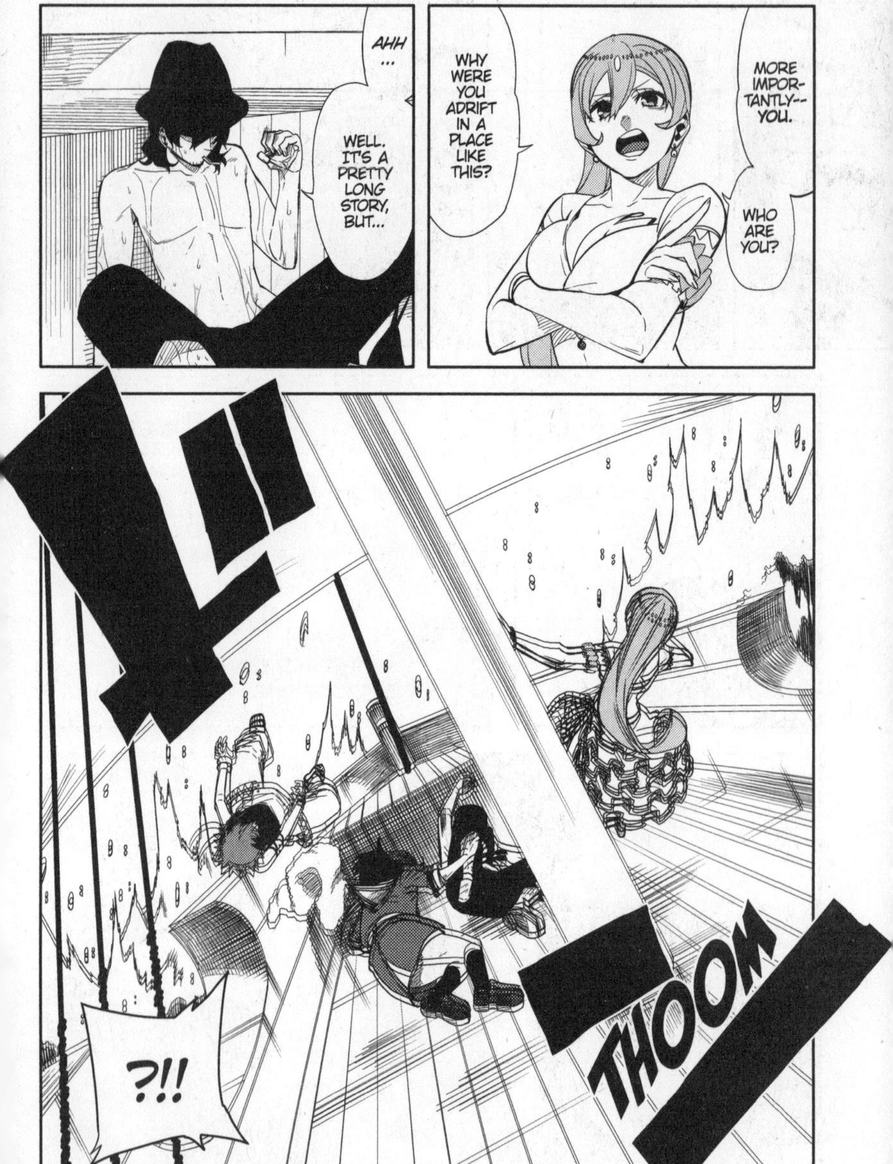
WHY WERE YOU ADRIFT IN A PLACE LIKE THIS?
MORE IMPORTANTLY-- YOU.
WHO ARE YOU?
AHH ...
WELL. IT'S A PRETTY LONG STORY, BUT...
THOOM
?!!

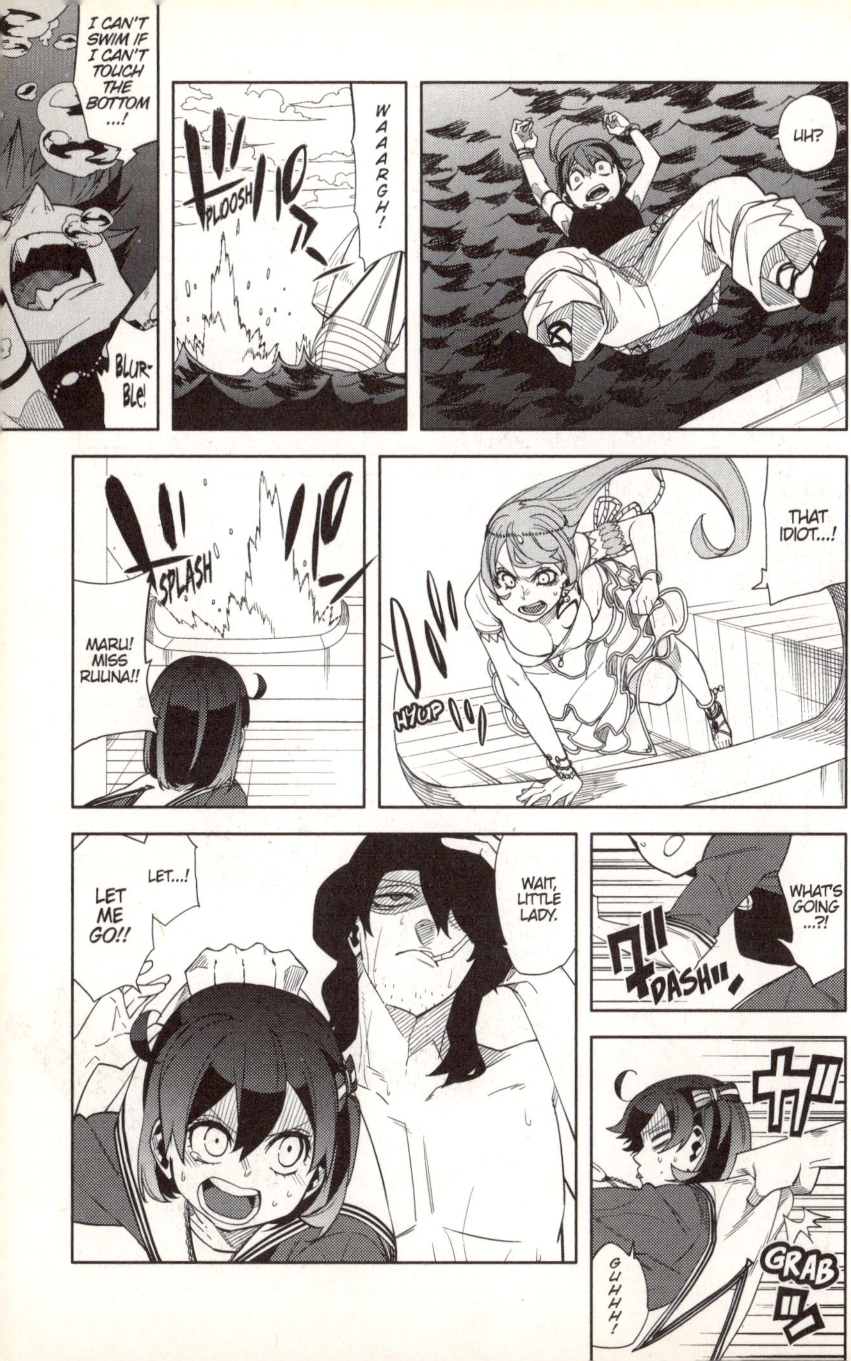
UH?
WAAAARGH!
PLOOSH
I CAN'T SWIM IF I CAN'T TOUCH THE BOTTOM ...!
BLURBLE!
THAT IDIOT...!
HYUP
SPLASH
MARU! MISS RUUNA!!
WHAT'S GOING ...?!
DASH
GRAB
GUHHH!
WAIT, LITTLE LADY.
LET...!
LET ME GO!!

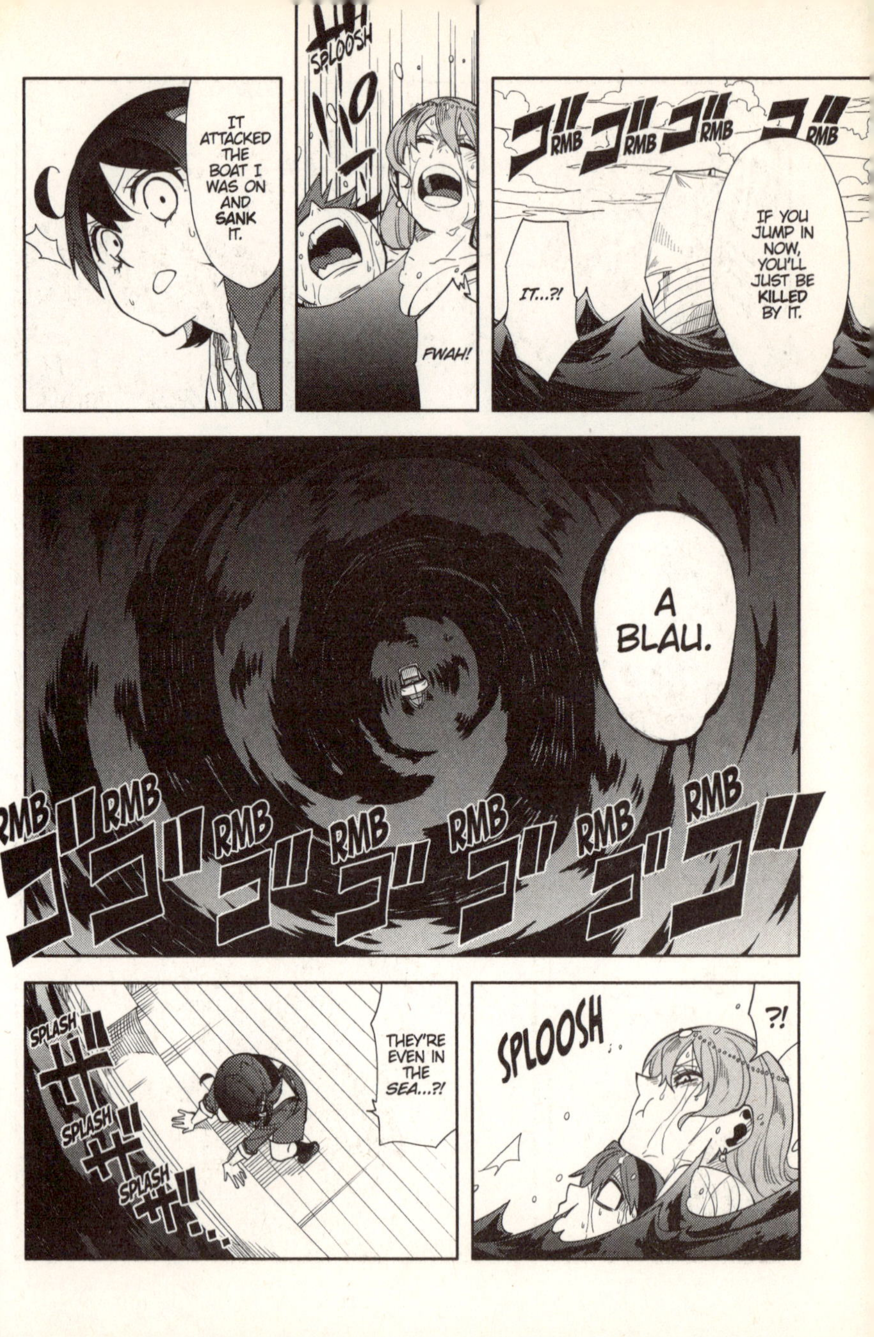

RMB RMB RMB RMB
IF YOU JUMP IN NOW, YOU'LL JUST BE KILLED BY IT.
IT...?!
SPLOOSH
FWAH!
IT ATTACKED THE BOAT I WAS ON AND SANK IT.
A BLAU.
RMB RMB RMB RMB RMB RMB RMB
?!
SPLOOSH
THEY'RE EVEN IN THE SEA...?!
SPLASH
SPLASH
SPLASH

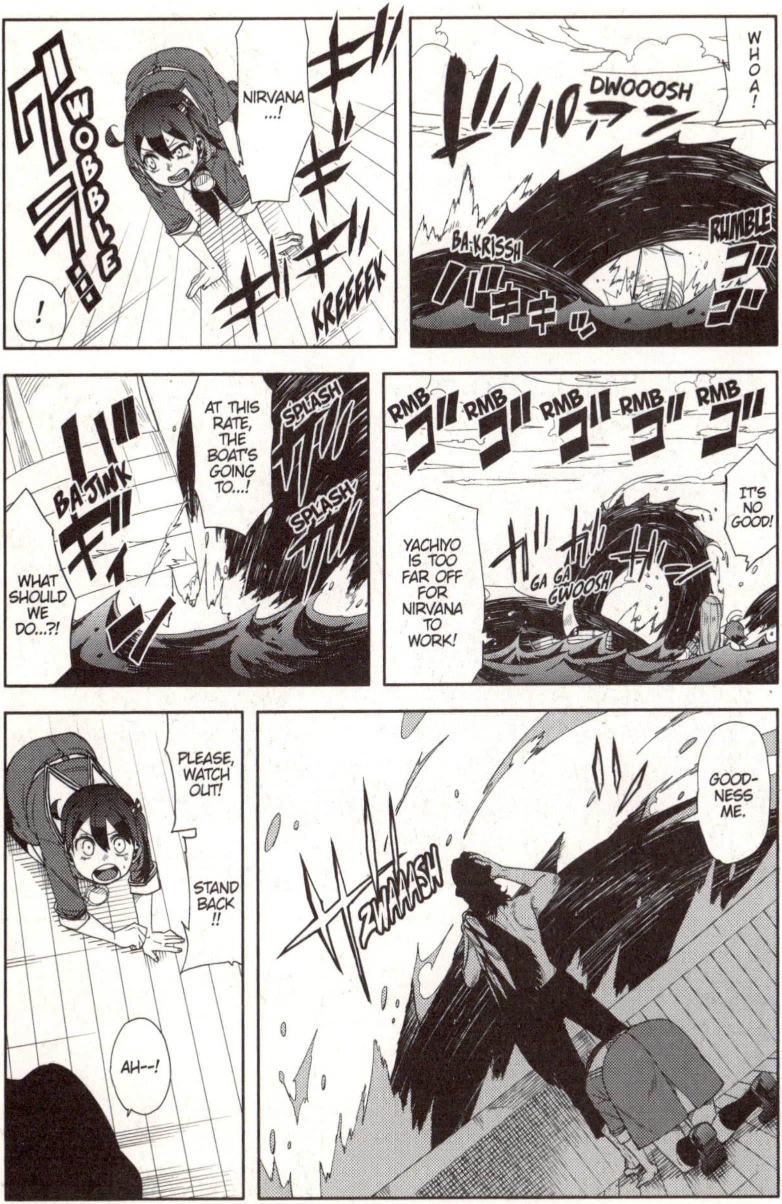
WHOA!
DWOOOSH
RUMBLE
BA-KRISSH
NIRVANA ...!
KREEEEK
WOBBLE
!
RMB RMB RMB RMB RMB
IT'S NO GOOD!
YACHIYO IS TOO FAR OFF FOR NIRVANA TO WORK!
GA GA GWOOSH
AT THIS RATE, THE BOAT'S GOING TO...!
SPLASH
SPLASH
BA-JINK
WHAT SHOULD WE DO...?!
GOOD-NESS ME.
ZWAAAASH
PLEASE, WATCH OUT!
STAND BACK !!
AH--!

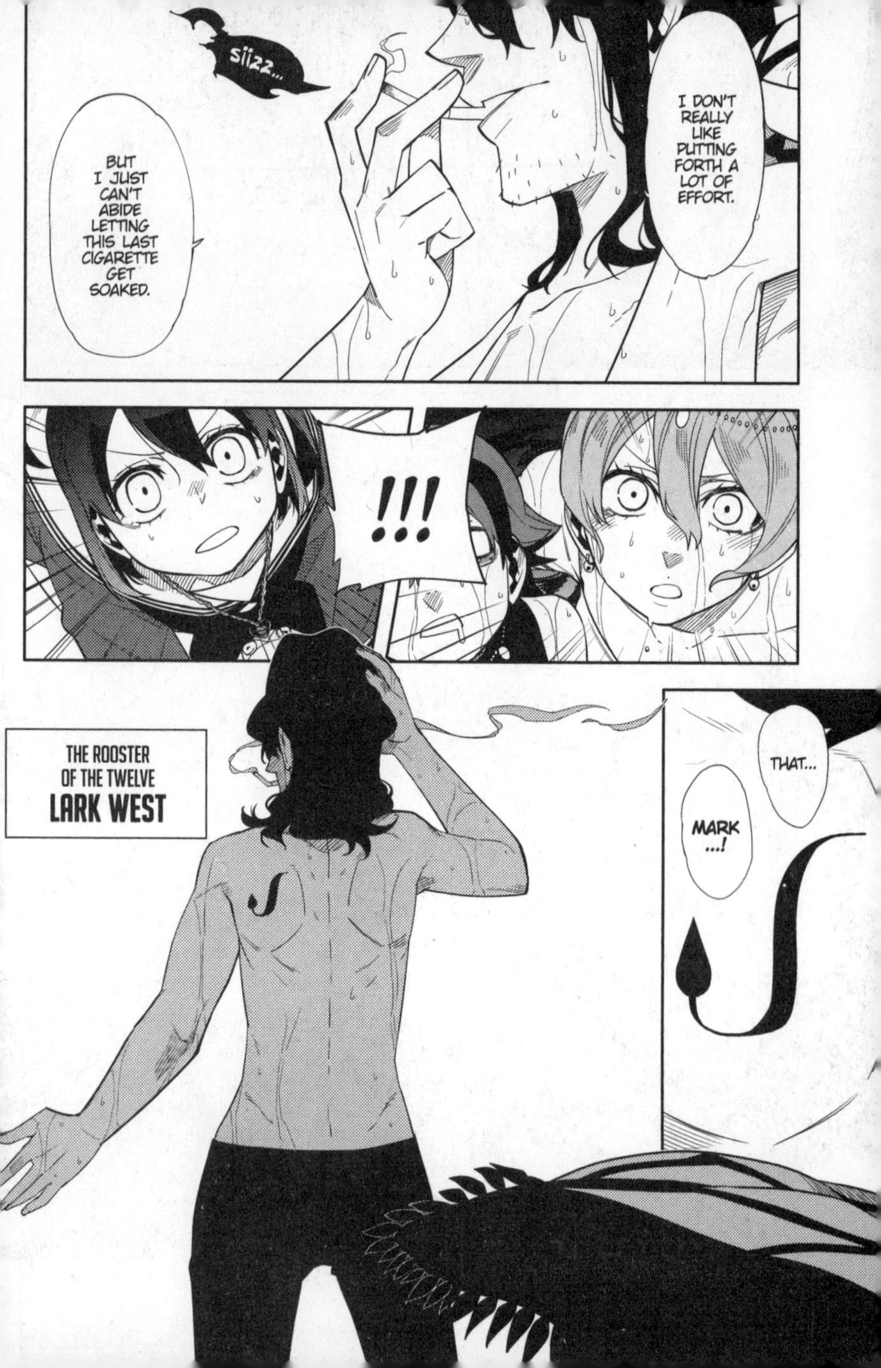
I DON'T REALLY LIKE PUTTING FORTH A LOT OF EFFORT.
siizz...
BUT I JUST CAN'T ABIDE LETTING THIS LAST CIGARETTE GET SOAKED.
!!!
THAT...
MARK ...!
THE ROOSTER OF THE TWELVE
LARK WEST

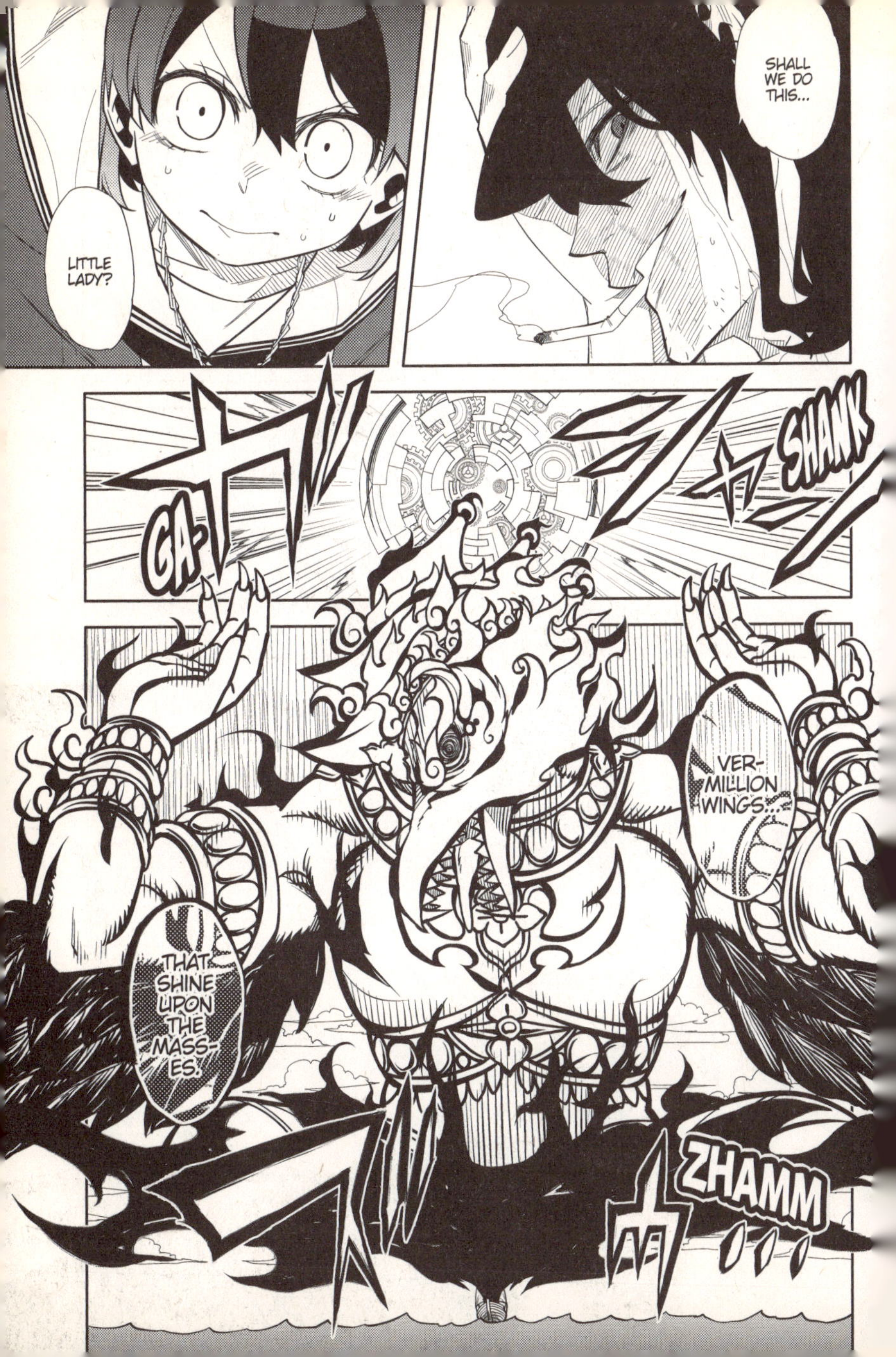
SHALL WE DO THIS...
LITTLE LADY?
CA-
SHANK
VER-MILLION WINGS...
THAT SHINE UPON THE MASS-ES.
ZHAMM

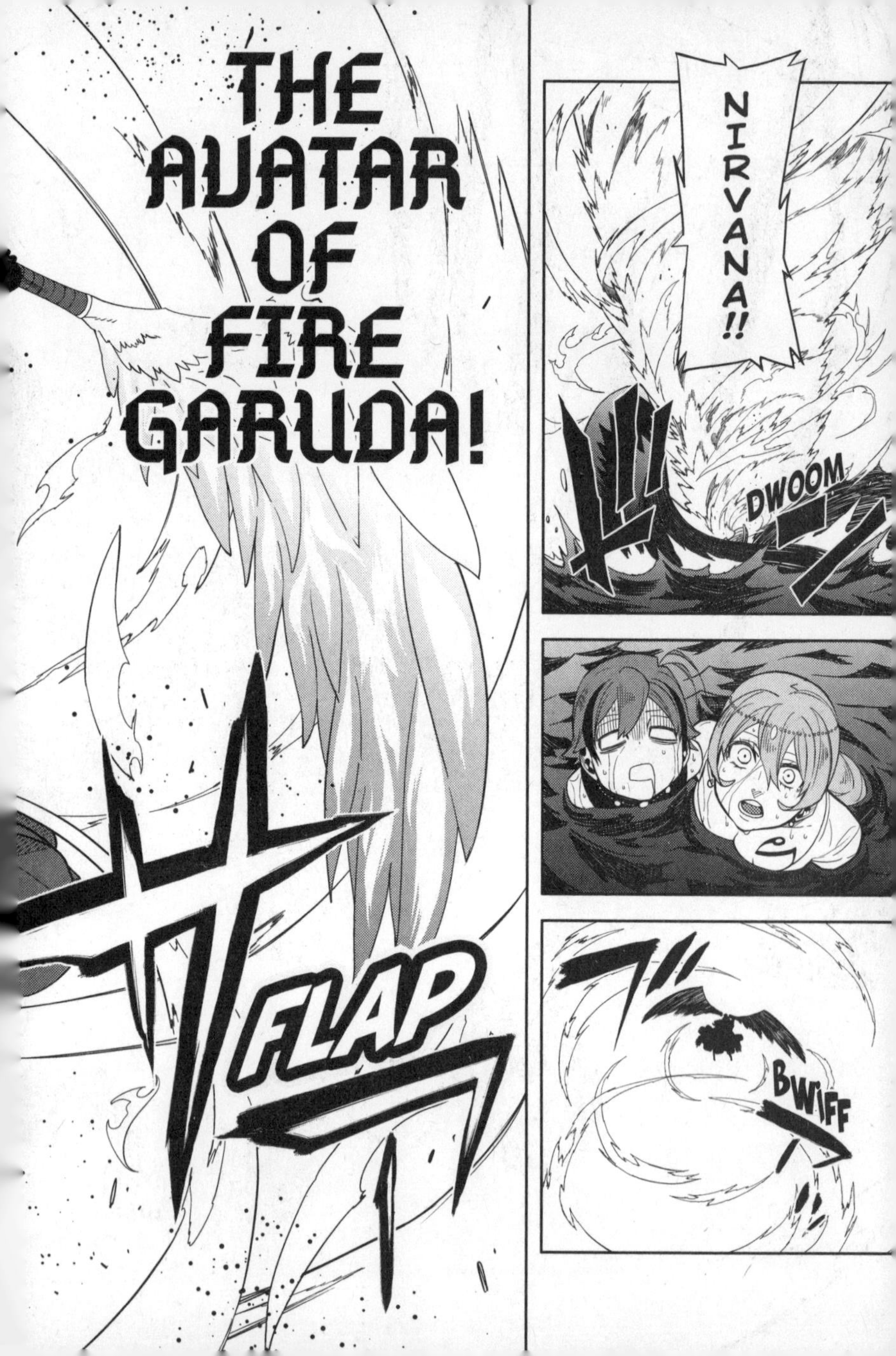
NIRVANA!!
DWOOM
BWIFF
THE AVATAR OF FIRE GARUDA!
FLAP

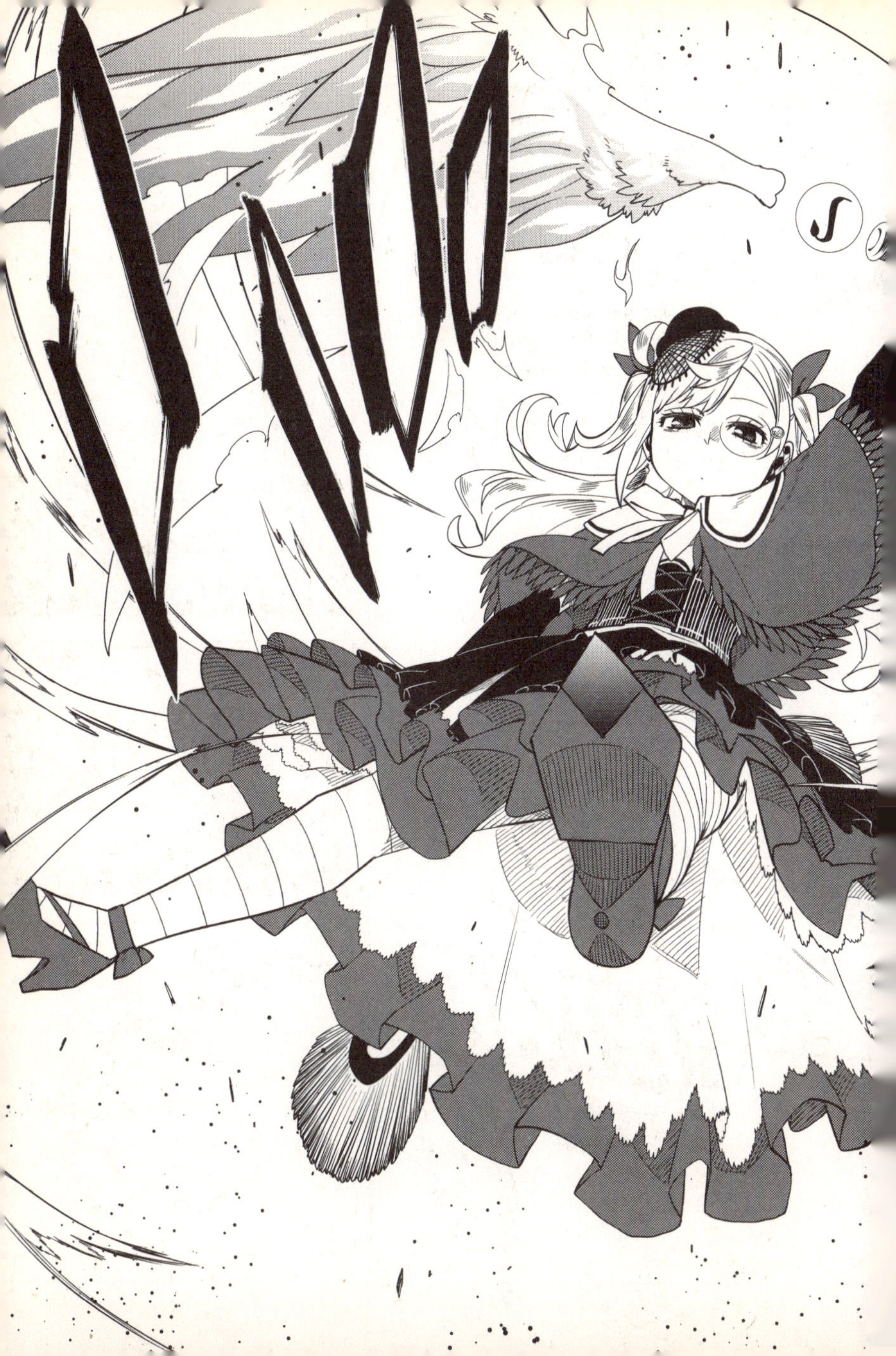

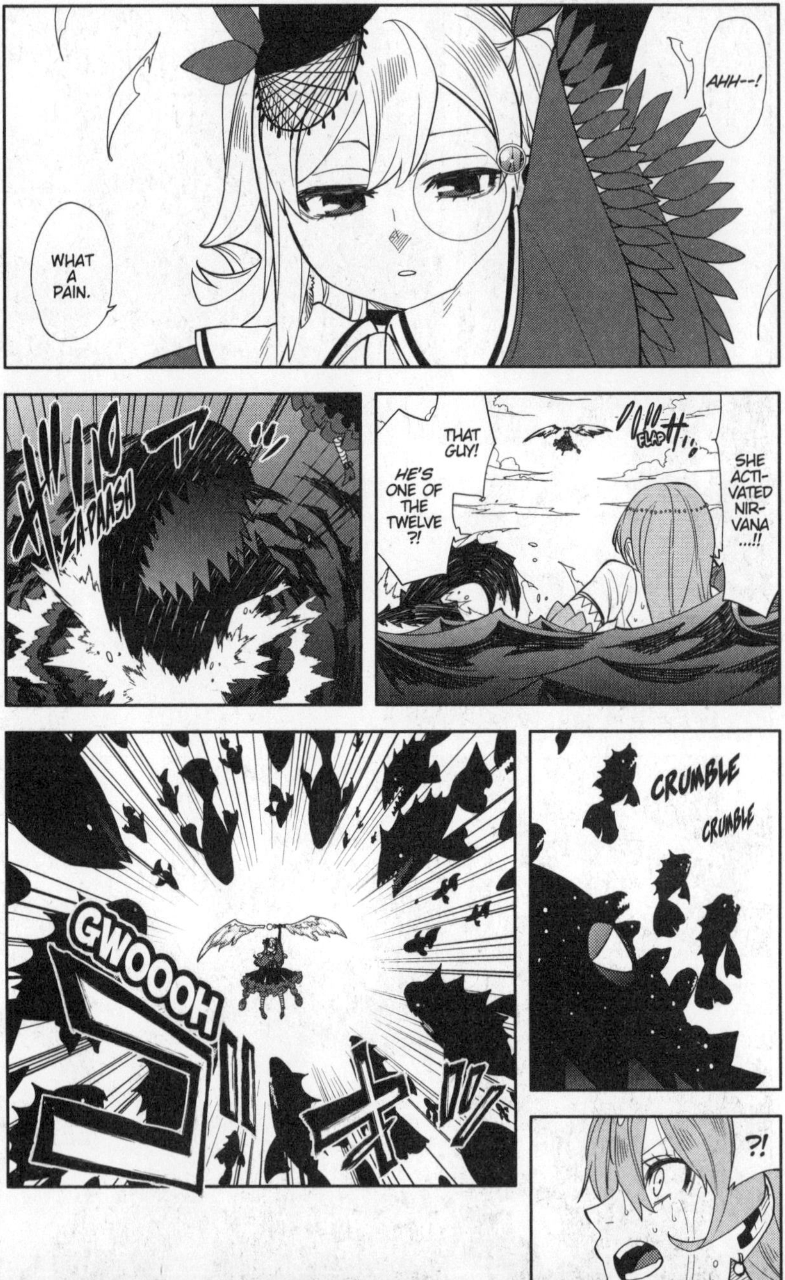
AHH--!
WHAT A PAIN.
FLAP
SHE ACTIVATED NIRVANA...!!
THAT GUY!
HE'S ONE OF THE TWELVE?!
ZA-PAASH
CRUMBLE
CRUMBLE
?!
GWOOOH

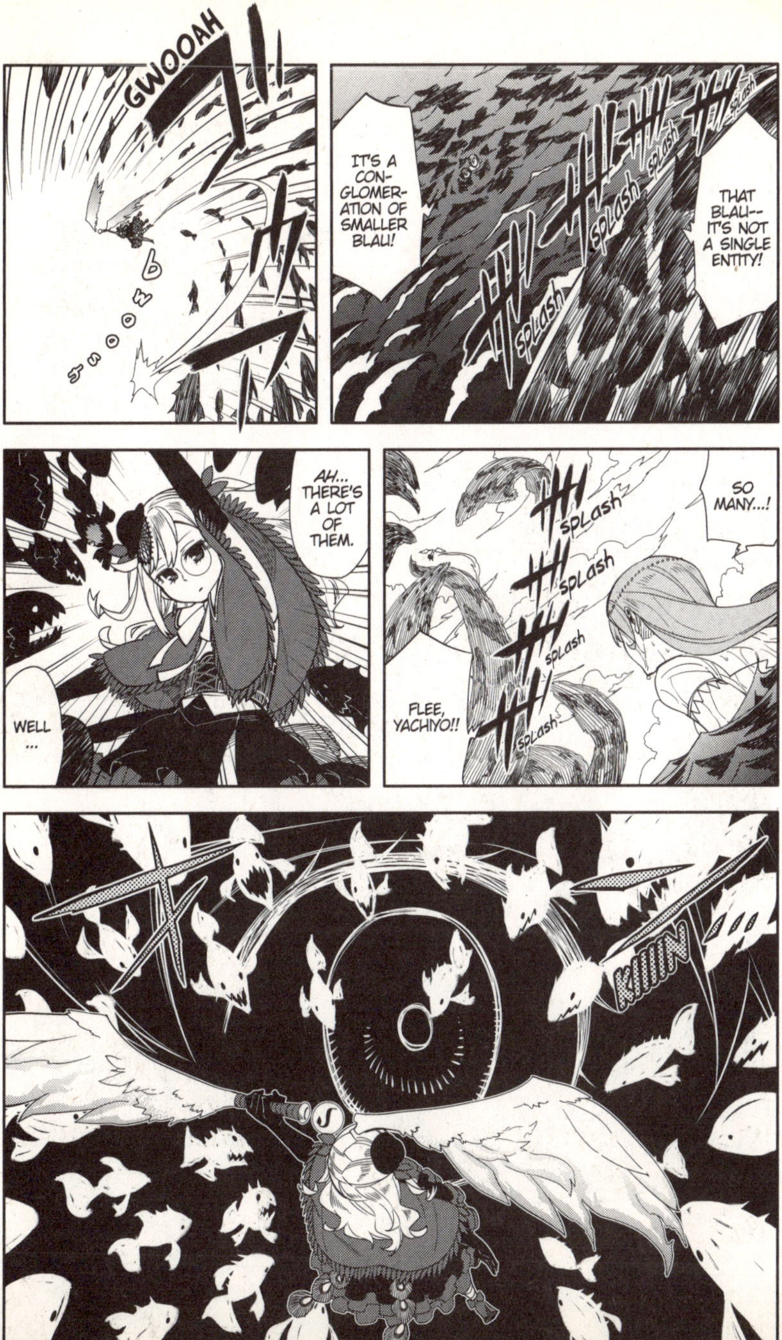
THAT BLAU-- IT'S NOT A SINGLE ENTITY!
splash splash splash splash splash
IT'S A CONGLOMERATION OF SMALLER BLAU!
GWOOAH
swoosh
SO MANY...!
splash splash splash splash
FLEE, YACHIYO!!
AH... THERE'S A LOT OF THEM.
WELL...
KIIIIN

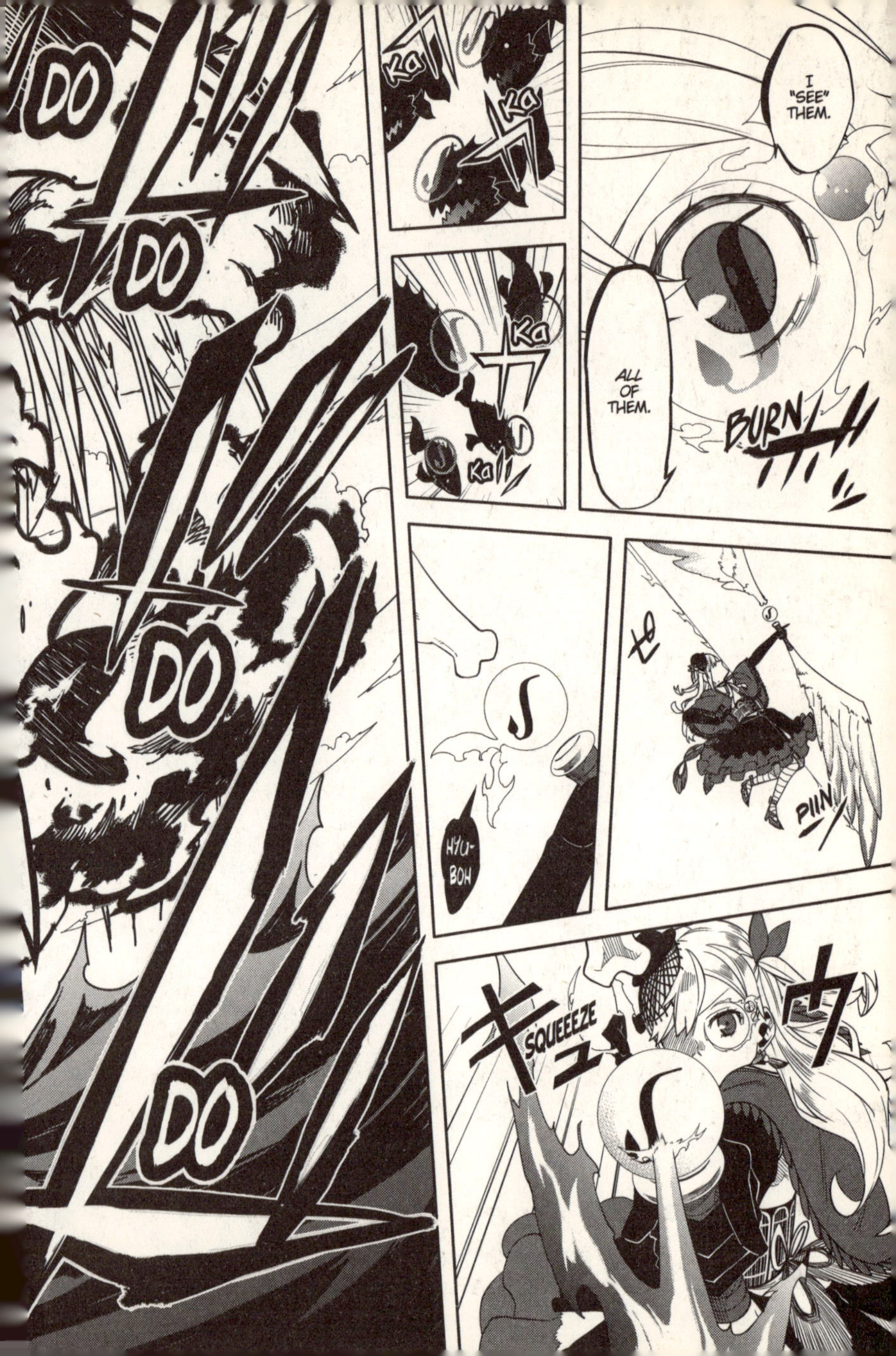

I "SEE" THEM.
ALL OF THEM.
BURN
KA
KA
KA
KA
PIIN
HYU-BOH
キュウ
SQUEEEZE
DO
DO
DO
DO

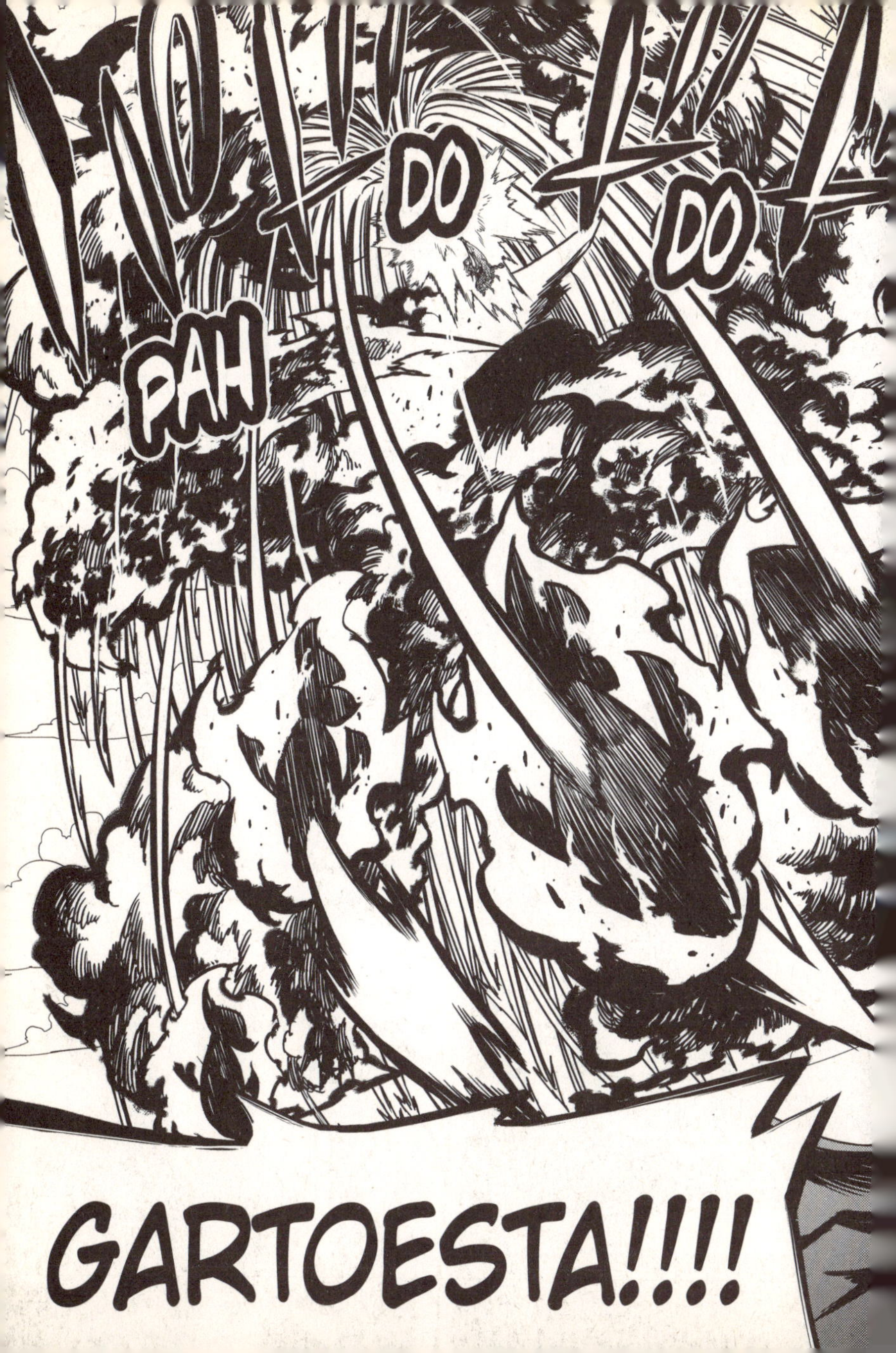
DO
DO
PAH
GARTOESTA!!!!

CRACKLE
CRACKLE
パララ
SCATTER
ボチャ
BLOSH
ボチャン
BLOSH
FLAP
AMAZ-ING...
FLO AT
TOK

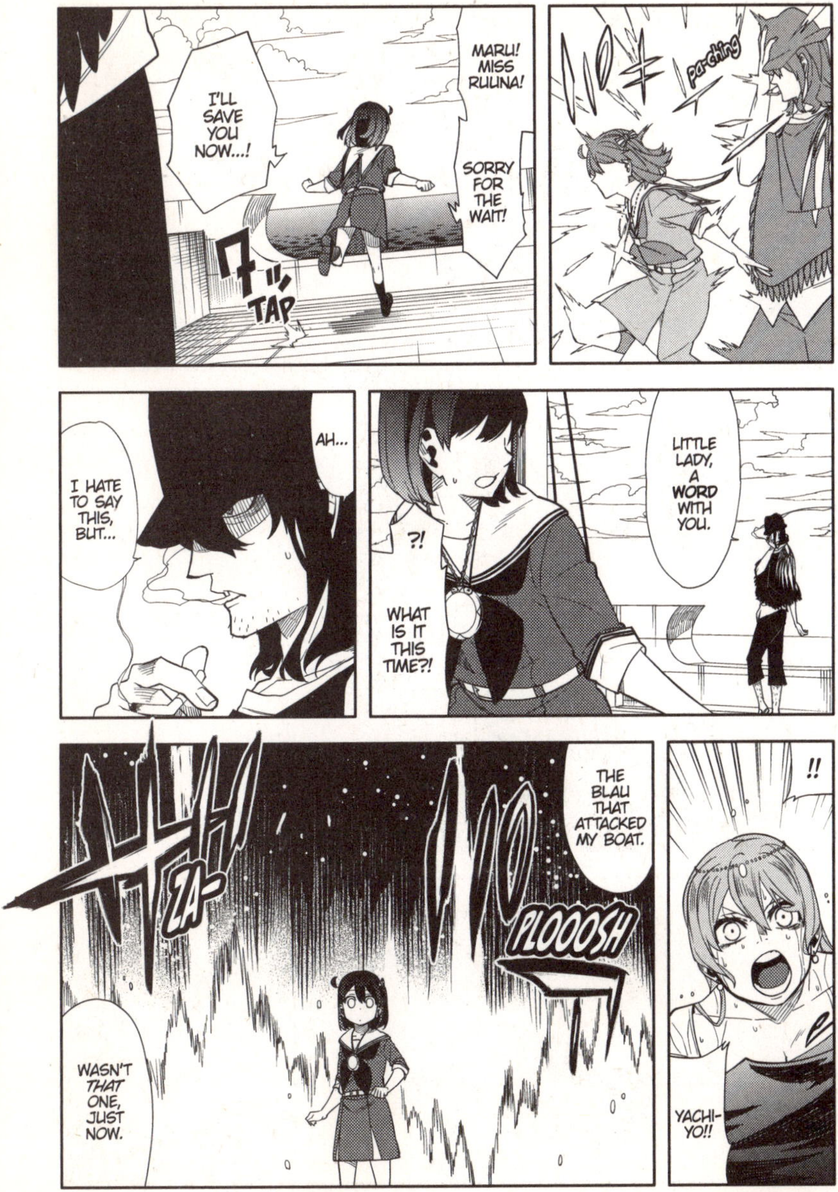
pa-ching
MARU! MISS RUUNA!
SORRY FOR THE WAIT!
I'LL SAVE YOU NOW...!
TAP
LITTLE LADY, A WORD WITH YOU.
?!
WHAT IS IT THIS TIME?!
AH...
I HATE TO SAY THIS, BUT...
!!
YACHI-YO!!
THE BLAU THAT ATTACKED MY BOAT.
PLOOOSH
ZA-
WASN'T *THAT* ONE, JUST NOW.

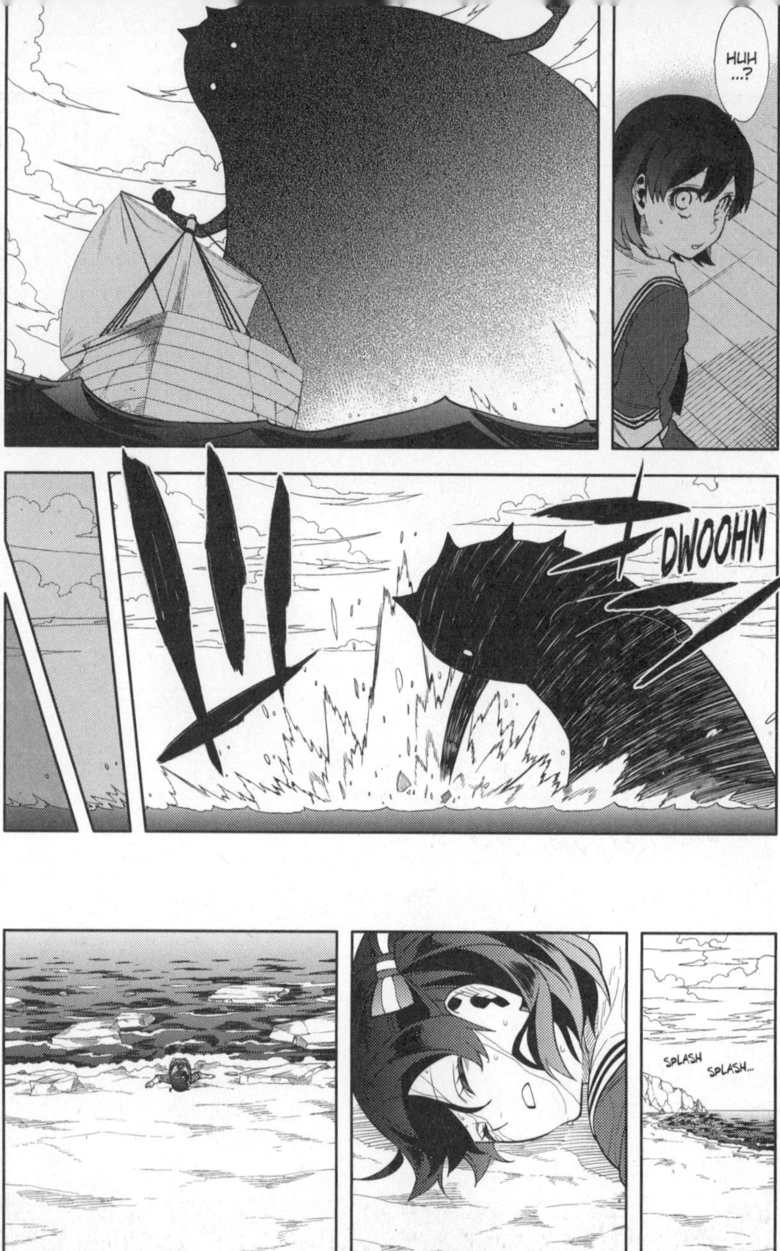
HUH ...?
DWOOHM
SPLASH
SPLASH...

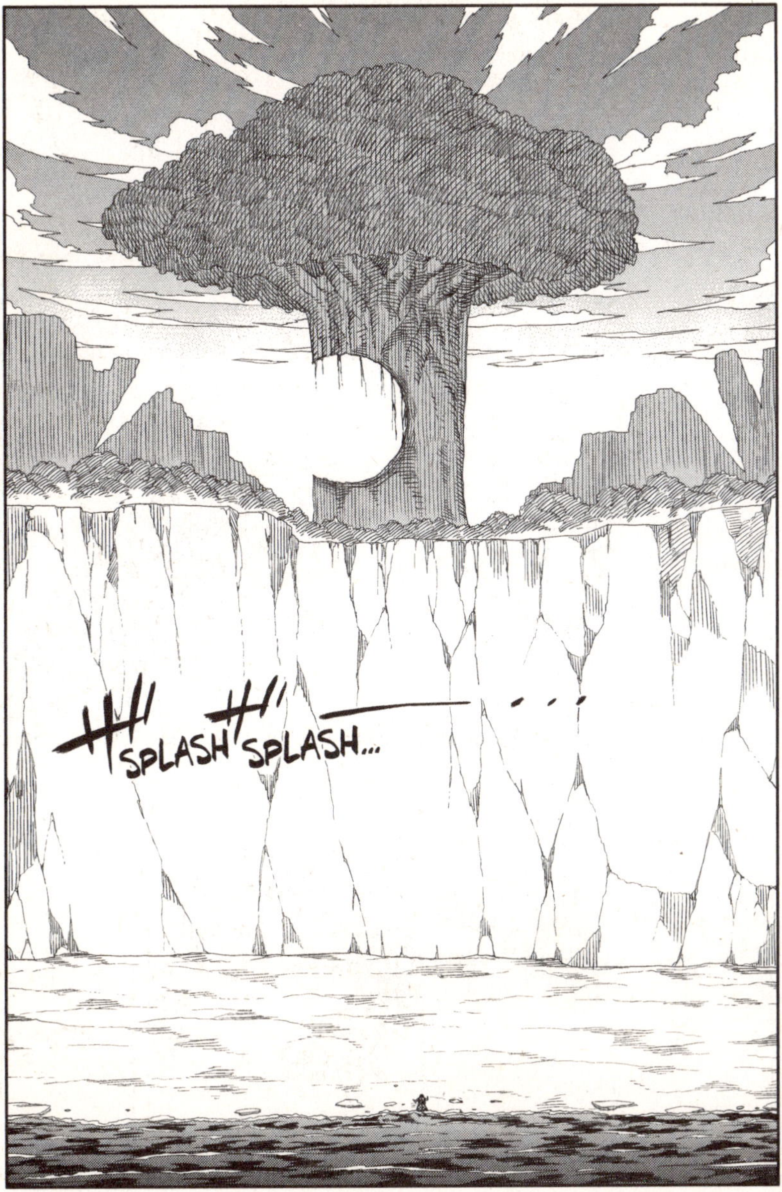
SPLASH SPLASH...

CHARACTER INTRODUCTION

Lark West

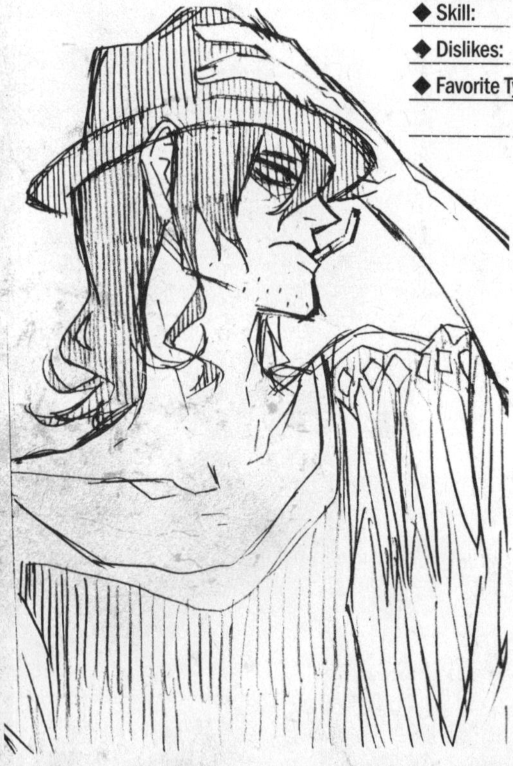

◆ Birthday:	10/11
◆ Age:	23
◆ Height:	181 cm
◆ Role/Job:	Rooster of the Twelve
◆ Hobbies:	Doing music performances
◆ Skill:	Can sleep anywhere
◆ Dislikes:	Cleaning Up
◆ Favorite Type of Woman:	
	One who's not too assertive

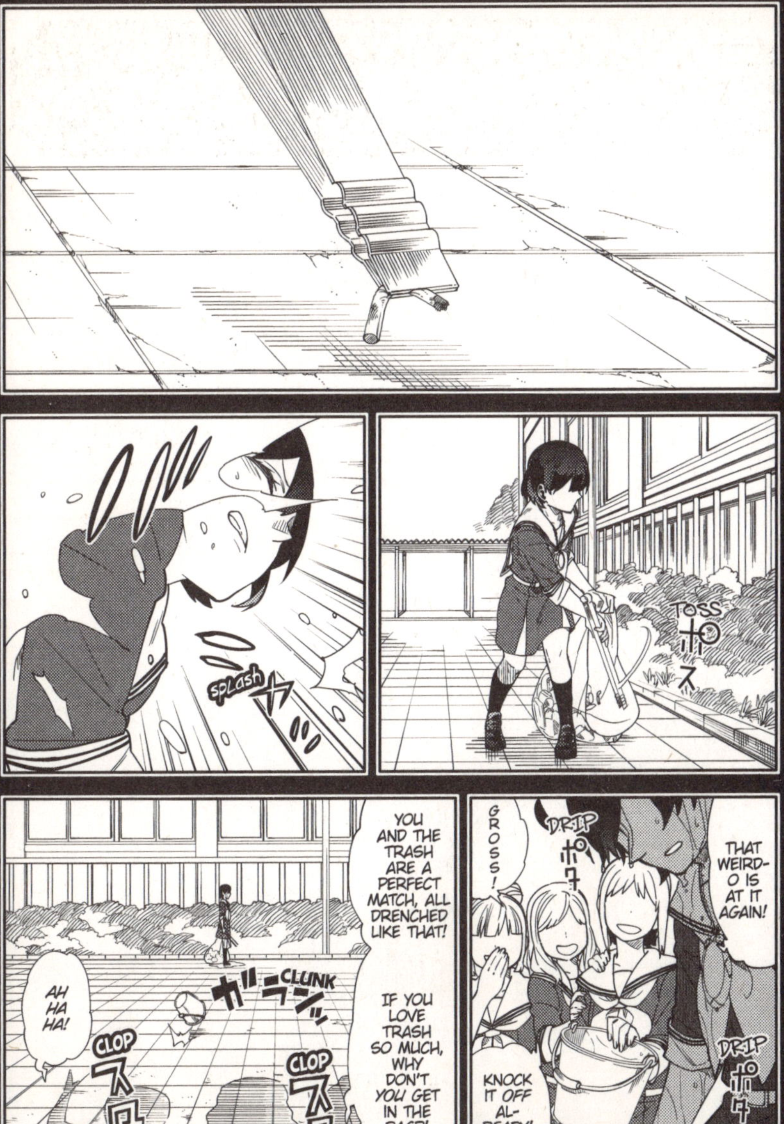

TOSS
splash
GROSS!
DRIP
THAT WEIRD-O IS AT IT AGAIN!
KNOCK IT OFF AL-READY! HEE HEE...!
DRIP
YOU AND THE TRASH ARE A PERFECT MATCH, ALL DRENCHED LIKE THAT!
IF YOU LOVE TRASH SO MUCH, WHY DON'T *YOU* GET IN THE BAG?!
CLUNK
AH HA HA!
CLOP
CLOP

IT'S OKAY.

THERE MUST BE SOMETHING THAT I CAN DO...

THERE MUST BE SOMETHING I CAN DO...

TO HELP OTHERS.

IS THAT HOW YOU REALLY FEEL?

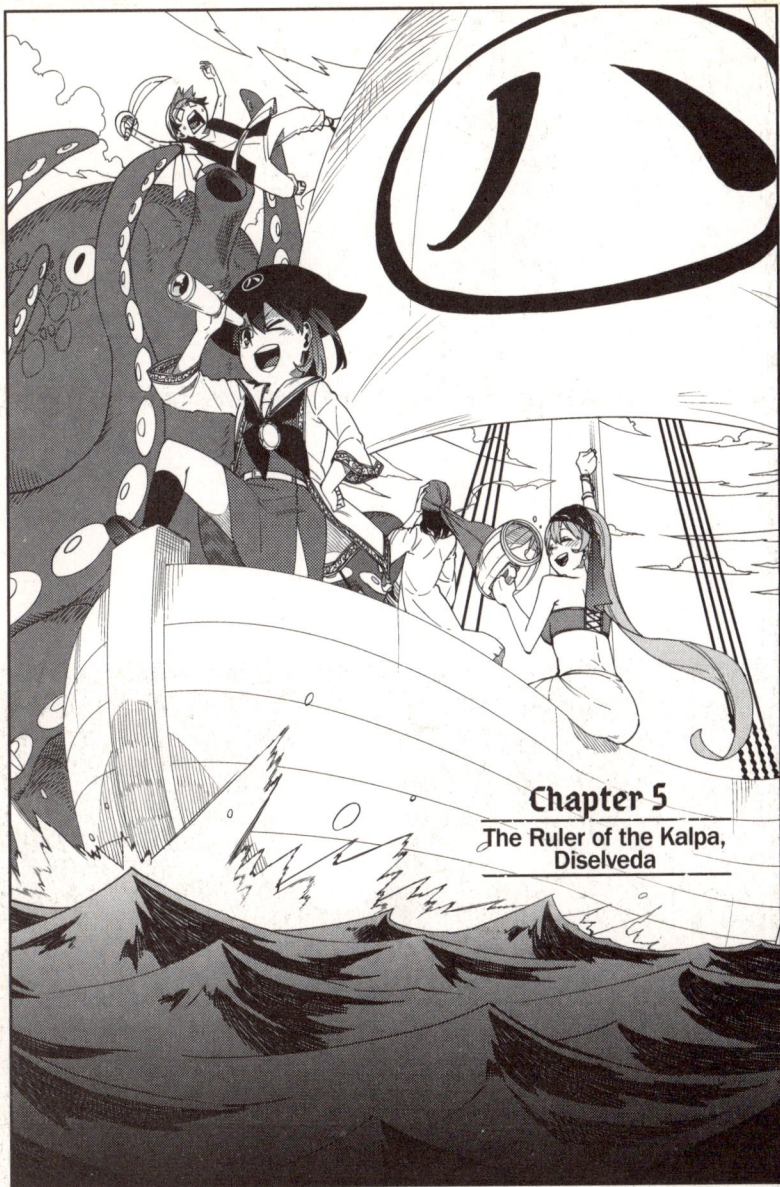

Chapter 5
The Ruler of the Kalpa, Diselveda

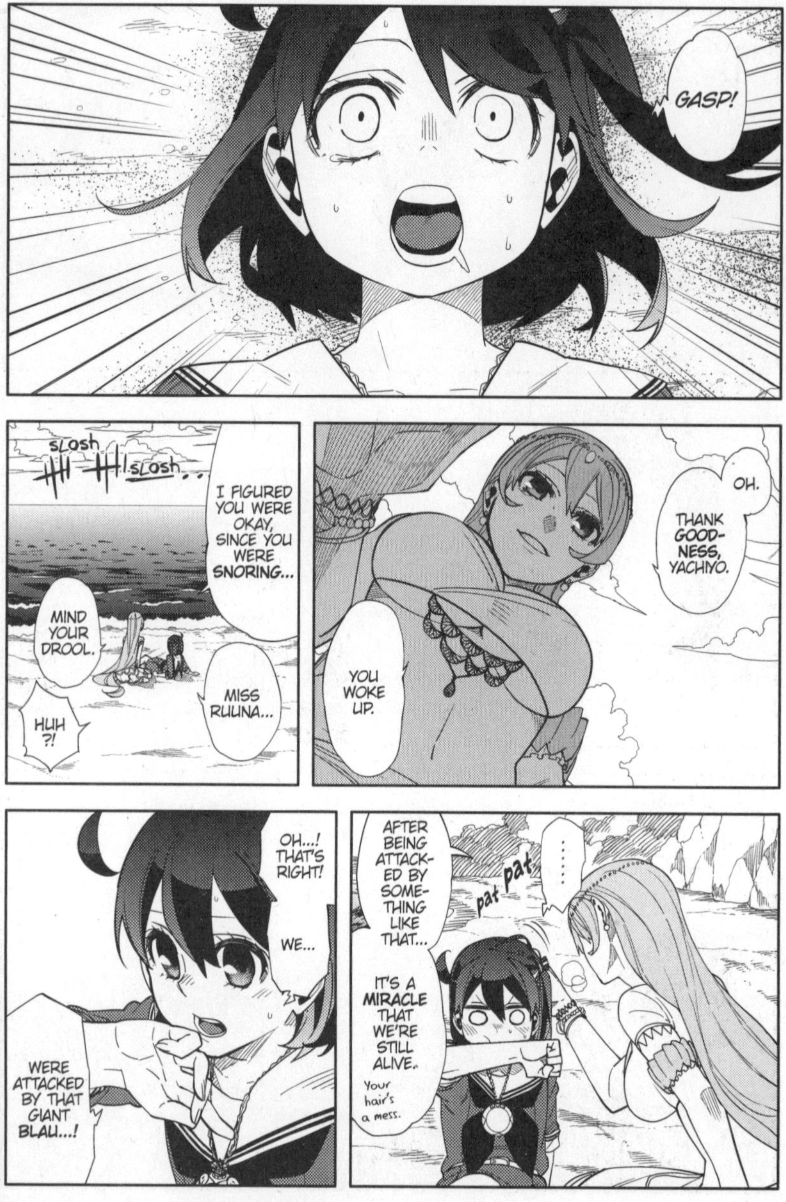
GASP!
OH.
THANK GOODNESS, YACHIYO.
YOU WOKE UP.
I FIGURED YOU WERE OKAY, SINCE YOU WERE SNORING...
SLOSH SLOSH...
MISS RUUNA...
MIND YOUR DROOL.
HUH?!
......
AFTER BEING ATTACKED BY SOMETHING LIKE THAT...
pat pat
IT'S A MIRACLE THAT WE'RE STILL ALIVE.
Your hair's a mess.
OH...! THAT'S RIGHT!
WE...
WERE ATTACKED BY THAT GIANT BLAU...!

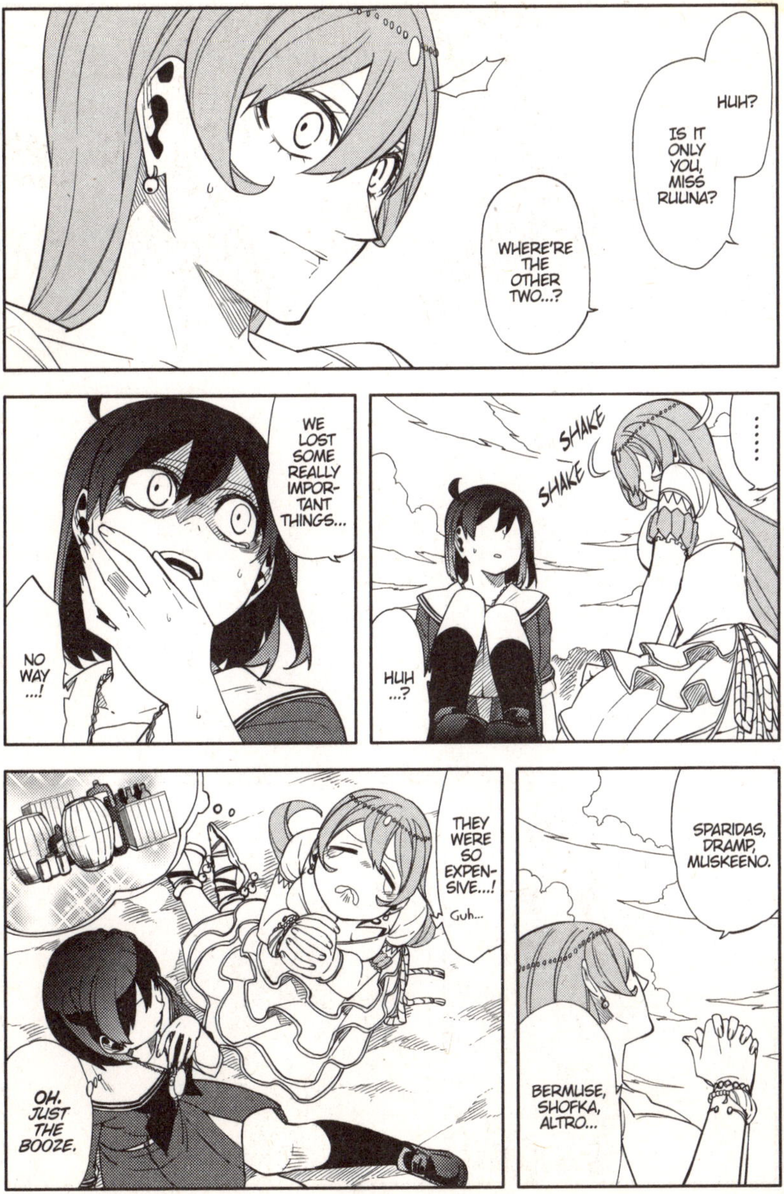
HUH?
IS IT ONLY YOU, MISS RUUNA?
WHERE'RE THE OTHER TWO...?
......
SHAKE
SHAKE
HUH ...?
WE LOST SOME REALLY IMPOR-TANT THINGS...
NO WAY ...!
SPARIDAS, DRAMP, MUSKEENO.
BERMUSE, SHOFKA, ALTRO...
THEY WERE SO EXPEN-SIVE...!
Guh...
OH. JUST THE BOOZE.

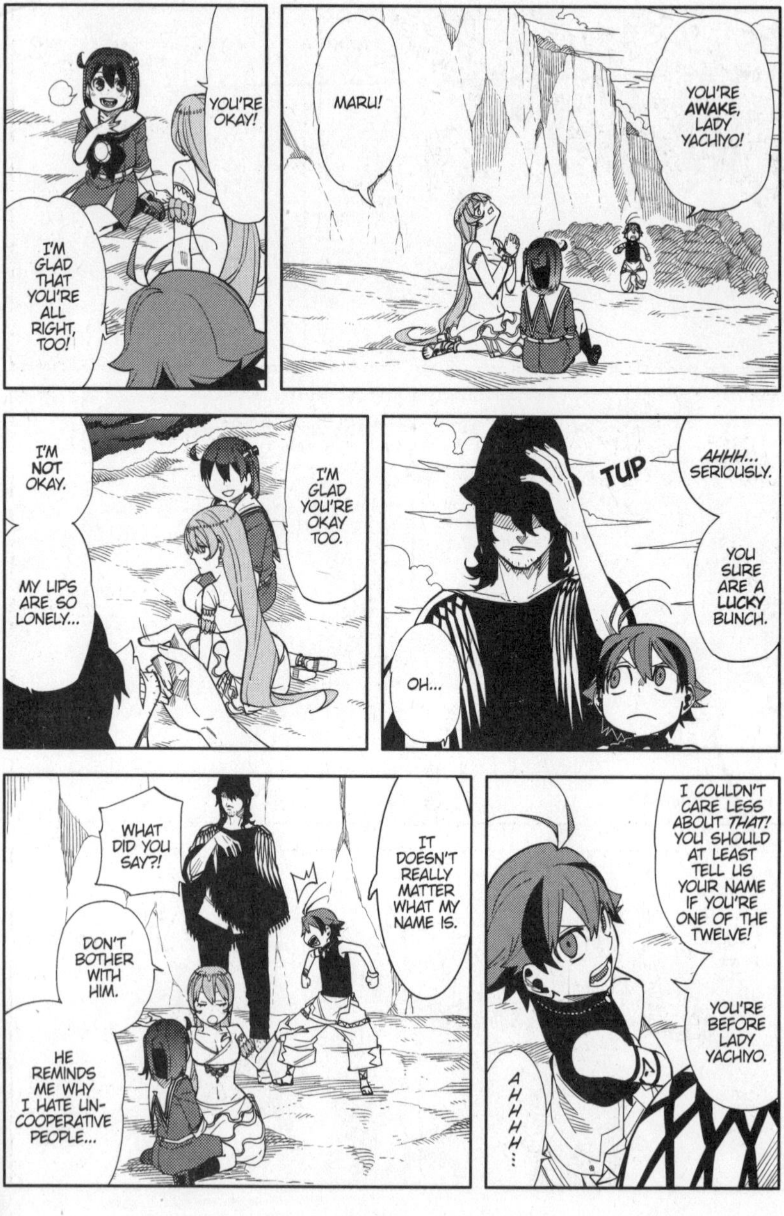

YOU'RE AWAKE, LADY YACHIYO!
MARU!
YOU'RE OKAY!
I'M GLAD THAT YOU'RE ALL RIGHT, TOO!
AHHH... SERIOUSLY.
TUP
YOU SURE ARE A **LUCKY** BUNCH.
OH...
I'M GLAD YOU'RE OKAY TOO.
I'M NOT OKAY.
MY LIPS ARE SO LONELY...
I COULDN'T CARE LESS ABOUT *THAT!* YOU SHOULD AT LEAST TELL US YOUR NAME IF YOU'RE ONE OF THE TWELVE!
YOU'RE BEFORE LADY YACHIYO.
AHHHH...
IT DOESN'T REALLY MATTER WHAT MY NAME IS.
WHAT DID YOU SAY?!
DON'T BOTHER WITH HIM.
HE REMINDS ME WHY I HATE UN-COOPERATIVE PEOPLE...

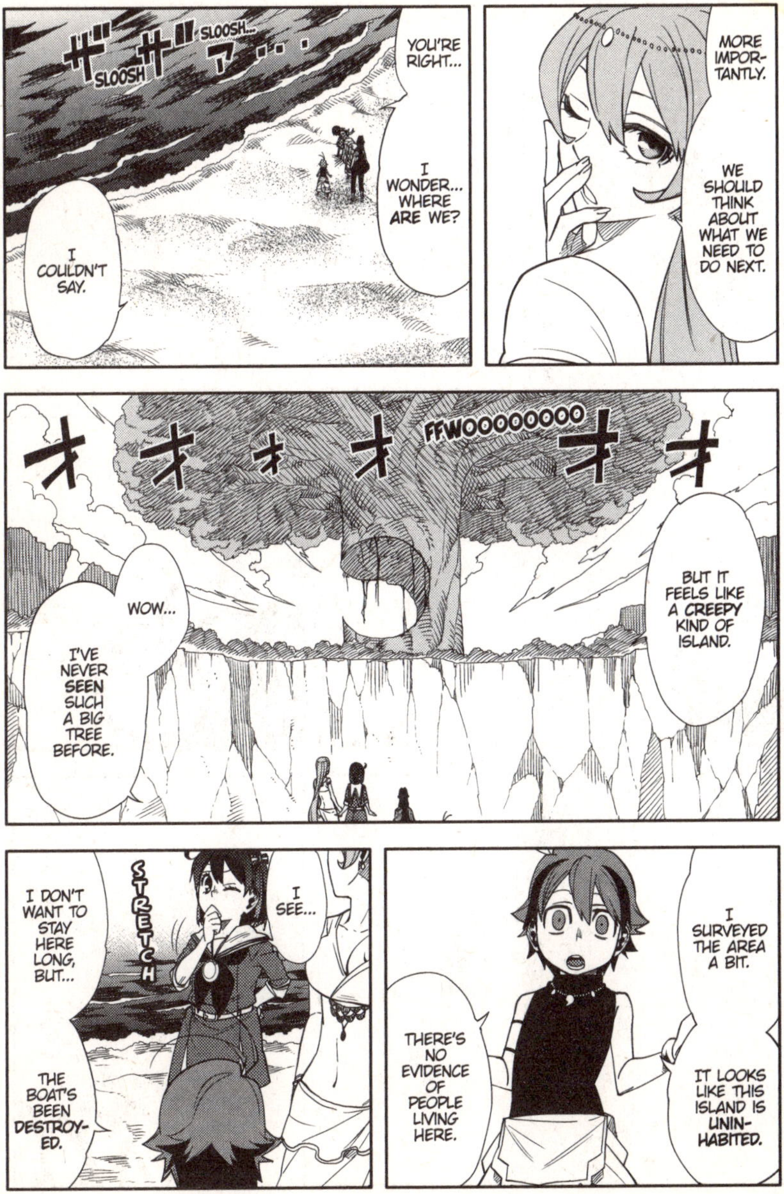

MORE IMPOR-TANTLY.
WE SHOULD THINK ABOUT WHAT WE NEED TO DO NEXT.
YOU'RE RIGHT...
I WONDER... WHERE ARE WE?
SLOOSH...
SLOOSH
I COULDN'T SAY.
FFWOOOOOOOO
BUT IT FEELS LIKE A CREEPY KIND OF ISLAND.
WOW...
I'VE NEVER SEEN SUCH A BIG TREE BEFORE.
I SURVEYED THE AREA A BIT.
IT LOOKS LIKE THIS ISLAND IS UNIN-HABITED.
THERE'S NO EVIDENCE OF PEOPLE LIVING HERE.
I SEE...
STRETCH
I DON'T WANT TO STAY HERE LONG, BUT...
THE BOAT'S BEEN DESTROY-ED.

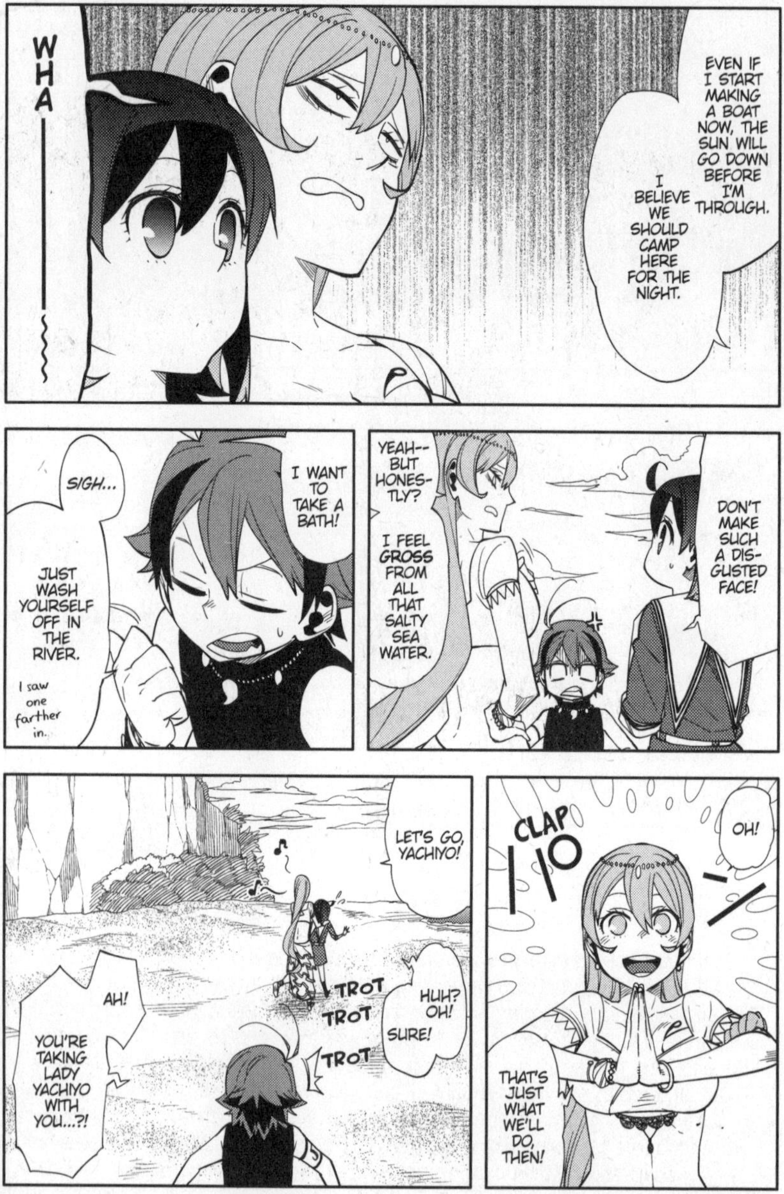
EVEN IF I START MAKING A BOAT NOW, THE SUN WILL GO DOWN BEFORE I'M THROUGH.
I BELIEVE WE SHOULD CAMP HERE FOR THE NIGHT.
WHA—
DON'T MAKE SUCH A DIS-GUSTED FACE!
YEAH-- BUT HONES-TLY?
I FEEL GROSS FROM ALL THAT SALTY SEA WATER.
I WANT TO TAKE A BATH!
SIGH...
JUST WASH YOURSELF OFF IN THE RIVER.
I saw one farther in.
OH!
CLAP
THAT'S JUST WHAT WE'LL DO, THEN!
LET'S GO, YACHIYO!
HUH? OH!
SURE!
TROT
TROT
TROT
AH!
YOU'RE TAKING LADY YACHIYO WITH YOU...?!

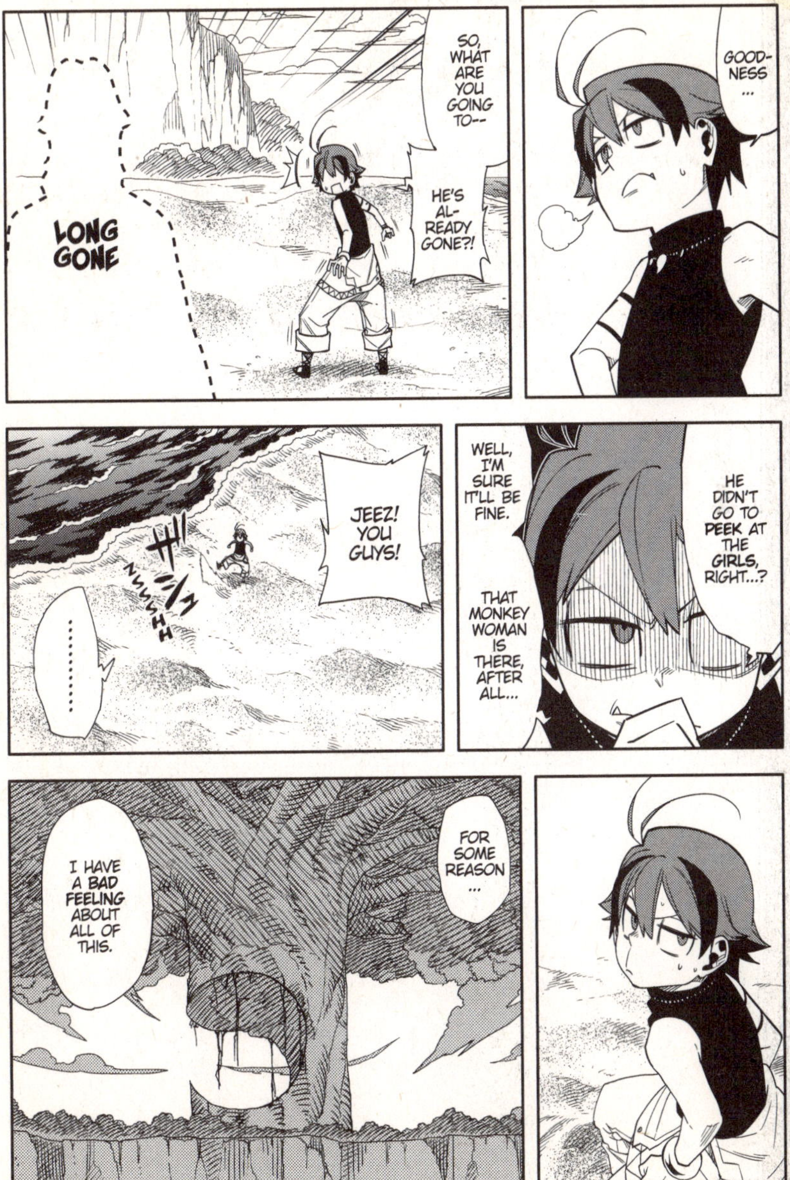

GOODNESS...
SO, WHAT ARE YOU GOING TO--
HE'S ALREADY GONE?!
LONG GONE
HE DIDN'T GO TO PEEK AT THE GIRLS, RIGHT...?
WELL, I'M SURE IT'LL BE FINE.
THAT MONKEY WOMAN IS THERE, AFTER ALL...
JEEZ! YOU GUYS!
NSSSHH
....
FOR SOME REASON...
I HAVE A BAD FEELING ABOUT ALL OF THIS.

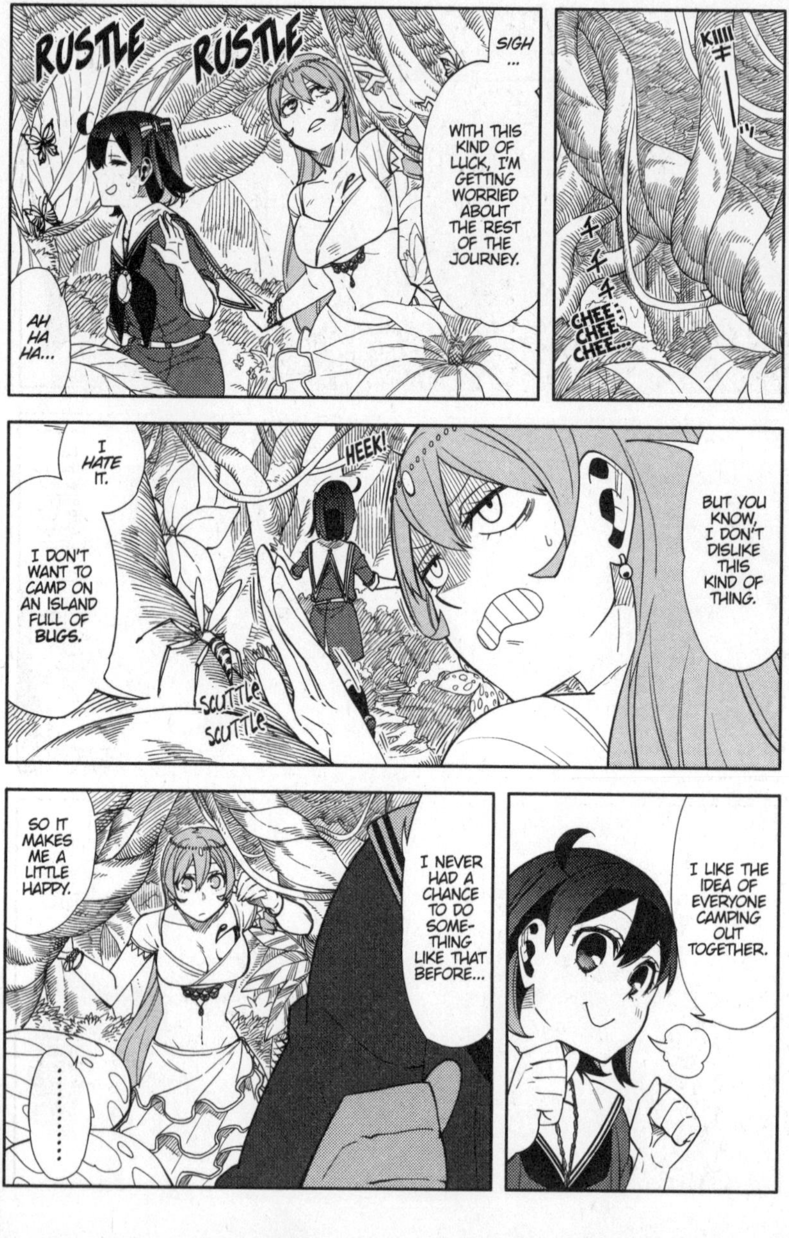
KIIII
キーッ
チチチ
CHEE CHEE CHEE...
SIGH ...
WITH THIS KIND OF LUCK, I'M GETTING WORRIED ABOUT THE REST OF THE JOURNEY.
RUSTLE RUSTLE
AH HA HA...
BUT YOU KNOW, I DON'T DISLIKE THIS KIND OF THING.
HEEK!
I HATE IT.
I DON'T WANT TO CAMP ON AN ISLAND FULL OF BUGS.
SCUTTLE SCUTTLE
I LIKE THE IDEA OF EVERYONE CAMPING OUT TOGETHER.
I NEVER HAD A CHANCE TO DO SOME-THING LIKE THAT BEFORE...
SO IT MAKES ME A LITTLE HAPPY.
....

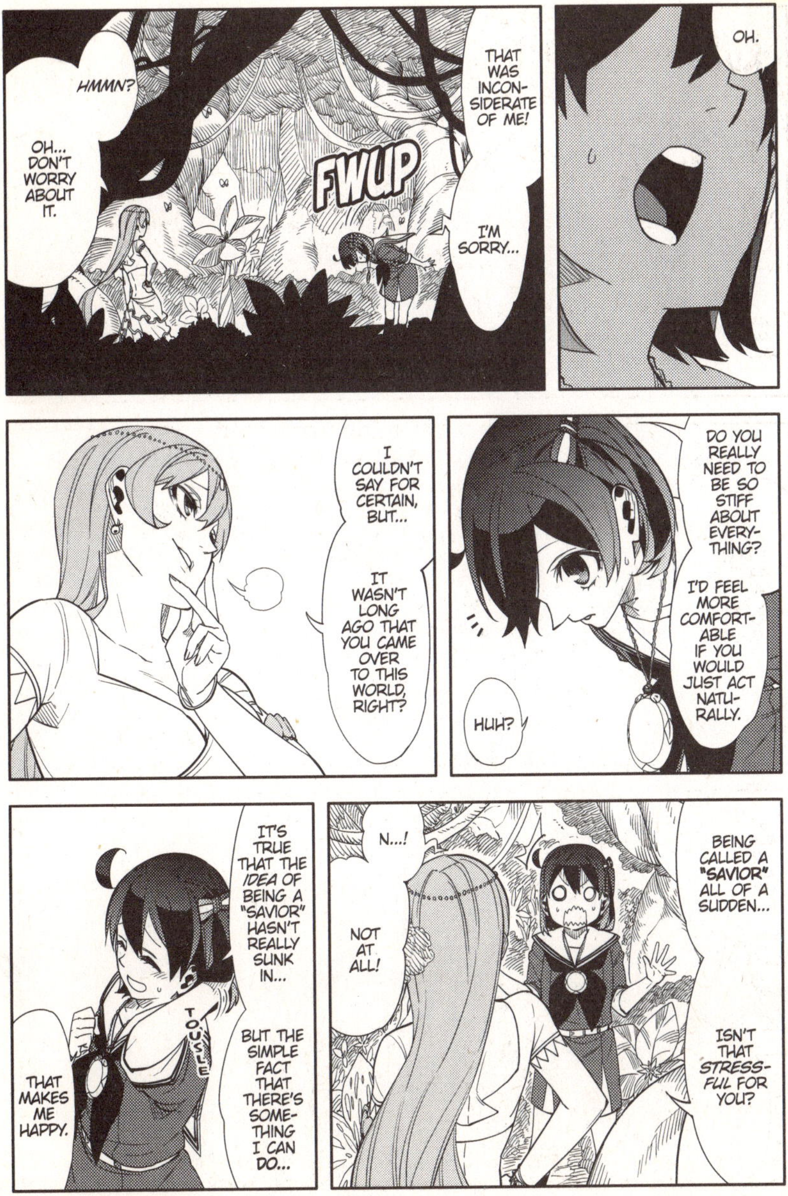

OH.
THAT WAS INCON-SIDERATE OF ME!
I'M SORRY...
FWUP
HMMN?
OH... DON'T WORRY ABOUT IT.
DO YOU REALLY NEED TO BE SO STIFF ABOUT EVERY-THING?
I'D FEEL MORE COMFORT-ABLE IF YOU WOULD JUST ACT NATU-RALLY.
HUH?
I COULDN'T SAY FOR CERTAIN, BUT...
IT WASN'T LONG AGO THAT YOU CAME OVER TO THIS WORLD, RIGHT?
BEING CALLED A "SAVIOR" ALL OF A SUDDEN...
ISN'T THAT STRESS-FUL FOR YOU?
N...!
NOT AT ALL!
IT'S TRUE THAT THE IDEA OF BEING A "SAVIOR" HASN'T REALLY SUNK IN...
BUT THE SIMPLE FACT THAT THERE'S SOME-THING I CAN DO...
TOUSLE
THAT MAKES ME HAPPY.

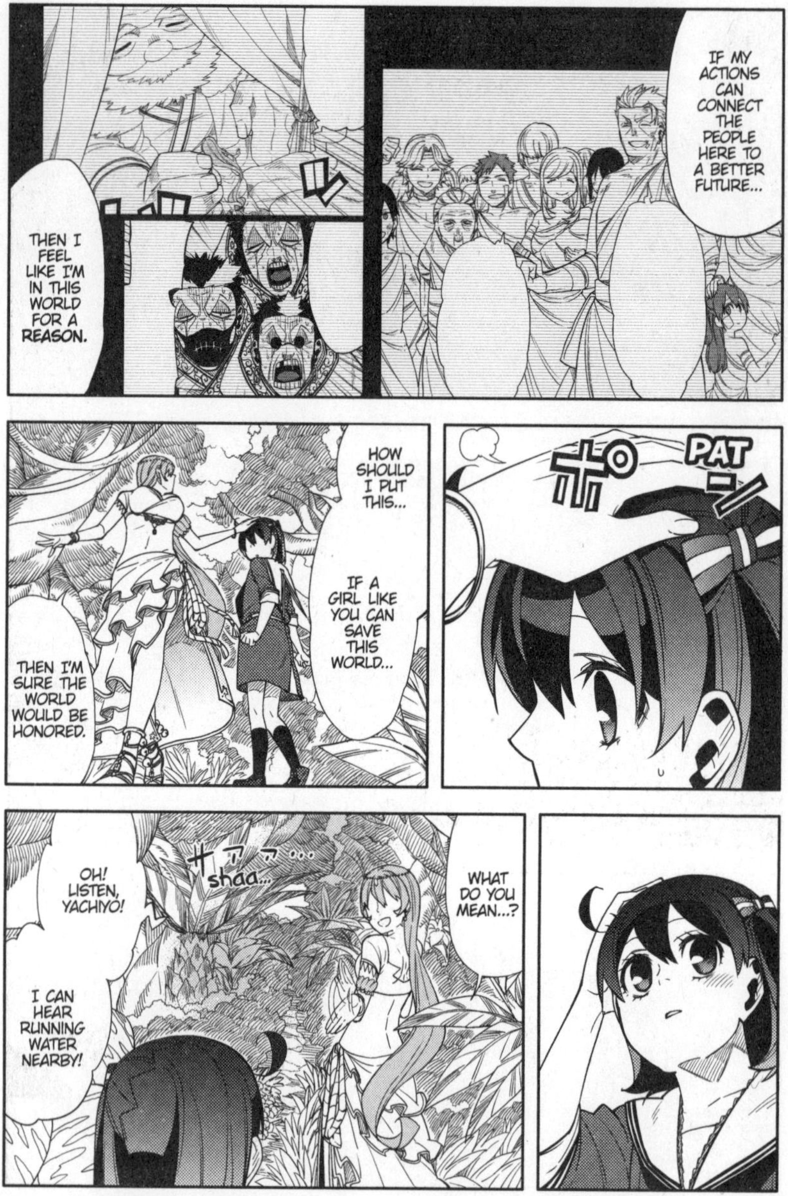
IF MY ACTIONS CAN CONNECT THE PEOPLE HERE TO A BETTER FUTURE...
THEN I FEEL LIKE I'M IN THIS WORLD FOR A REASON.
PAT
HOW SHOULD I PUT THIS...
IF A GIRL LIKE YOU CAN SAVE THIS WORLD...
THEN I'M SURE THE WORLD WOULD BE HONORED.
WHAT DO YOU MEAN...?
shaa...
OH! LISTEN, YACHIYO!
I CAN HEAR RUNNING WATER NEARBY!

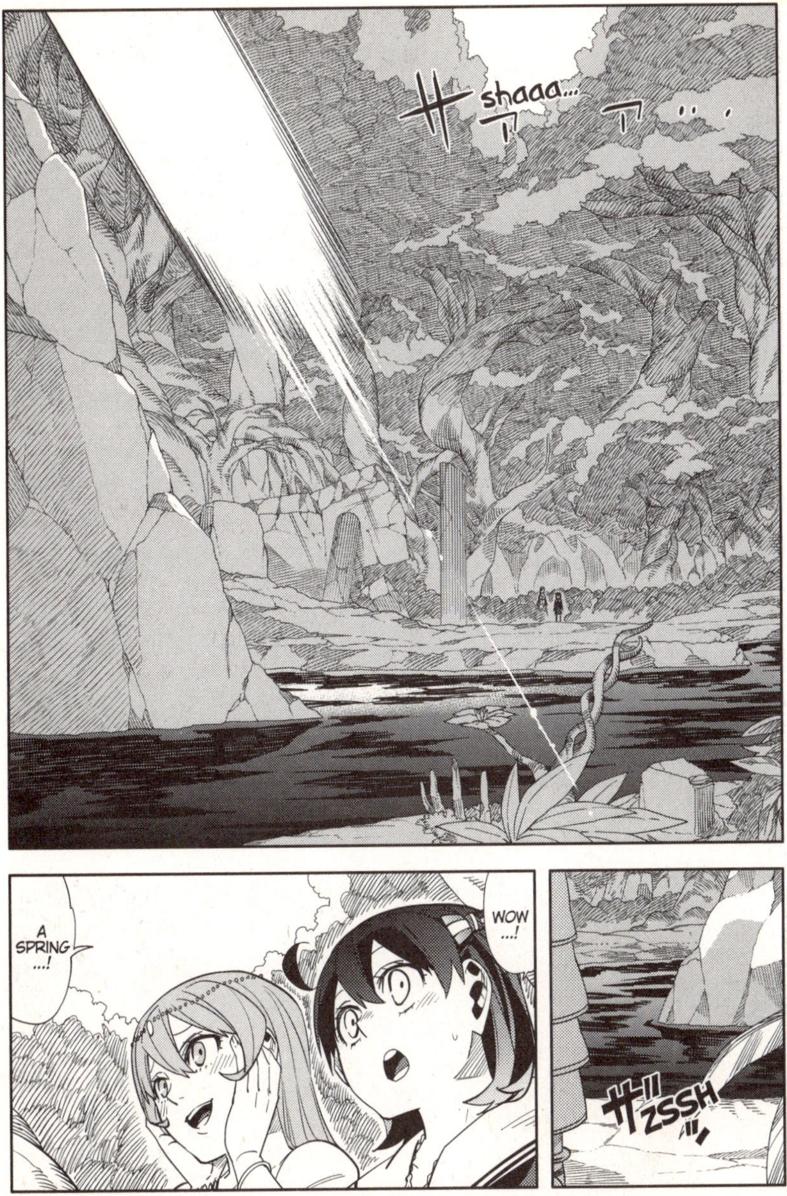
shaaa...
ZSSH
WOW ...!
A SPRING ...!

SO PRETTY...

...............!

THIS IS A LOT BETTER THAN I EXPECTED!

PLSSH

YAHOO!

THIS IS GREAT! THIS IS SO GREAT!

IS THERE SOMETHING WRITTEN ON IT...?

$$\lambda - \alpha \times \omega \times \lambda - \phi$$

$$\Pi \cup \rtimes \rtimes = \bullet - \times \Lambda \cup$$

$$L \times \phi \oplus \cup = 0 \cdot \vee$$

THAT ROCK...

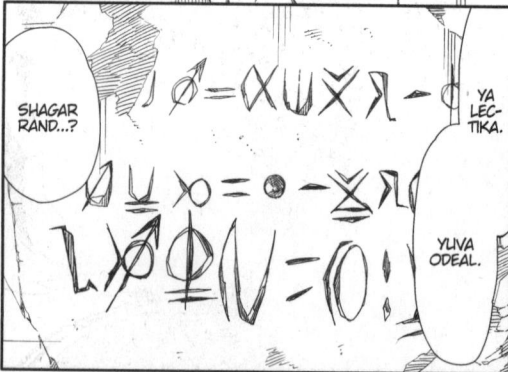

SHAGAR RAND...?

$$\lambda - \alpha \times \omega \times \lambda - \phi$$

$$\Pi \cup \rtimes \rtimes = \bullet - \times \Lambda \cup$$

$$L \times \phi \oplus \cup = 0 \cdot \vee$$

YA LEC-TIKA.

YUVA ODEAL.

WHAT IS IT, YACHI-YO?

HM?

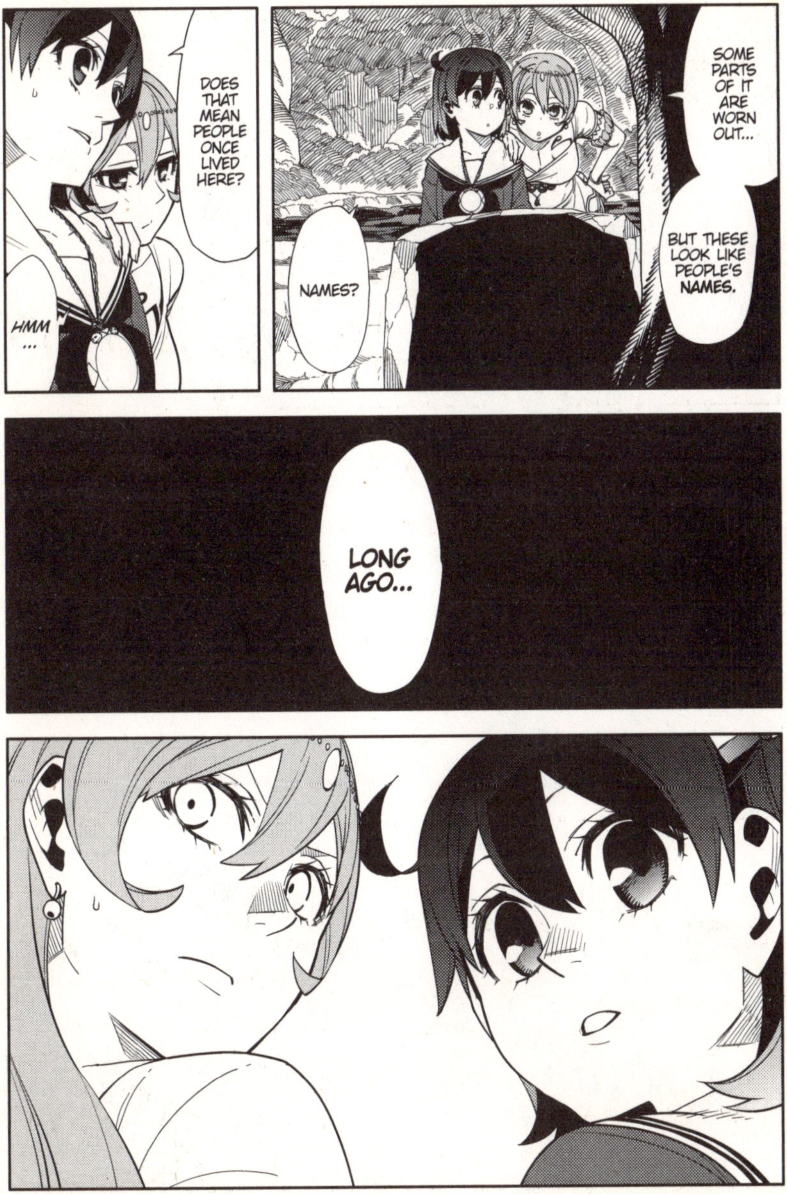
SOME PARTS OF IT ARE WORN OUT...
BUT THESE LOOK LIKE PEOPLE'S NAMES.
NAMES?
DOES THAT MEAN PEOPLE ONCE LIVED HERE?
HMM...
LONG AGO...

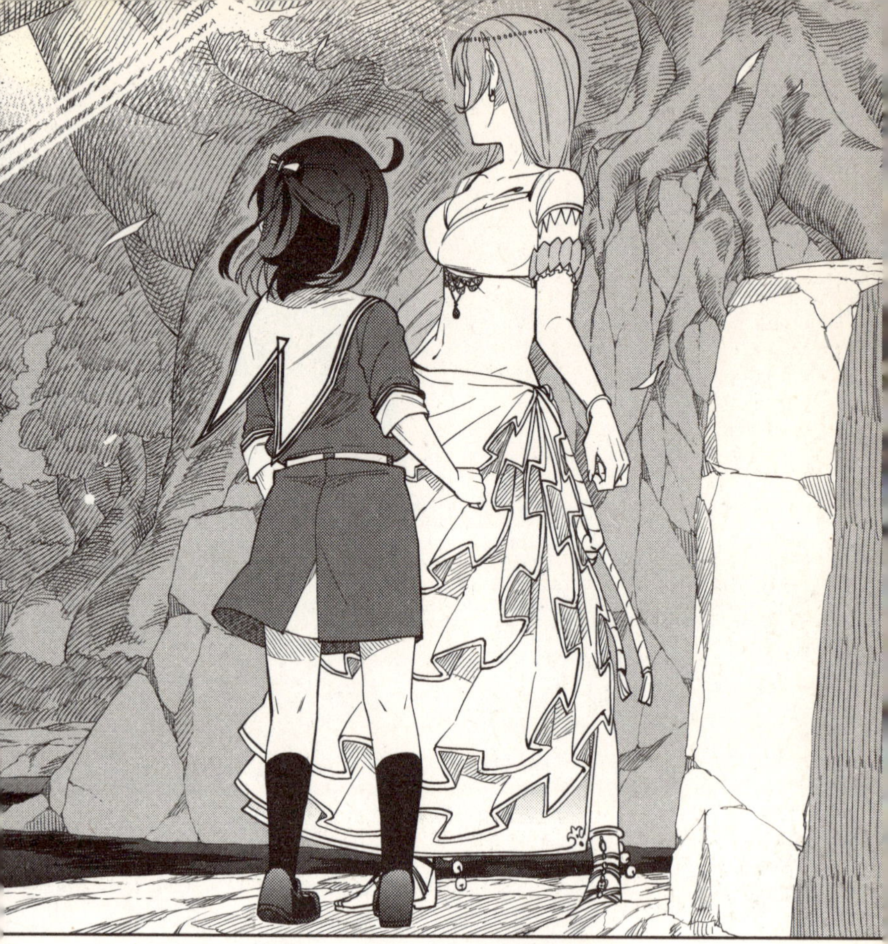

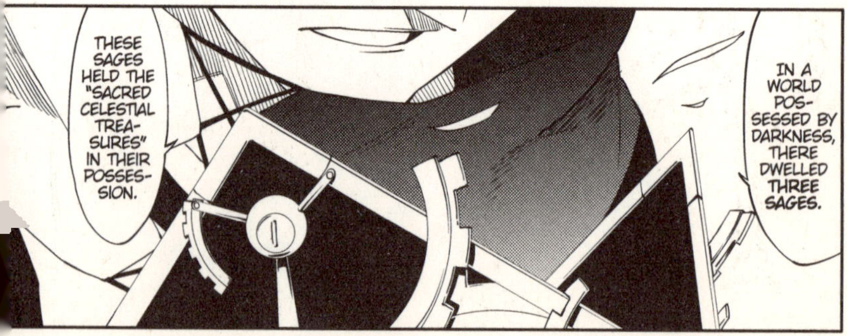
IN A WORLD POS-SESSED BY DARKNESS, THERE DWELLED THREE SAGES.
THESE SAGES HELD THE "SACRED CELESTIAL TREA-SURES" IN THEIR POSSES-SION.

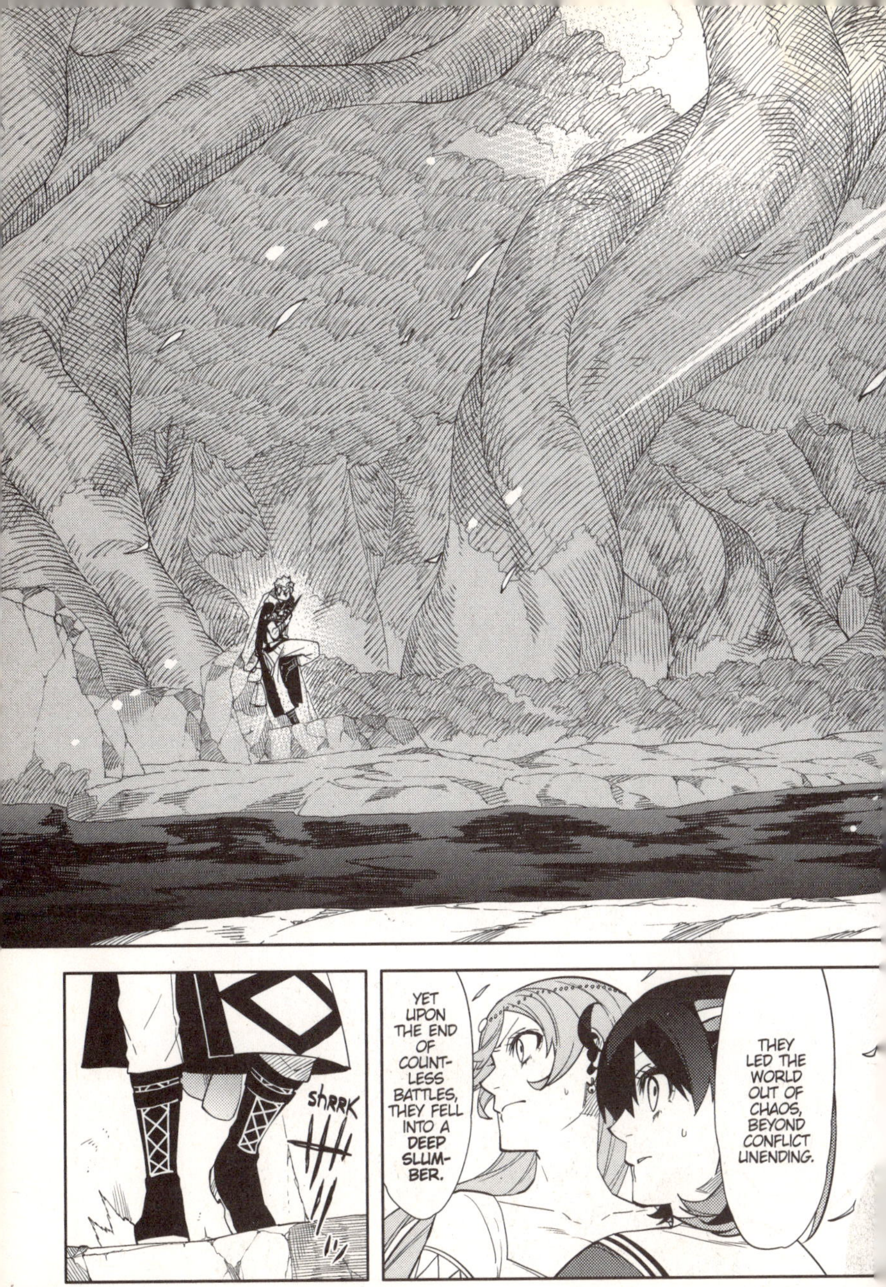
THEY LED THE WORLD OUT OF CHAOS, BEYOND CONFLICT UNENDING.
YET UPON THE END OF COUNT-LESS BATTLES, THEY FELL INTO A DEEP SLUM-BER.
SHRRK

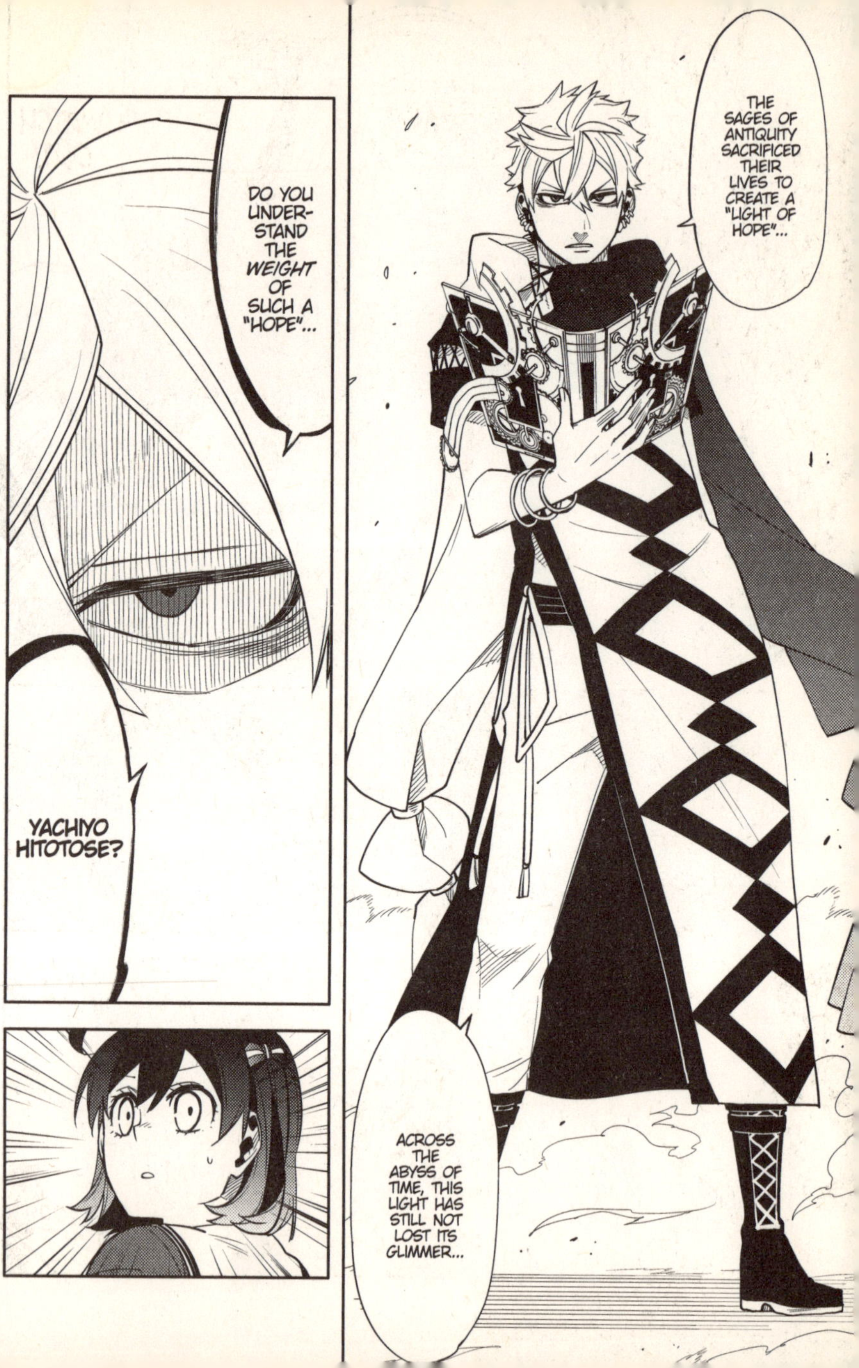
THE SAGES OF ANTIQUITY SACRIFICED THEIR LIVES TO CREATE A "LIGHT OF HOPE"...
ACROSS THE ABYSS OF TIME, THIS LIGHT HAS STILL NOT LOST ITS GLIMMER...
DO YOU UNDER-STAND THE *WEIGHT* OF SUCH A "HOPE"...
YACHIYO HITOTOSE?

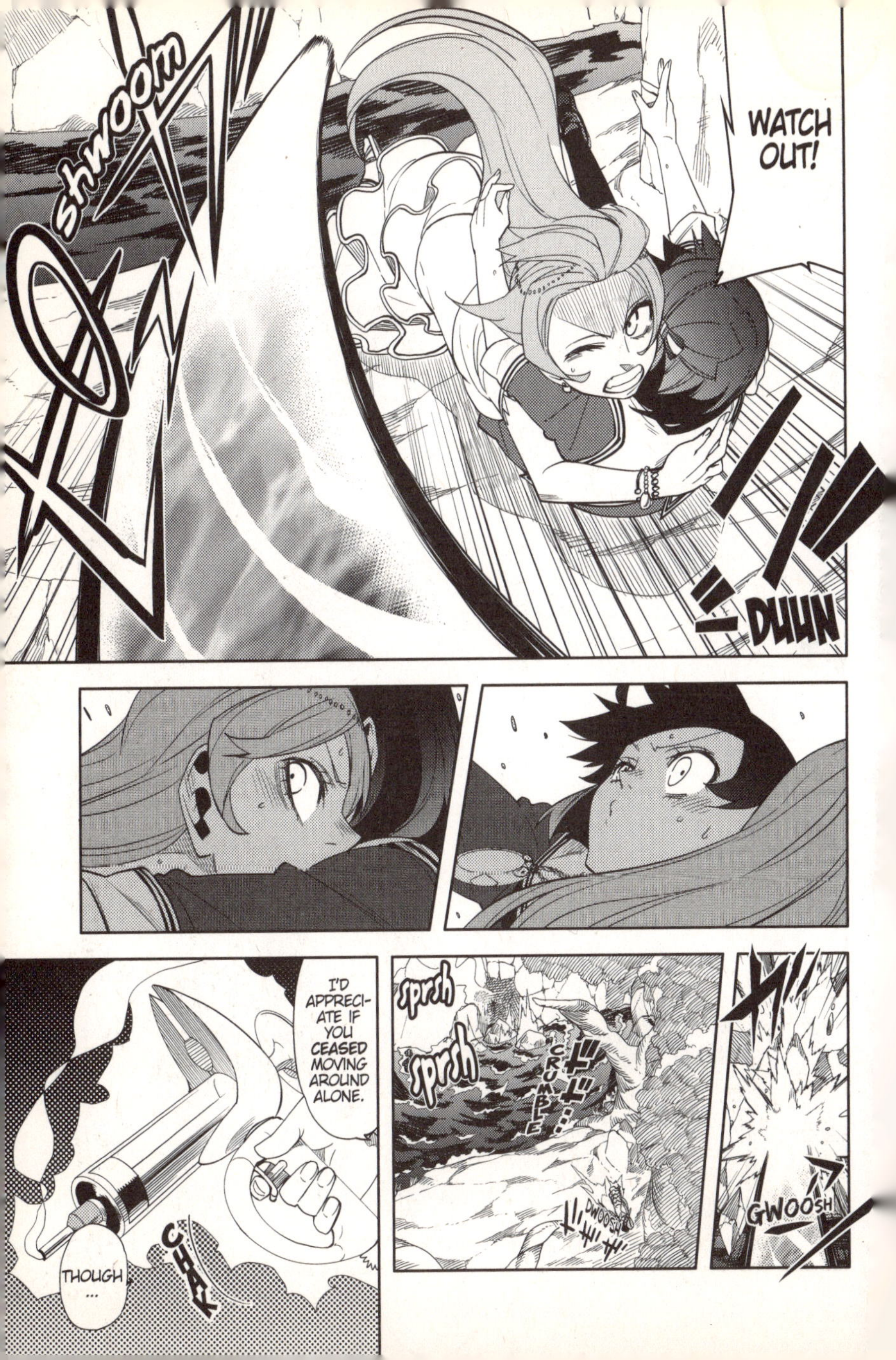
WATCH OUT!
shwoom
DUUN
GWOOSH
sprsh
sprsh
CRUMBLE...
DWOOSH
I'D APPRECIATE IF YOU CEASED MOVING AROUND ALONE.
CHAK
THOUGH...

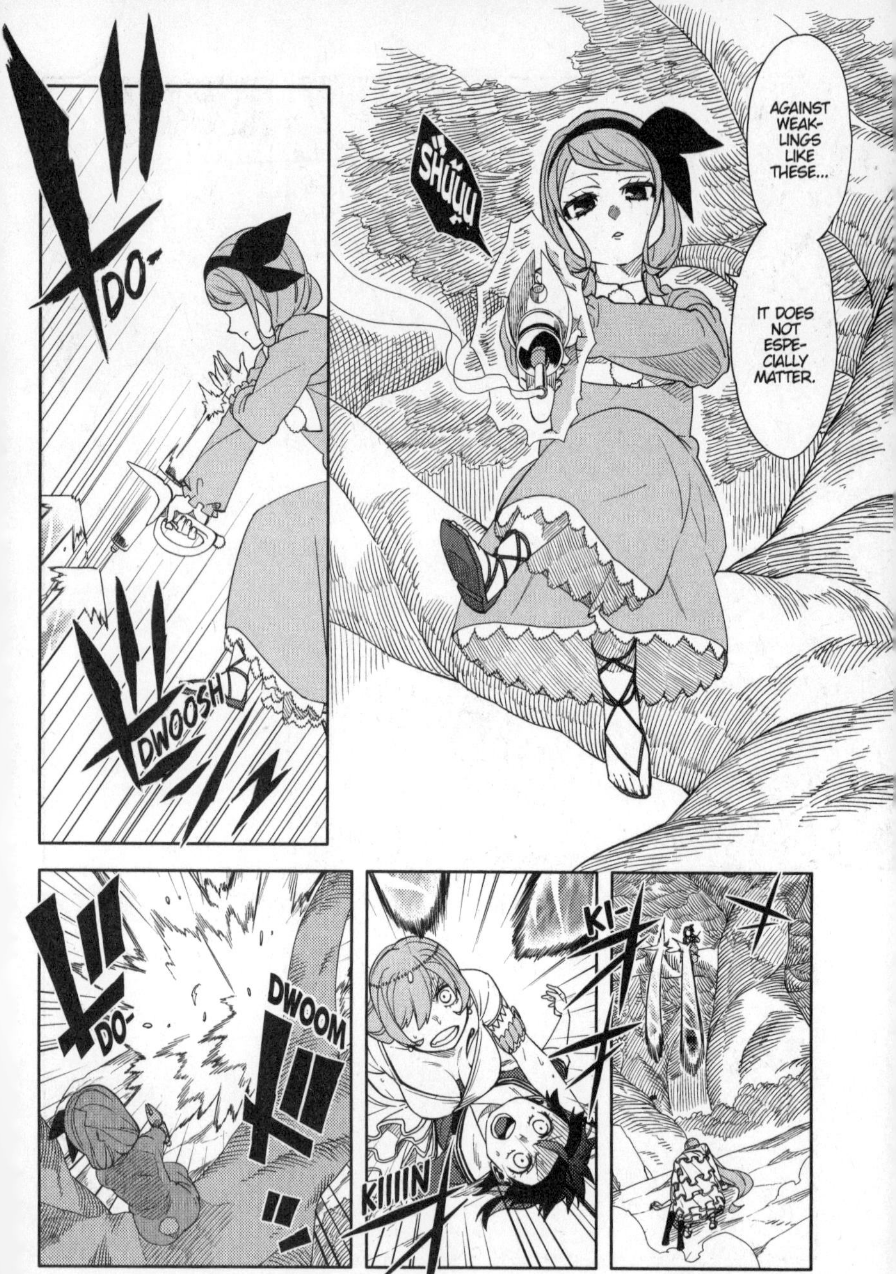
SHUUU
AGAINST WEAK-LINGS LIKE THESE...
IT DOES NOT ESPE-CIALLY MATTER.
DO-
DWOOSH
KI-
KIIIIN
DO-
DWOOM

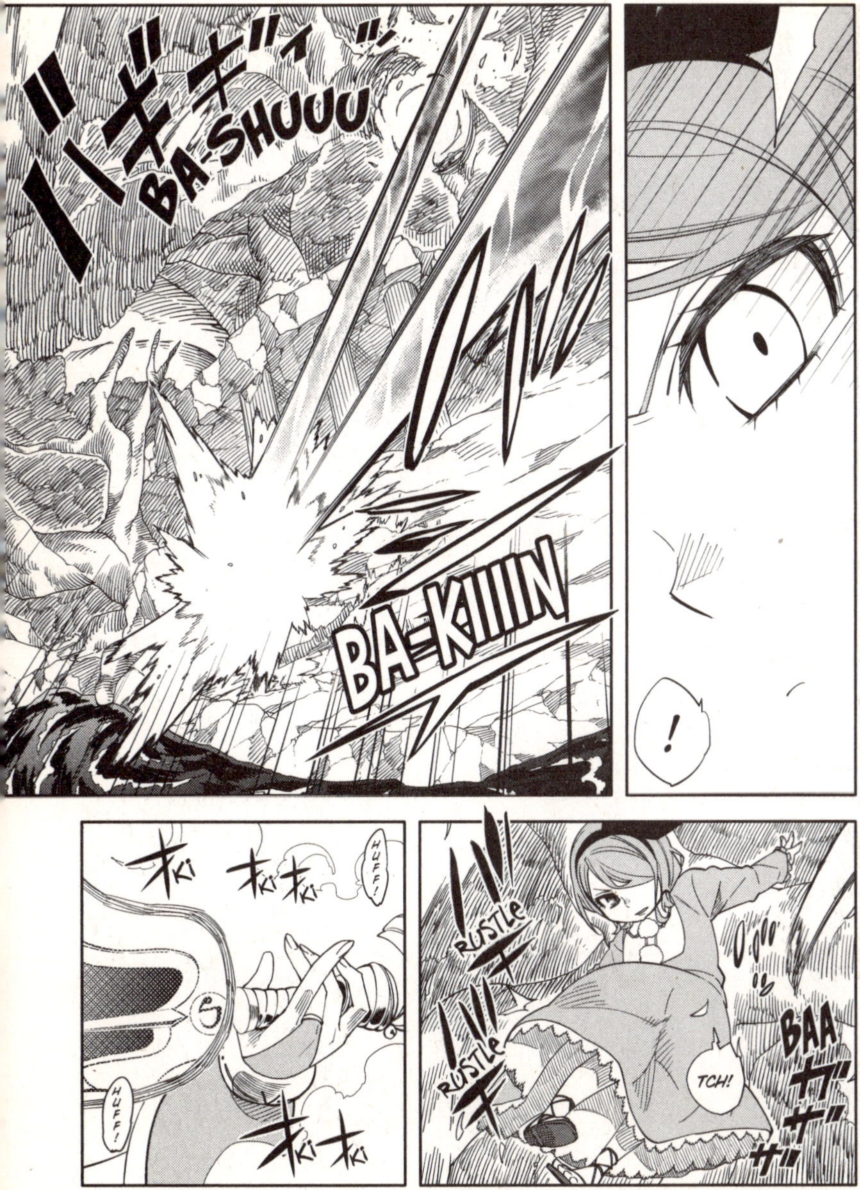
!
BA-SHUUU
BA-KIIIIN
RUSTLE
RUSTLE
TCH!
BAA
KI KI KI
HUFF!
HUFF!
KI KI

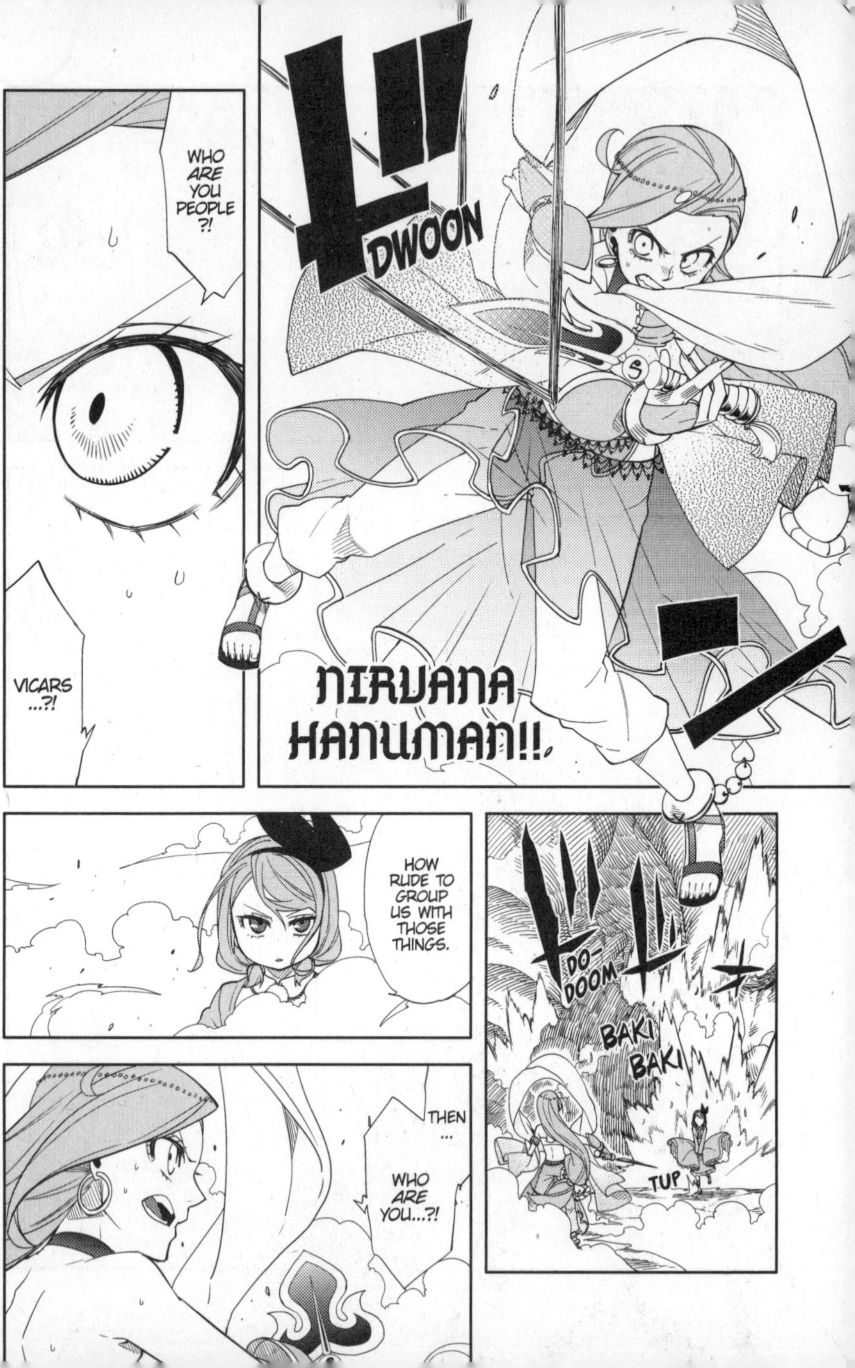
DWOON
NIRVANA HANUMAN!!
WHO ARE YOU PEOPLE?!
VICARS...?!
DO-DOOM
BAKI BAKI
TUP
HOW RUDE TO GROUP US WITH THOSE THINGS.
THEN...
WHO ARE YOU...?!

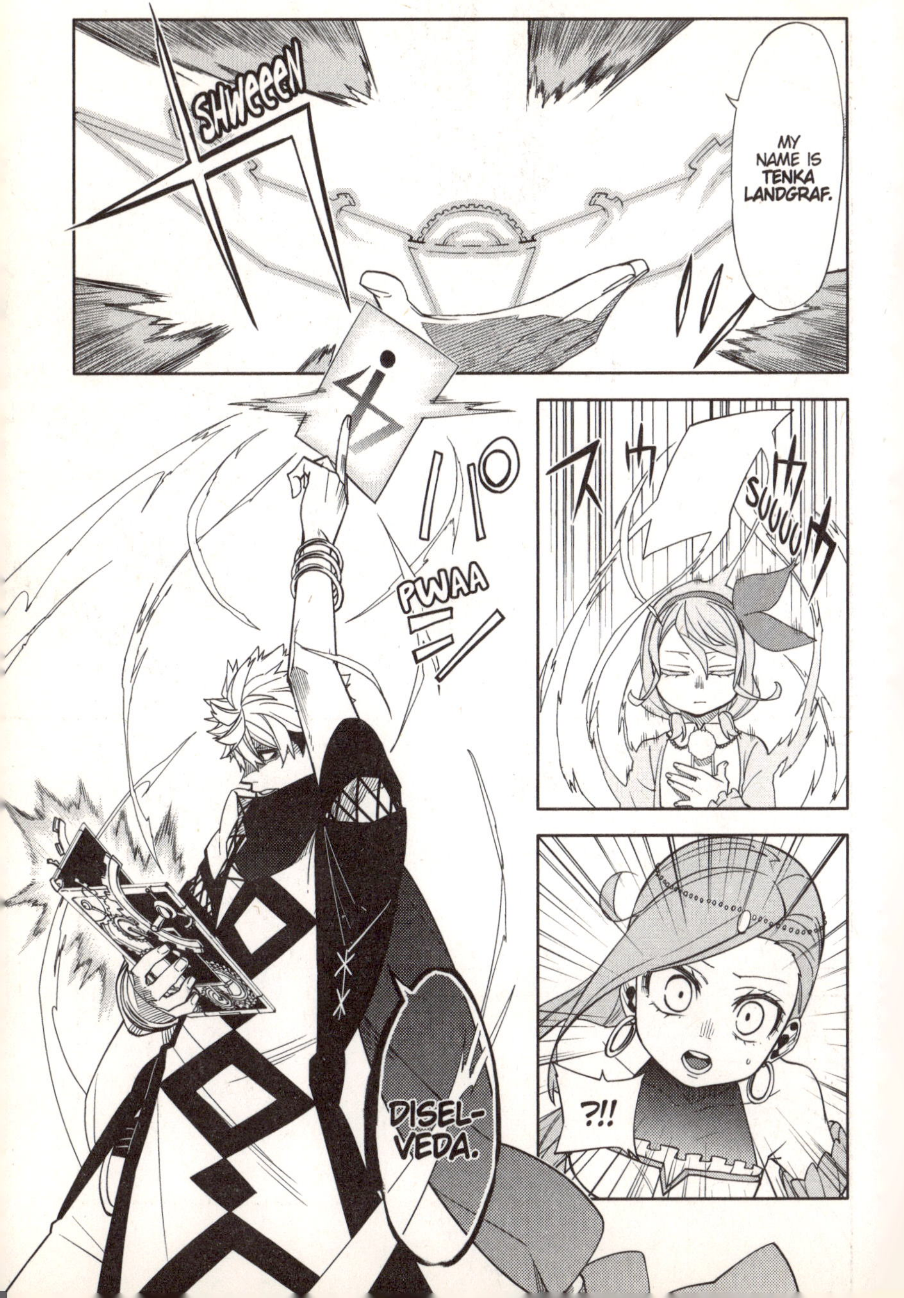
MY NAME IS TENKA LANDGRAF.
SHWEEEN
SUUUUU
?!!
PWAA
DISEL-VEDA.

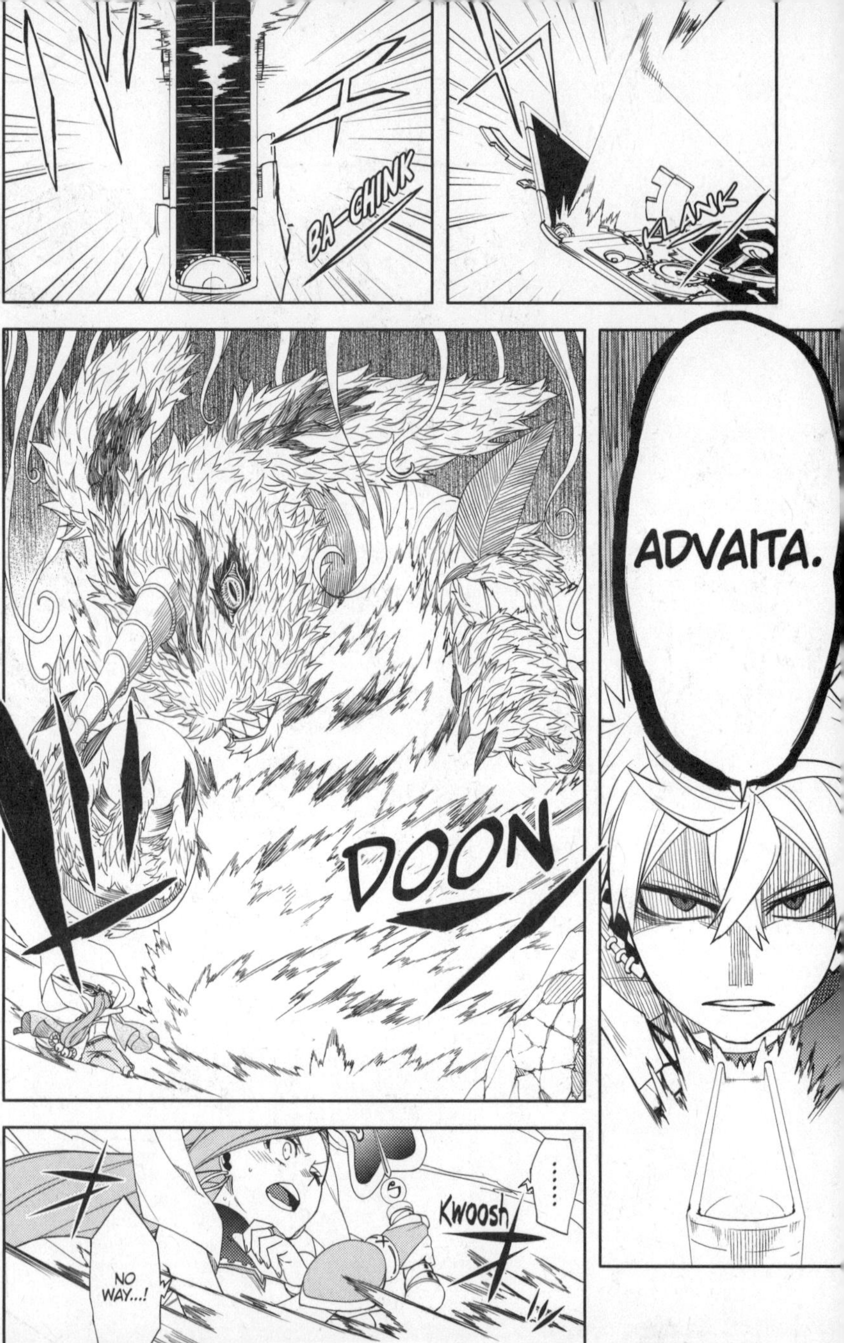
KLANK
BA-CHINK
ADVAITA.
DOON
......
Kwoosh
NO WAY...!

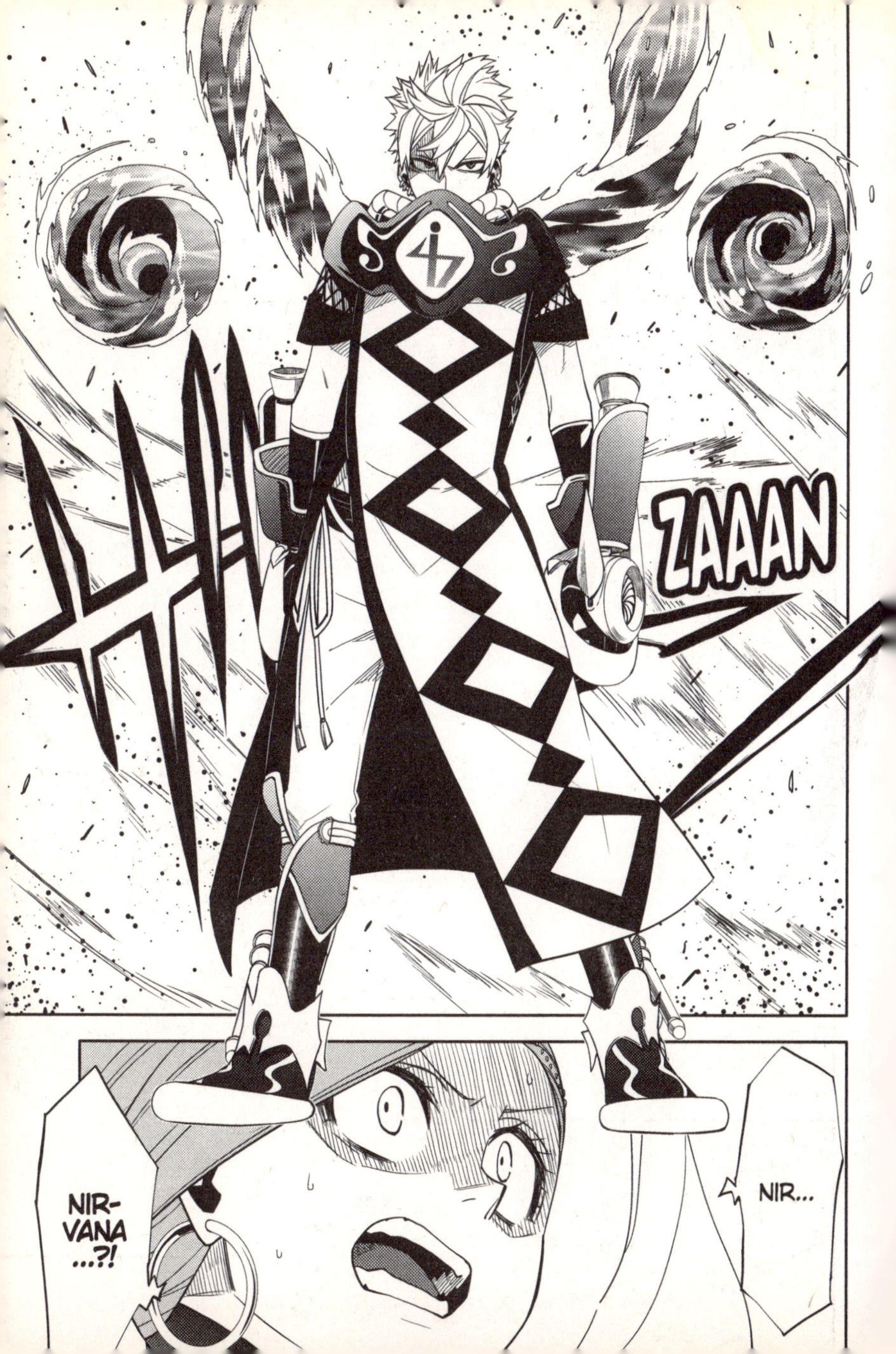
ZAAAN
NIR...
NIR-
VANA
...?!

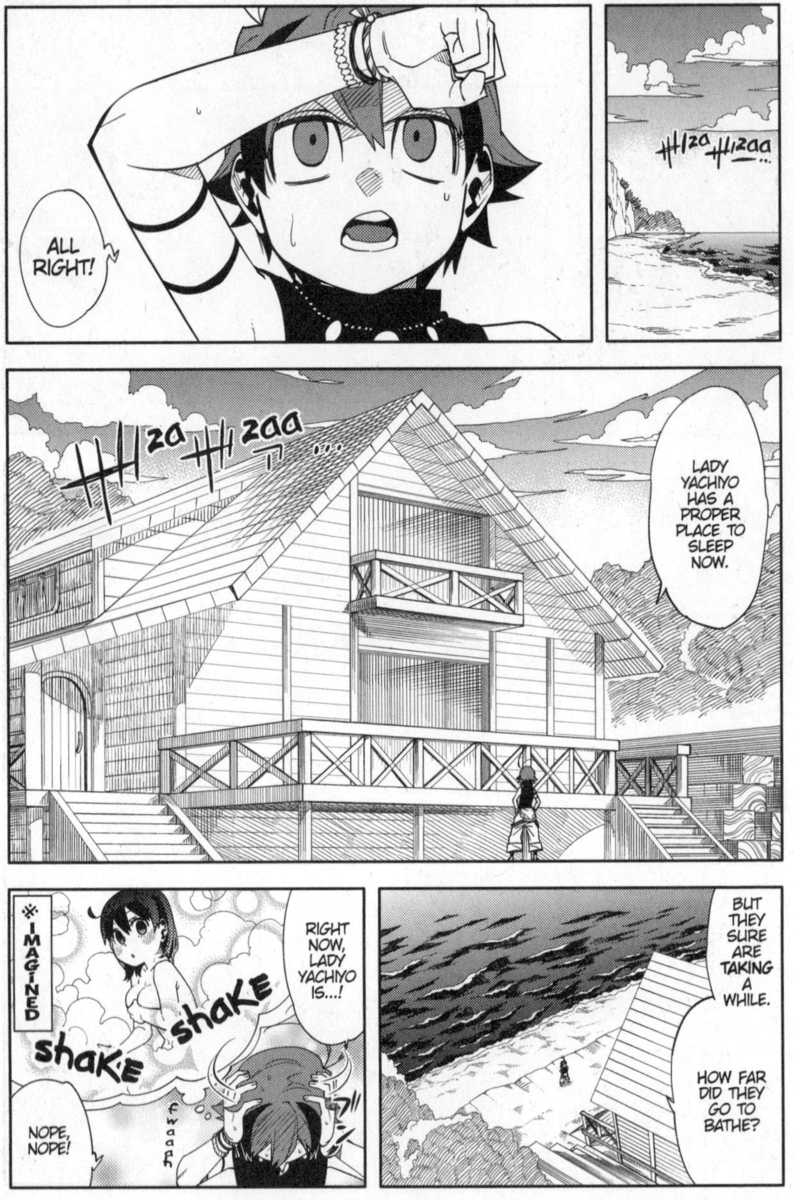
za zaa...
ALL RIGHT!
za zaa...
LADY YACHIYO HAS A PROPER PLACE TO SLEEP NOW.
BUT THEY SURE ARE TAKING A WHILE.
HOW FAR DID THEY GO TO BATHE?
※IMAGINED
RIGHT NOW, LADY YACHIYO IS...!
shake shake
fwaaah
NOPE, NOPE!

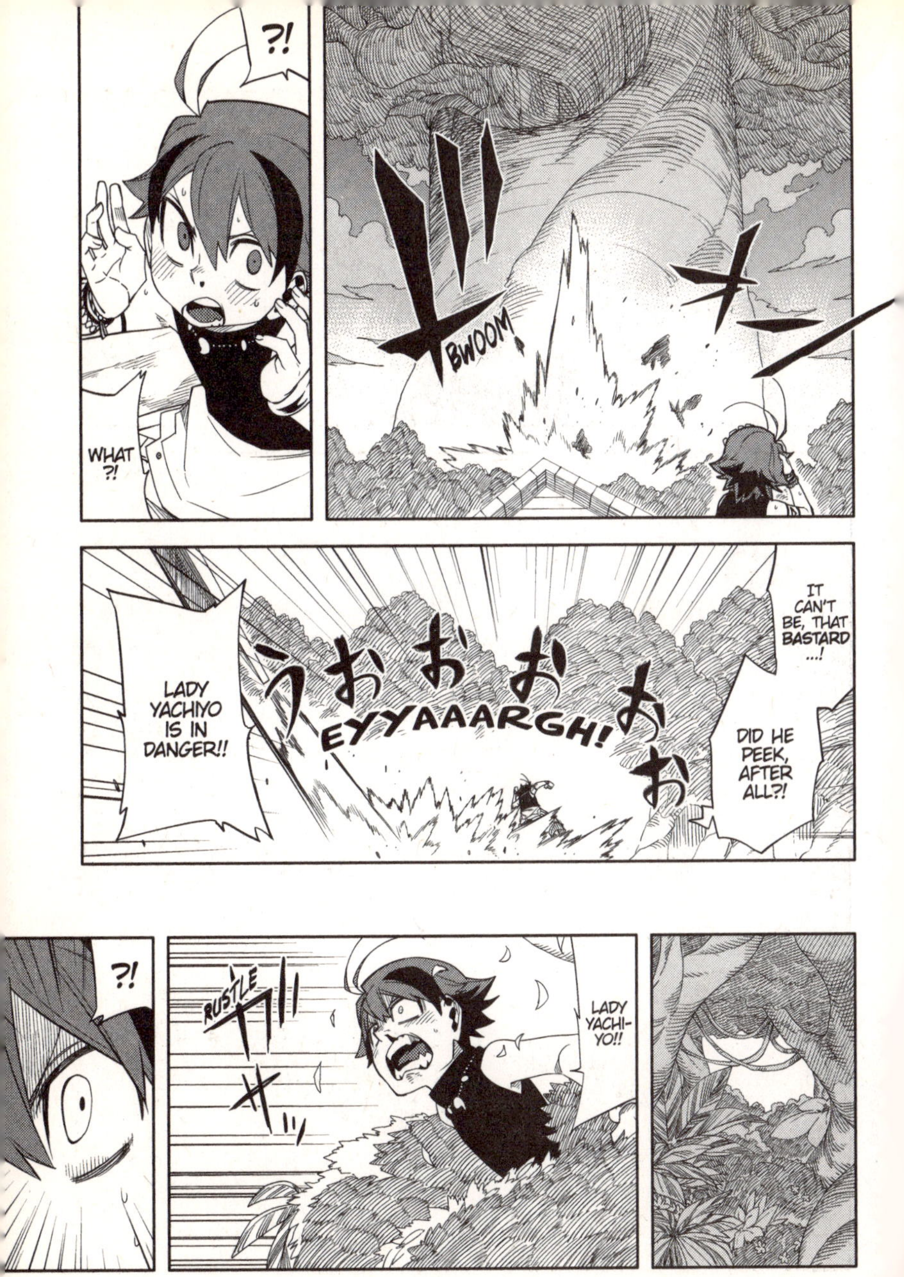
BWOOM
?!
WHAT ?!
IT CAN'T BE, THAT BASTARD ...!
DID HE PEEK, AFTER ALL?!
うおおおおお
EYYAAARGH!
LADY YACHIYO IS IN DANGER!!
LADY YACHI-YO!!
RUSTLE
?!

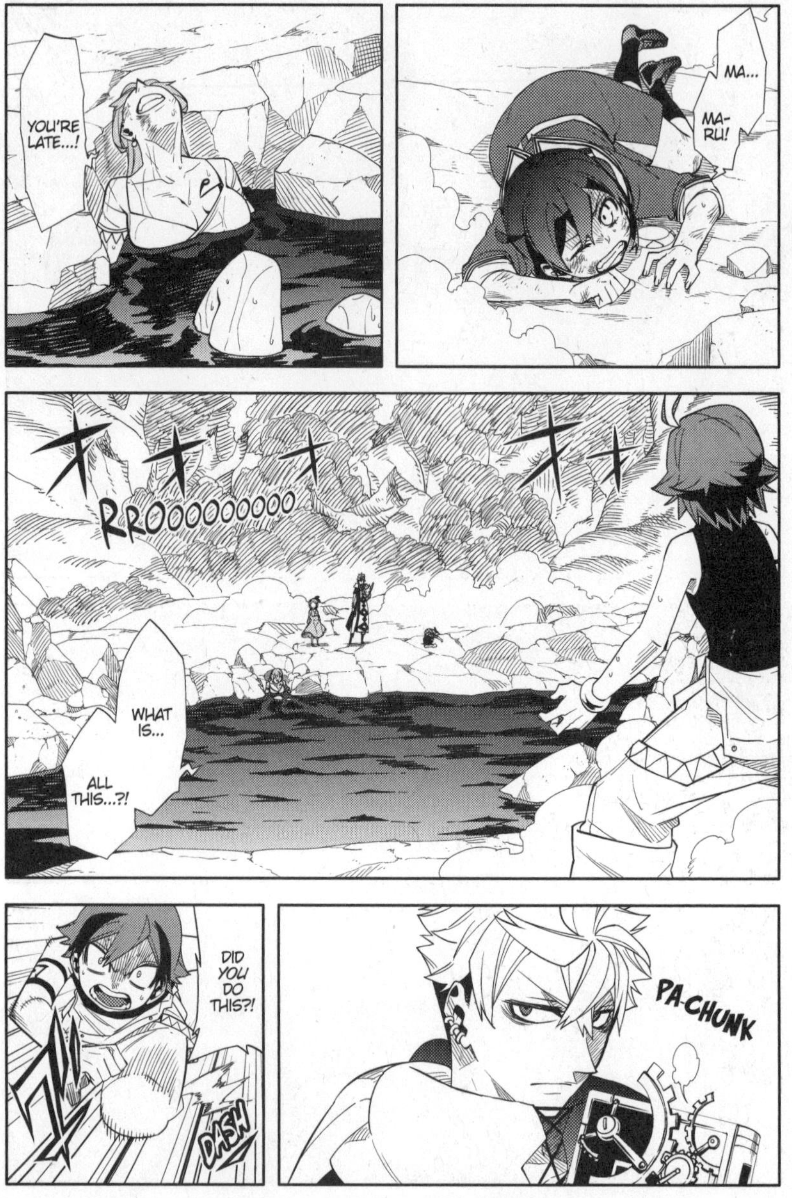

MA...
MA-RU!
YOU'RE LATE...!
RROOOOOOOOO
WHAT IS...
ALL THIS...?!
PA-CHUNK
DID YOU DO THIS?!
DASH

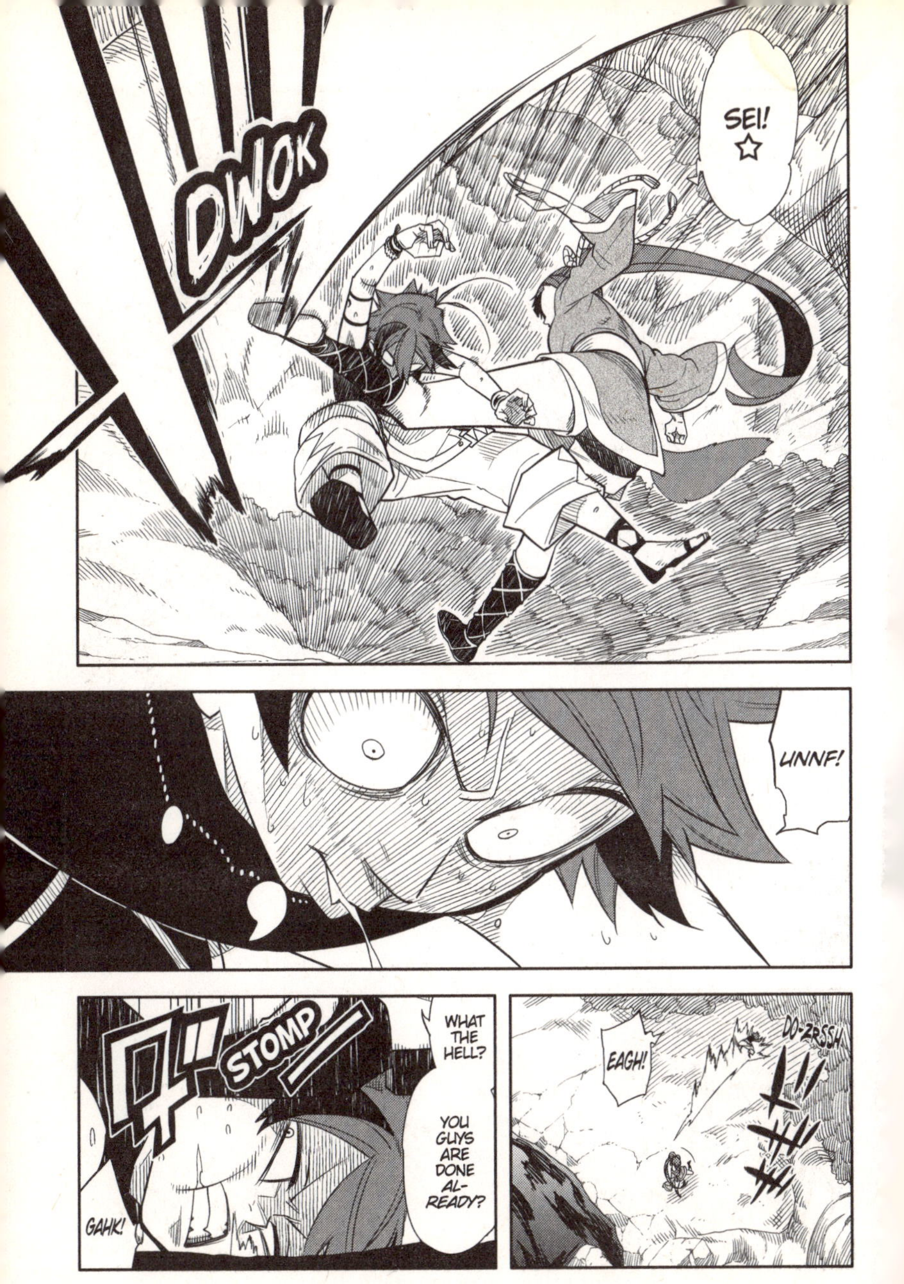
SEI! ☆
DWOK
UNNF!
DO-ZRSSH
EAGH!
WHAT THE HELL?
YOU GUYS ARE DONE AL-READY?
STOMP
GAHK!

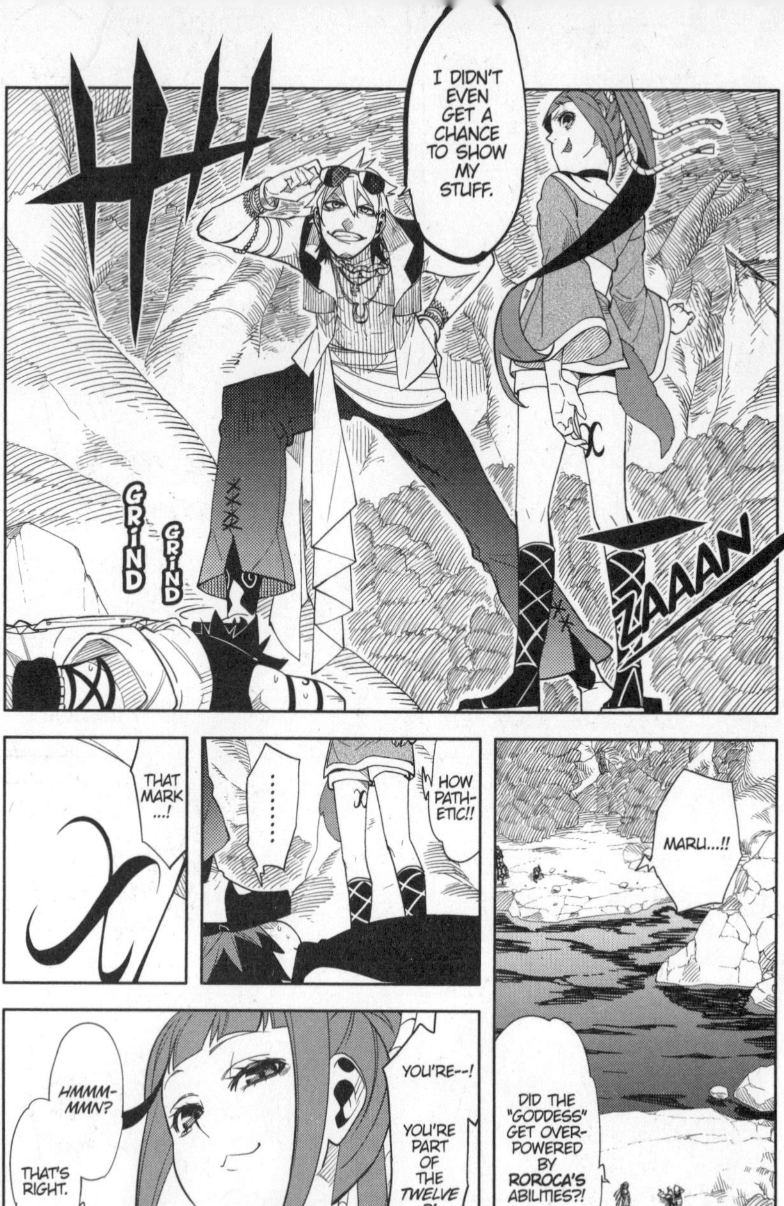
I DIDN'T EVEN GET A CHANCE TO SHOW MY STUFF.
ZAAAN
GRIND GRIND
MARU...!!
DID THE "GODDESS" GET OVER-POWERED BY ROROCA'S ABILITIES?!
HOW PATH-ETIC!!
......
THAT MARK ...!
YOU'RE--!
YOU'RE PART OF THE TWELVE ?!
HMMM-MMN?
THAT'S RIGHT.

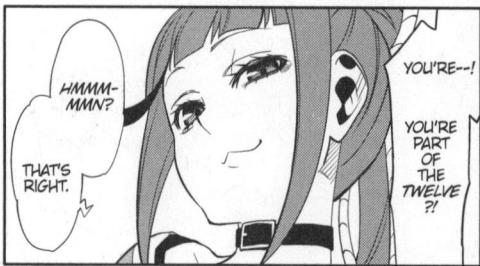

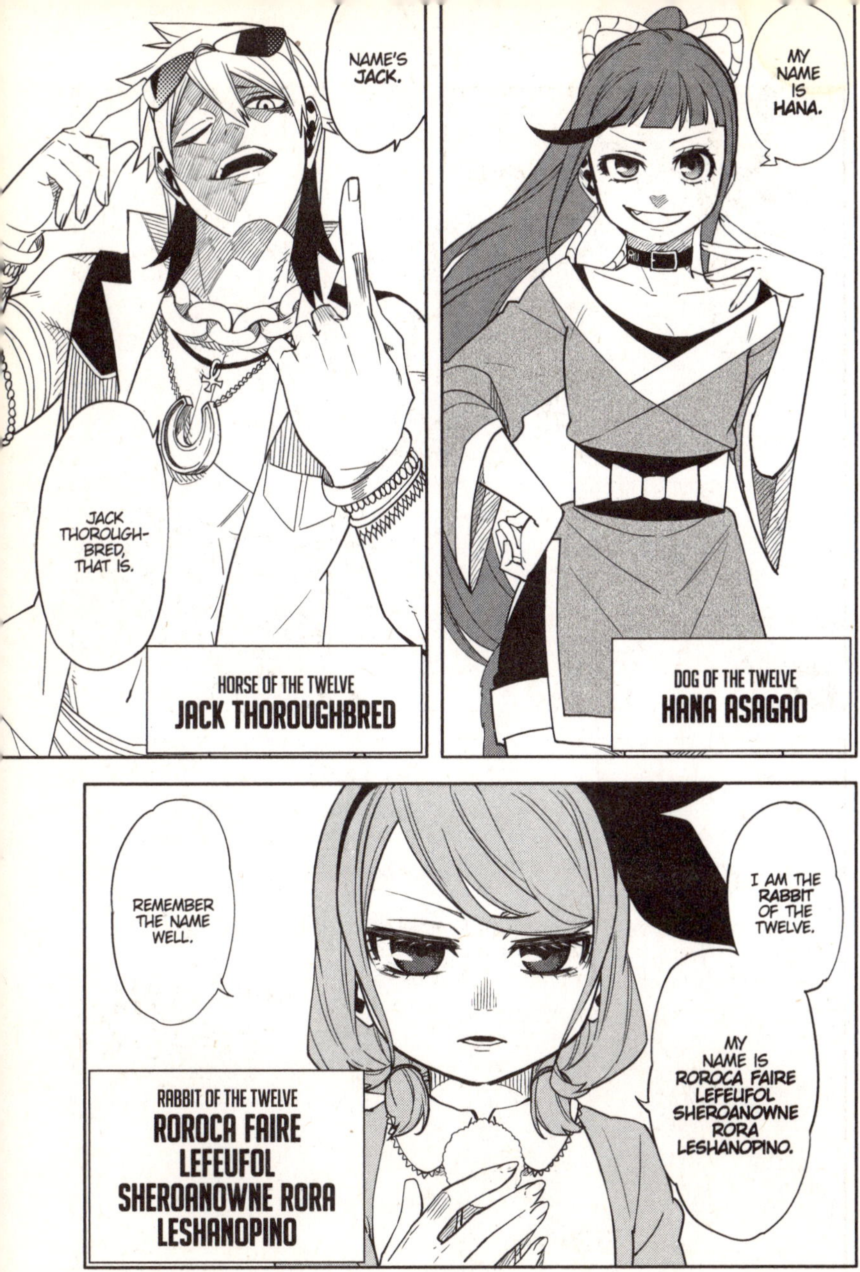
MY NAME IS HANA.
DOG OF THE TWELVE
HANA ASAGAO
NAME'S JACK.
JACK THOROUGHBRED, THAT IS.
HORSE OF THE TWELVE
JACK THOROUGHBRED
I AM THE RABBIT OF THE TWELVE.
MY NAME IS ROROCA FAIRE LEFEUFOL SHEROANOWNE RORA LESHANOPINO.
REMEMBER THE NAME WELL.
RABBIT OF THE TWELVE
ROROCA FAIRE LEFEUFOL SHEROANOWNE RORA LESHANOPINO

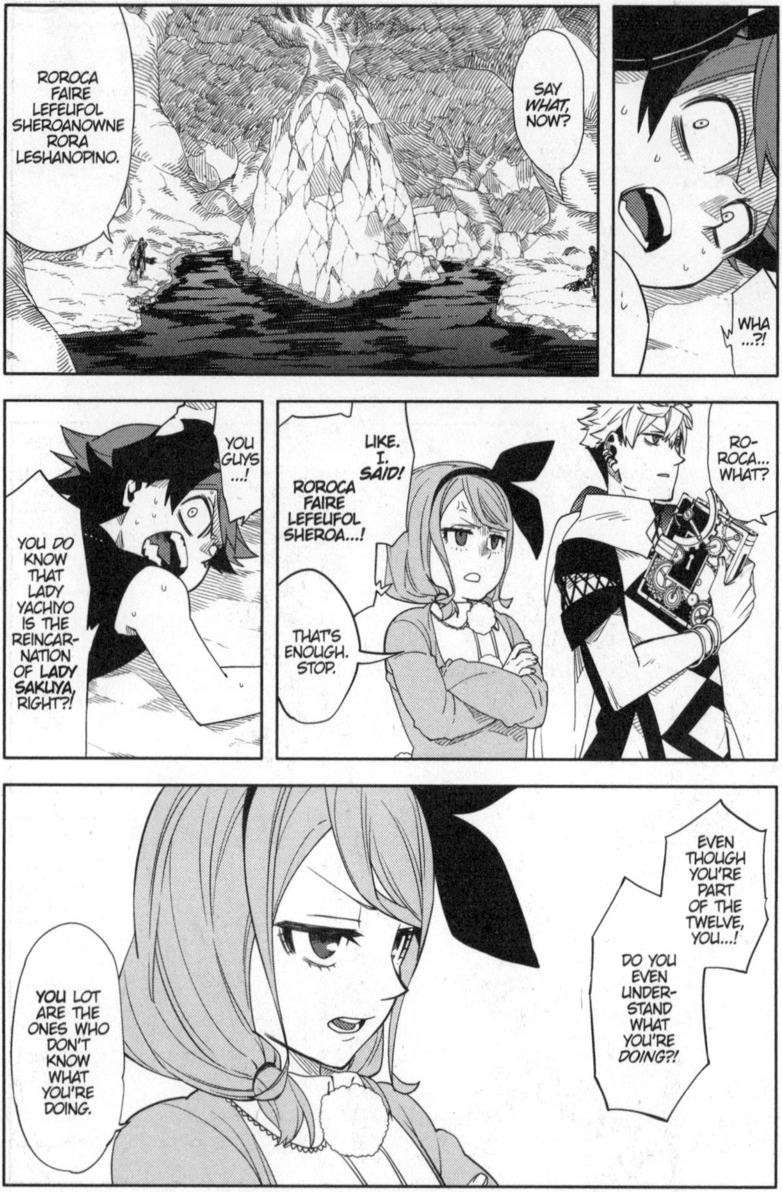
WHA ...?!
SAY WHAT, NOW?
ROROCA FAIRE LEFEUFOL SHEROANOWNE RORA LESHANOPINO.
RO-ROCA... WHAT?
LIKE. I. SAID!
ROROCA FAIRE LEFEUFOL SHEROA...!
THAT'S ENOUGH. STOP.
YOU GUYS ...!
YOU DO KNOW THAT LADY YACHIYO IS THE REINCAR-NATION OF LADY SAKUYA, RIGHT?!
EVEN THOUGH YOU'RE PART OF THE TWELVE, YOU...!
DO YOU EVEN UNDER-STAND WHAT YOU'RE DOING?!
YOU LOT ARE THE ONES WHO DON'T KNOW WHAT YOU'RE DOING.

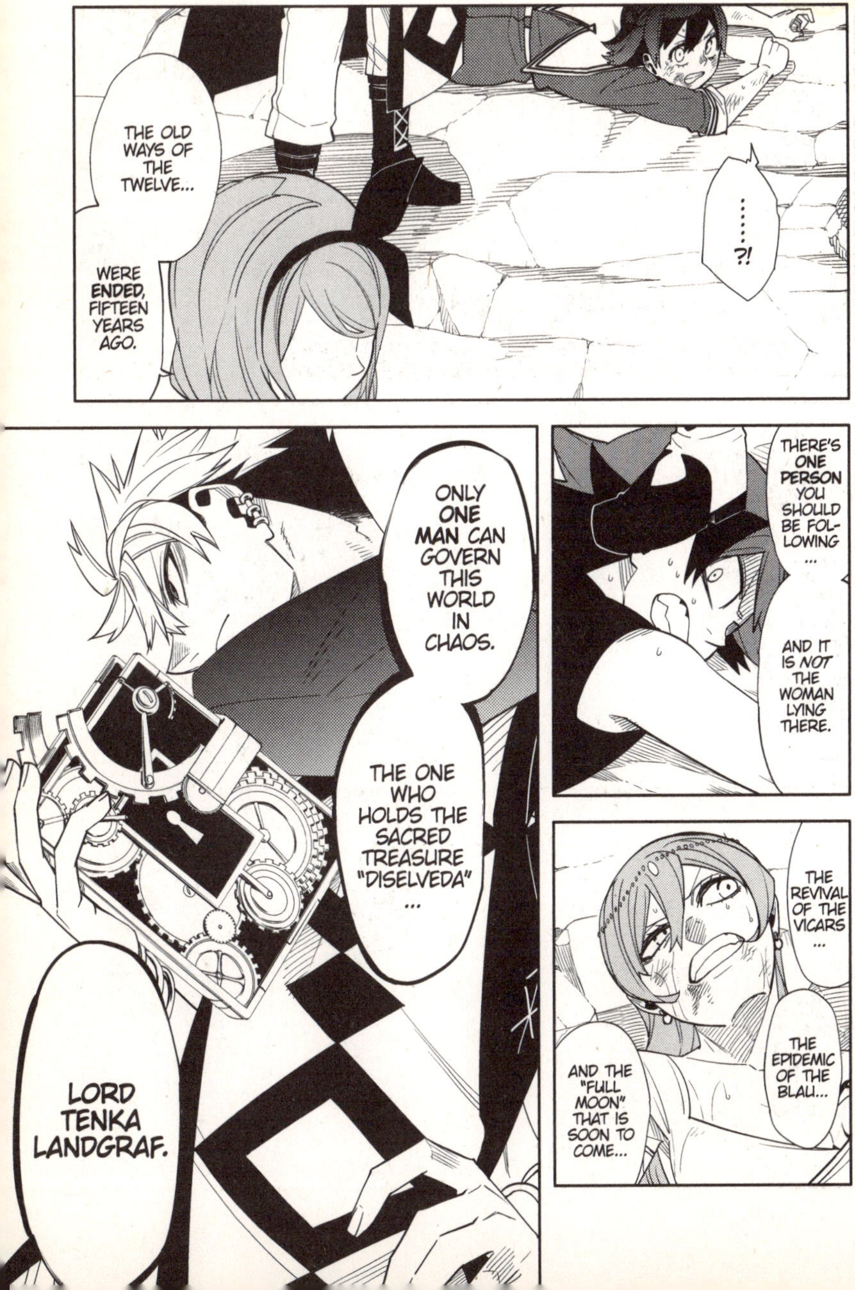
THE OLD WAYS OF THE TWELVE...
WERE ENDED, FIFTEEN YEARS AGO.
......?!
THERE'S ONE PERSON YOU SHOULD BE FOL-LOWING ...
AND IT IS NOT THE WOMAN LYING THERE.
THE REVIVAL OF THE VICARS ...
THE EPIDEMIC OF THE BLAU...
AND THE "FULL MOON" THAT IS SOON TO COME...
ONLY ONE MAN CAN GOVERN THIS WORLD IN CHAOS.
THE ONE WHO HOLDS THE SACRED TREASURE "DISELVEDA" ...
LORD TENKA LANDGRAF.

Avatar Introduction

The Avatar of Fire

Garuda

◆ Weapon Name: Raktapaksha

◆ Specialty: Conjuration of Fire

Super-Sight

◆ Special Skill: Gartoesta

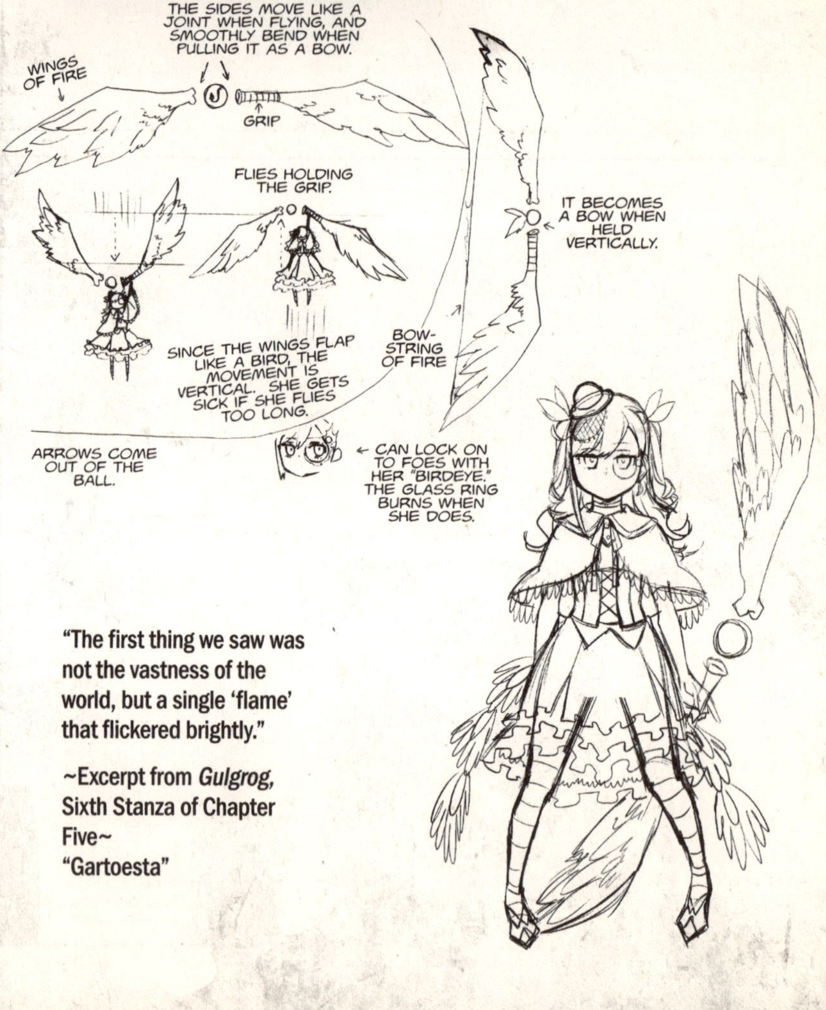

THE SIDES MOVE LIKE A JOINT WHEN FLYING, AND SMOOTHLY BEND WHEN PULLING IT AS A BOW.
WINGS OF FIRE
GRIP
FLIES HOLDING THE GRIP.
IT BECOMES A BOW WHEN HELD VERTICALLY.
BOW-STRING OF FIRE
SINCE THE WINGS FLAP LIKE A BIRD, THE MOVEMENT IS VERTICAL. SHE GETS SICK IF SHE FLIES TOO LONG.
ARROWS COME OUT OF THE BALL.
← CAN LOCK ON TO FOES WITH HER "BIRDEYE." THE GLASS RING BURNS WHEN SHE DOES.

"The first thing we saw was not the vastness of the world, but a single 'flame' that flickered brightly."

~Excerpt from *Gulgrog,* Sixth Stanza of Chapter Five~
"Gartoesta"

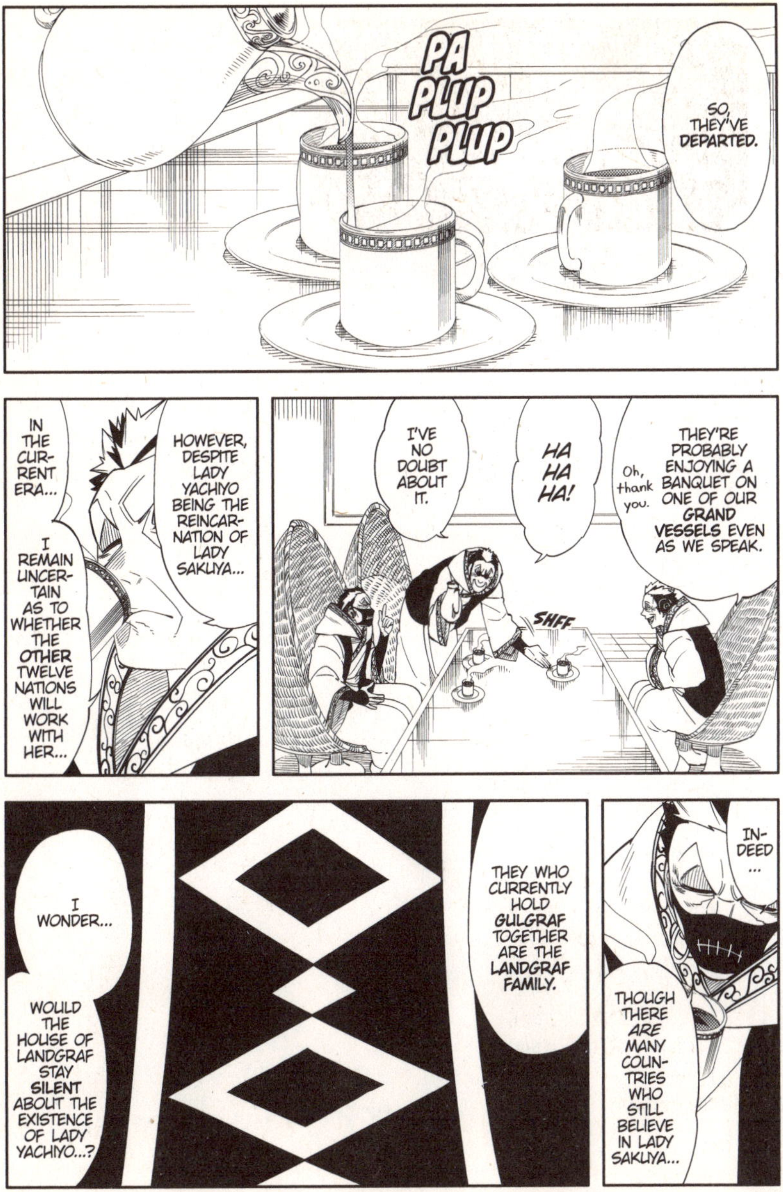
SO, THEY'VE DEPARTED.
PA PLUP PLUP
THEY'RE PROBABLY ENJOYING A BANQUET ON ONE OF OUR GRAND VESSELS EVEN AS WE SPEAK.
Oh, thank you.
HA HA HA!
I'VE NO DOUBT ABOUT IT.
SHFF
HOWEVER, DESPITE LADY YACHIYO BEING THE REINCARNATION OF LADY SAKUYA...
IN THE CURRENT ERA...
I REMAIN UNCERTAIN AS TO WHETHER THE OTHER TWELVE NATIONS WILL WORK WITH HER...
INDEED...
THOUGH THERE ARE MANY COUNTRIES WHO STILL BELIEVE IN LADY SAKUYA...
THEY WHO CURRENTLY HOLD GULGRAF TOGETHER ARE THE LANDGRAF FAMILY.
I WONDER...
WOULD THE HOUSE OF LANDGRAF STAY SILENT ABOUT THE EXISTENCE OF LADY YACHIYO...?

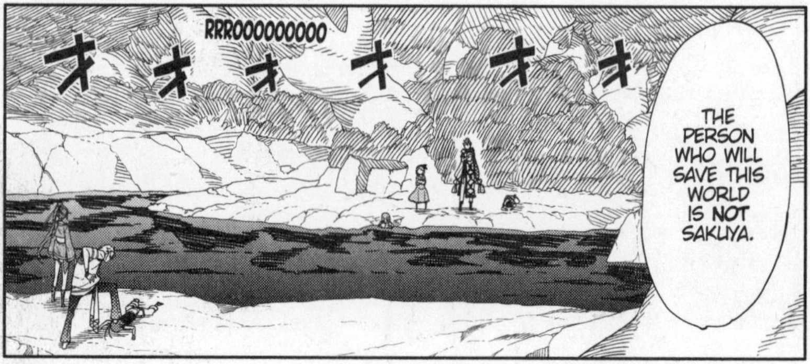
THE PERSON WHO WILL SAVE THIS WORLD IS NOT SAKUYA.
RRROOOOOOOOO

Chapter 6

Fake Savior

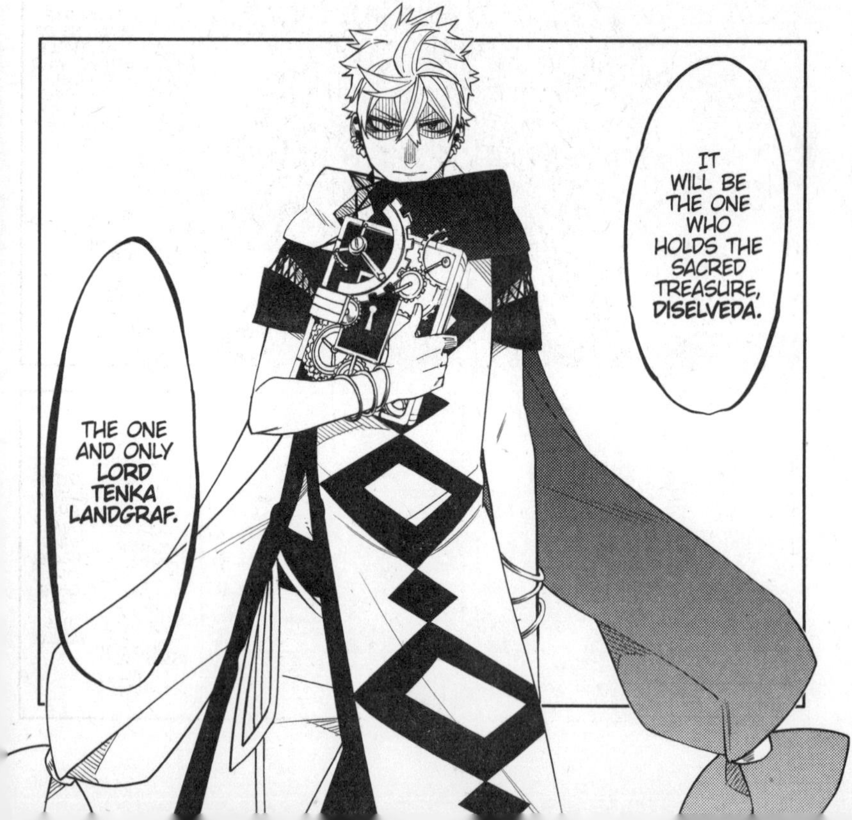
IT WILL BE THE ONE WHO HOLDS THE SACRED TREASURE, DISELVEDA.
THE ONE AND ONLY LORD TENKA LANDGRAF.

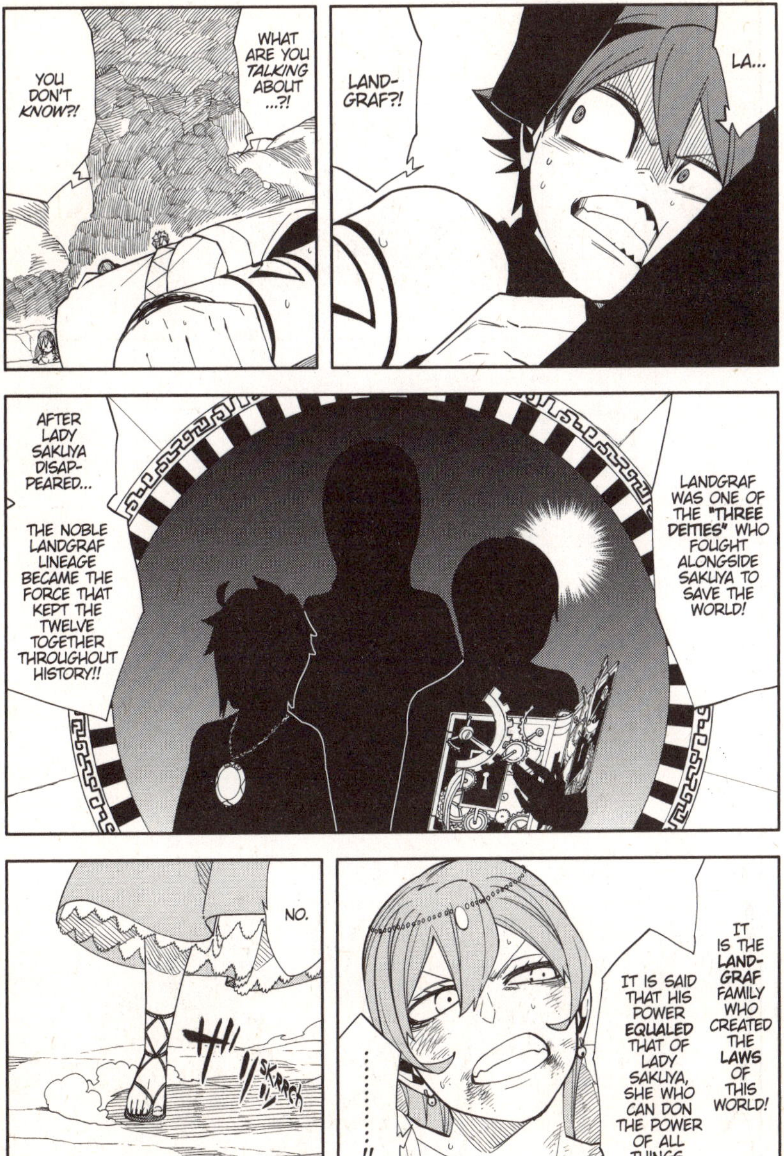

LA...
LAND-GRAF?!
WHAT ARE YOU TALKING ABOUT ...?!
YOU DON'T KNOW?!
LANDGRAF WAS ONE OF THE "THREE DEITIES" WHO FOUGHT ALONGSIDE SAKUYA TO SAVE THE WORLD!
AFTER LADY SAKUYA DISAP-PEARED...
THE NOBLE LANDGRAF LINEAGE BECAME THE FORCE THAT KEPT THE TWELVE TOGETHER THROUGHOUT HISTORY!!
IT IS THE LAND-GRAF FAMILY WHO CREATED THE LAWS OF THIS WORLD!
IT IS SAID THAT HIS POWER EQUALED THAT OF LADY SAKUYA, SHE WHO CAN DON THE POWER OF ALL THINGS.
......!!
NO.
SKRRCH

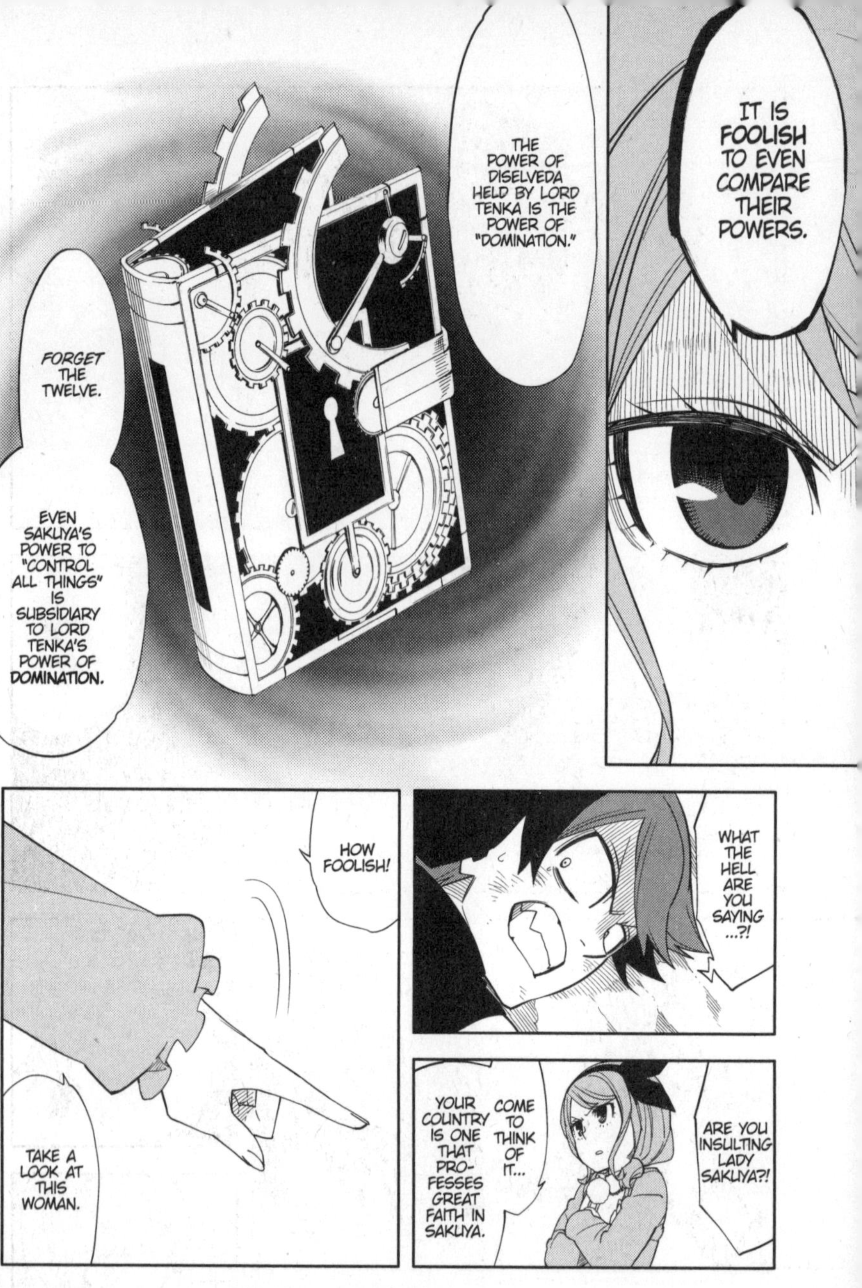
IT IS FOOLISH TO EVEN COMPARE THEIR POWERS.
THE POWER OF DISELVEDA HELD BY LORD TENKA IS THE POWER OF "DOMINATION."
FORGET THE TWELVE.
EVEN SAKUYA'S POWER TO "CONTROL ALL THINGS" IS SUBSIDIARY TO LORD TENKA'S POWER OF DOMINATION.
WHAT THE HELL ARE YOU SAYING ...?!
ARE YOU INSULTING LADY SAKUYA?!
COME TO THINK OF IT...
YOUR COUNTRY IS ONE THAT PRO-FESSES GREAT FAITH IN SAKUYA.
HOW FOOLISH!
TAKE A LOOK AT THIS WOMAN.

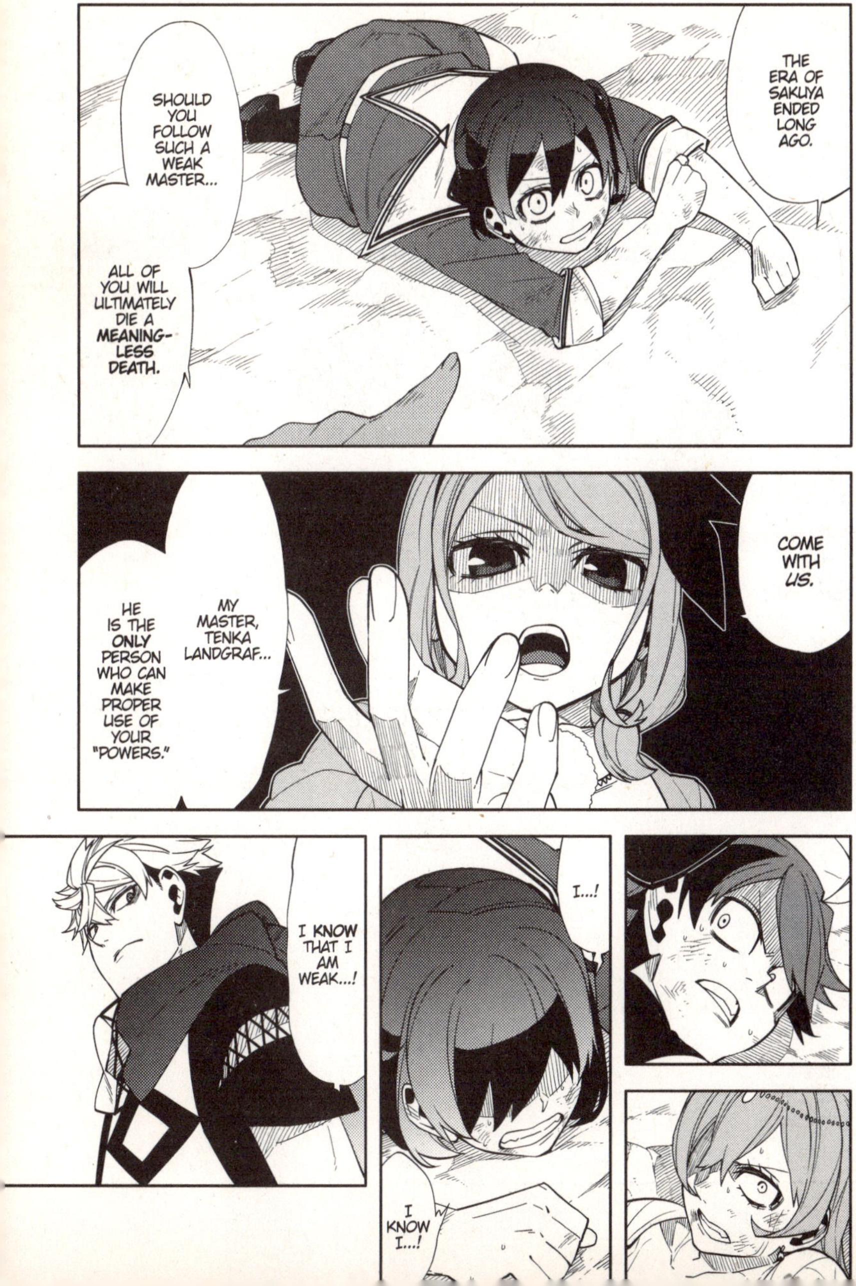
THE ERA OF SAKUYA ENDED LONG AGO.
SHOULD YOU FOLLOW SUCH A WEAK MASTER...
ALL OF YOU WILL ULTIMATELY DIE A MEANING-LESS DEATH.
COME WITH US.
MY MASTER, TENKA LANDGRAF...
HE IS THE ONLY PERSON WHO CAN MAKE PROPER USE OF YOUR "POWERS."
I...!
I KNOW I...!
I KNOW THAT I AM WEAK...!

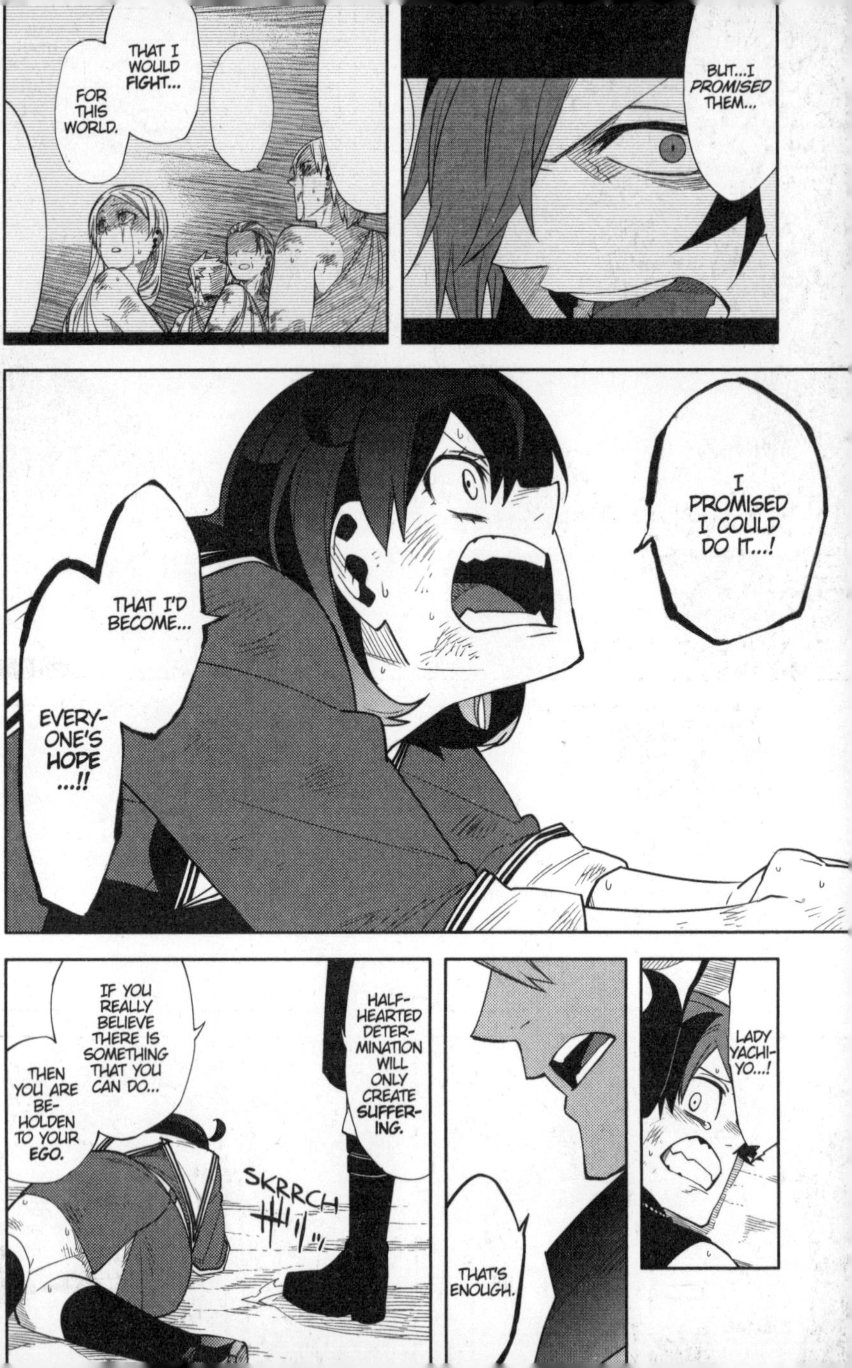
BUT...I *PROMISED* THEM...
THAT I WOULD FIGHT...
FOR THIS WORLD.
I PROMISED I COULD DO IT...!
THAT I'D BECOME...
EVERYONE'S HOPE ...!!
LADY YACHIYO...!
THAT'S ENOUGH.
HALF-HEARTED DETERMINATION WILL ONLY CREATE SUFFERING.
IF YOU REALLY BELIEVE THERE IS SOMETHING THAT YOU CAN DO...
THEN YOU ARE BEHOLDEN TO YOUR EGO.
SKRRCH

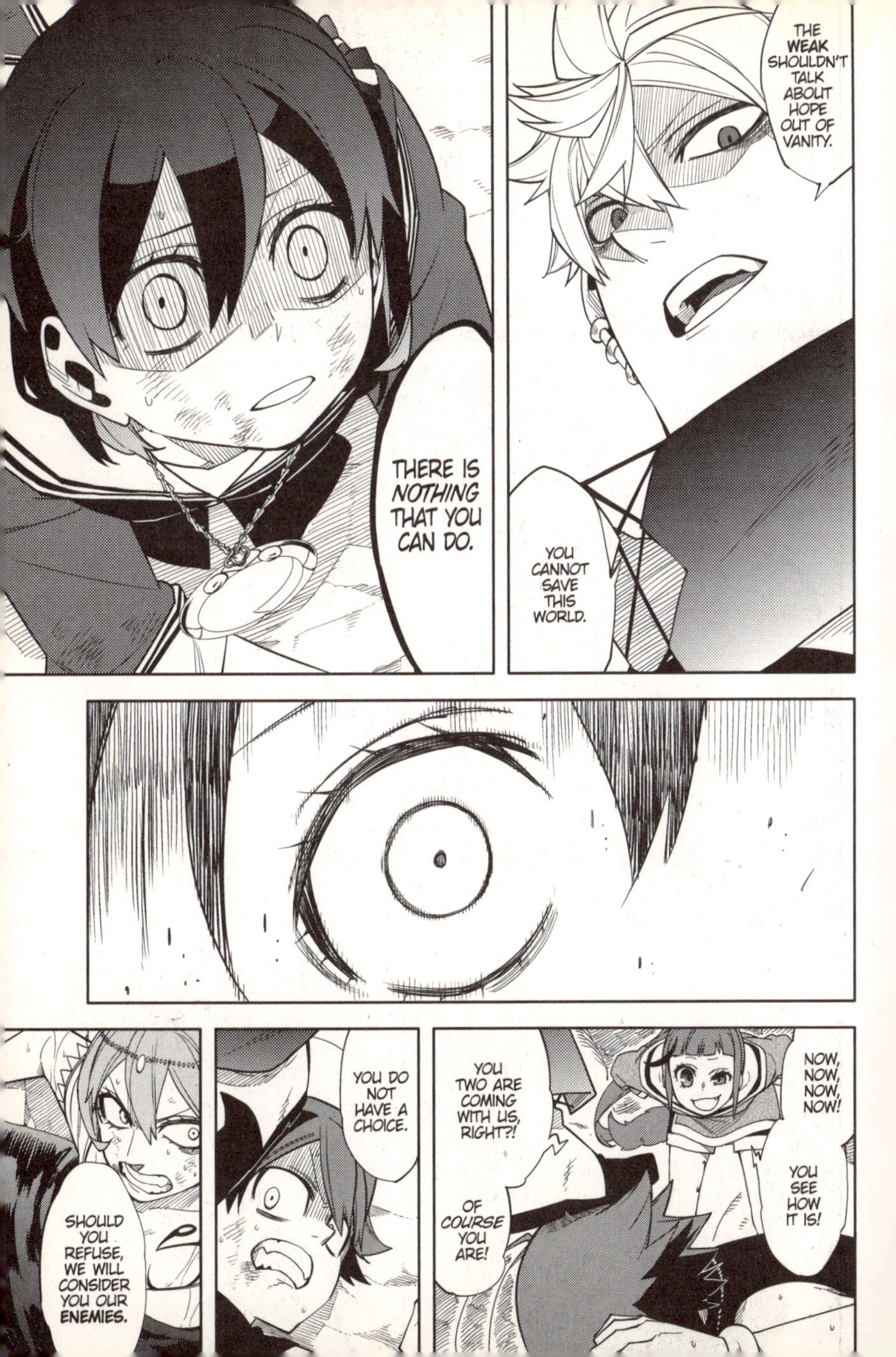
THE WEAK SHOULDN'T TALK ABOUT HOPE OUT OF VANITY.
YOU CANNOT SAVE THIS WORLD.
THERE IS *NOTHING* THAT YOU CAN DO.
NOW, NOW, NOW, NOW!
YOU SEE HOW IT IS!
YOU TWO ARE COMING WITH US, RIGHT?!
OF COURSE YOU ARE!
YOU DO NOT HAVE A CHOICE.
SHOULD YOU REFUSE, WE WILL CONSIDER YOU OUR ENEMIES.

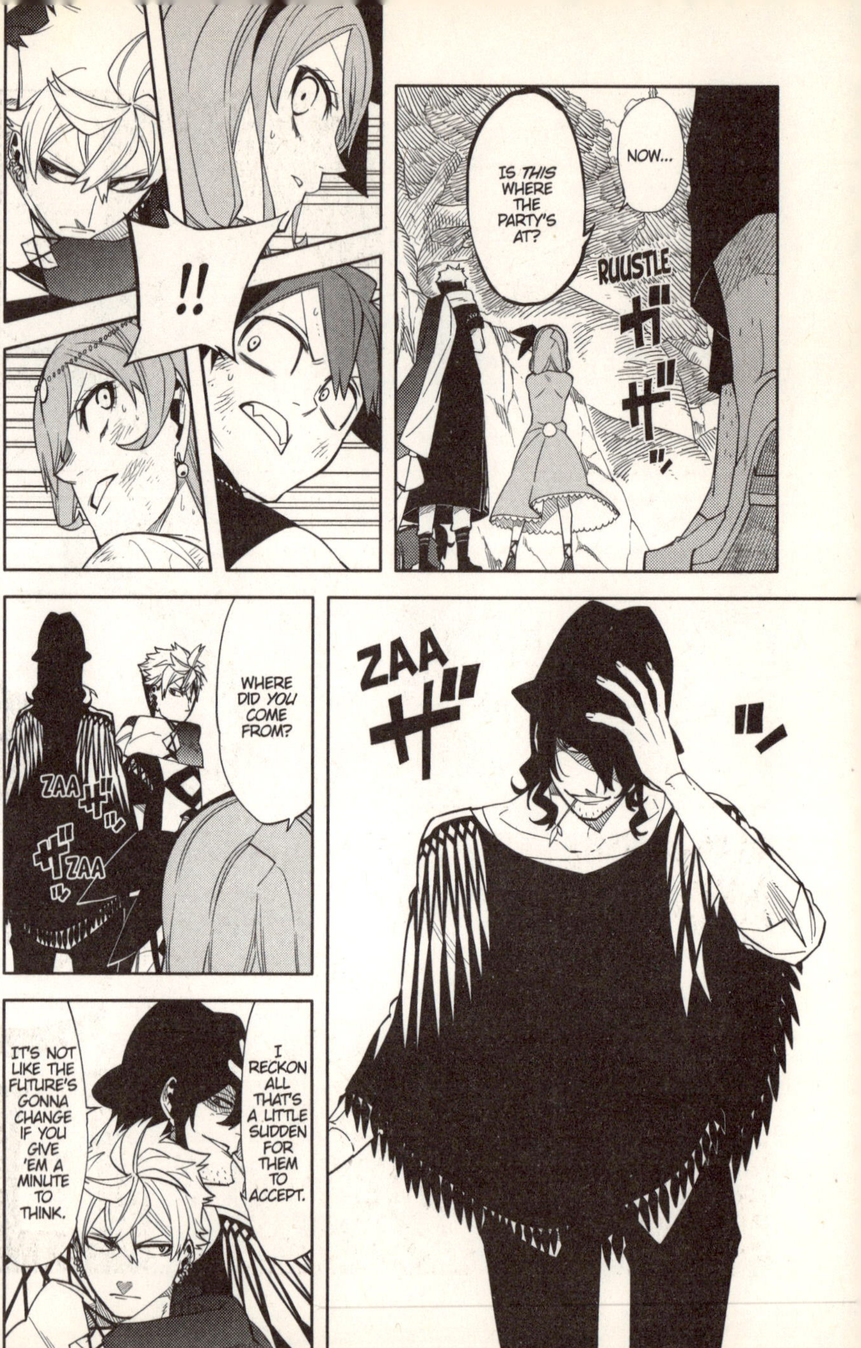

NOW...
IS THIS WHERE THE PARTY'S AT?
RUUSTLE
ガザザ
!!
ZAA
ザ
WHERE DID YOU COME FROM?
ZAA
ZAA
I RECKON ALL THAT'S A LITTLE SUDDEN FOR THEM TO ACCEPT.
IT'S NOT LIKE THE FUTURE'S GONNA CHANGE IF YOU GIVE 'EM A MINUTE TO THINK.

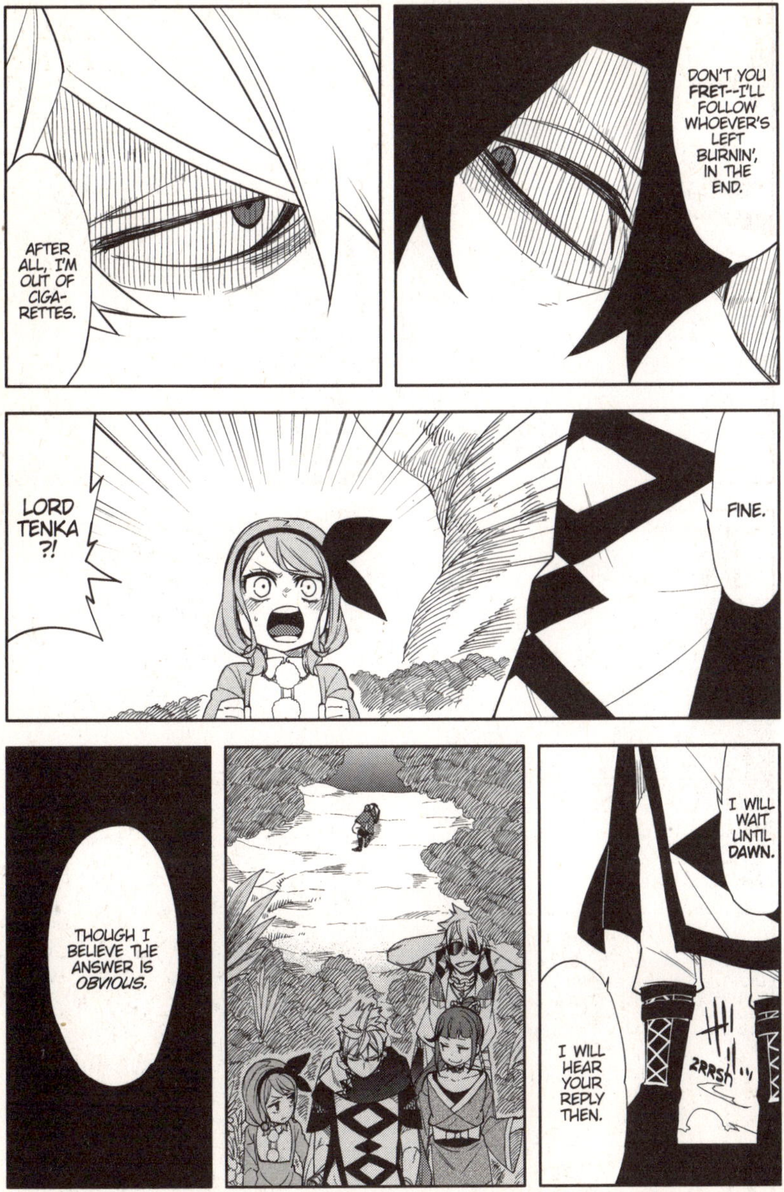
DON'T YOU FRET--I'LL FOLLOW WHOEVER'S LEFT BURNIN', IN THE END.
AFTER ALL, I'M OUT OF CIGA-RETTES.
FINE.
LORD TENKA ?!
I WILL WAIT UNTIL DAWN.
I WILL HEAR YOUR REPLY THEN.
ZRRSh
THOUGH I BELIEVE THE ANSWER IS *OBVIOUS.*

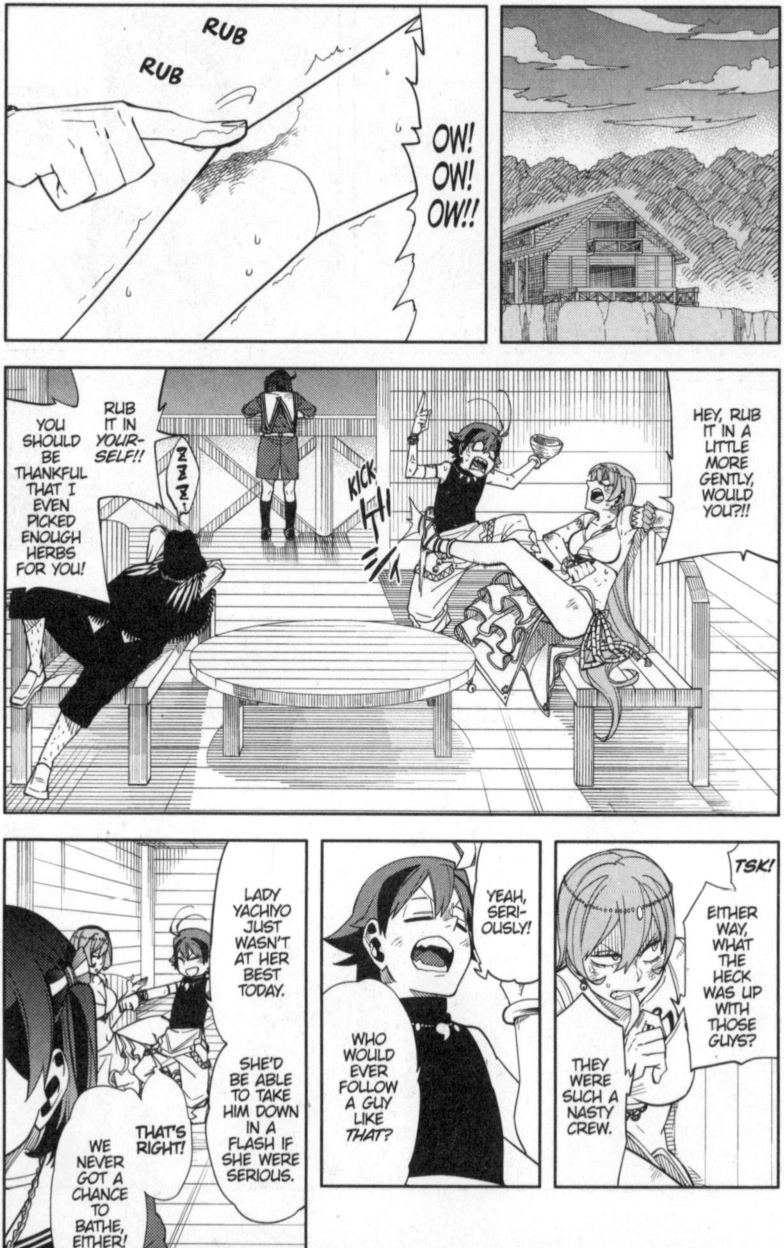
RUB
RUB
OW! OW! OW!!
HEY, RUB IT IN A LITTLE MORE GENTLY, WOULD YOU?!!
KICK
RUB IT IN *YOURSELF*!!
ZZZ...
YOU SHOULD BE THANKFUL THAT I EVEN PICKED ENOUGH HERBS FOR YOU!
TSK!
EITHER WAY, WHAT THE HECK WAS UP WITH THOSE GUYS?
THEY WERE SUCH A NASTY CREW.
YEAH, SERIOUSLY!
WHO WOULD EVER FOLLOW A GUY LIKE *THAT*?
LADY YACHIYO JUST WASN'T AT HER BEST TODAY.
SHE'D BE ABLE TO TAKE HIM DOWN IN A FLASH IF SHE WERE SERIOUS.
THAT'S RIGHT!
WE NEVER GOT A CHANCE TO BATHE, EITHER!

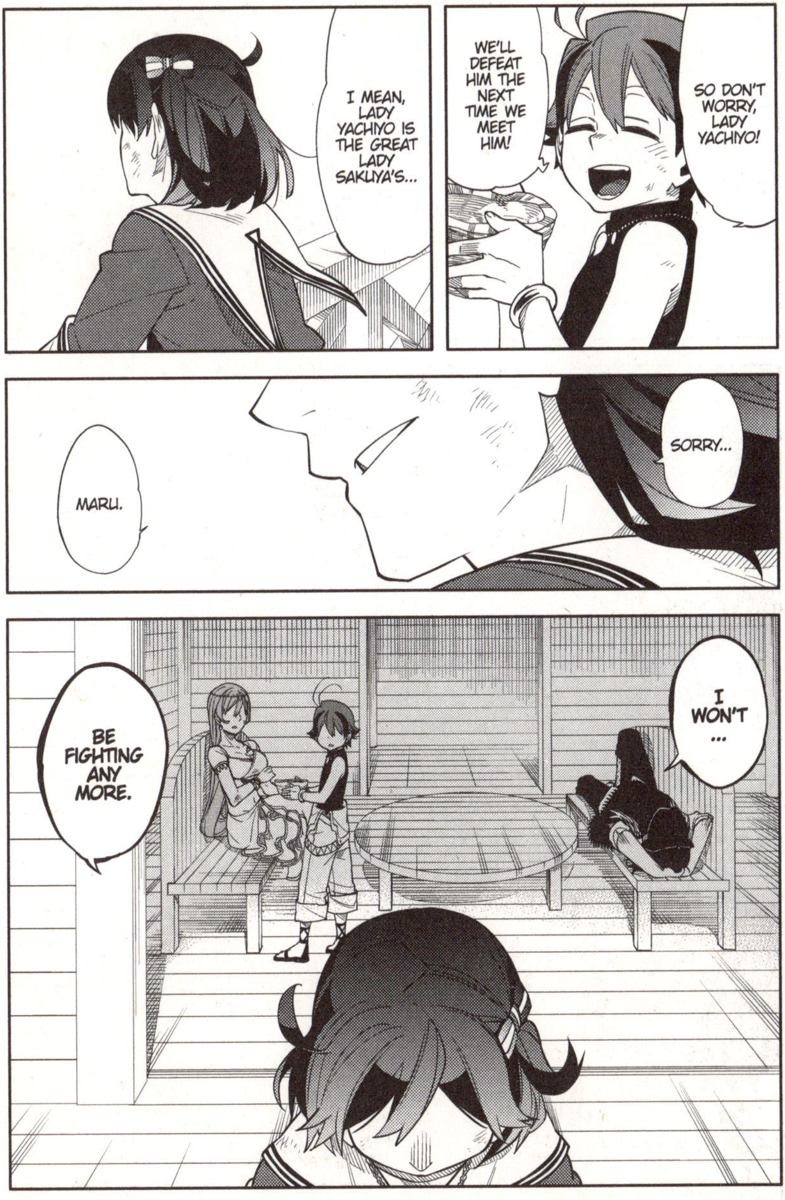
SO DON'T WORRY, LADY YACHIYO!
WE'LL DEFEAT HIM THE NEXT TIME WE MEET HIM!
I MEAN, LADY YACHIYO IS THE GREAT LADY SAKUYA'S...
SORRY...
MARU.
I WON'T ...
BE FIGHTING ANY MORE.

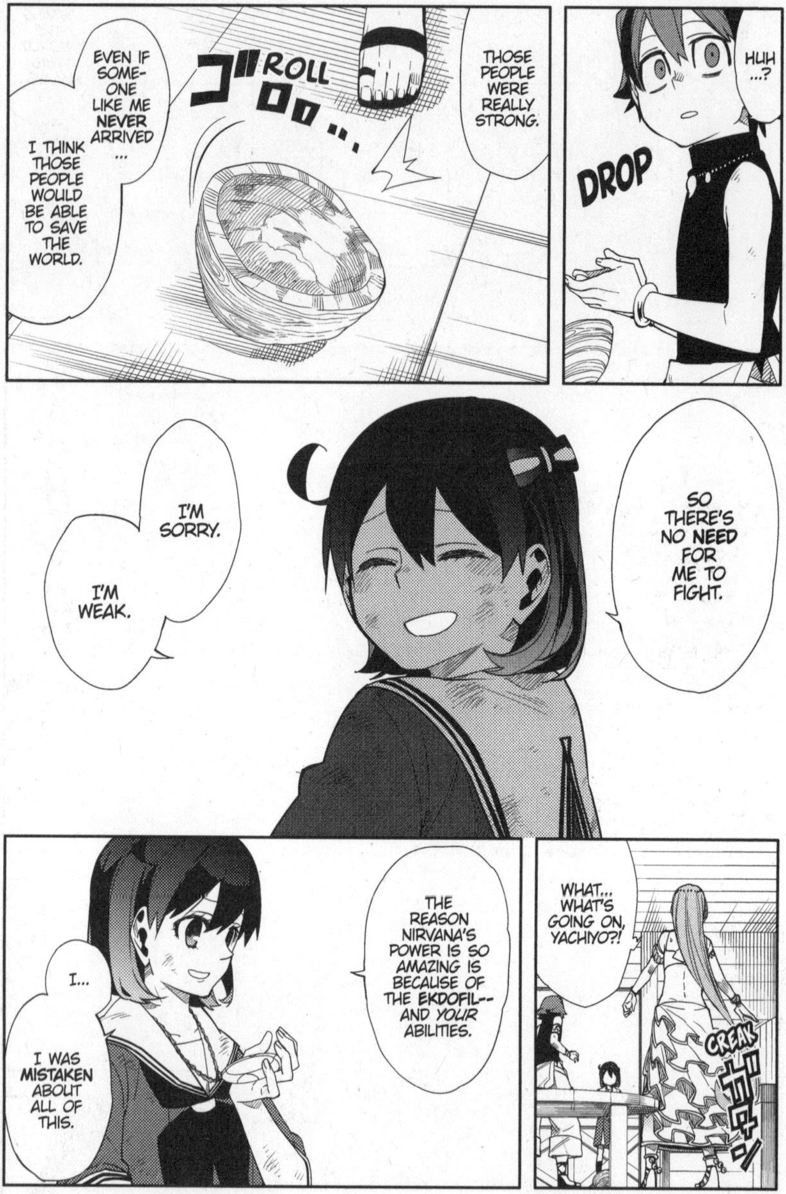
HUH ...?
DROP
THOSE PEOPLE WERE REALLY STRONG.
ROLL
EVEN IF SOME-ONE LIKE ME NEVER ARRIVED ...
I THINK THOSE PEOPLE WOULD BE ABLE TO SAVE THE WORLD.
SO THERE'S NO NEED FOR ME TO FIGHT.
I'M SORRY.
I'M WEAK.
WHAT... WHAT'S GOING ON, YACHIYO?!
CREAK
THE REASON NIRVANA'S POWER IS SO AMAZING IS BECAUSE OF THE EKDOFIL-- AND YOUR ABILITIES.
I...
I WAS MISTAKEN ABOUT ALL OF THIS.

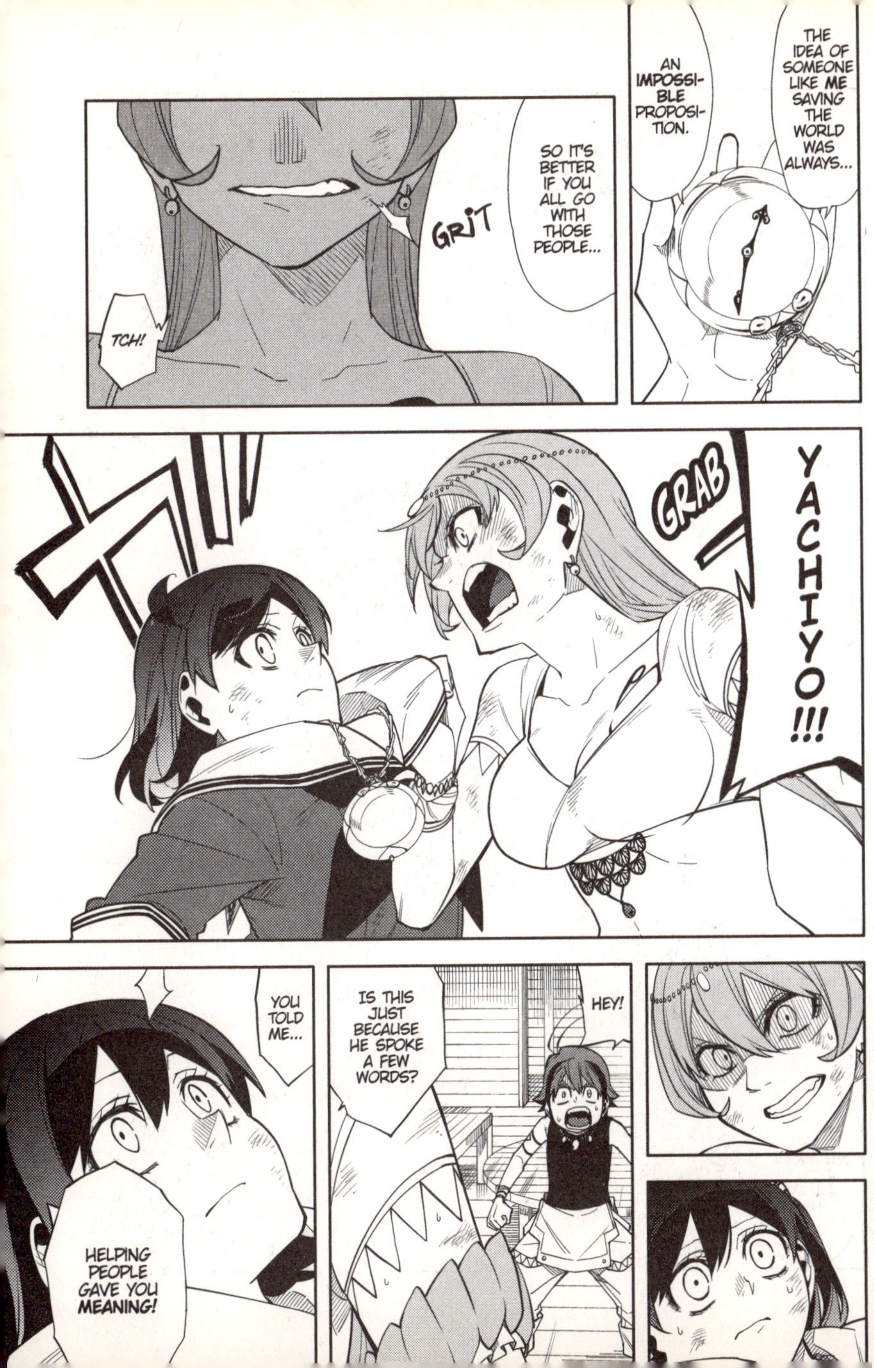
THE IDEA OF SOMEONE LIKE ME SAVING THE WORLD WAS ALWAYS...
AN IMPOSSIBLE PROPOSITION.
SO IT'S BETTER IF YOU ALL GO WITH THOSE PEOPLE...
GRIT
TCH!
YACHIYO!!!
GRAB
HEY!
IS THIS JUST BECAUSE HE SPOKE A FEW WORDS?
YOU TOLD ME...
HELPING PEOPLE GAVE YOU MEANING!

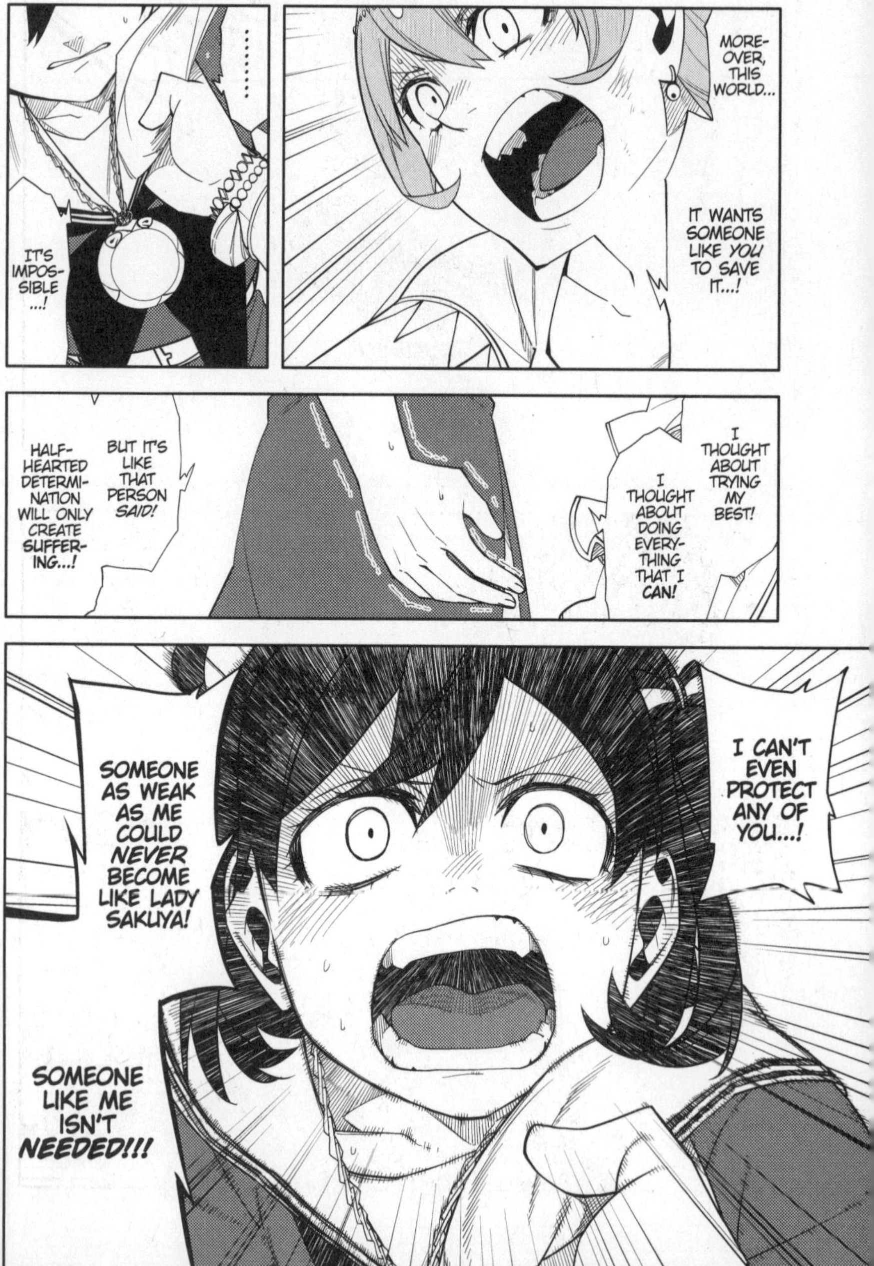
MOREOVER, THIS WORLD...
IT WANTS SOMEONE LIKE *YOU* TO SAVE IT...!
......
IT'S IMPOSSIBLE...!
I THOUGHT ABOUT TRYING MY BEST!
I THOUGHT ABOUT DOING EVERYTHING THAT I CAN!
BUT IT'S LIKE THAT PERSON *SAID!*
HALF-HEARTED DETERMINATION WILL ONLY CREATE SUFFERING...!
I CAN'T EVEN PROTECT ANY OF YOU...!
SOMEONE AS WEAK AS ME COULD *NEVER* BECOME LIKE LADY SAKUYA!
SOMEONE LIKE ME ISN'T *NEEDED!!!*

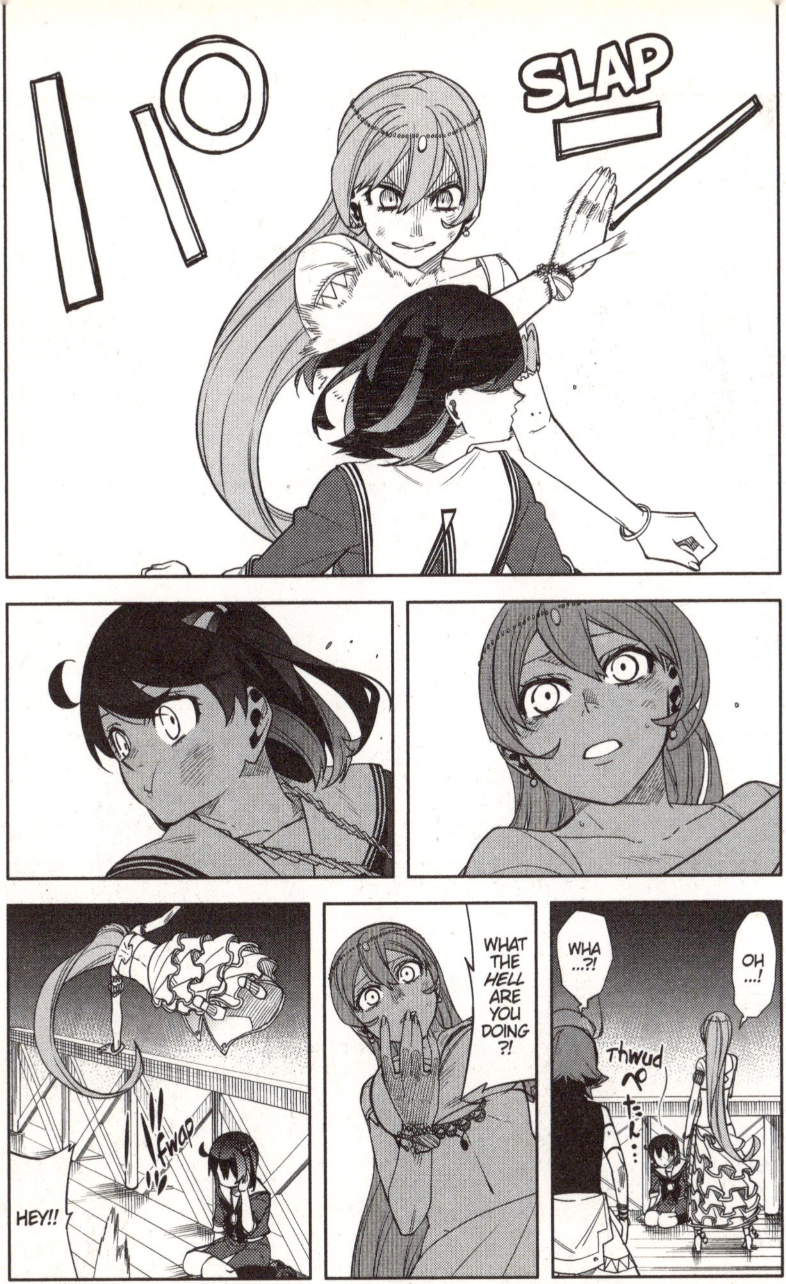
SLAP
OH ...!
WHA ...?!
Thwud
WHAT THE HELL ARE YOU DOING ?!
fwap
HEY!!

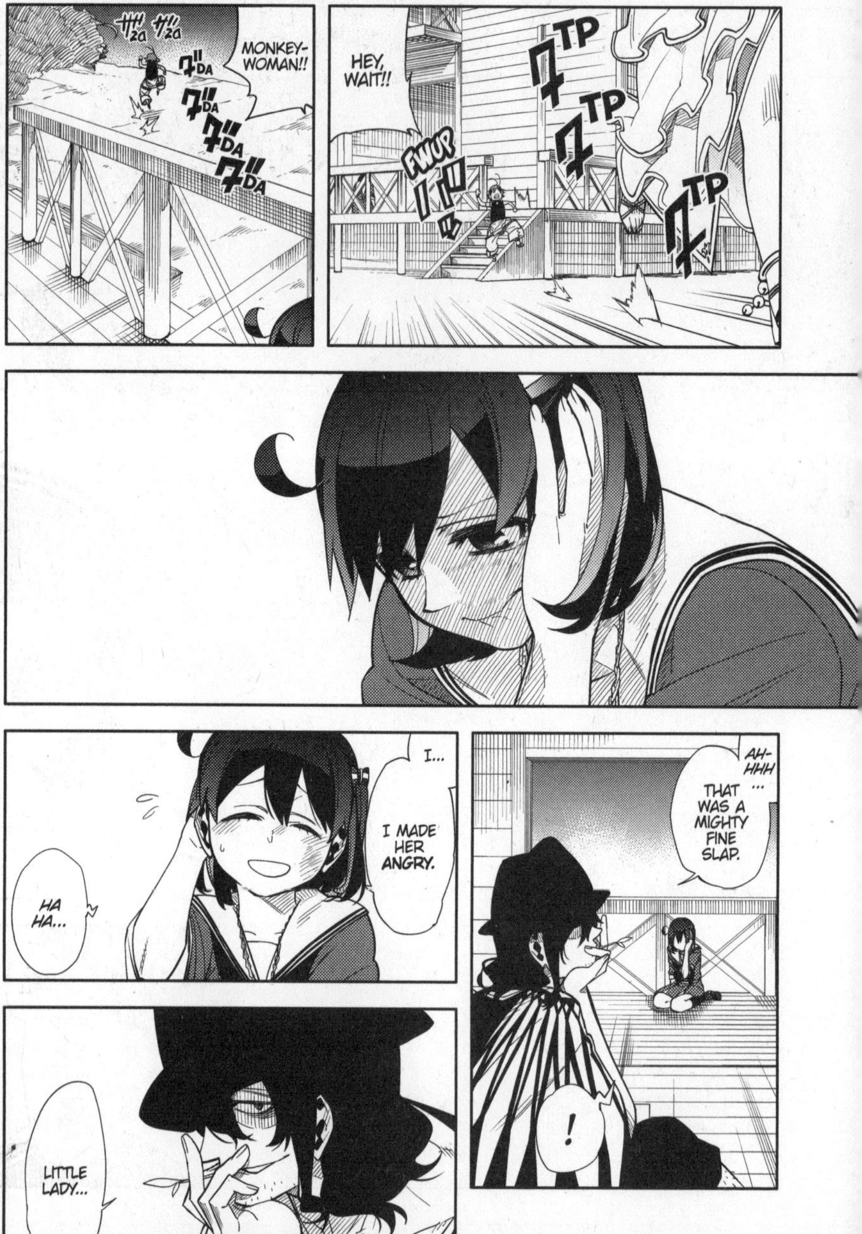

HEY, WAIT!!
TP
TP
TP
FWUP
MONKEY-WOMAN!!
za za
DA
DA
DA
DA
AH-HHH...
THAT WAS A MIGHTY FINE SLAP.
!
I...
I MADE HER ANGRY.
HA HA...
LITTLE LADY...

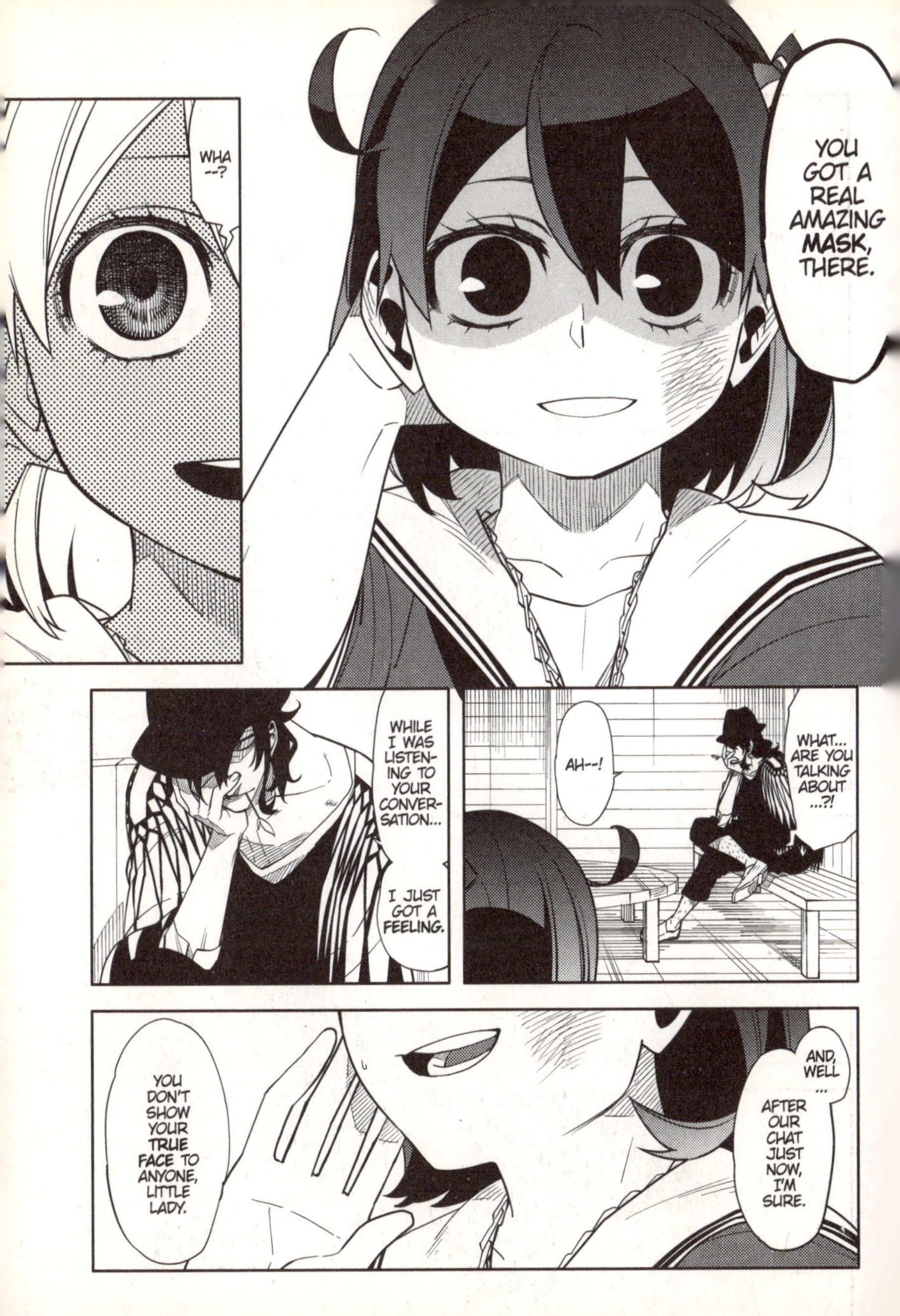
YOU GOT A REAL AMAZING MASK, THERE.
WHA--?
WHAT... ARE YOU TALKING ABOUT...?!
AH--!
WHILE I WAS LISTENING TO YOUR CONVERSATION...
I JUST GOT A FEELING.
AND, WELL...
AFTER OUR CHAT JUST NOW, I'M SURE.
YOU DON'T SHOW YOUR TRUE FACE TO ANYONE, LITTLE LADY.

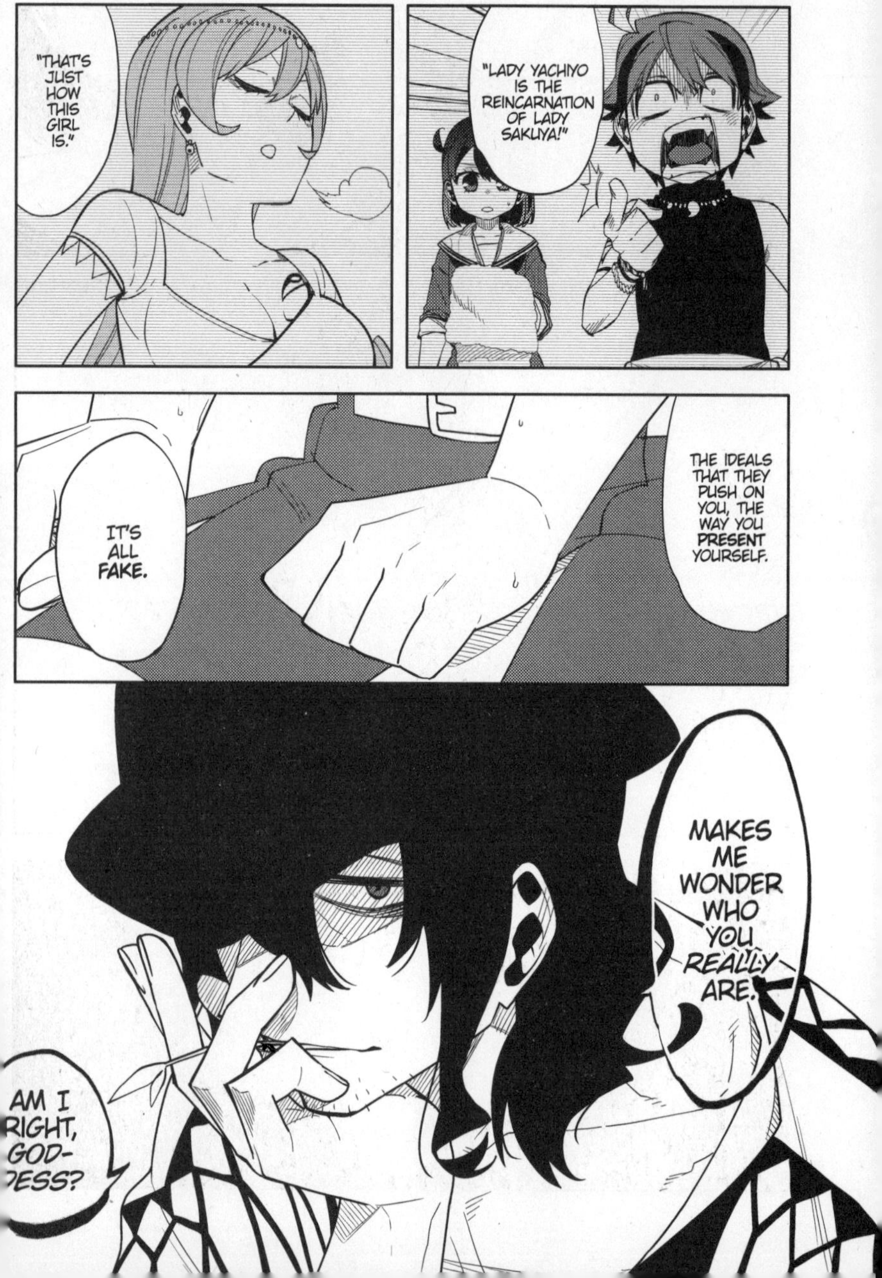
"LADY YACHIYO IS THE REINCARNATION OF LADY SAKUYA!"
"THAT'S JUST HOW THIS GIRL IS."
THE IDEALS THAT THEY PUSH ON YOU, THE WAY YOU PRESENT YOURSELF.
IT'S ALL FAKE.
MAKES ME WONDER WHO YOU REALLY ARE.
AM I RIGHT, GOD-DESS?

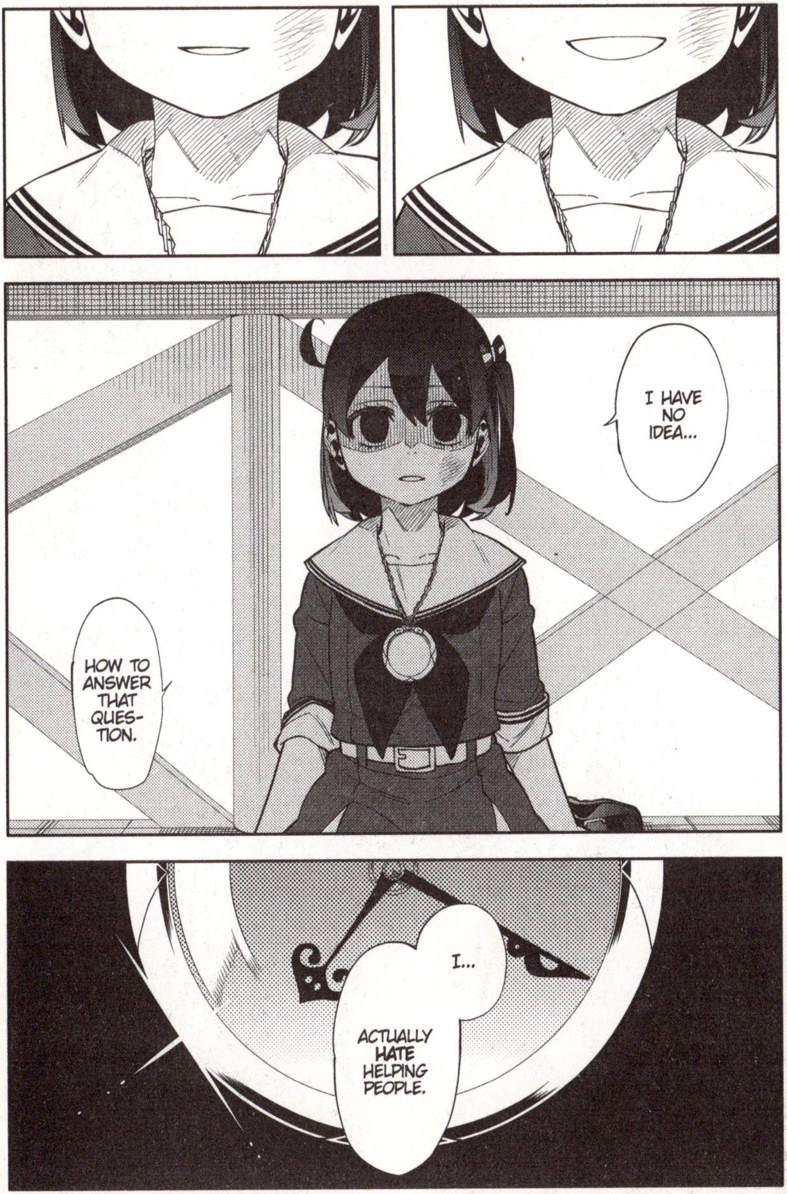
I HAVE NO IDEA...
HOW TO ANSWER THAT QUES-TION.
I...
ACTUALLY HATE HELPING PEOPLE.

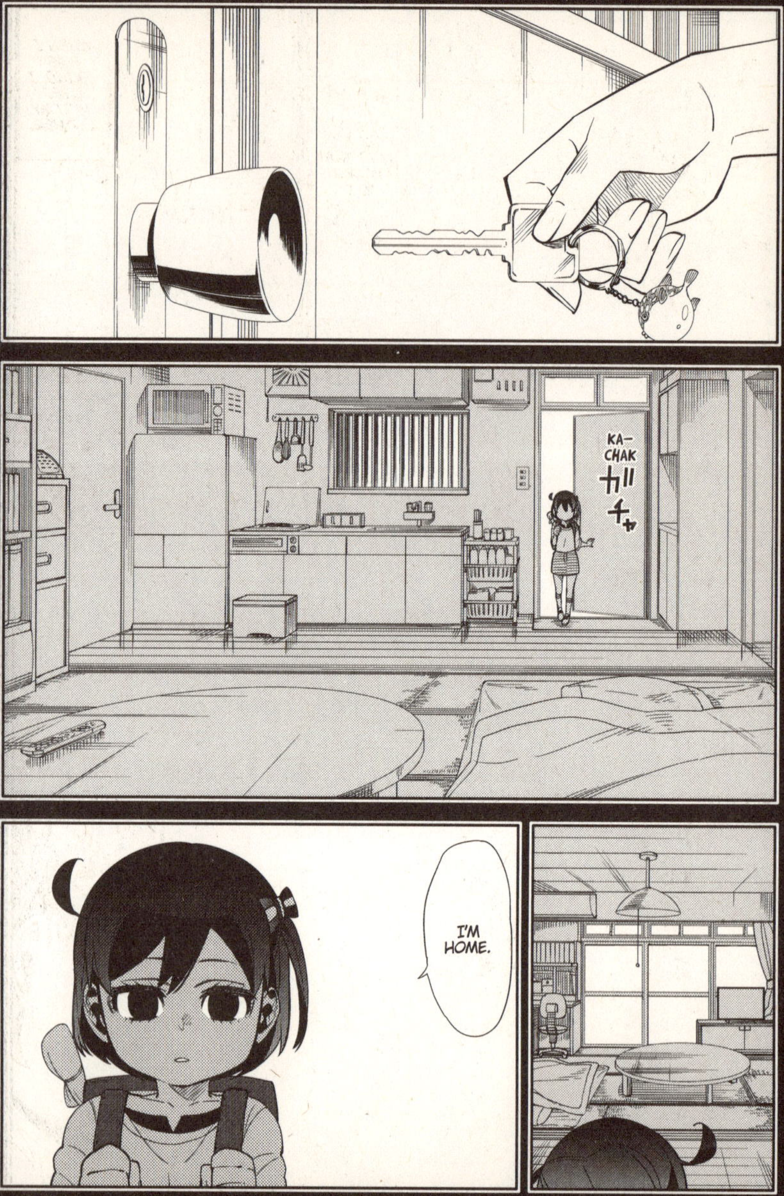
KA-CHAK
カリチャ
I'M HOME.

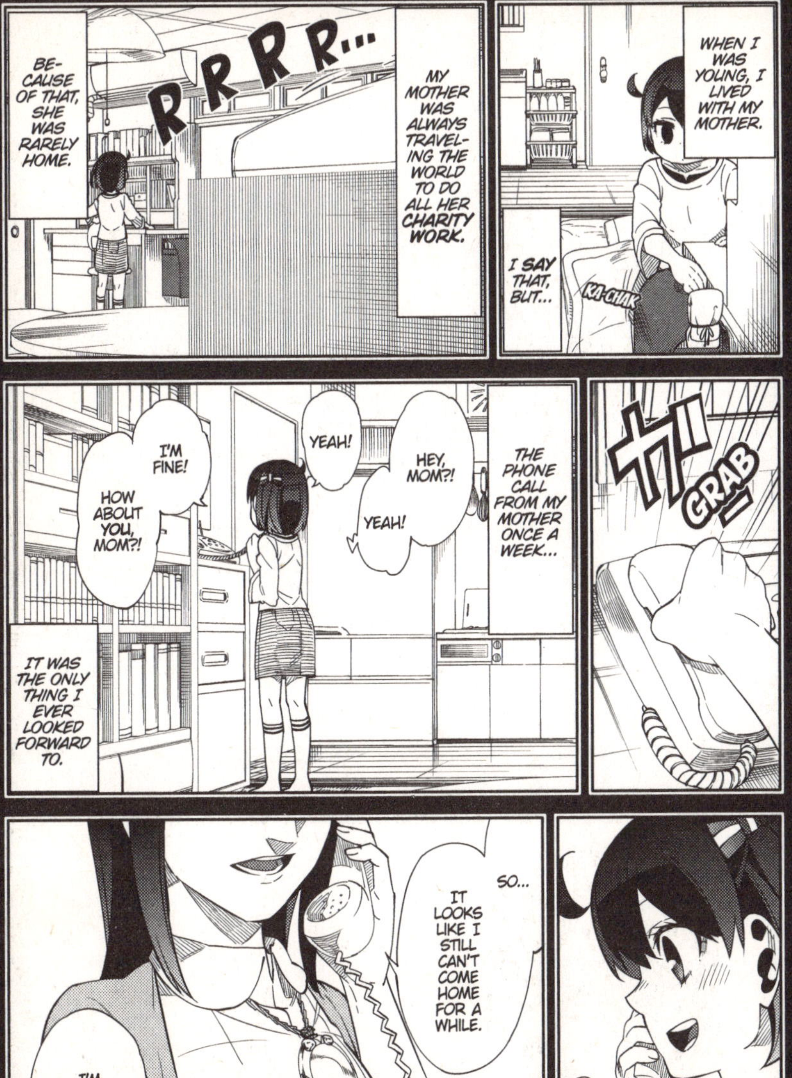
WHEN I WAS YOUNG, I LIVED WITH MY MOTHER.
I SAY THAT, BUT...
KA-CHAK
MY MOTHER WAS ALWAYS TRAVELING THE WORLD TO DO ALL HER CHARITY WORK.
RRRR...
BE-CAUSE OF THAT, SHE WAS RARELY HOME.
GRAB
THE PHONE CALL FROM MY MOTHER ONCE A WEEK...
HEY, MOM?!
YEAH!
YEAH!
I'M FINE! HOW ABOUT YOU, MOM?!
IT WAS THE ONLY THING I EVER LOOKED FORWARD TO.
I SEE.
SO... IT LOOKS LIKE I STILL CAN'T COME HOME FOR A WHILE.
I'M SORRY, YACHIYO.

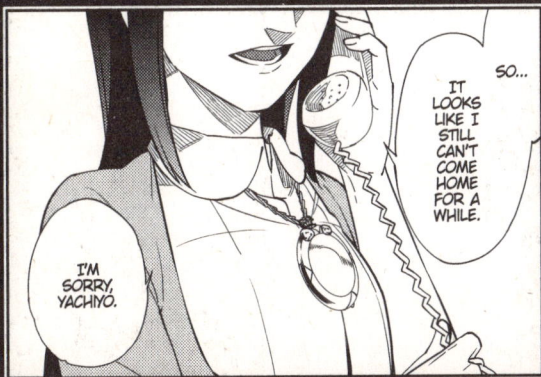

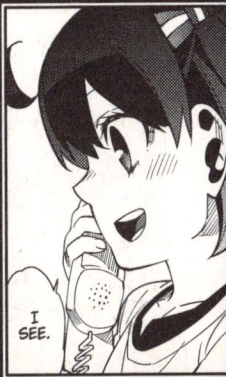

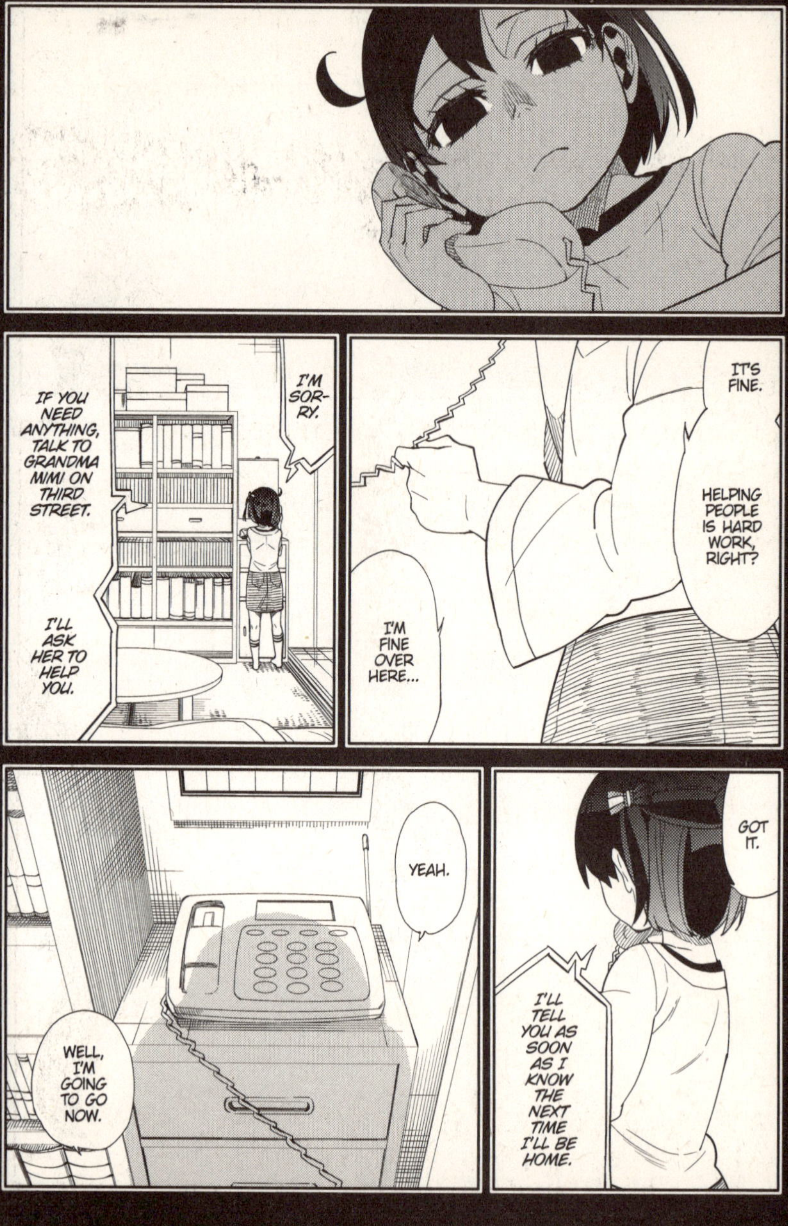
IT'S FINE.
HELPING PEOPLE IS HARD WORK, RIGHT?
I'M FINE OVER HERE...
I'M SORRY.
IF YOU NEED ANYTHING, TALK TO GRANDMA MIMI ON THIRD STREET.
I'LL ASK HER TO HELP YOU.
GOT IT.
I'LL TELL YOU AS SOON AS I KNOW THE NEXT TIME I'LL BE HOME.
YEAH.
WELL, I'M GOING TO GO NOW.

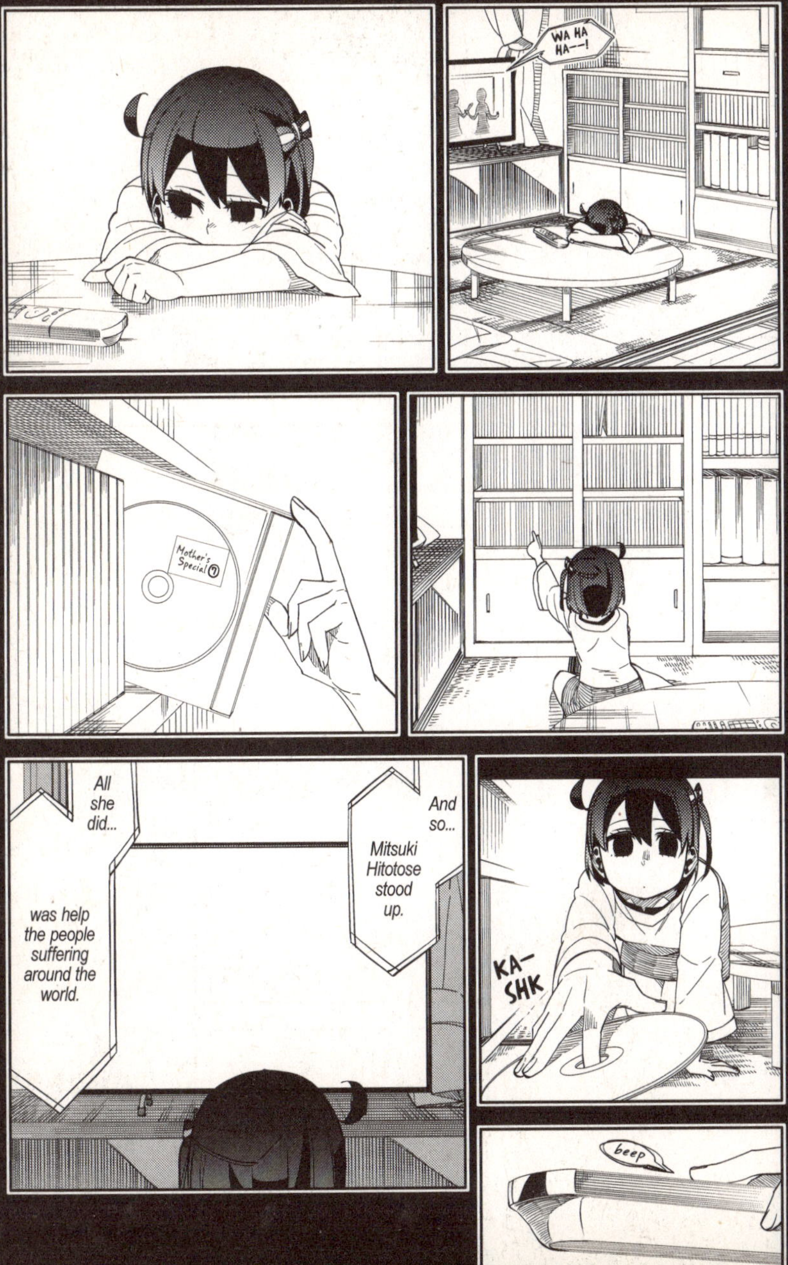
WA HA HA--!
Mother's Special 7
KA-SHK
beep
All she did...
was help the people suffering around the world.
And so...
Mitsuki Hitotose stood up.

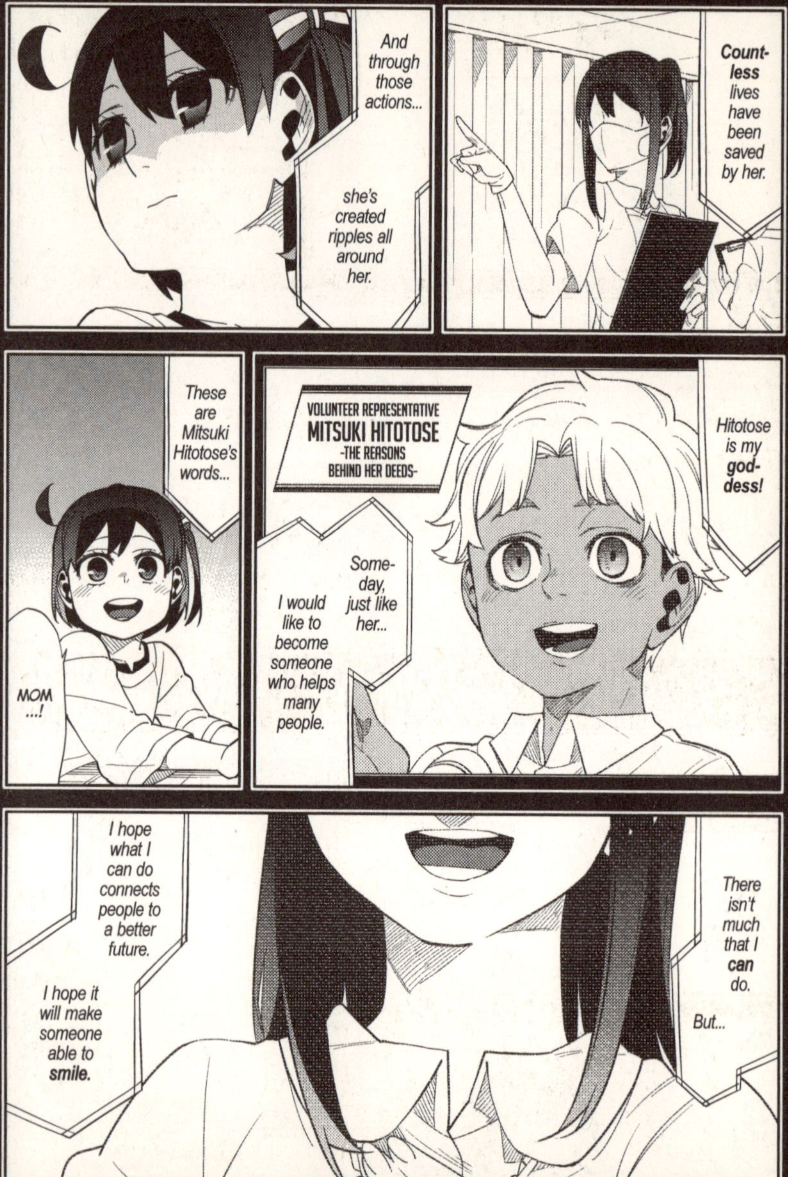
Countless lives have been saved by her.
And through those actions...
she's created ripples all around her.
Hitotose is my goddess!
VOLUNTEER REPRESENTATIVE MITSUKI HITOTOSE -THE REASONS BEHIND HER DEEDS-
Someday, just like her...
I would like to become someone who helps many people.
These are Mitsuki Hitotose's words...
MOM ...!
There isn't much that I can do.
But...
I hope what I can do connects people to a better future.
I hope it will make someone able to smile.

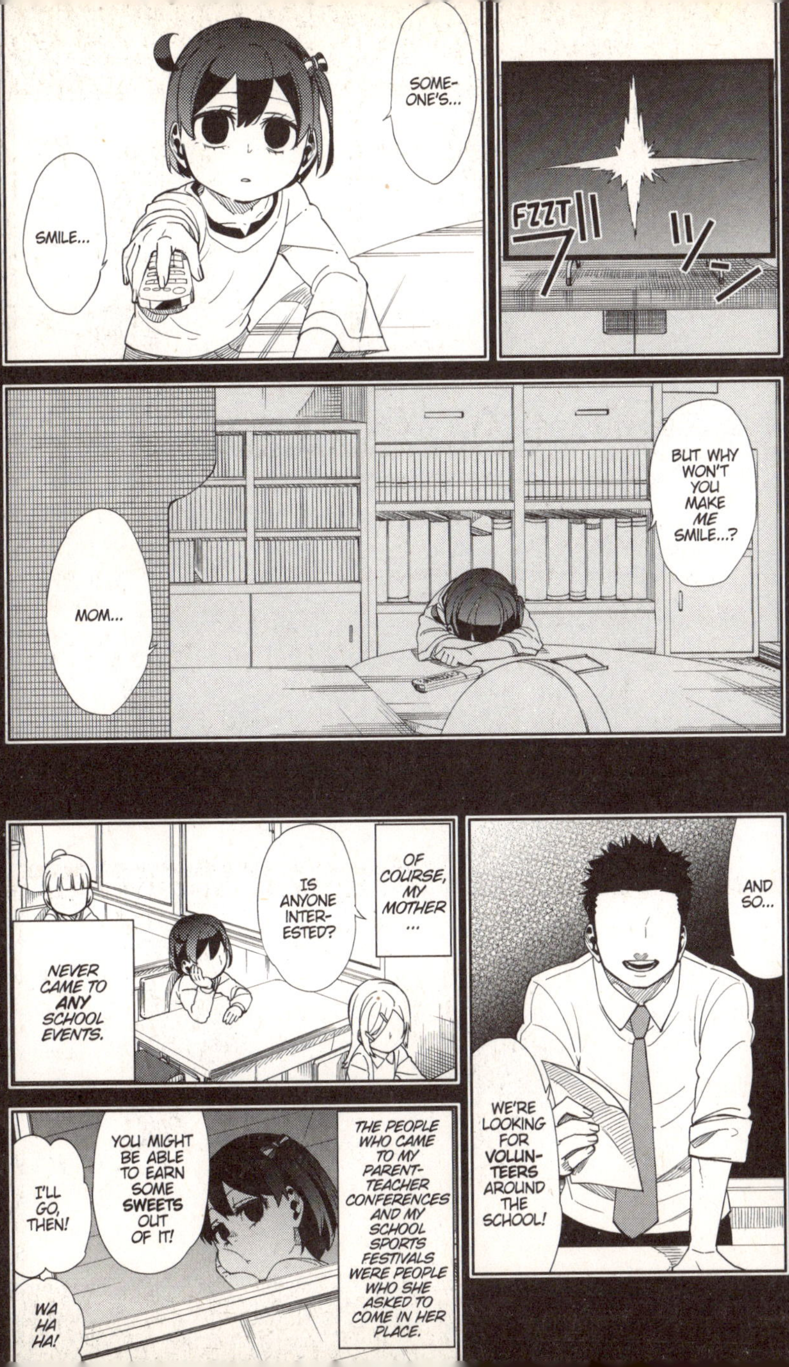
FZZT
SOME-ONE'S...
SMILE...
BUT WHY WON'T YOU MAKE ME SMILE...?
MOM...
AND SO...
WE'RE LOOKING FOR **VOLUNTEERS** AROUND THE SCHOOL!
OF COURSE, MY MOTHER...
IS ANYONE INTERESTED?
NEVER CAME TO **ANY** SCHOOL EVENTS.
THE PEOPLE WHO CAME TO MY PARENT-TEACHER CONFERENCES AND MY SCHOOL SPORTS FESTIVALS WERE PEOPLE WHO SHE ASKED TO COME IN HER PLACE.
YOU MIGHT BE ABLE TO EARN SOME **SWEETS** OUT OF IT!
I'LL GO, THEN!
WA HA HA!

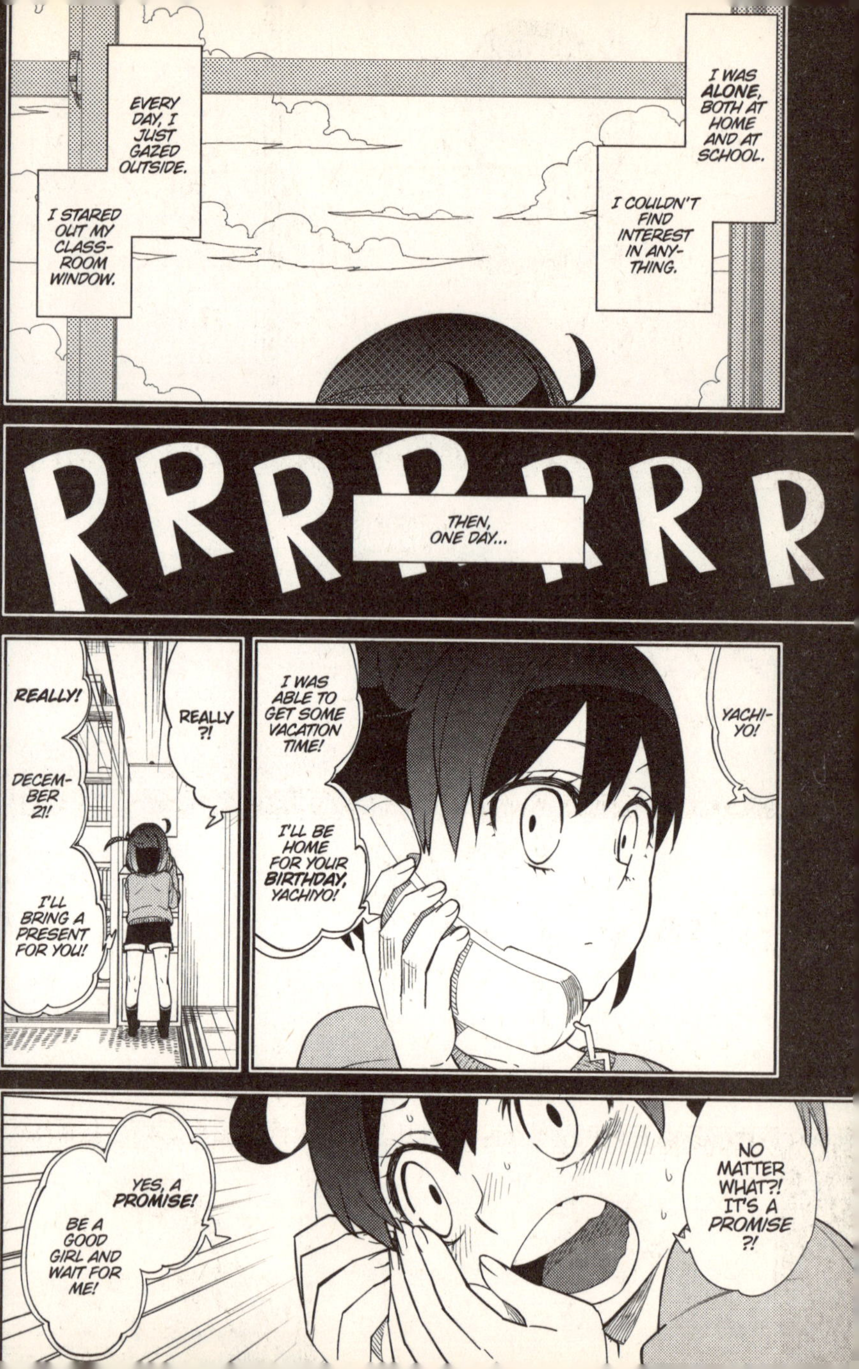
I WAS ALONE, BOTH AT HOME AND AT SCHOOL.
I COULDN'T FIND INTEREST IN ANY-THING.
EVERY DAY, I JUST GAZED OUTSIDE.
I STARED OUT MY CLASS-ROOM WINDOW.
RRRRRR
THEN, ONE DAY...
YACHI-YO!
I WAS ABLE TO GET SOME VACATION TIME!
I'LL BE HOME FOR YOUR BIRTHDAY, YACHIYO!
REALLY ?!
REALLY!
DECEM-BER 21!
I'LL BRING A PRESENT FOR YOU!
NO MATTER WHAT?! IT'S A PROMISE ?!
YES, A PROMISE!
BE A GOOD GIRL AND WAIT FOR ME!

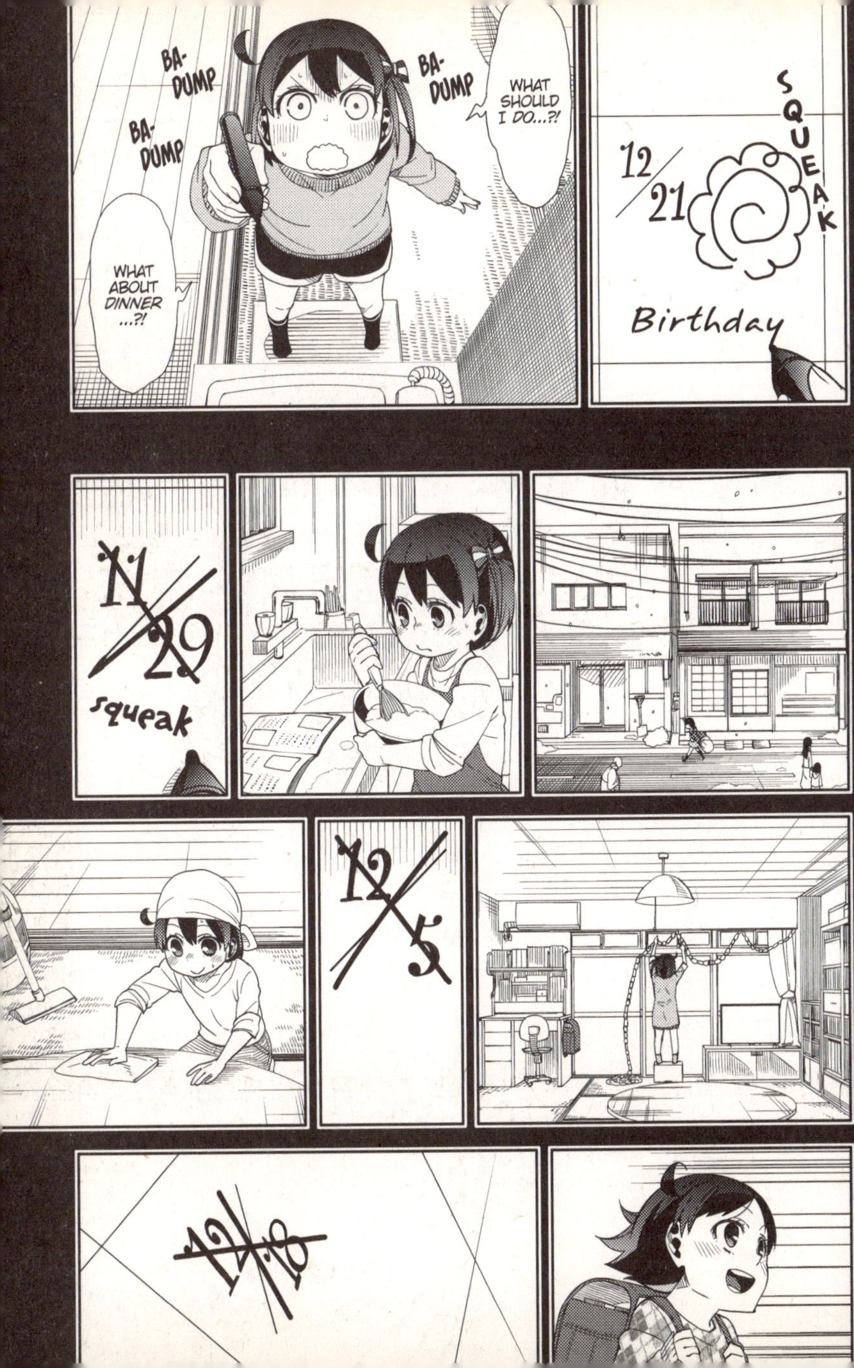
12/21
SQUEAK
Birthday
WHAT SHOULD I DO...?!
BA-DUMP
BA-DUMP
BA-DUMP
WHAT ABOUT DINNER ...?!
11/29
squeak
12/5
12/8

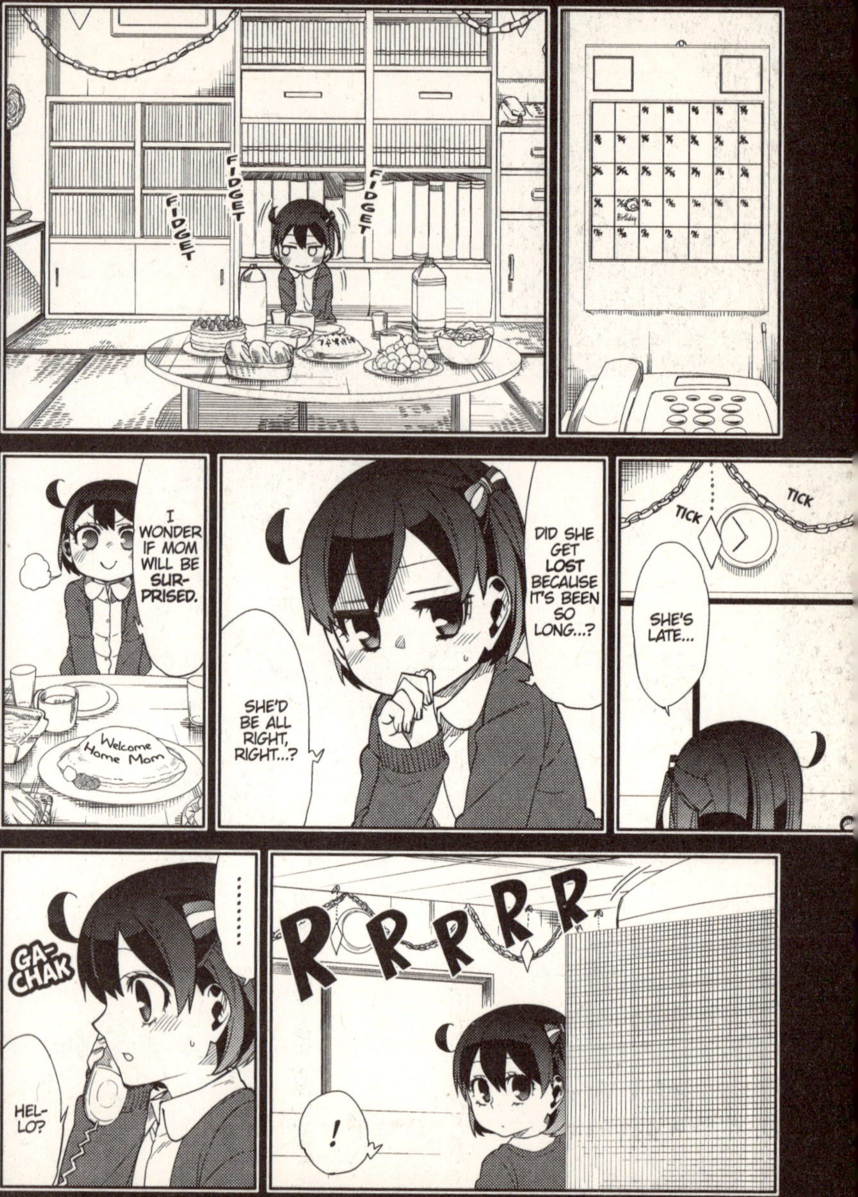
FIDGET
FIDGET
FIDGET
TICK
TICK
SHE'S LATE...
DID SHE GET LOST BECAUSE IT'S BEEN SO LONG...?
SHE'D BE ALL RIGHT, RIGHT...?
I WONDER IF MOM WILL BE SURPRISED.
Welcome Home Mom
RRRRR
!
......
GA-CHAK
HEL-LO?

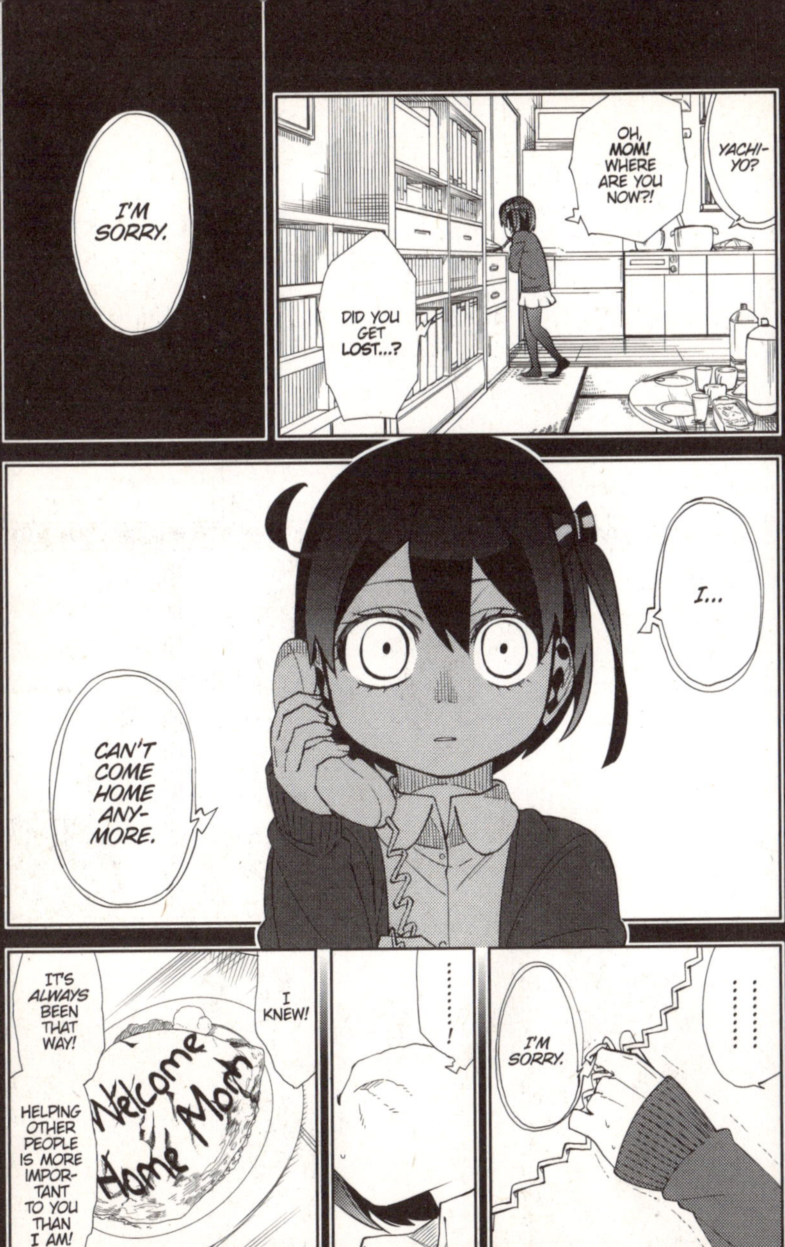
YACHI-YO?
OH, MOM! WHERE ARE YOU NOW?!
DID YOU GET LOST...?
I'M SORRY.
I...
CAN'T COME HOME ANYMORE.
......
I'M SORRY.
......!
I KNEW!
IT'S ALWAYS BEEN THAT WAY!
Welcome Home Mom
HELPING OTHER PEOPLE IS MORE IMPORTANT TO YOU THAN I AM!

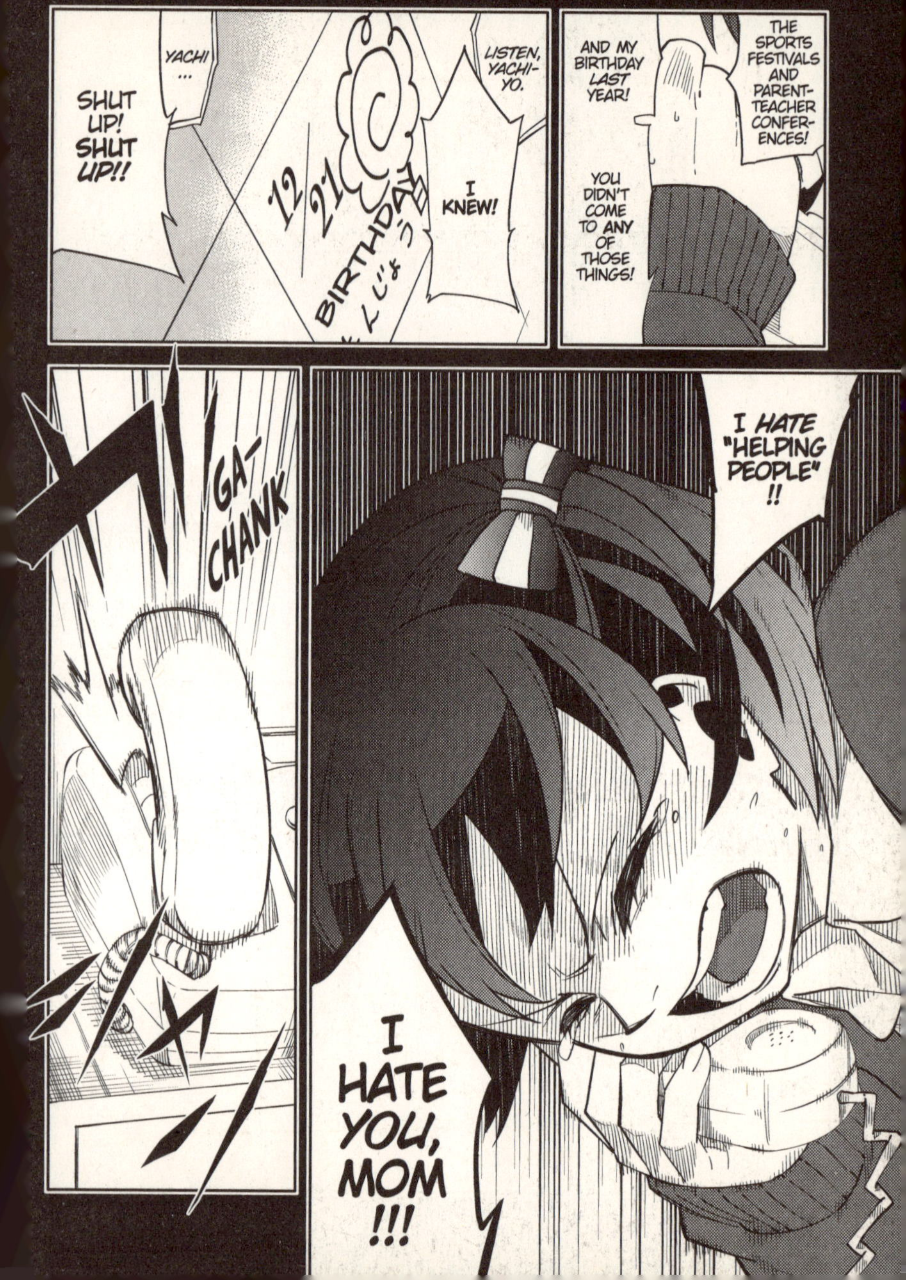
THE SPORTS FESTIVALS AND PARENT-TEACHER CONFER-ENCES!
AND MY BIRTHDAY LAST YEAR!
YOU DIDN'T COME TO ANY OF THOSE THINGS!
LISTEN, YACHI-YO.
I KNEW!
12
21
YACHI ...
SHUT UP! SHUT UP!!
I HATE "HELPING PEOPLE" !!
I HATE YOU, MOM !!!
GA-CHANK

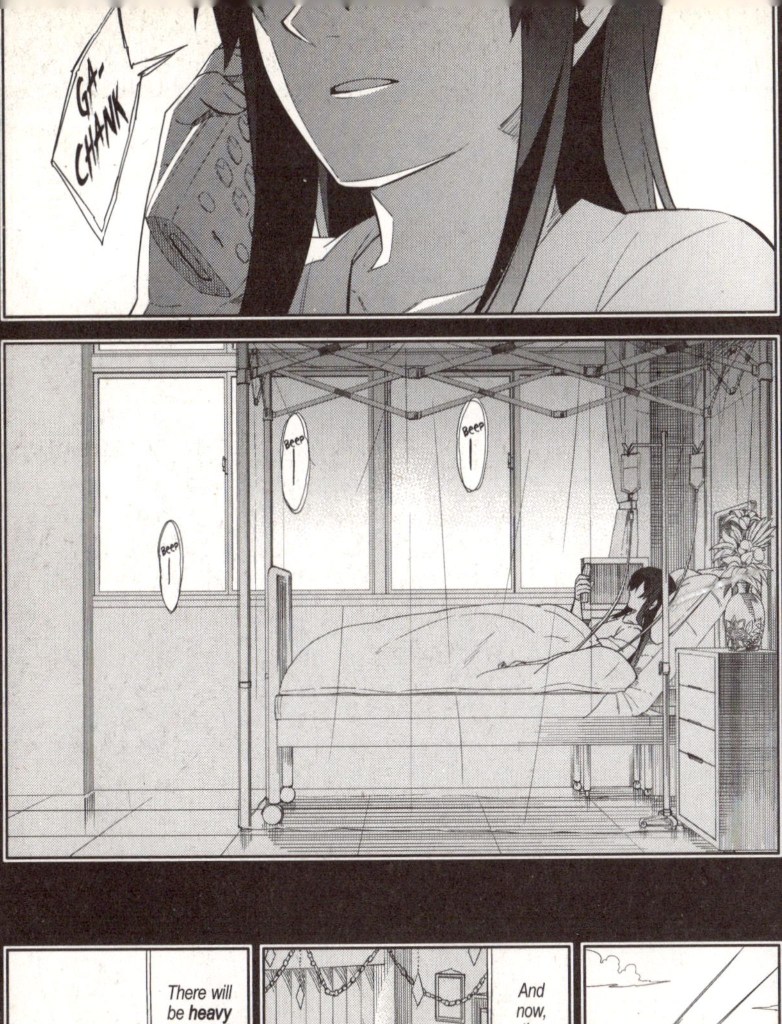
GA-CHANK
Beep
Beep
Beep
CHIRP CHIRP
CHIRP...
And now, the weather.
There will be **heavy snowfall** starting this week--
RISE...

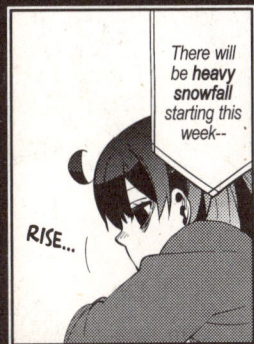

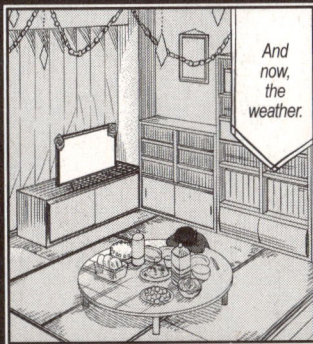

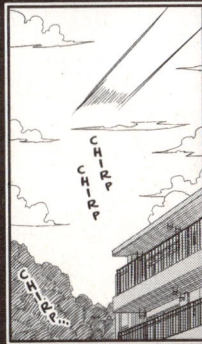

And now for the news.

バ
タ
ン
KA-TUNK

SCHOOL.

I HAVE
TO GO...

チ
TIK

チ
TIK

チ
TIK

*Miss **Mitsuki Hitotose**, long at the forefront of voluntary charity work...*

***passed away** this morning at her current volunteer location.*

Chapter 7: How to Create Hope

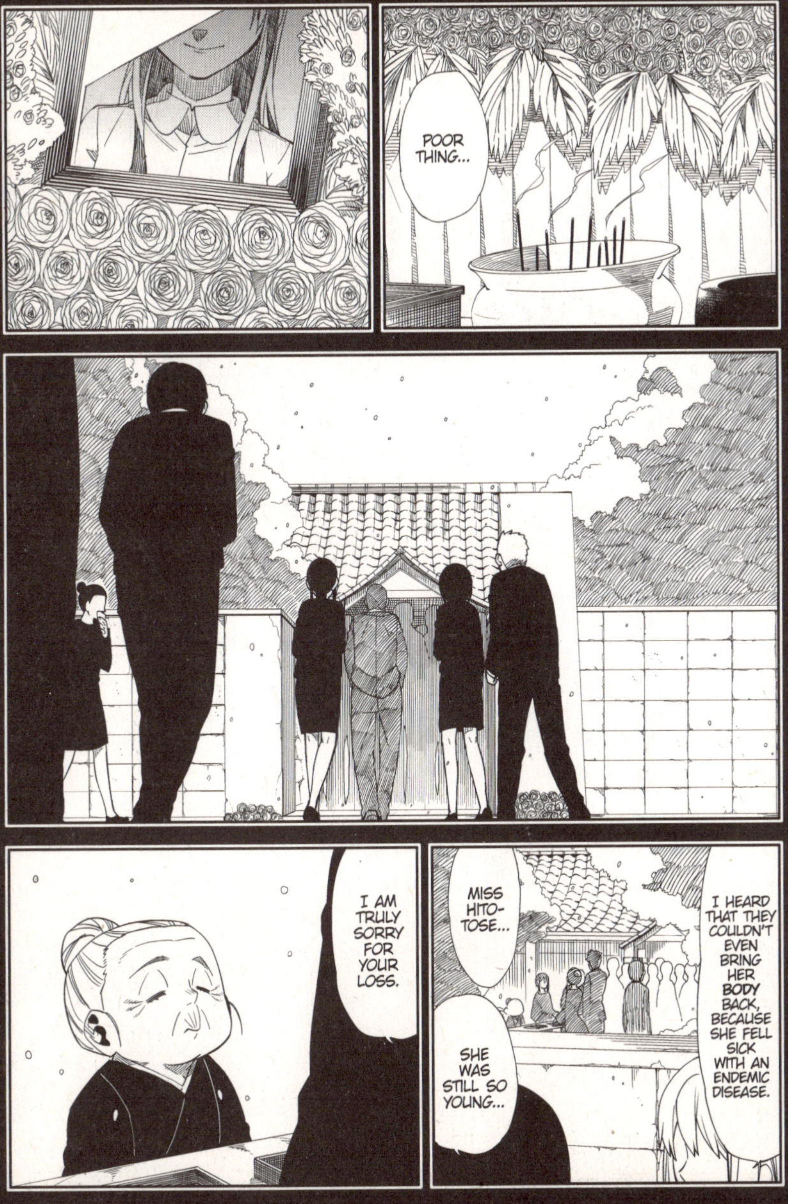
POOR THING...
I HEARD THAT THEY COULDN'T EVEN BRING HER BODY BACK, BECAUSE SHE FELL SICK WITH AN ENDEMIC DISEASE.
MISS HITO-TOSE...
SHE WAS STILL SO YOUNG...
I AM TRULY SORRY FOR YOUR LOSS.

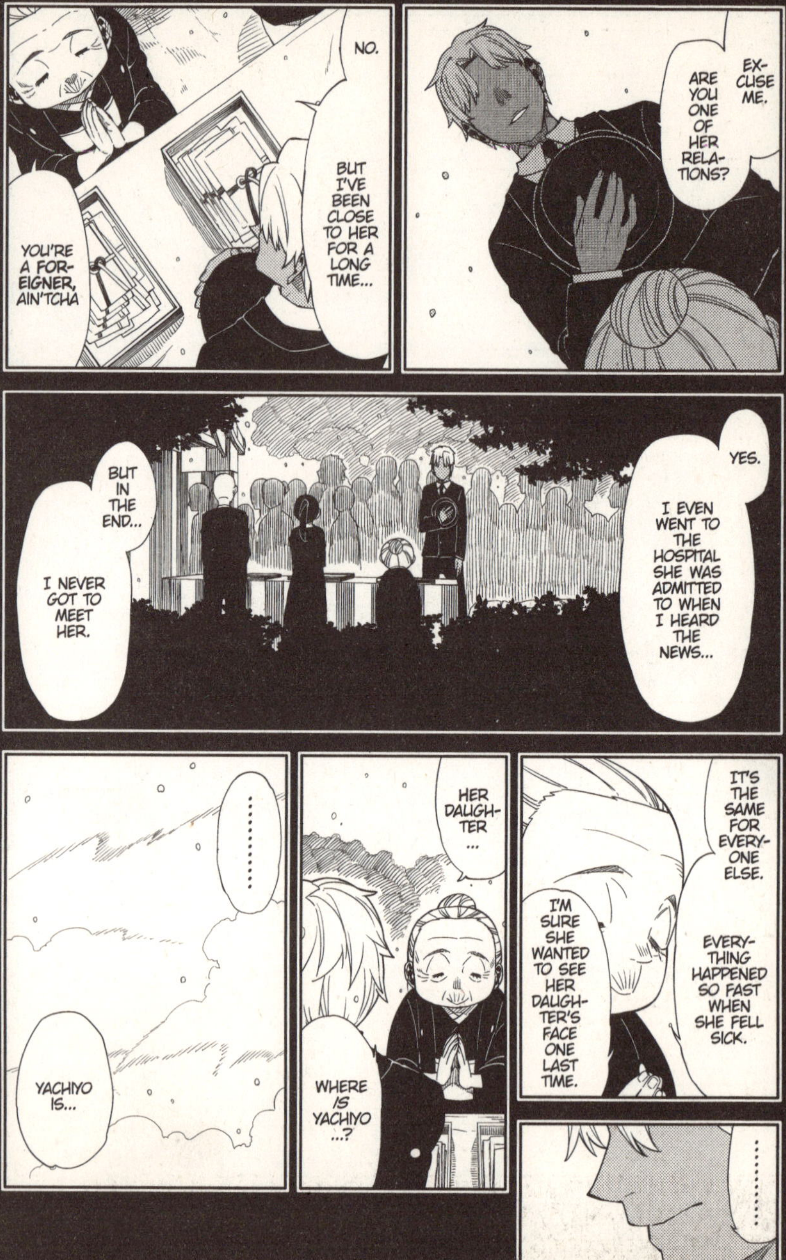
EX-CUSE ME.
ARE YOU ONE OF HER RELA-TIONS?
NO.
BUT I'VE BEEN CLOSE TO HER FOR A LONG TIME...
YOU'RE A FOR-EIGNER, AIN'TCHA
YES.
I EVEN WENT TO THE HOSPITAL SHE WAS ADMITTED TO WHEN I HEARD THE NEWS...
BUT IN THE END...
I NEVER GOT TO MEET HER.
IT'S THE SAME FOR EVERY-ONE ELSE.
EVERY-THING HAPPENED SO FAST WHEN SHE FELL SICK.
I'M SURE SHE WANTED TO SEE HER DAUGH-TER'S FACE ONE LAST TIME.
......
HER DAUGH-TER ...
WHERE IS YACHIYO ...?
....
YACHIYO IS...

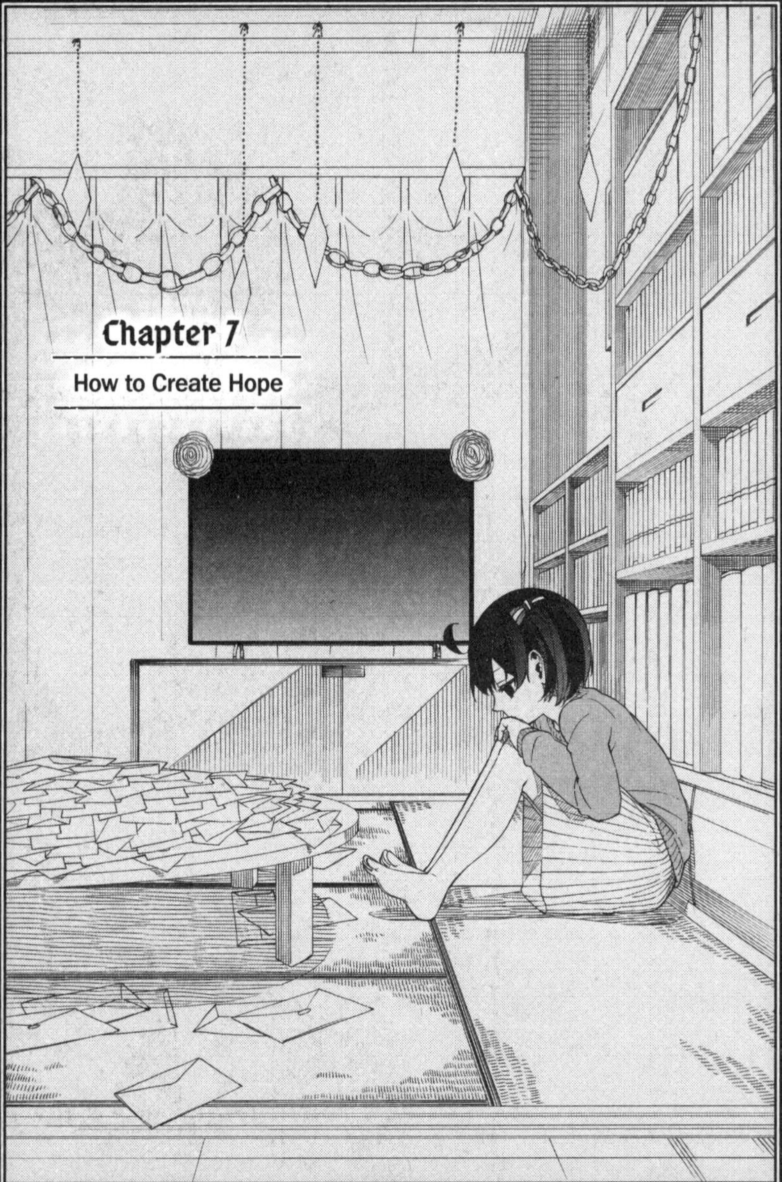
Chapter 7
How to Create Hope

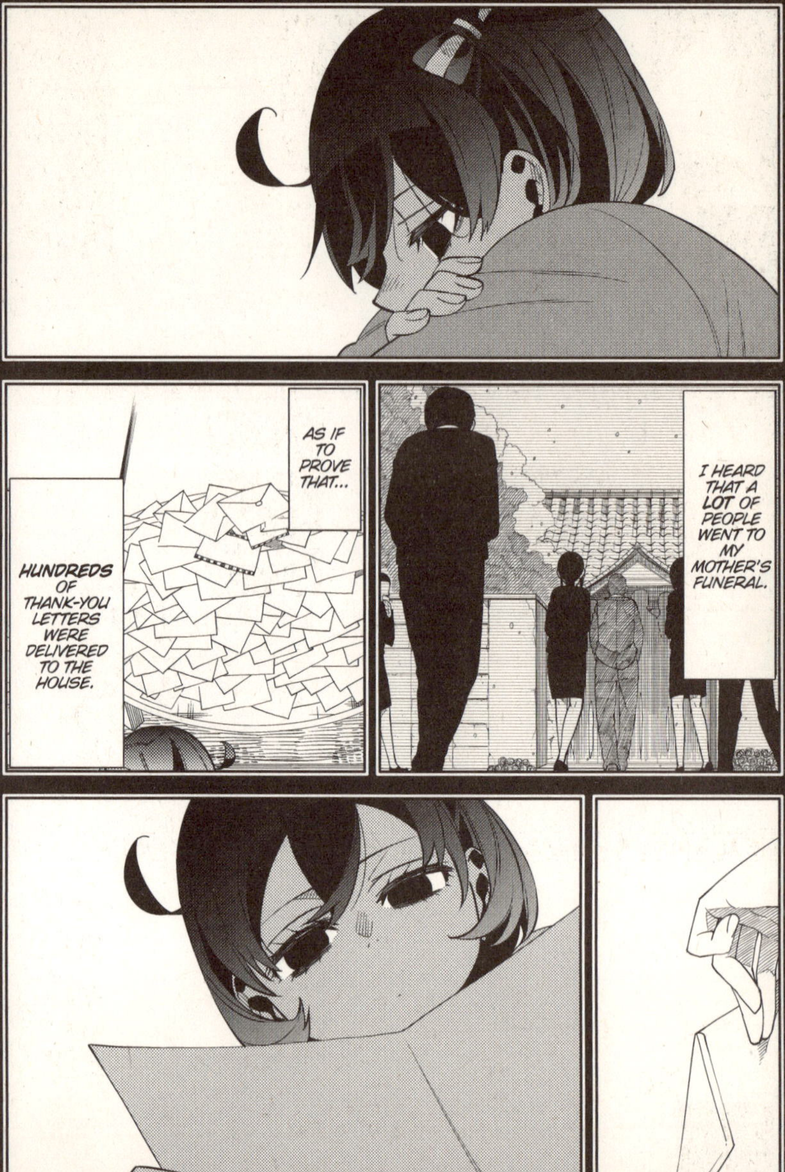
I HEARD THAT A LOT OF PEOPLE WENT TO MY MOTHER'S FUNERAL.
AS IF TO PROVE THAT...
HUNDREDS OF THANK-YOU LETTERS WERE DELIVERED TO THE HOUSE.

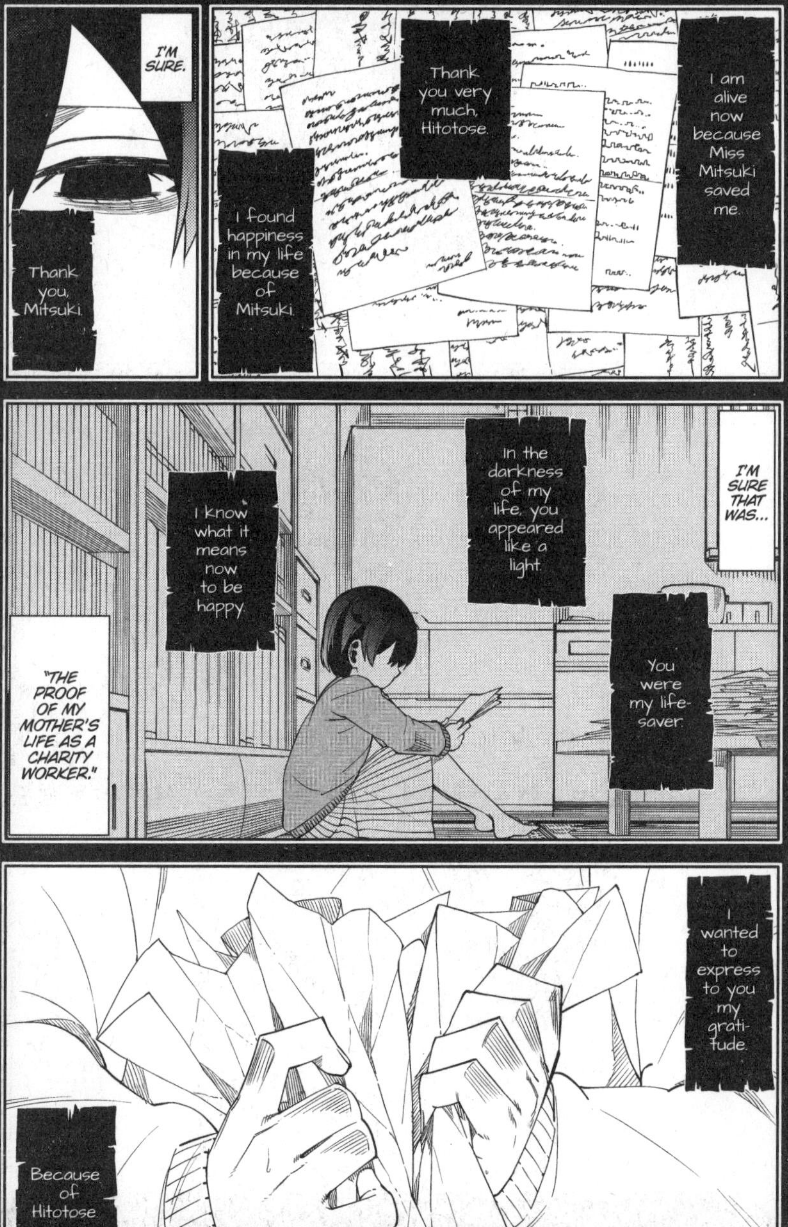
I am alive now because Miss Mitsuki saved me.
Thank you very much, Hitotose.
I found happiness in my life because of Mitsuki.
I'M SURE.
Thank you, Mitsuki.
I'M SURE THAT WAS...
You were my life-saver.
In the darkness of my life, you appeared like a light.
I know what it means now to be happy.
"THE PROOF OF MY MOTHER'S LIFE AS A CHARITY WORKER."
I wanted to express to you my gratitude.
Because of Hitotose.

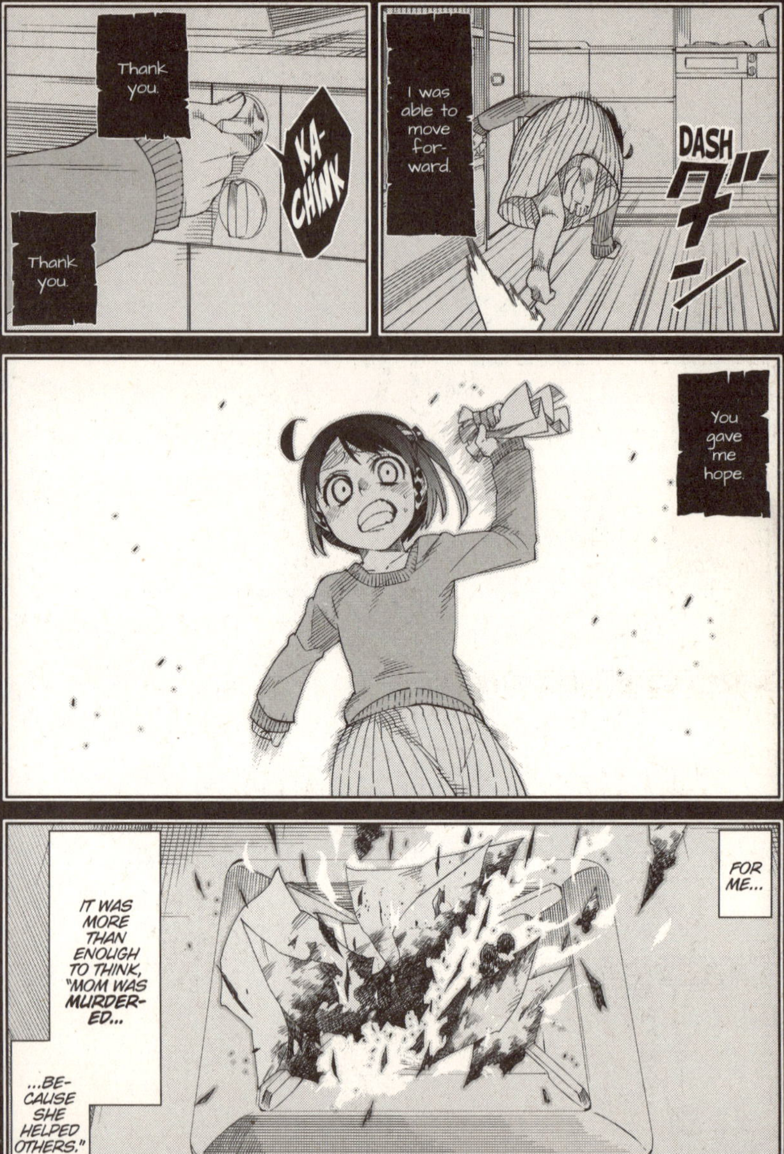

I was able to move for-ward.
DASH
ダーン
Thank you.
KA-CHINK
Thank you.
You gave me hope.
FOR ME...
IT WAS MORE THAN ENOUGH TO THINK, "MOM WAS MURDER-ED...
...BE-CAUSE SHE HELPED OTHERS."

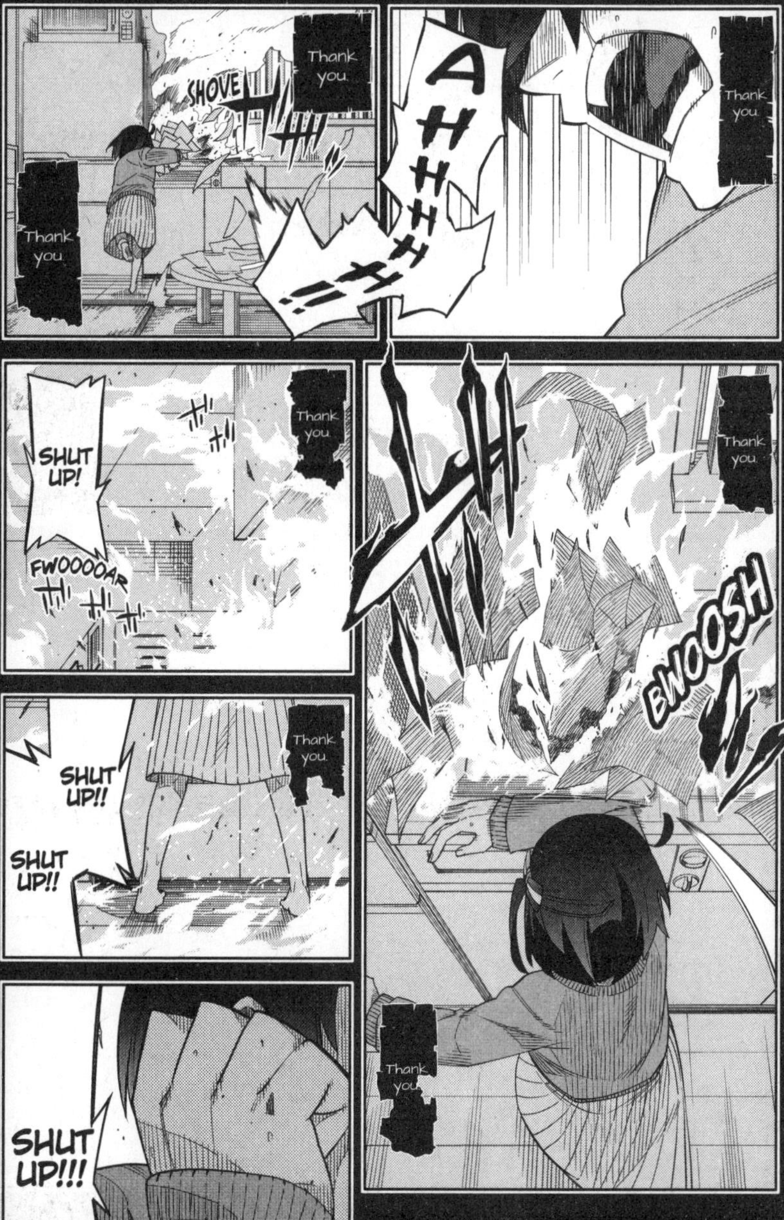
Thank you.
AHHHHHHH!!
Thank you.
SHOVE
Thank you.
Thank you.
BWOOSH
Thank you.
Thank you.
SHUT UP!
FWOOOOAR
Thank you.
SHUT UP!!
SHUT UP!!
SHUT UP!!!

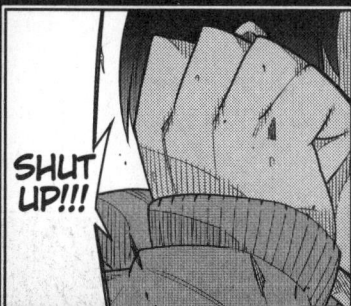

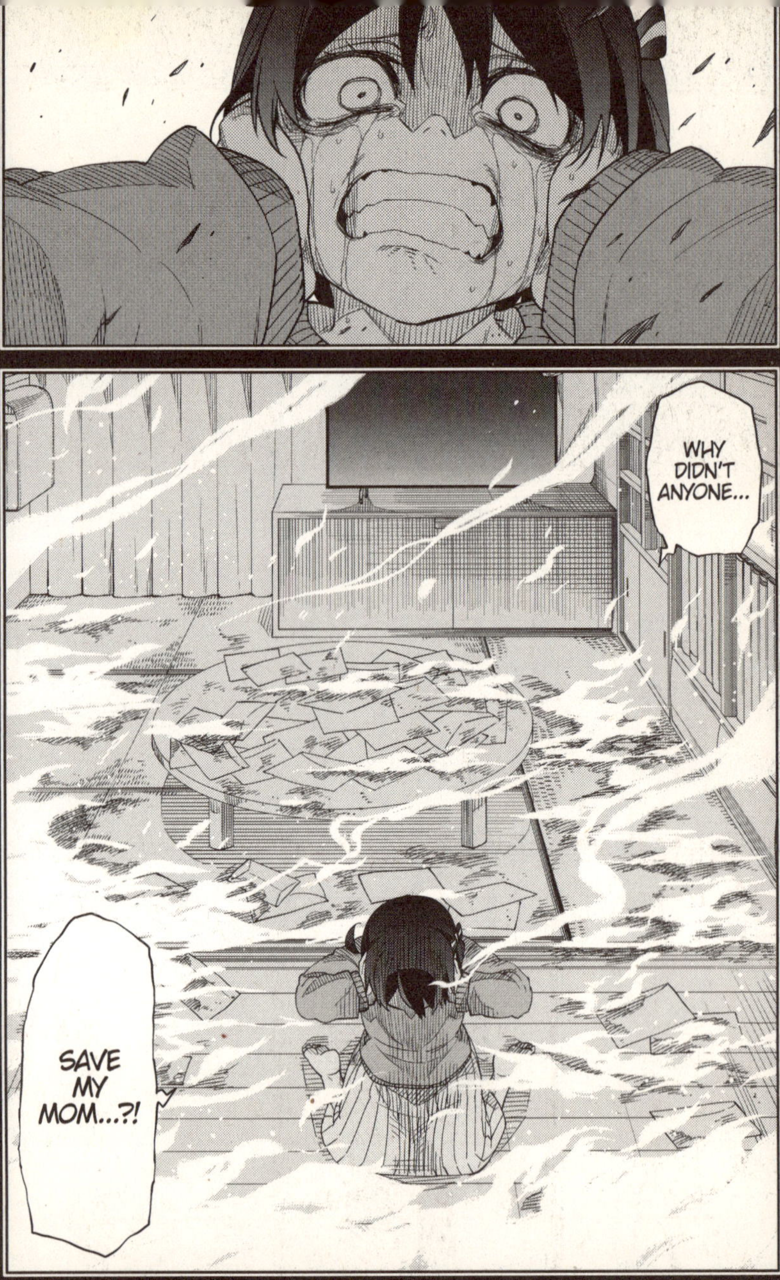
WHY DIDN'T ANYONE...
SAVE MY MOM...?!

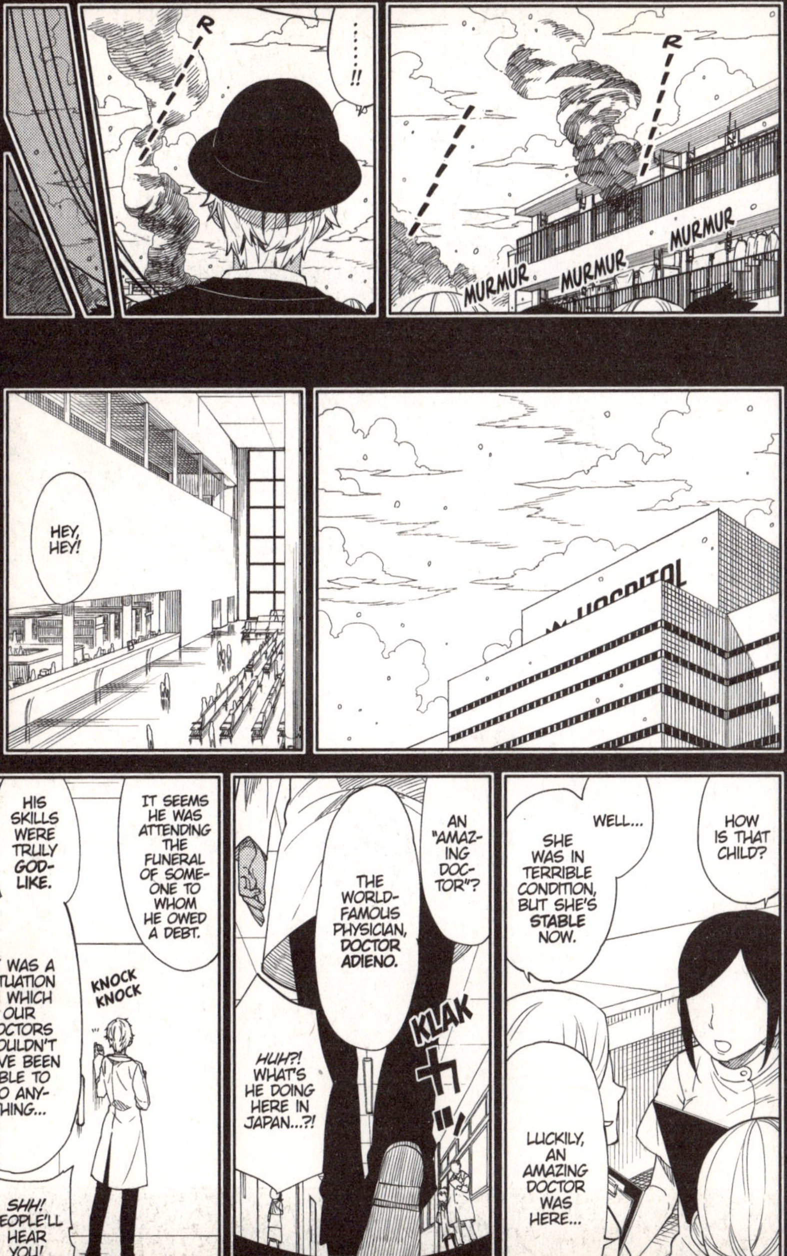
R--
MURMUR MURMUR MURMUR
R--
......!!
HEY, HEY!
HOW IS THAT CHILD?
WELL...
SHE WAS IN TERRIBLE CONDITION, BUT SHE'S STABLE NOW.
LUCKILY, AN AMAZING DOCTOR WAS HERE...
AN "AMAZ-ING DOC-TOR"?
THE WORLD-FAMOUS PHYSICIAN, DOCTOR ADIENO.
KLAK
HUH?! WHAT'S HE DOING HERE IN JAPAN...?!
IT SEEMS HE WAS ATTENDING THE FUNERAL OF SOME-ONE TO WHOM HE OWED A DEBT.
HIS SKILLS WERE TRULY GOD-LIKE.
IT WAS A SITUATION IN WHICH OUR DOCTORS WOULDN'T HAVE BEEN ABLE TO DO ANY-THING...
KNOCK KNOCK
SHH! PEOPLE'LL HEAR YOU!

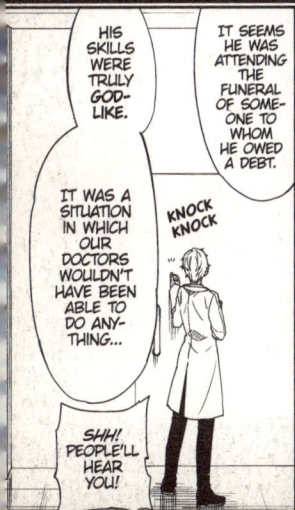

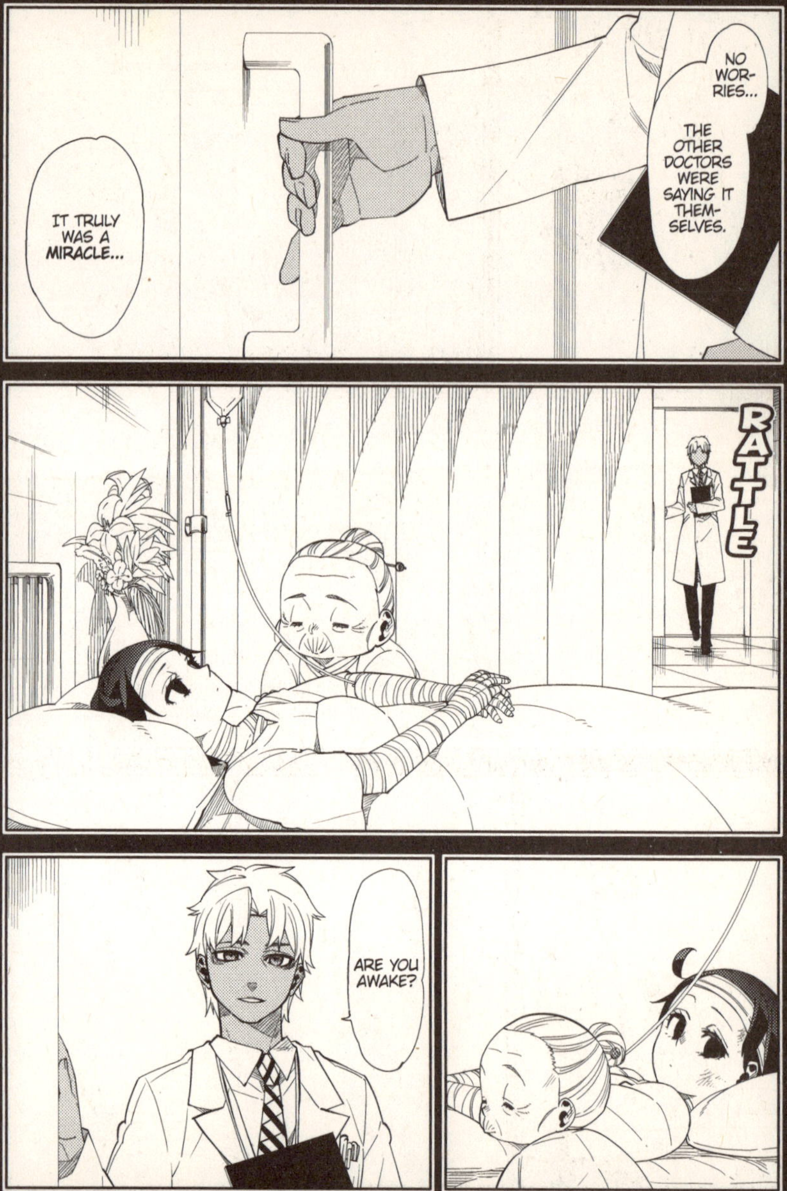
NO WORRIES...
THE OTHER DOCTORS WERE SAYING IT THEMSELVES.
IT TRULY WAS A MIRACLE...
RATTLE
ARE YOU AWAKE?

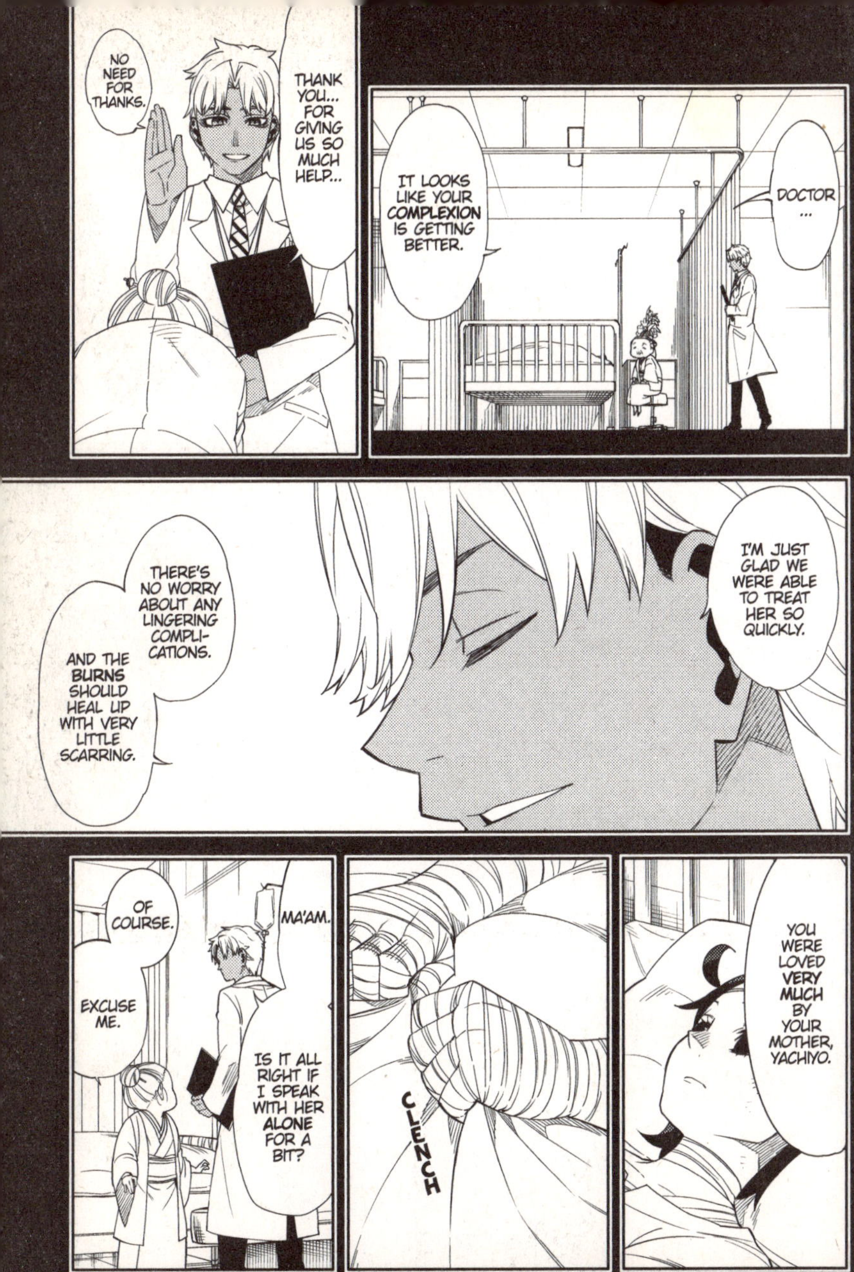
DOCTOR ...
IT LOOKS LIKE YOUR COMPLEXION IS GETTING BETTER.
THANK YOU... FOR GIVING US SO MUCH HELP...
NO NEED FOR THANKS.
I'M JUST GLAD WE WERE ABLE TO TREAT HER SO QUICKLY.
THERE'S NO WORRY ABOUT ANY LINGERING COMPLI-CATIONS.
AND THE BURNS SHOULD HEAL UP WITH VERY LITTLE SCARRING.
YOU WERE LOVED VERY MUCH BY YOUR MOTHER, YACHIYO.
CLENCH
MA'AM.
IS IT ALL RIGHT IF I SPEAK WITH HER ALONE FOR A BIT?
OF COURSE.
EXCUSE ME.

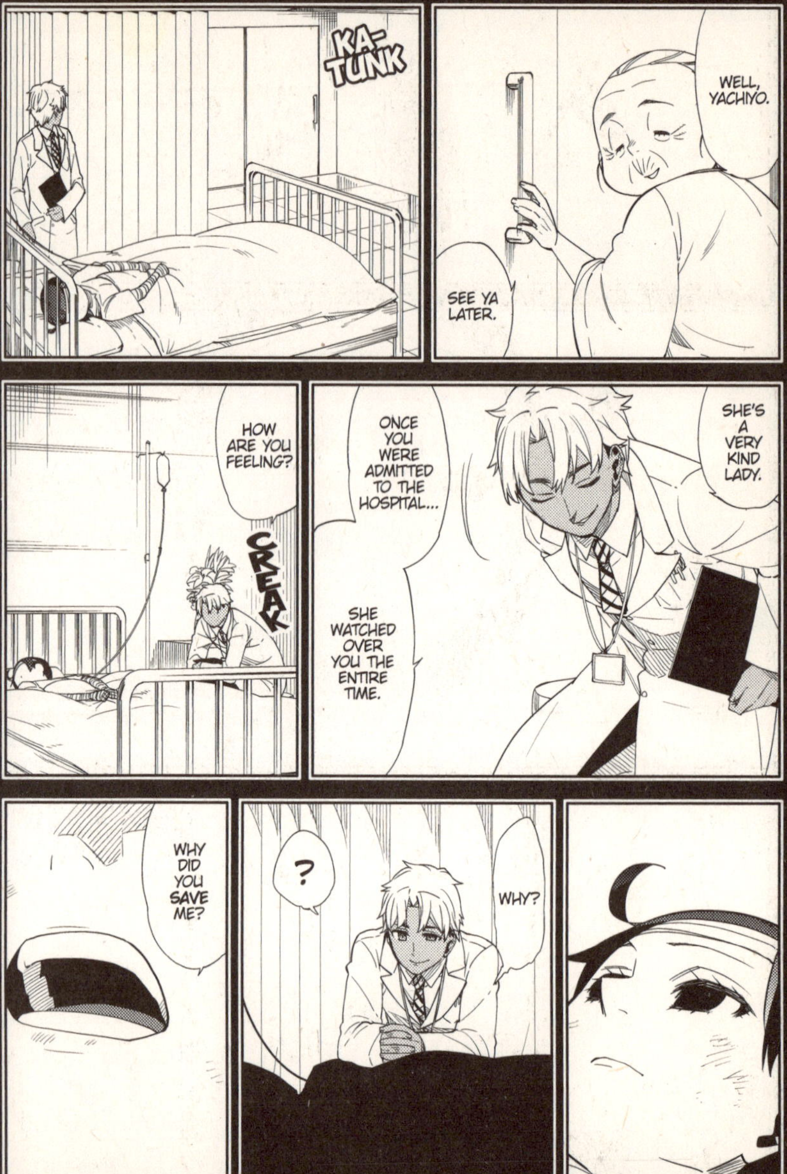
WELL, YACHIYO.
SEE YA LATER.
KA-TUNK
SHE'S A VERY KIND LADY.
ONCE YOU WERE ADMITTED TO THE HOSPITAL...
SHE WATCHED OVER YOU THE ENTIRE TIME.
HOW ARE YOU FEELING?
CREAK
WHY?
?
WHY DID YOU SAVE ME?

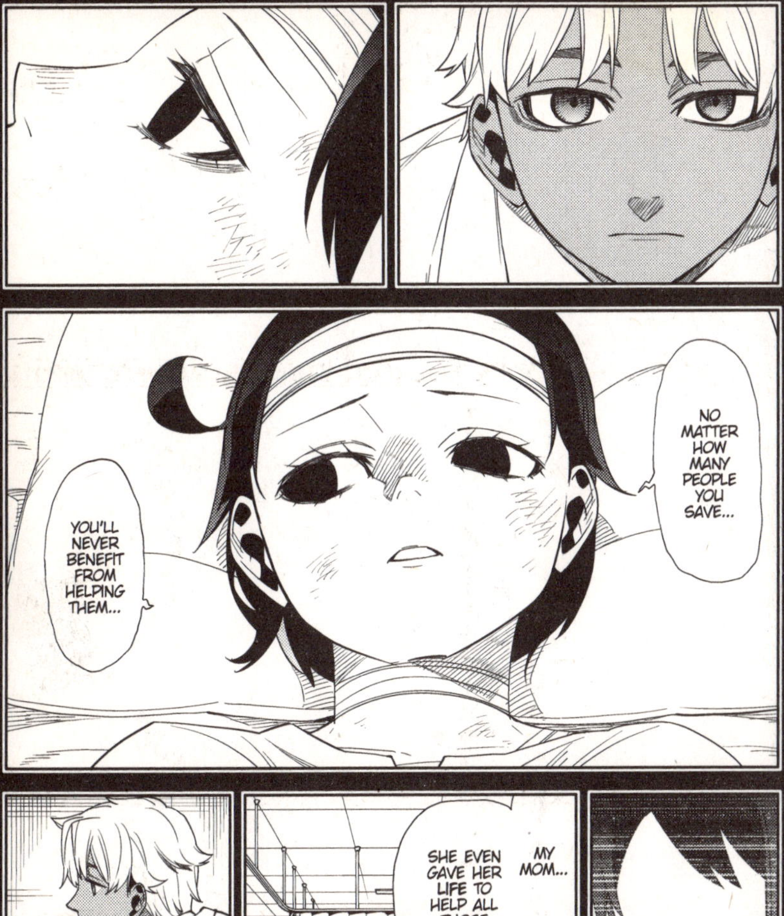
NO MATTER HOW MANY PEOPLE YOU SAVE...
YOU'LL NEVER BENEFIT FROM HELPING THEM...
MY MOM...
SHE EVEN GAVE HER LIFE TO HELP ALL THOSE PEOPLE...
BUT IN THE END, NO ONE HELPED *HER*.

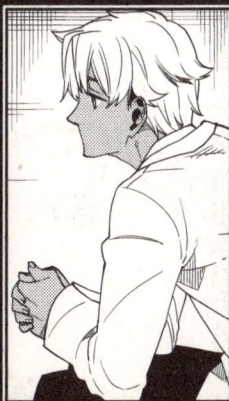

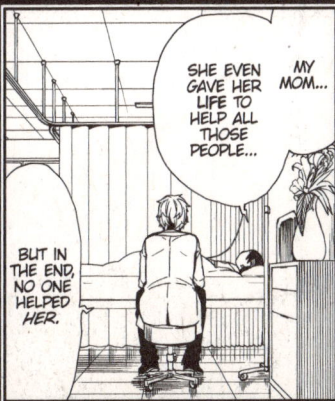

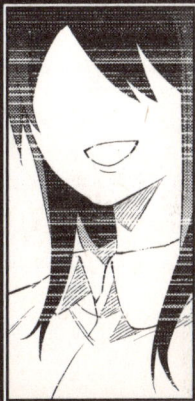

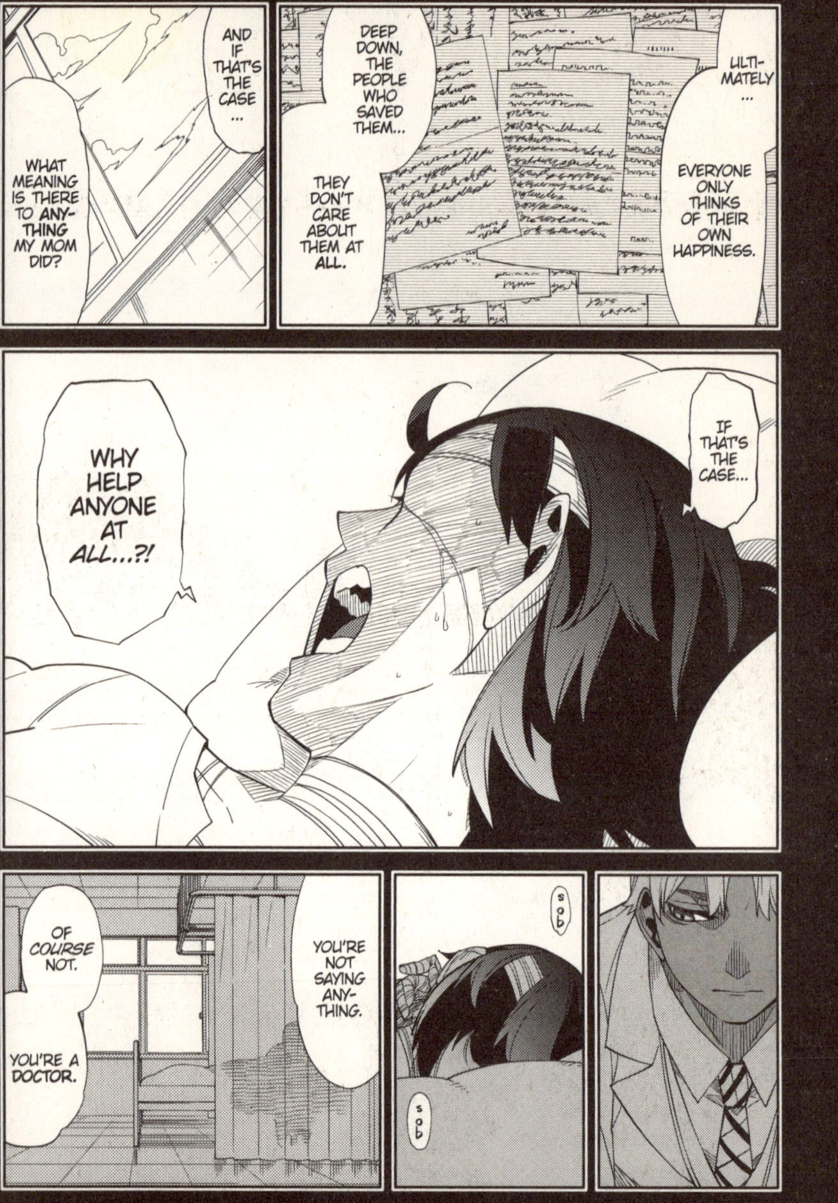
ULTI-MATELY...
EVERYONE ONLY THINKS OF THEIR OWN HAPPINESS.
DEEP DOWN, THE PEOPLE WHO SAVED THEM...
THEY DON'T CARE ABOUT THEM AT ALL.
AND IF THAT'S THE CASE...
WHAT MEANING IS THERE TO ANYTHING MY MOM DID?
IF THAT'S THE CASE...
WHY HELP ANYONE AT ALL...?!
sob
sob
YOU'RE NOT SAYING ANYTHING.
OF COURSE NOT.
YOU'RE A DOCTOR.

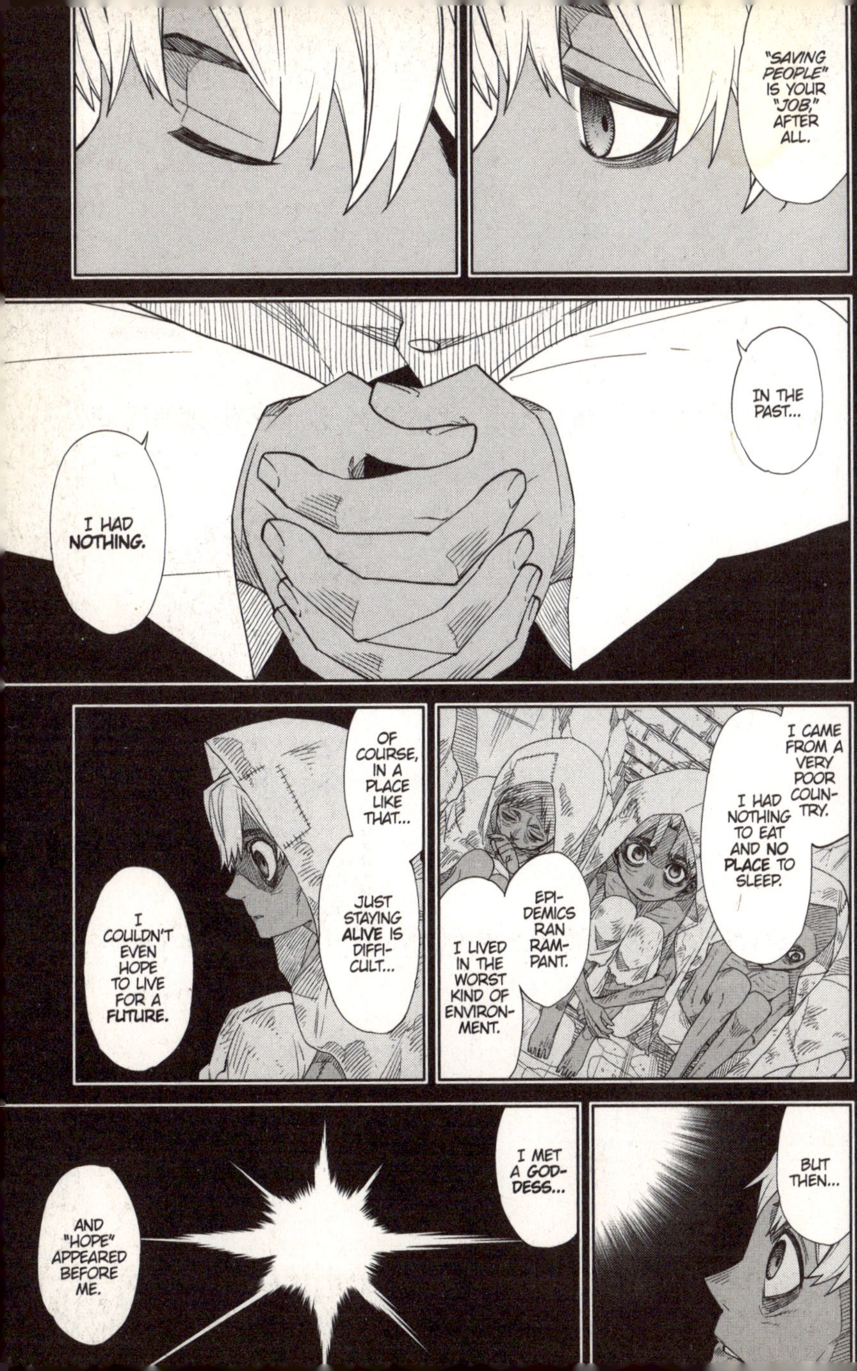
"SAVING PEOPLE" IS YOUR "JOB," AFTER ALL.
IN THE PAST...
I HAD NOTHING.
I CAME FROM A VERY POOR COUNTRY.
I HAD NOTHING TO EAT AND NO PLACE TO SLEEP.
EPIDEMICS RAN RAMPANT.
I LIVED IN THE WORST KIND OF ENVIRONMENT.
OF COURSE, IN A PLACE LIKE THAT...
JUST STAYING ALIVE IS DIFFICULT...
I COULDN'T EVEN HOPE TO LIVE FOR A FUTURE.
BUT THEN...
I MET A GODDESS...
AND "HOPE" APPEARED BEFORE ME.

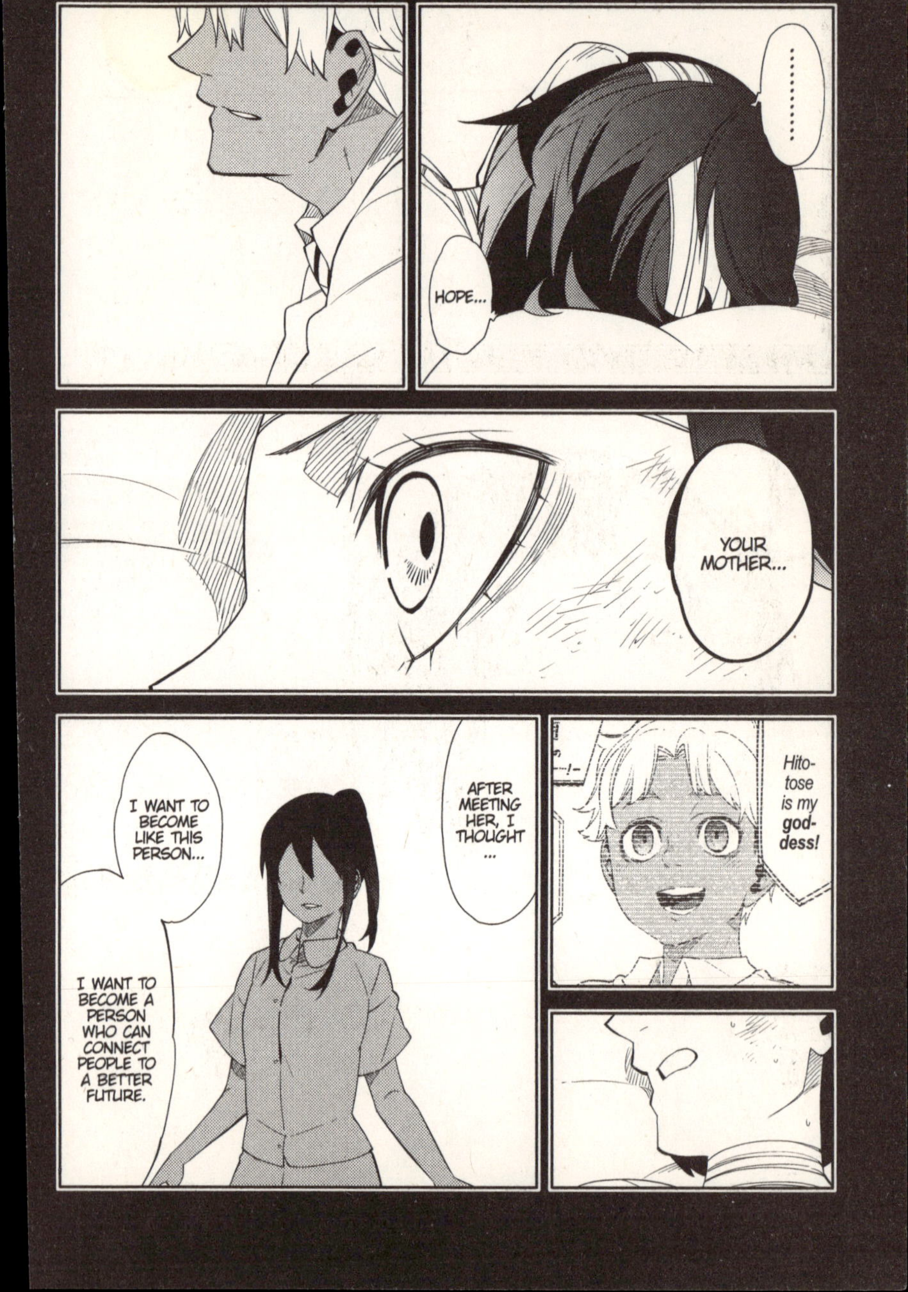
......
HOPE...
YOUR MOTHER...
Hito-tose is my god-dess!
AFTER MEETING HER, I THOUGHT ...
I WANT TO BECOME LIKE THIS PERSON...
I WANT TO BECOME A PERSON WHO CAN CONNECT PEOPLE TO A BETTER FUTURE.

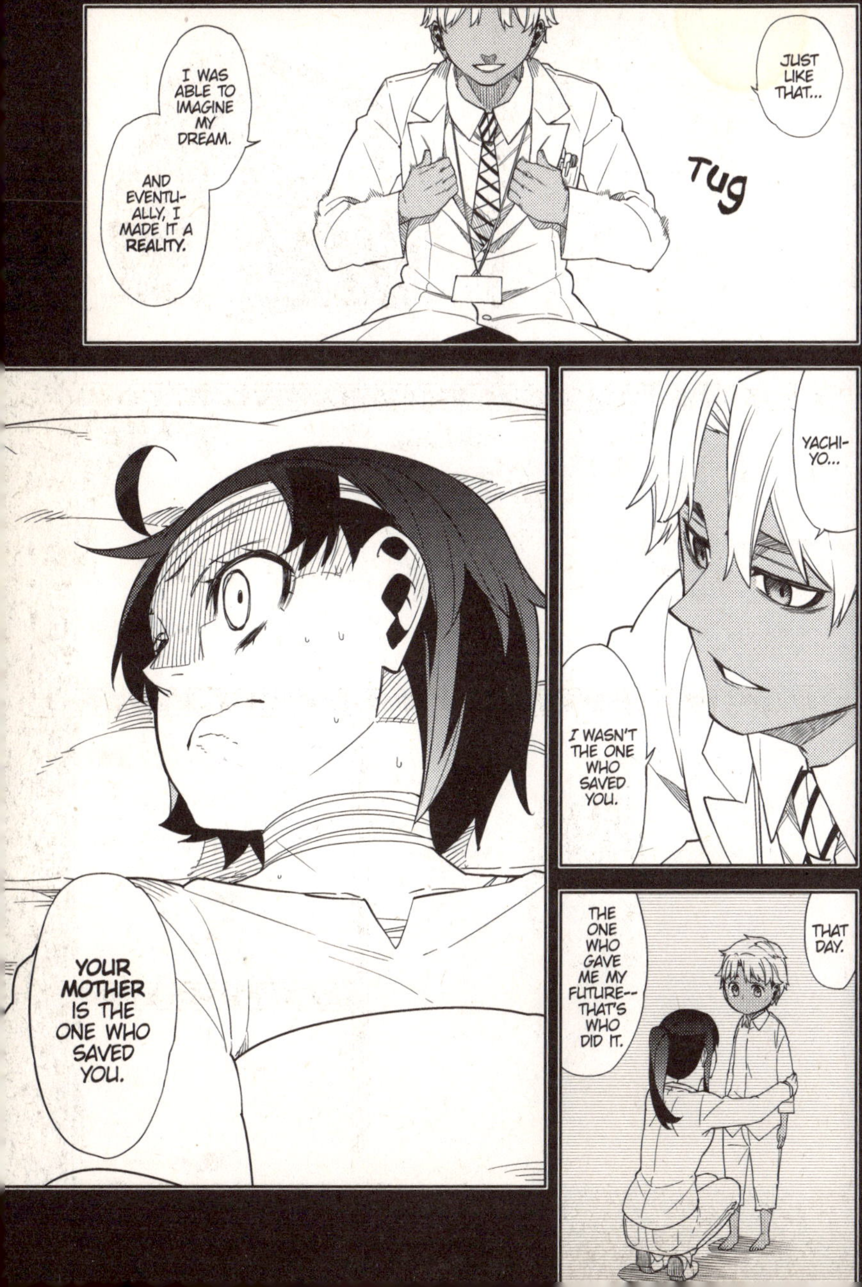

JUST LIKE THAT...
Tug
I WAS ABLE TO IMAGINE MY DREAM.
AND EVENTUALLY, I MADE IT A REALITY.
YACHIYO...
I WASN'T THE ONE WHO SAVED YOU.
THAT DAY.
THE ONE WHO GAVE ME MY FUTURE--THAT'S WHO DID IT.
YOUR MOTHER IS THE ONE WHO SAVED YOU.

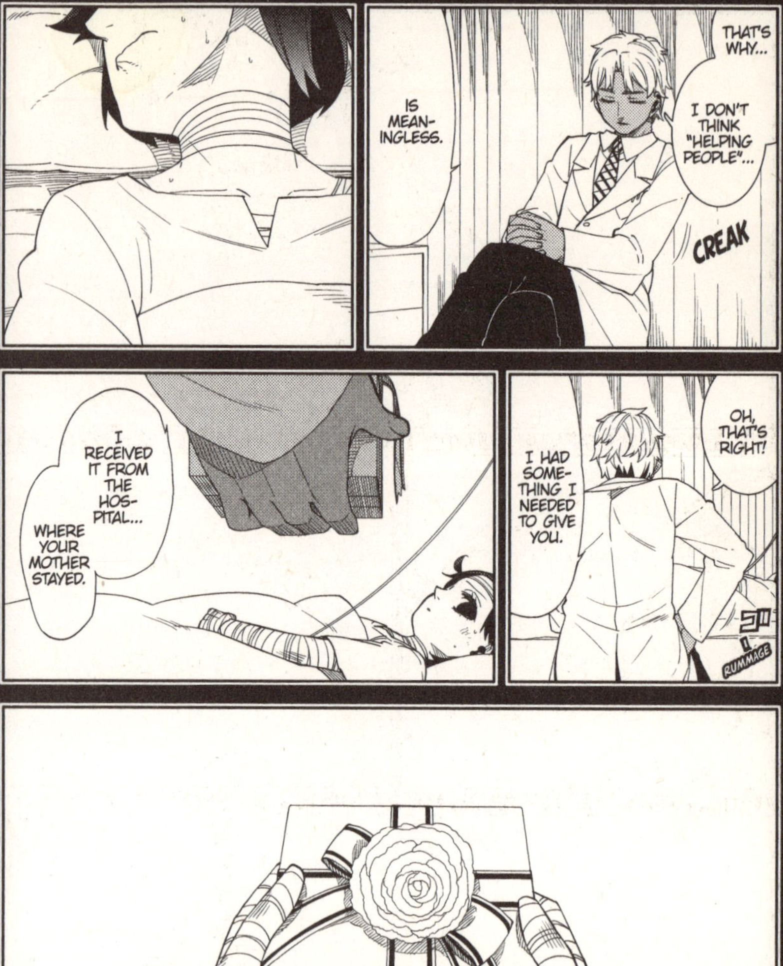
THAT'S WHY...
I DON'T THINK "HELPING PEOPLE"...
CREAK
IS MEANINGLESS.
OH, THAT'S RIGHT!
I HAD SOMETHING I NEEDED TO GIVE YOU.
RUMMAGE
I RECEIVED IT FROM THE HOSPITAL...
WHERE YOUR MOTHER STAYED.

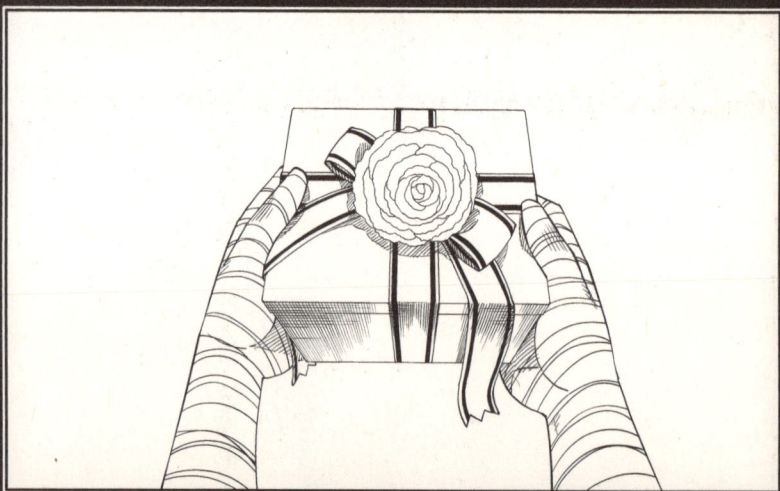

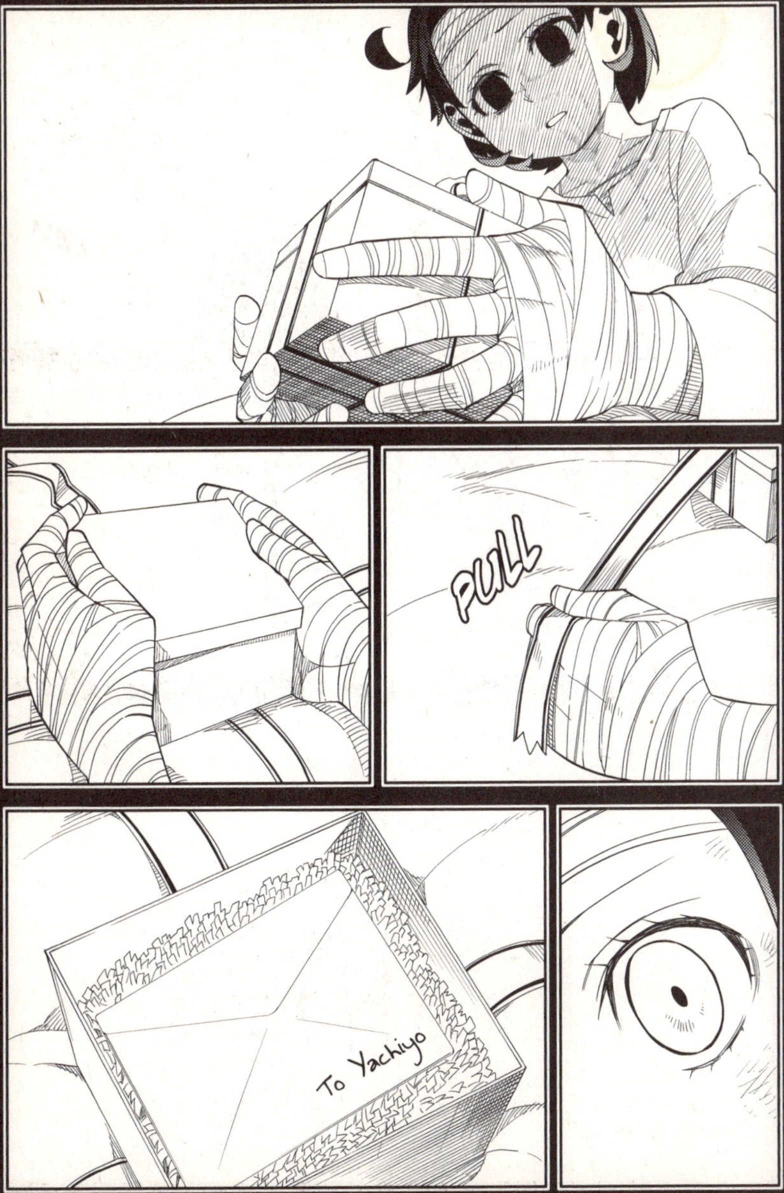
PULL
To Yachiyo

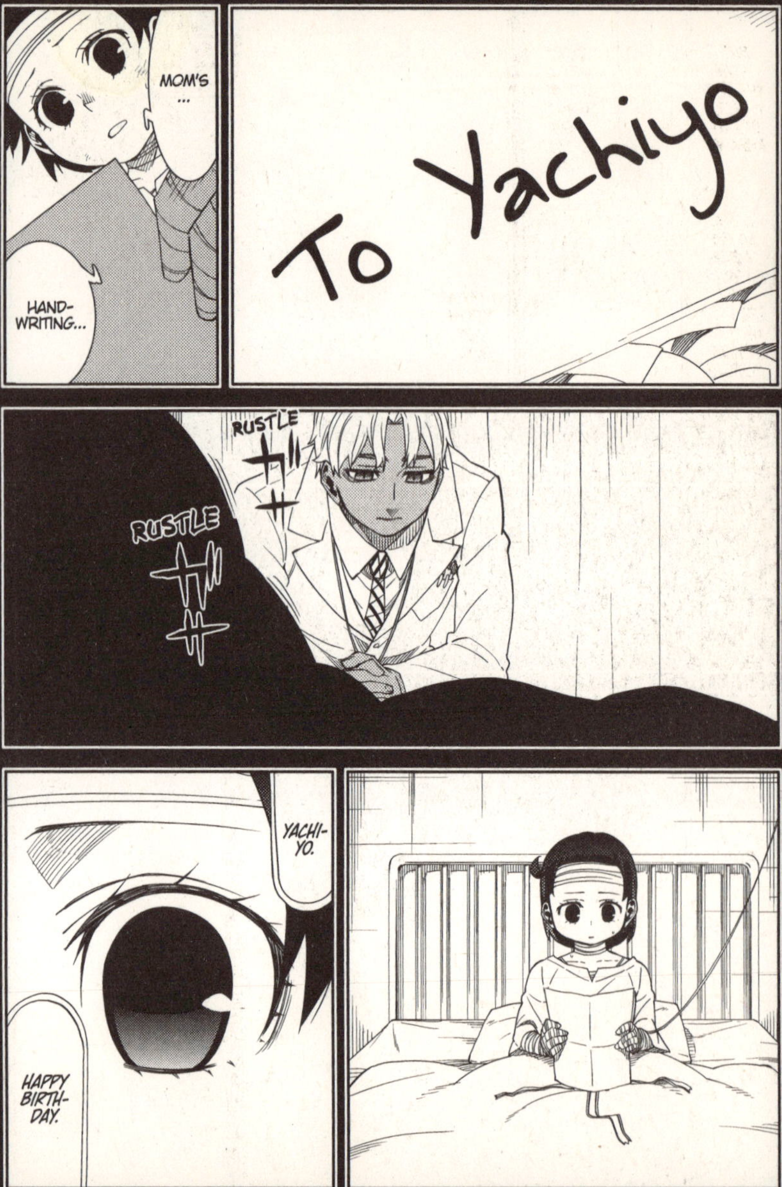
To Yachiyo
MOM'S ...
HAND-WRITING...
RUSTLE
RUSTLE
YACHI-YO.
HAPPY BIRTH-DAY.

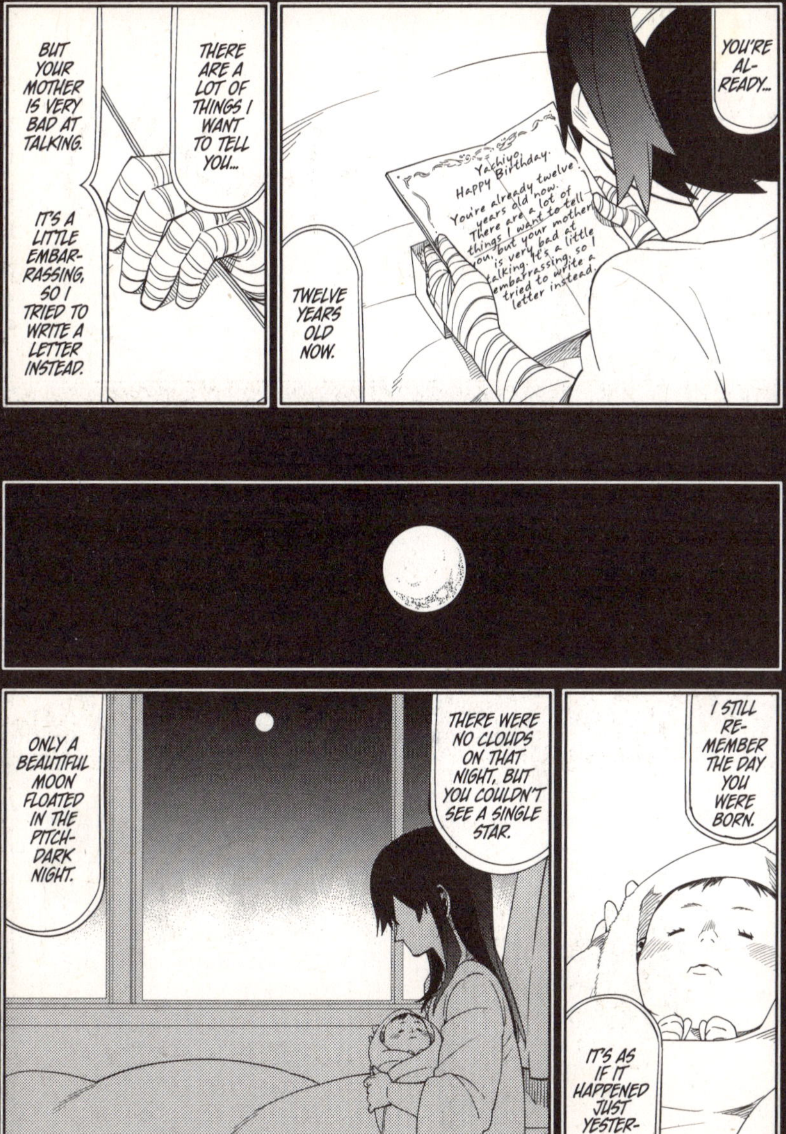
YOU'RE AL-READY...
Yachiyo, Happy Birthday. You're already twelve years old now. There are a lot of things I want to tell you, but your mother is very bad at talking. It's a little embarrassing, so I tried to write a letter instead.
TWELVE YEARS OLD NOW.
THERE ARE A LOT OF THINGS I WANT TO TELL YOU...
BUT YOUR MOTHER IS VERY BAD AT TALKING.
IT'S A LITTLE EMBAR-RASSING, SO I TRIED TO WRITE A LETTER INSTEAD.
I STILL RE-MEMBER THE DAY YOU WERE BORN.
IT'S AS IF IT HAPPENED JUST YESTER-DAY.
THERE WERE NO CLOUDS ON THAT NIGHT, BUT YOU COULDN'T SEE A SINGLE STAR.
ONLY A BEAUTIFUL MOON FLOATED IN THE PITCH-DARK NIGHT.

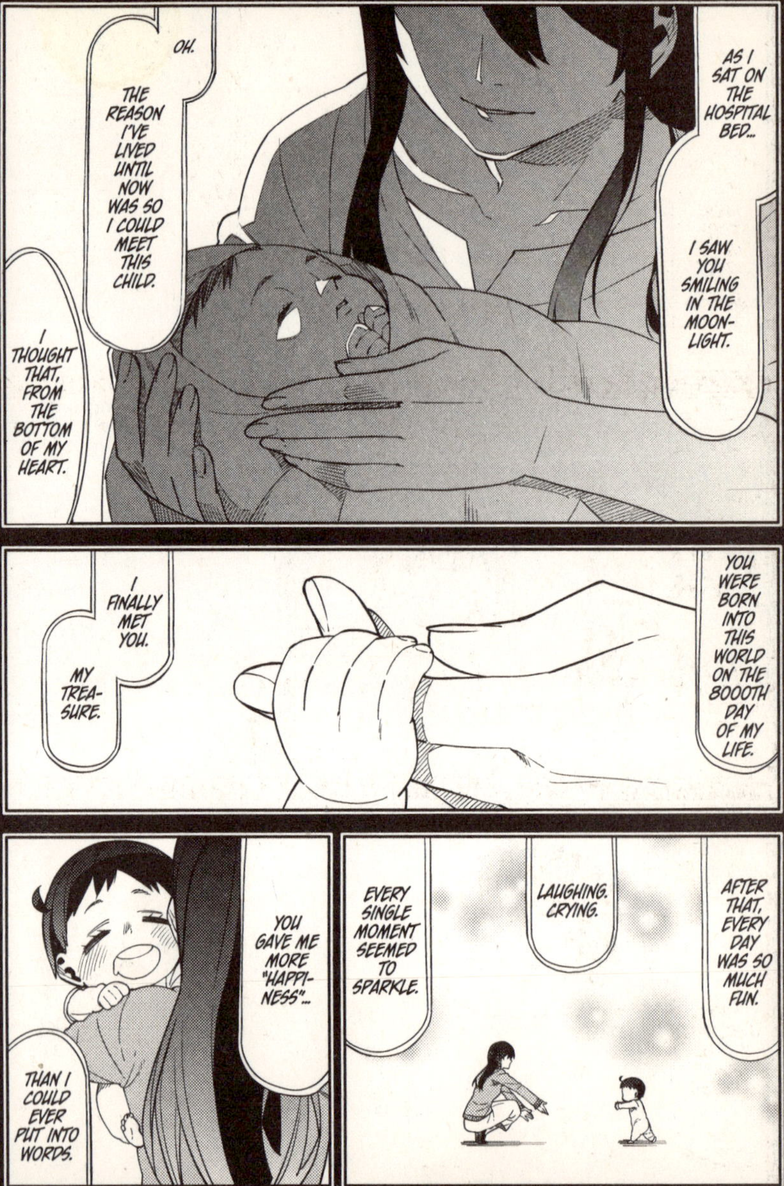
AS I SAT ON THE HOSPITAL BED...
I SAW YOU SMILING IN THE MOONLIGHT.
OH.
THE REASON I'VE LIVED UNTIL NOW WAS SO I COULD MEET THIS CHILD.
I THOUGHT THAT, FROM THE BOTTOM OF MY HEART.
YOU WERE BORN INTO THIS WORLD ON THE 8000TH DAY OF MY LIFE.
I FINALLY MET YOU.
MY TREASURE.
AFTER THAT, EVERY DAY WAS SO MUCH FUN.
LAUGHING. CRYING.
EVERY SINGLE MOMENT SEEMED TO SPARKLE.
YOU GAVE ME MORE "HAPPINESS"...
THAN I COULD EVER PUT INTO WORDS.

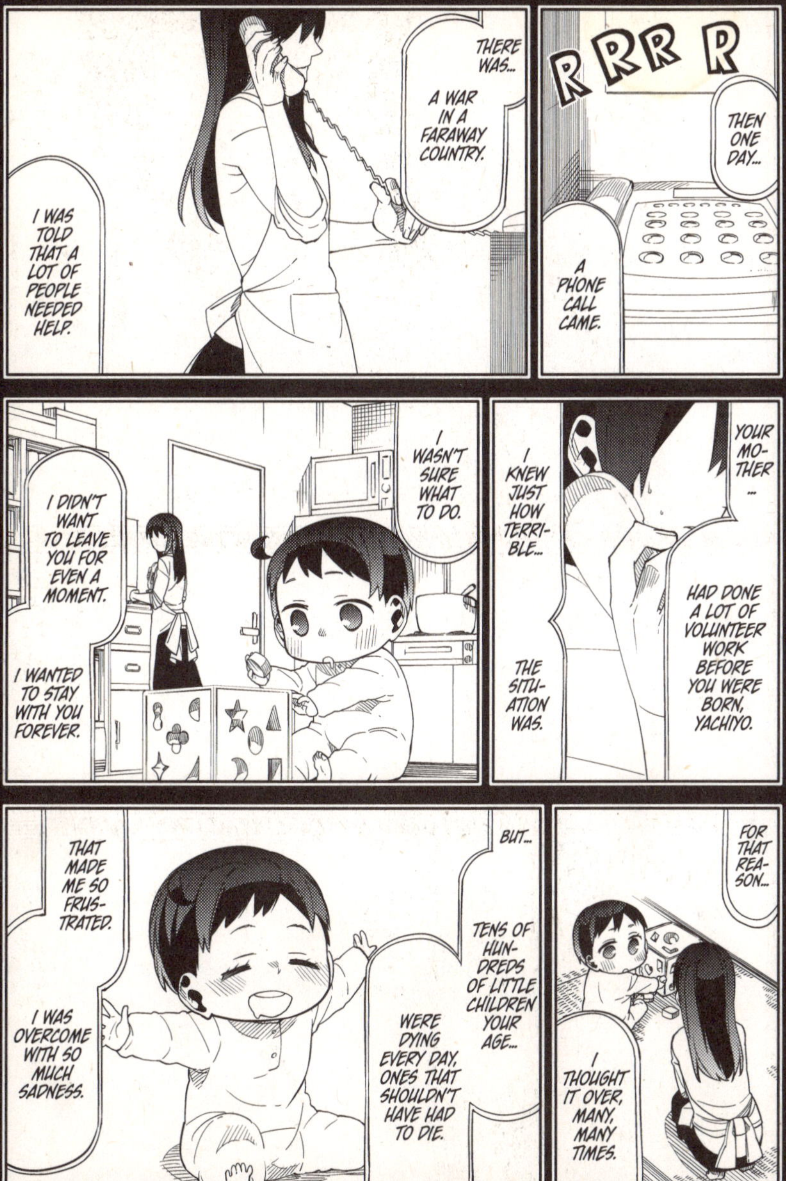
RRRR
THEN ONE DAY...
A PHONE CALL CAME.
THERE WAS...
A WAR IN A FARAWAY COUNTRY.
I WAS TOLD THAT A LOT OF PEOPLE NEEDED HELP.
YOUR MOTHER...
HAD DONE A LOT OF VOLUNTEER WORK BEFORE YOU WERE BORN, YACHIYO.
I KNEW JUST HOW TERRIBLE...
THE SITUATION WAS.
I WASN'T SURE WHAT TO DO.
I DIDN'T WANT TO LEAVE YOU FOR EVEN A MOMENT.
I WANTED TO STAY WITH YOU FOREVER.
FOR THAT REASON...
I THOUGHT IT OVER, MANY, MANY TIMES.
BUT...
TENS OF HUNDREDS OF LITTLE CHILDREN YOUR AGE...
WERE DYING EVERY DAY, ONES THAT SHOULDN'T HAVE HAD TO DIE.
THAT MADE ME SO FRUSTRATED.
I WAS OVERCOME WITH SO MUCH SADNESS.

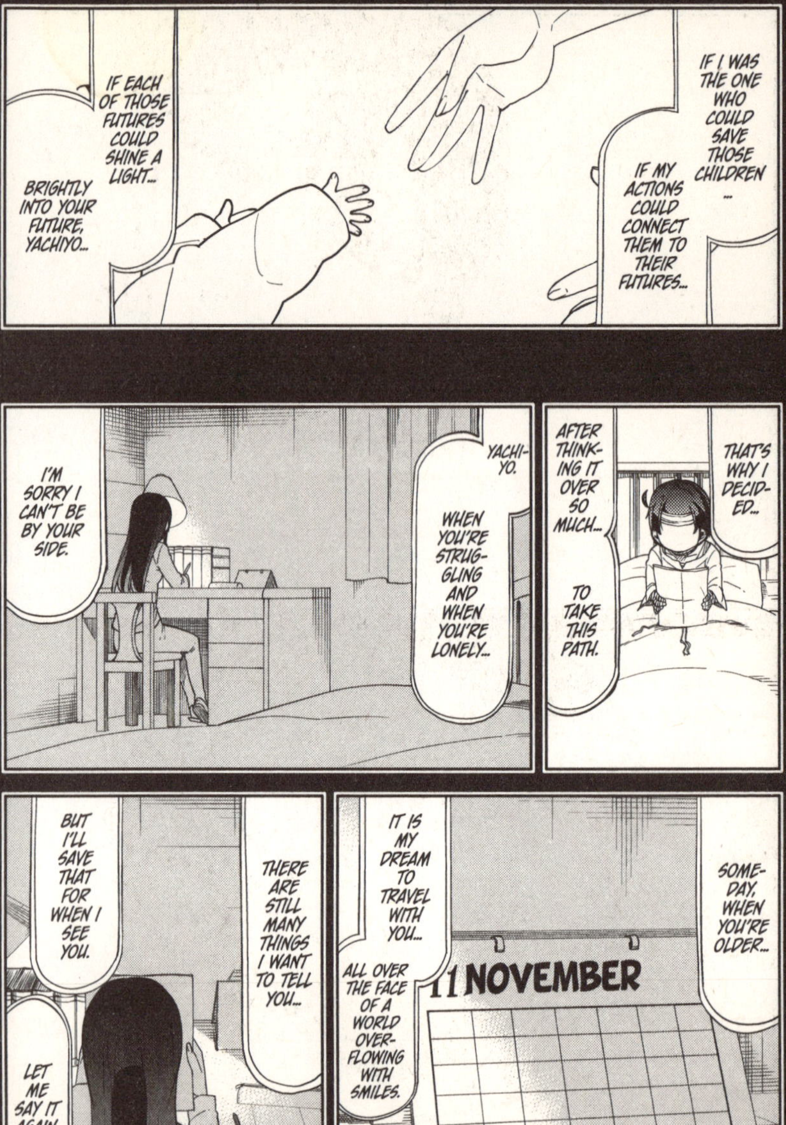
IF I WAS THE ONE WHO COULD SAVE THOSE CHILDREN ...
IF MY ACTIONS COULD CONNECT THEM TO THEIR FUTURES...
IF EACH OF THOSE FUTURES COULD SHINE A LIGHT...
BRIGHTLY INTO YOUR FUTURE, YACHIYO...
THAT'S WHY I DECIDED...
AFTER THINKING IT OVER SO MUCH...
TO TAKE THIS PATH.
YACHIYO.
WHEN YOU'RE STRUGGLING AND WHEN YOU'RE LONELY...
I'M SORRY I CAN'T BE BY YOUR SIDE.
SOMEDAY, WHEN YOU'RE OLDER...
IT IS MY DREAM TO TRAVEL WITH YOU...
ALL OVER THE FACE OF A WORLD OVERFLOWING WITH SMILES.
11 NOVEMBER
THERE ARE STILL MANY THINGS I WANT TO TELL YOU...
BUT I'LL SAVE THAT FOR WHEN I SEE YOU.
LET ME SAY IT AGAIN.

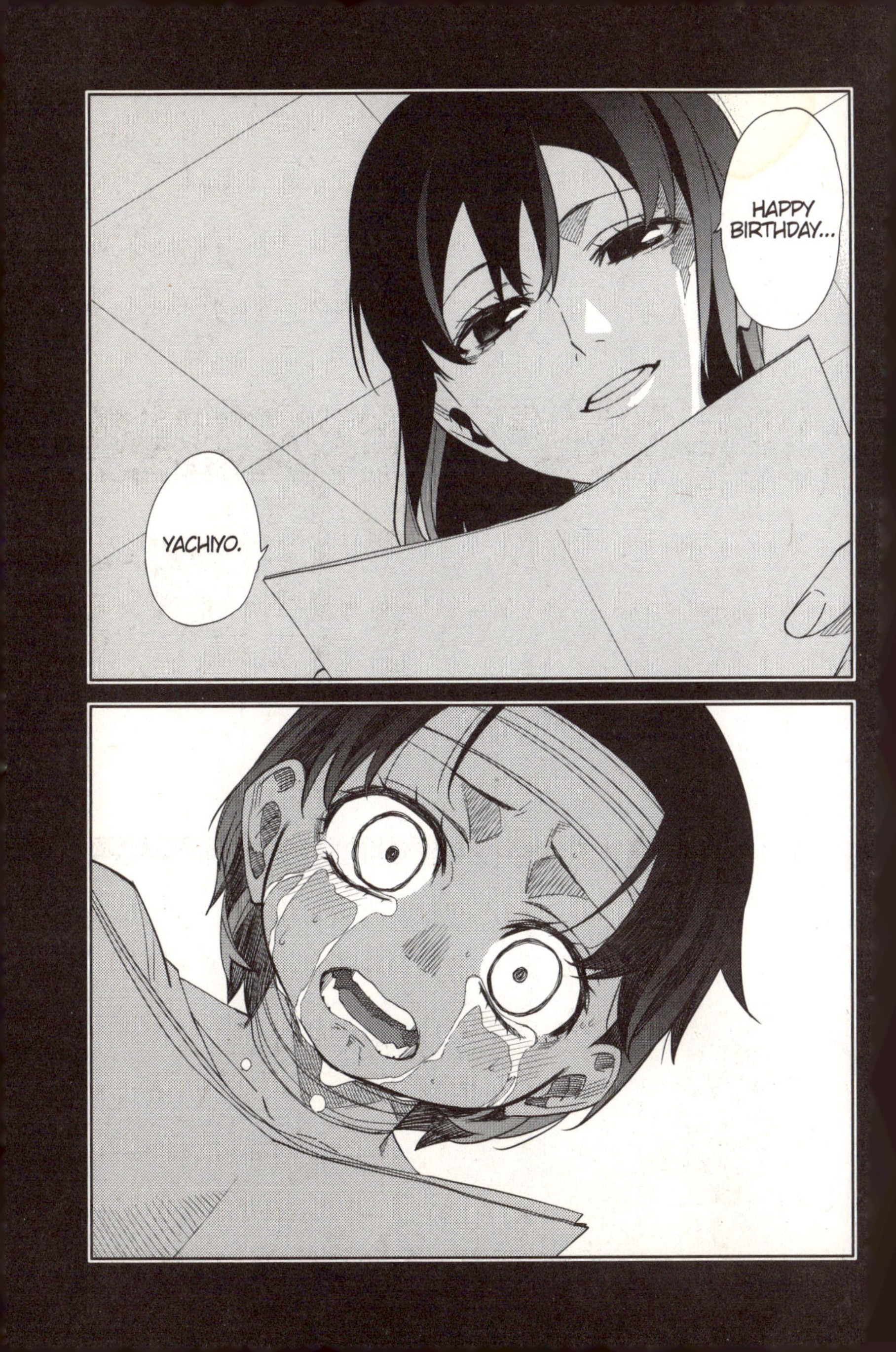
HAPPY BIRTHDAY...
YACHIYO.

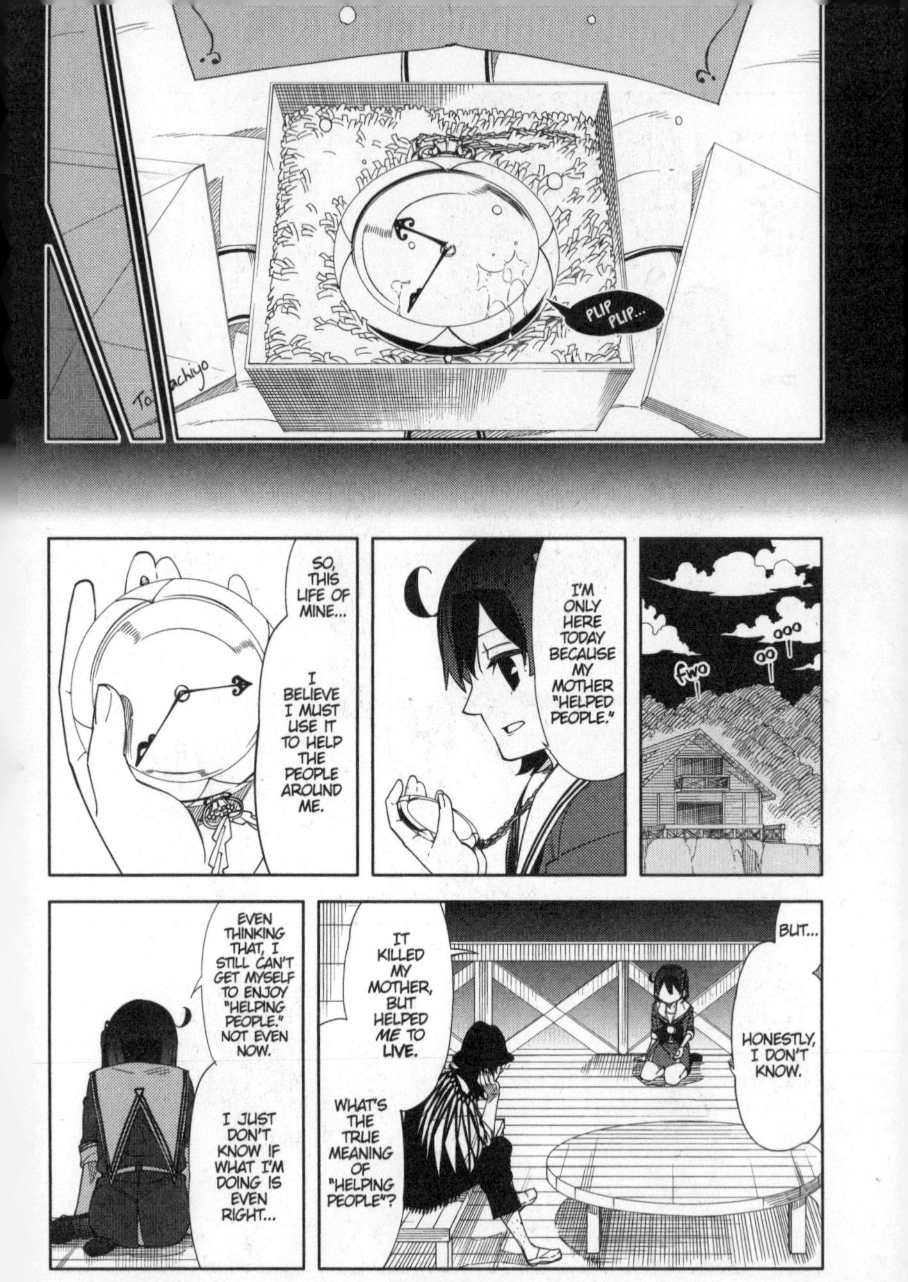
PLIP PLIP...
fwo
oo
ooo
I'M ONLY HERE TODAY BECAUSE MY MOTHER "HELPED PEOPLE."
SO, THIS LIFE OF MINE...
I BELIEVE I MUST USE IT TO HELP THE PEOPLE AROUND ME.
BUT...
HONESTLY, I DON'T KNOW.
IT KILLED MY MOTHER, BUT HELPED *ME* TO LIVE.
WHAT'S THE TRUE MEANING OF "HELPING PEOPLE"?
EVEN THINKING THAT, I STILL CAN'T GET MYSELF TO ENJOY "HELPING PEOPLE." NOT EVEN NOW.
I JUST DON'T KNOW IF WHAT I'M DOING IS EVEN RIGHT...

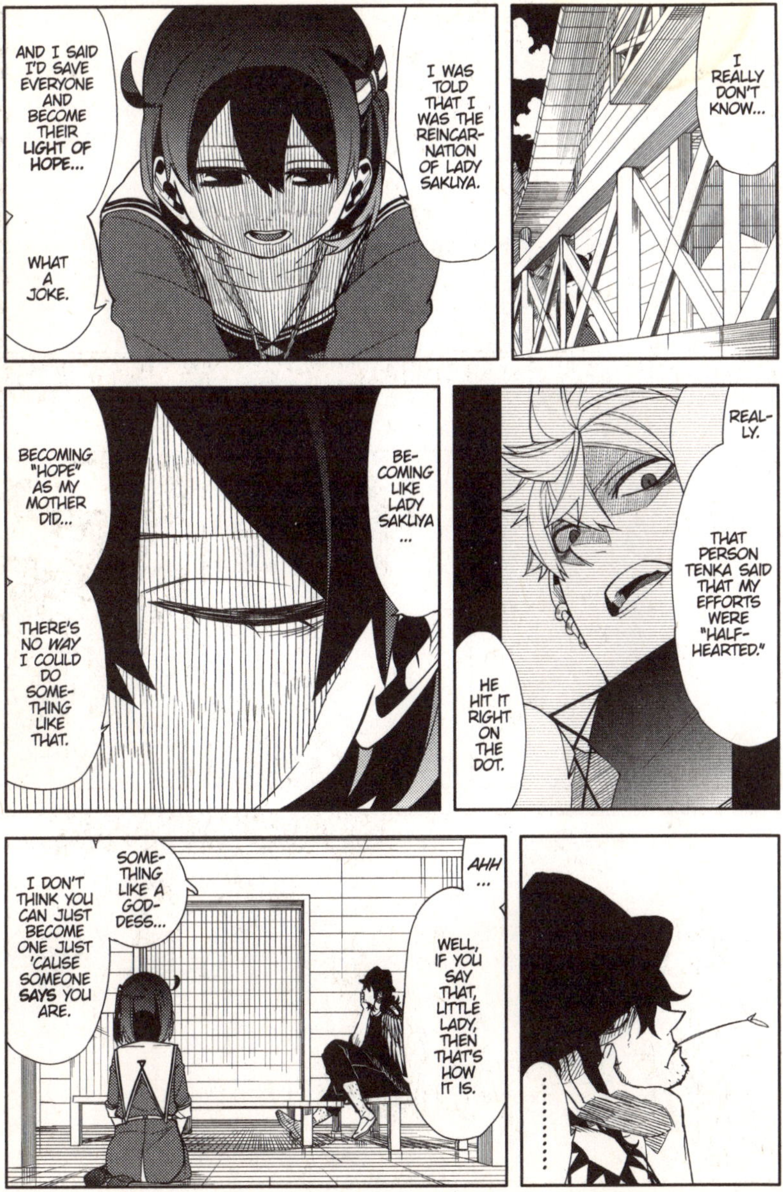
I REALLY DON'T KNOW...
I WAS TOLD THAT I WAS THE REINCARNATION OF LADY SAKUYA.
AND I SAID I'D SAVE EVERYONE AND BECOME THEIR LIGHT OF HOPE...
WHAT A JOKE.
REALLY.
THAT PERSON TENKA SAID THAT MY EFFORTS WERE "HALF-HEARTED."
HE HIT IT RIGHT ON THE DOT.
BECOMING LIKE LADY SAKUYA...
BECOMING "HOPE" AS MY MOTHER DID...
THERE'S NO WAY I COULD DO SOMETHING LIKE THAT.
......
AHH...
WELL, IF YOU SAY THAT, LITTLE LADY, THEN THAT'S HOW IT IS.
SOMETHING LIKE A GODDESS...
I DON'T THINK YOU CAN JUST BECOME ONE JUST 'CAUSE SOMEONE SAYS YOU ARE.

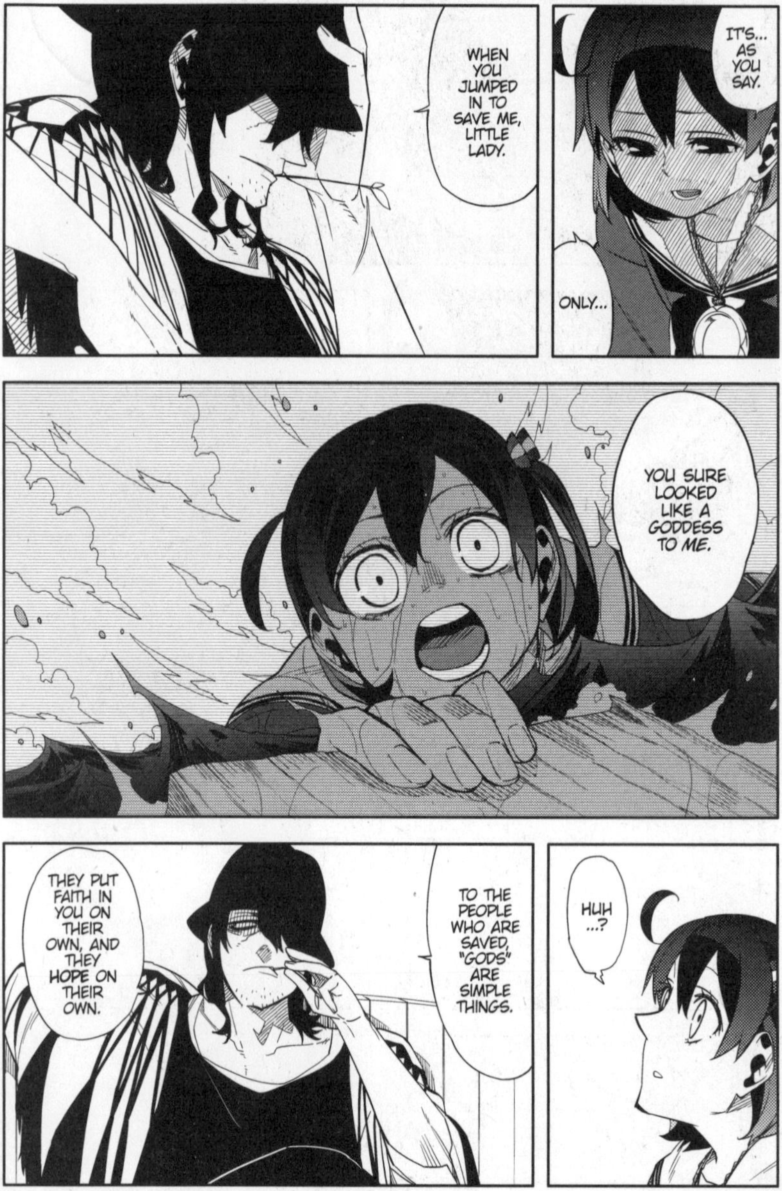
IT'S... AS YOU SAY.
ONLY...
WHEN YOU JUMPED IN TO SAVE ME, LITTLE LADY.
YOU SURE LOOKED LIKE A GODDESS TO ME.
HUH ...?
TO THE PEOPLE WHO ARE SAVED, "GODS" ARE SIMPLE THINGS.
THEY PUT FAITH IN YOU ON THEIR OWN, AND THEY HOPE ON THEIR OWN.

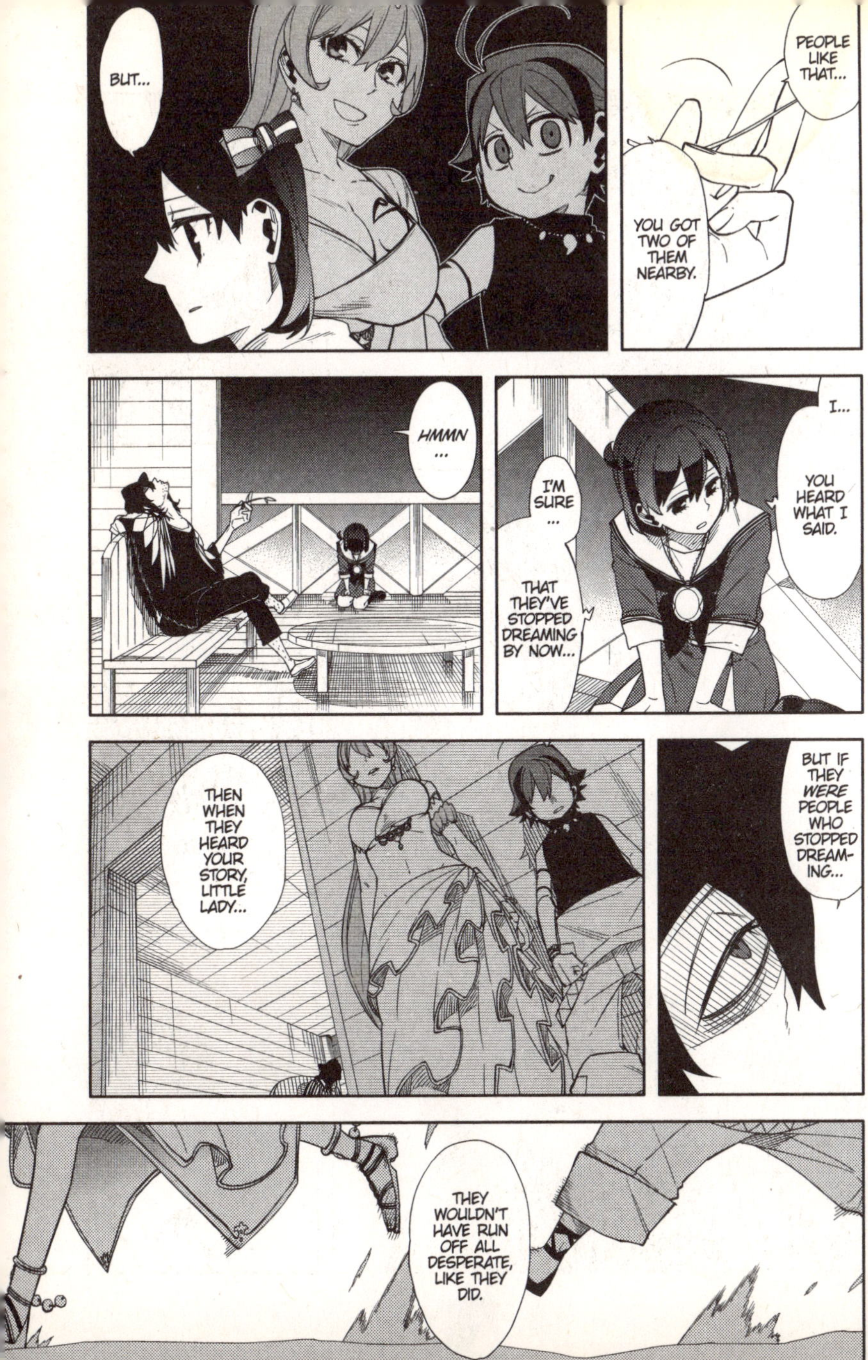
PEOPLE LIKE THAT...
YOU GOT TWO OF THEM NEARBY.
BUT...
I...
YOU HEARD WHAT I SAID.
I'M SURE ...
THAT THEY'VE STOPPED DREAMING BY NOW...
HMMN ...
BUT IF THEY *WERE* PEOPLE WHO STOPPED DREAM-ING...
THEN WHEN THEY HEARD YOUR STORY, LITTLE LADY...
THEY WOULDN'T HAVE RUN OFF ALL DESPERATE, LIKE THEY DID.

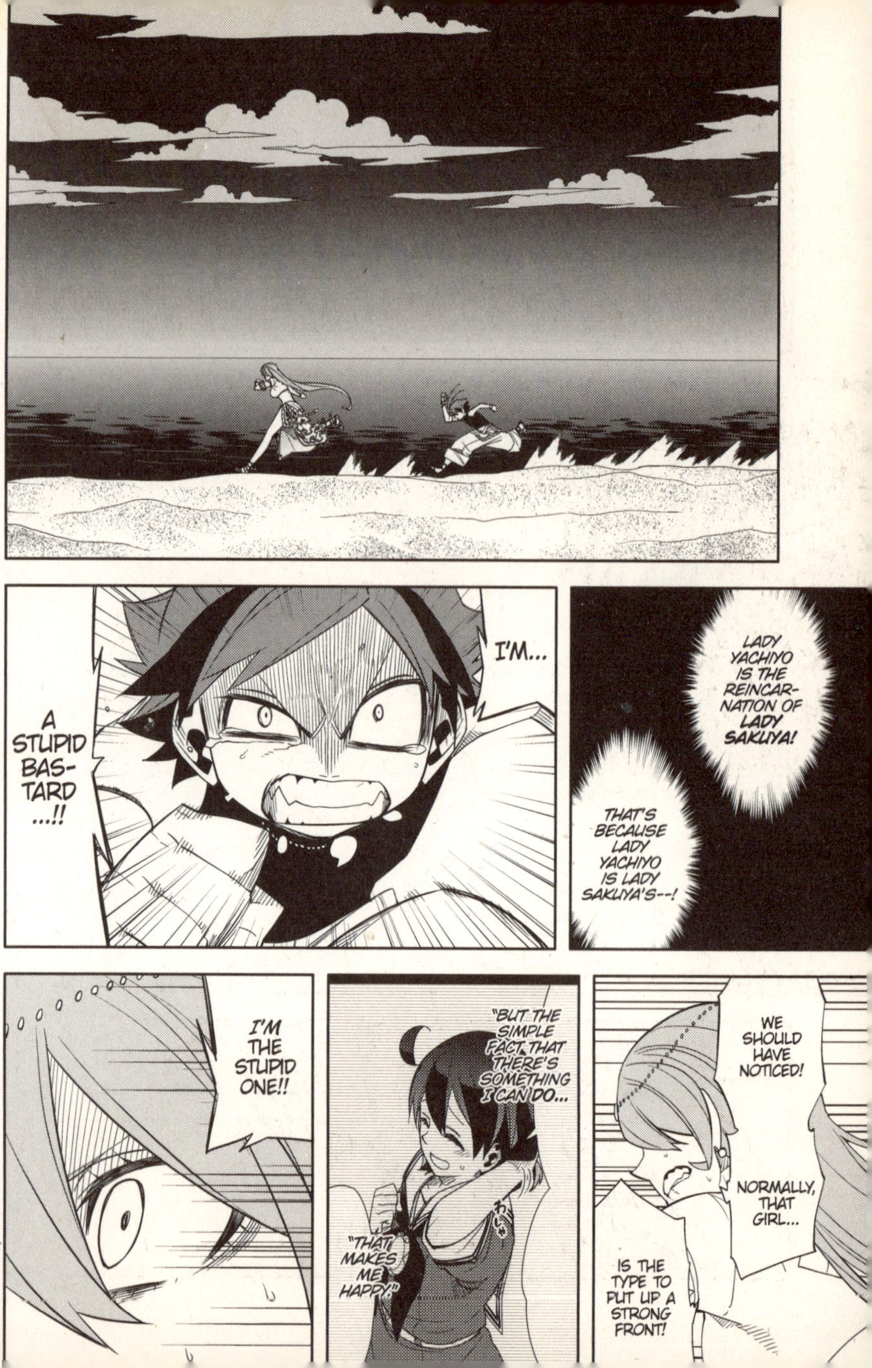
LADY YACHIYO IS THE REINCAR-NATION OF LADY SAKUYA!
THAT'S BECAUSE LADY YACHIYO IS LADY SAKUYA'S--!
I'M...
A STUPID BAS-TARD ...!!
WE SHOULD HAVE NOTICED!
NORMALLY, THAT GIRL...
IS THE TYPE TO PUT UP A STRONG FRONT!
"BUT THE SIMPLE FACT THAT THERE'S SOMETHING I CAN DO...
"THAT MAKES ME HAPPY!"
I'M THE STUPID ONE!!

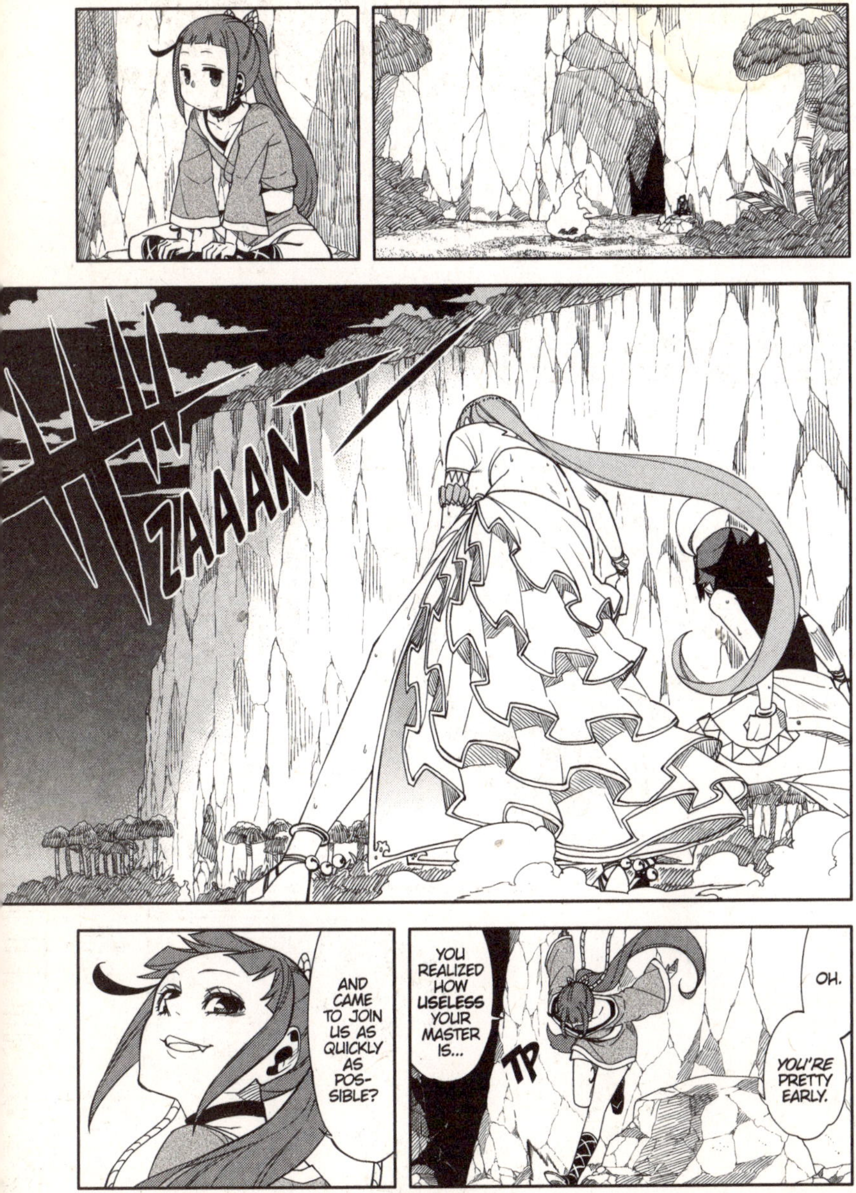
ZAAAN
OH.
YOU'RE PRETTY EARLY.
YOU REALIZED HOW USELESS YOUR MASTER IS...
TP
AND CAME TO JOIN US AS QUICKLY AS POS-SIBLE?

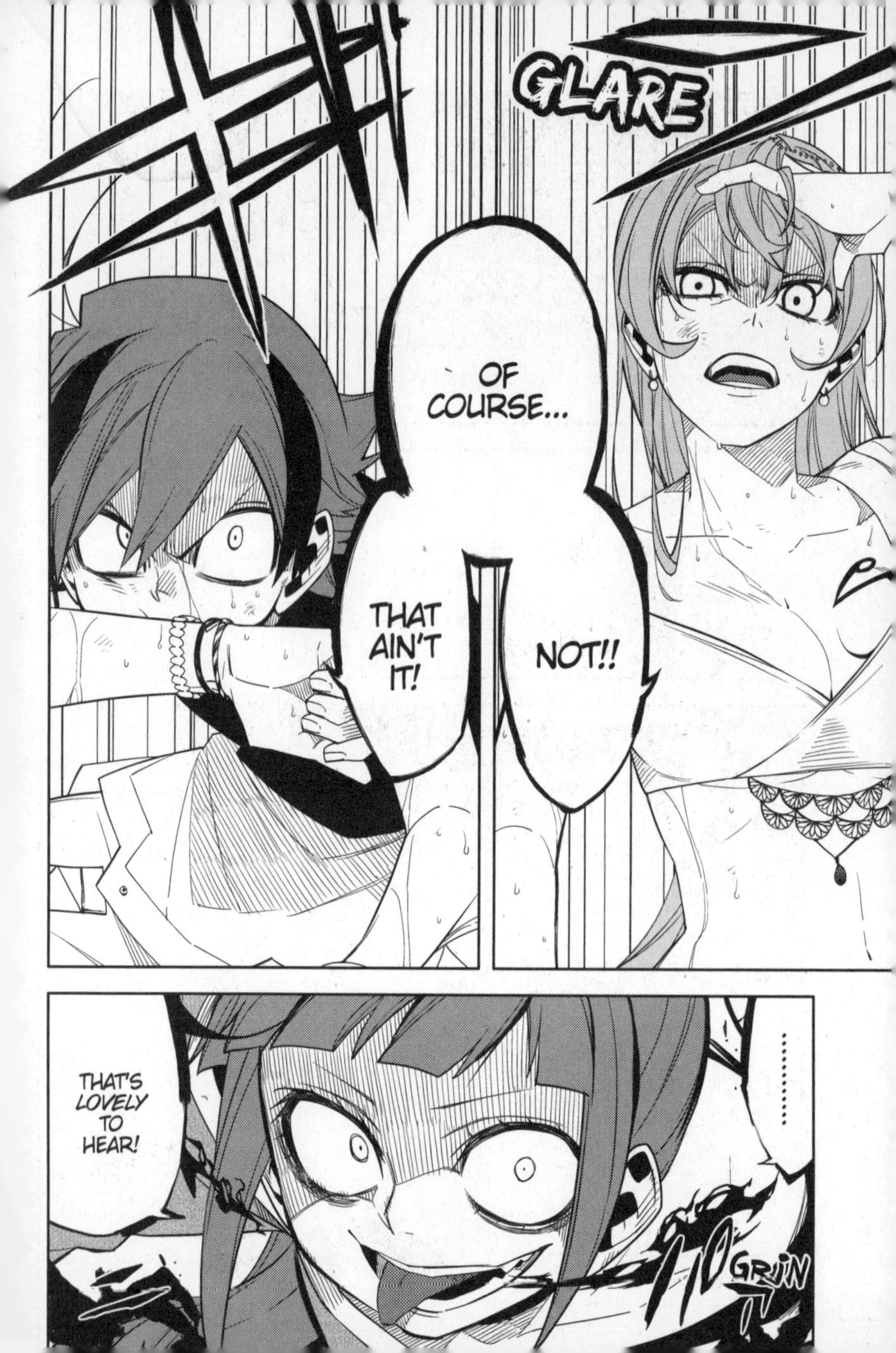
GLARE
OF COURSE...
NOT!!
THAT AIN'T IT!
....
THAT'S LOVELY TO HEAR!
GRIN

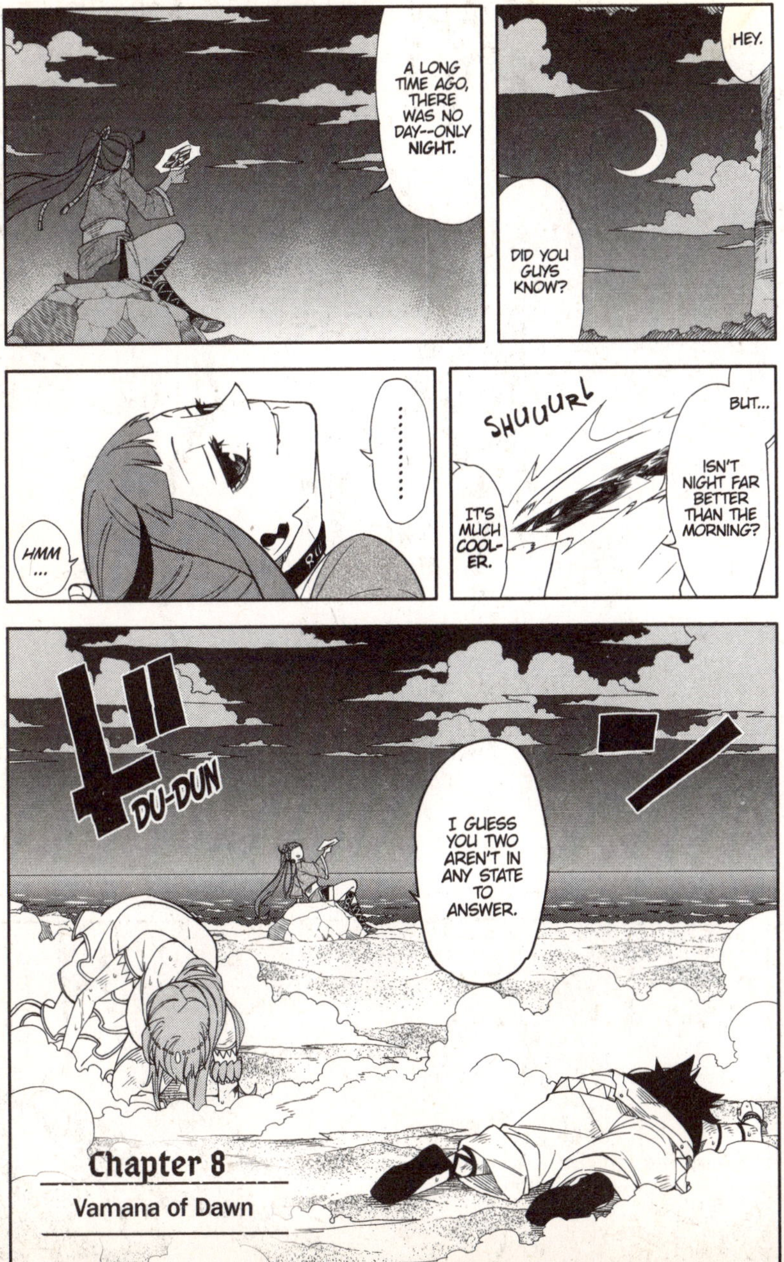
HEY.
DID YOU GUYS KNOW?
A LONG TIME AGO, THERE WAS NO DAY--ONLY NIGHT.
BUT...
ISN'T NIGHT FAR BETTER THAN THE MORNING?
SHUUURL
IT'S MUCH COOL-ER.
......
HMM ...
I GUESS YOU TWO AREN'T IN ANY STATE TO ANSWER.
DU-DUN

Chapter 8

Vamana of Dawn

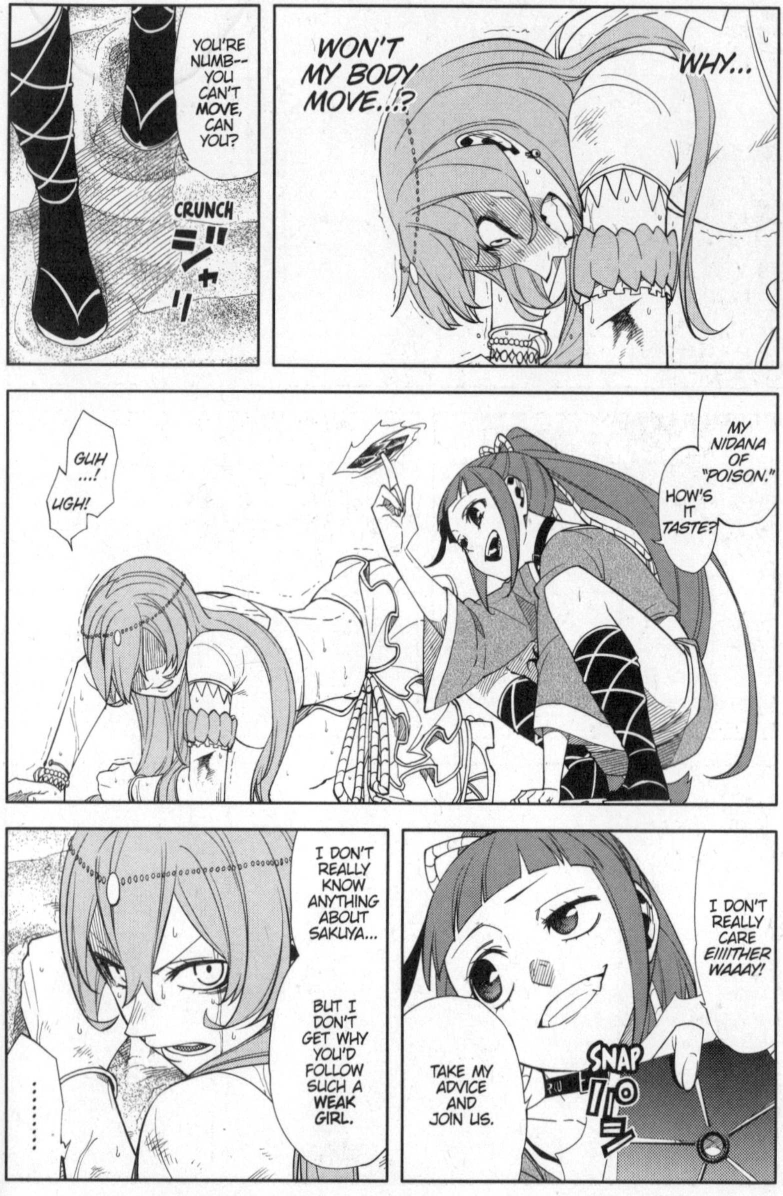
WHY...
WON'T MY BODY MOVE...?
YOU'RE NUMB-- YOU CAN'T MOVE, CAN YOU?
CRUNCH
ジャリ
MY NIDANA OF "POISON."
HOW'S IT TASTE?
GUH ...! UGH!
I DON'T REALLY CARE EIIIITHER WAAAY!
SNAP
TAKE MY ADVICE AND JOIN US.
I DON'T REALLY KNOW ANYTHING ABOUT SAKUYA...
BUT I DON'T GET WHY YOU'D FOLLOW SUCH A WEAK GIRL.
......

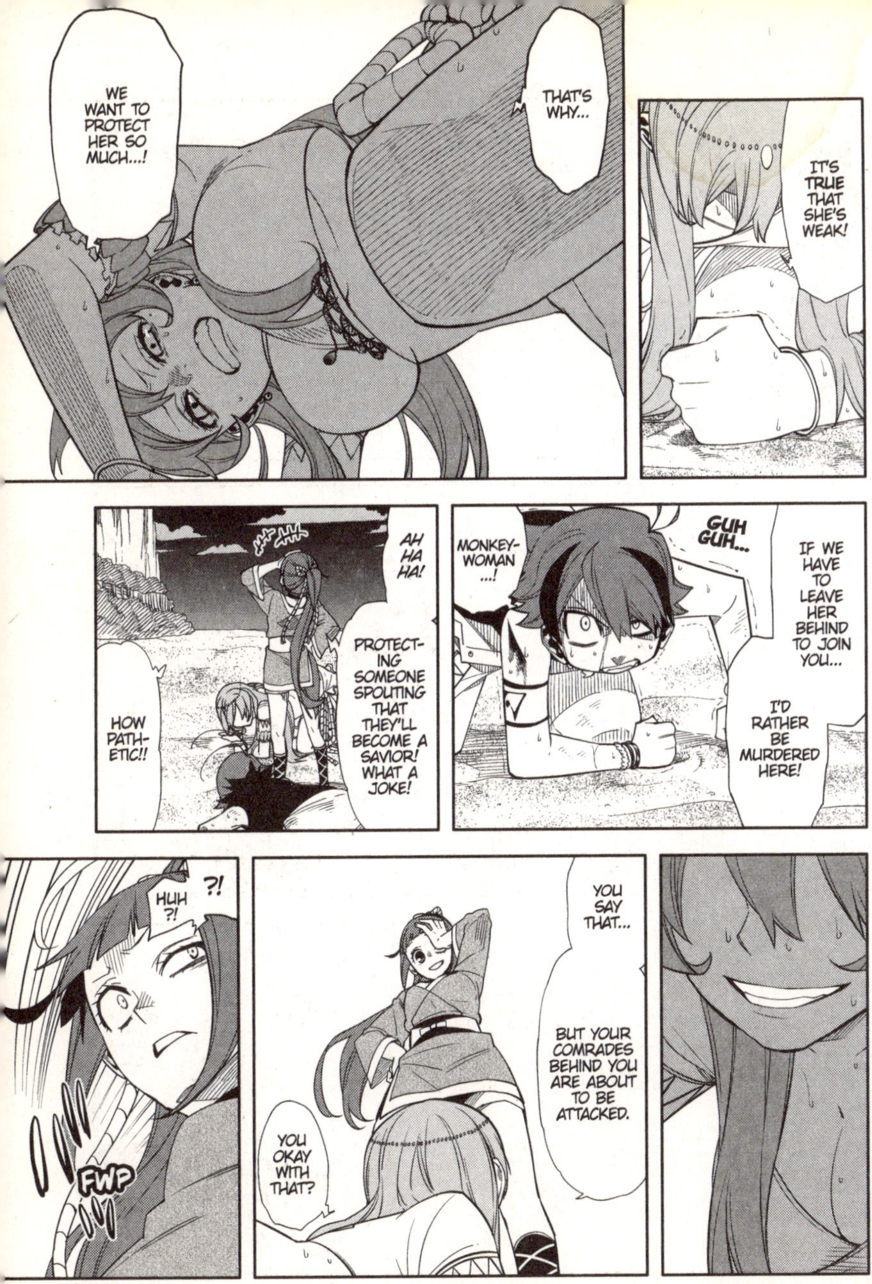
IT'S TRUE THAT SHE'S WEAK!
THAT'S WHY...
WE WANT TO PROTECT HER SO MUCH...!
IF WE HAVE TO LEAVE HER BEHIND TO JOIN YOU...
GUH GUH...
MONKEY-WOMAN...!
I'D RATHER BE MURDERED HERE!
AH HA HA!
PROTECT-ING SOMEONE SPOUTING THAT THEY'LL BECOME A SAVIOR! WHAT A JOKE!
HOW PATH-ETIC!!
YOU SAY THAT...
BUT YOUR COMRADES BEHIND YOU ARE ABOUT TO BE ATTACKED.
YOU OKAY WITH THAT?
?!
HUH ?!
FWP

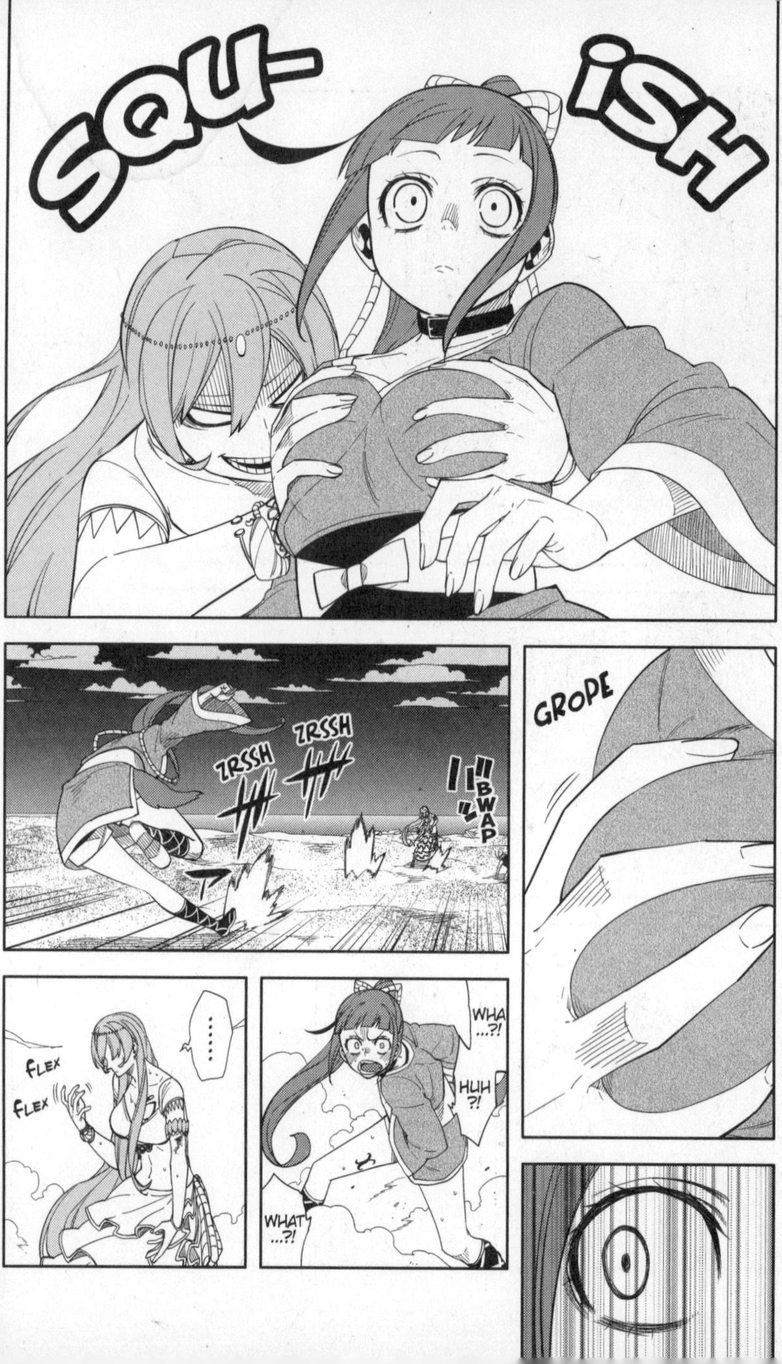
SQU-
ISH
GROPE
ZRSSH
ZRSSH
BWAP
WHA ...?!
HUH ?!
WHAT ...?!
......
FLEX
FLEX

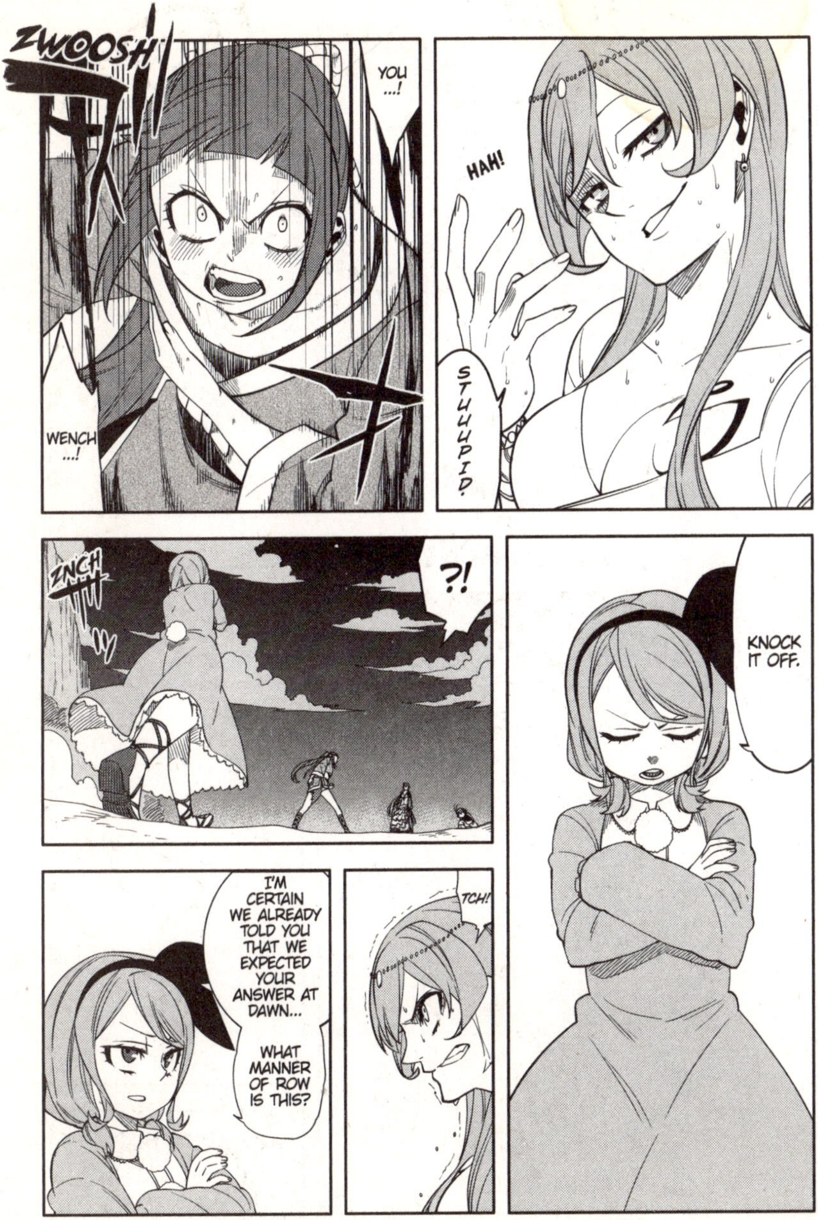
HAH!
STUUUPID.
ZWOOSH!
YOU ...!
WENCH ...!
KNOCK IT OFF.
?!
ZNCH
TCH!
I'M CERTAIN WE ALREADY TOLD YOU THAT WE EXPECTED YOUR ANSWER AT DAWN...
WHAT MANNER OF ROW IS THIS?

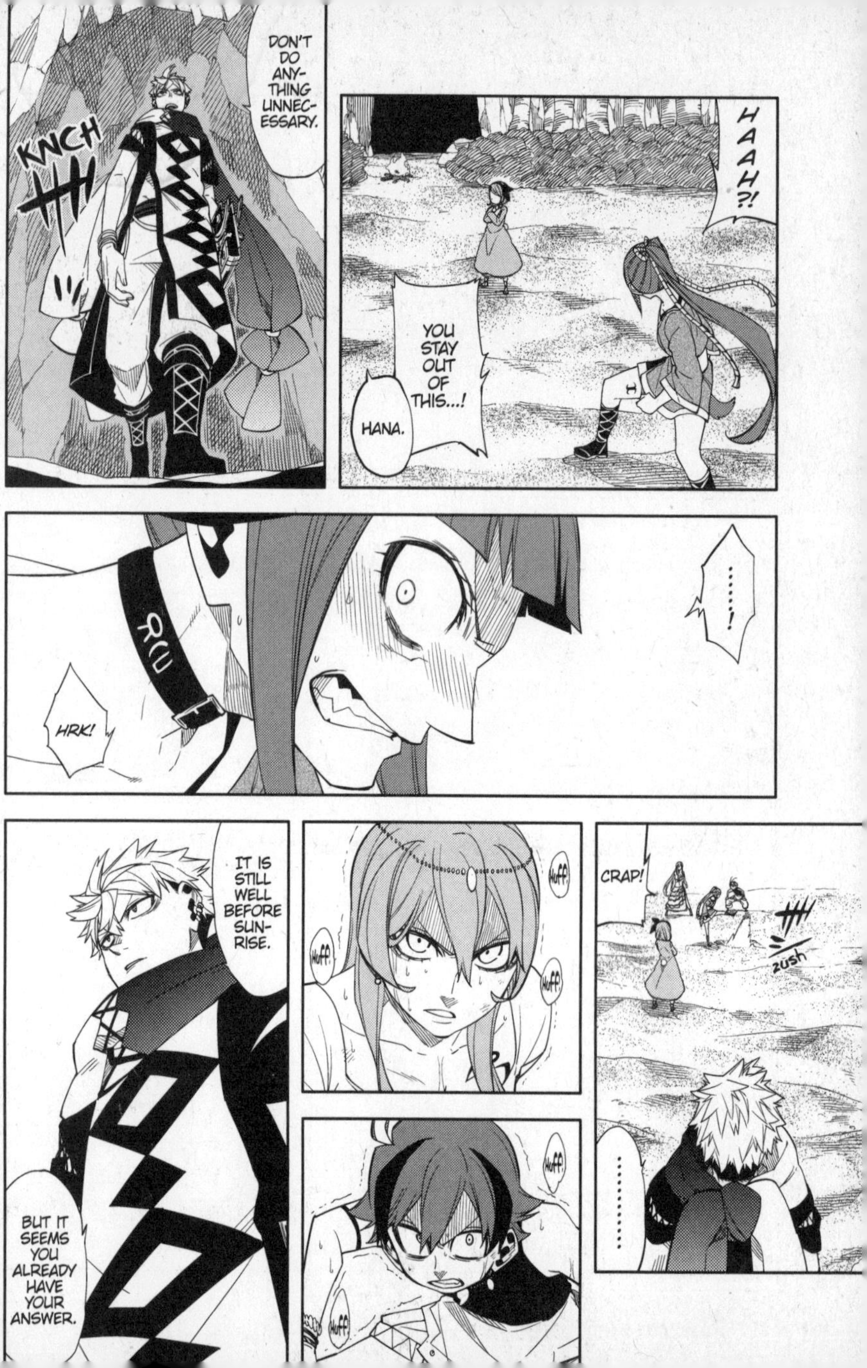
HAAAH?!
YOU STAY OUT OF THIS...!
HANA.
DON'T DO ANYTHING UNNECESSARY.
KNCH
......!
HRK!
CRAP!
zush
......
Huff
Huff
Huff
Huff
Huff
IT IS STILL WELL BEFORE SUNRISE.
BUT IT SEEMS YOU ALREADY HAVE YOUR ANSWER.

YOU SAW YOUR MASTER LOSE AND FAIL.
WHAT CAN YOU POSSIBLY EXPECT FROM YACHIYO HITOTOSE?
I'M NOT EXPECTING HER TO DO ANYTHING!
I ADMIRE LADY YACHIYO'S KINDNESS!
WHO'D FOLLOW A GUY WHO DOESN'T UNDERSTAND THE FEELINGS OF OTHERS?!
SO THAT IS WHAT YOU PUT FAITH IN.
LET ME TELL YOU A STORY.
ABOUT ONE OF YOU.
ABOUT ONE OF THE TWELVE.

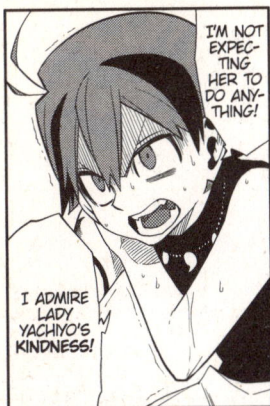

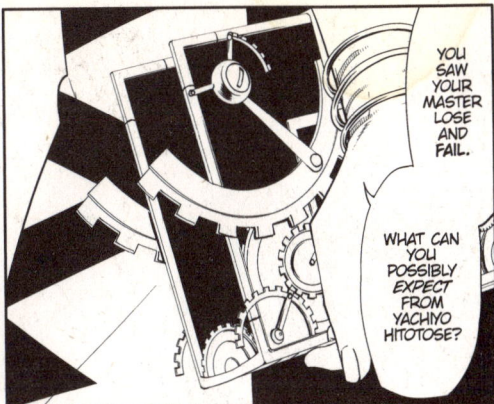

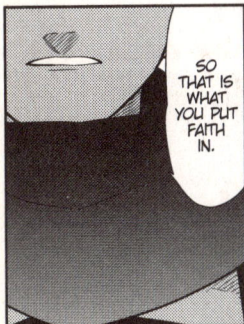

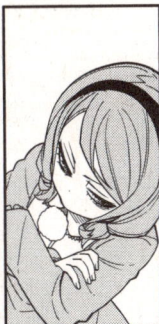

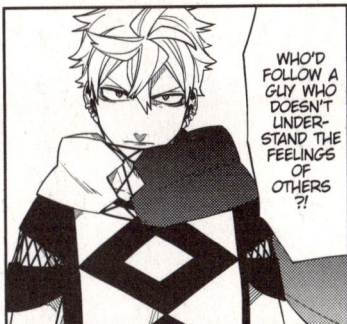

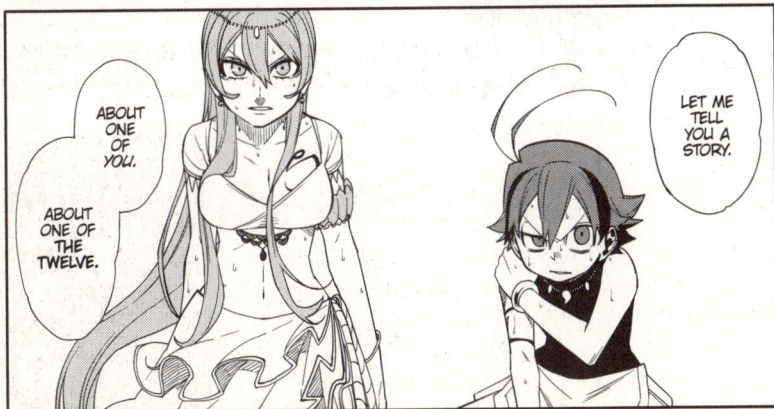

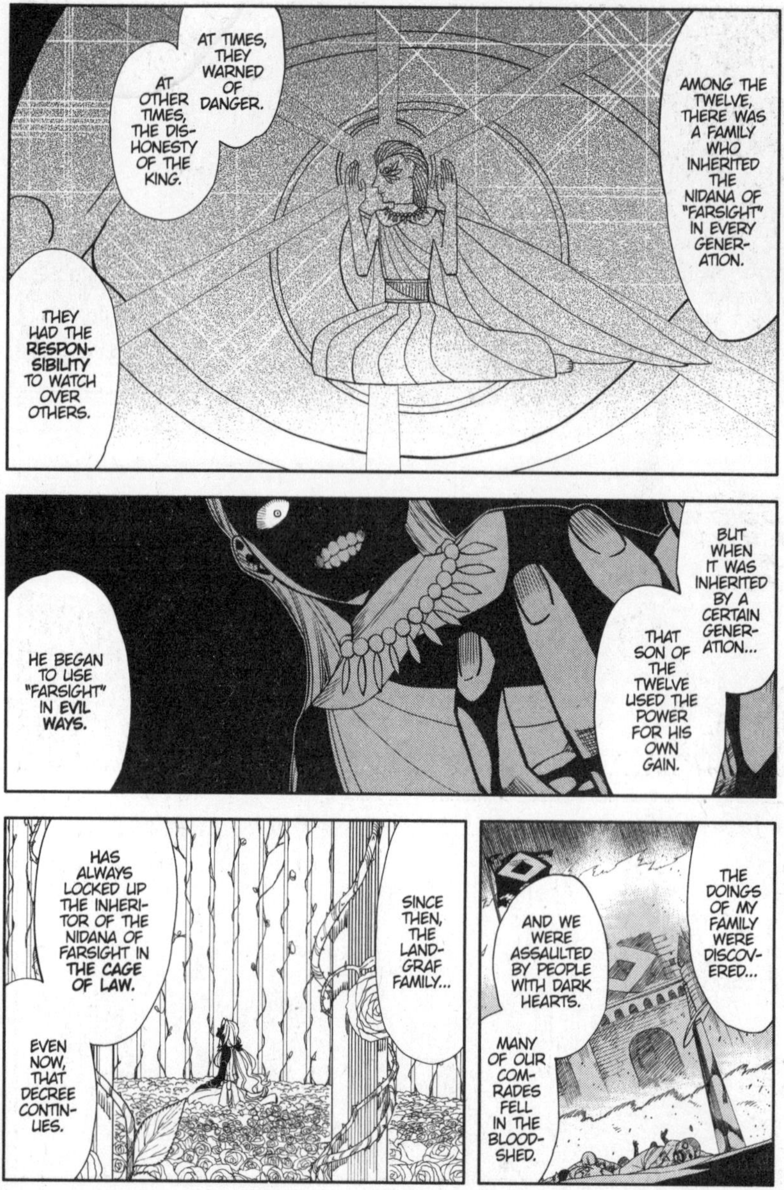
AMONG THE TWELVE, THERE WAS A FAMILY WHO INHERITED THE NIDANA OF "FARSIGHT" IN EVERY GENERATION.
AT TIMES, THEY WARNED OF DANGER.
AT OTHER TIMES, THE DISHONESTY OF THE KING.
THEY HAD THE **RESPONSIBILITY** TO WATCH OVER OTHERS.
BUT WHEN IT WAS INHERITED BY A CERTAIN GENERATION...
THAT SON OF THE TWELVE USED THE POWER FOR HIS OWN GAIN.
HE BEGAN TO USE "FARSIGHT" IN EVIL WAYS.
THE DOINGS OF MY FAMILY WERE DISCOVERED...
AND WE WERE ASSAULTED BY PEOPLE WITH DARK HEARTS.
MANY OF OUR COMRADES FELL IN THE BLOODSHED.
SINCE THEN, THE LANDGRAF FAMILY...
HAS ALWAYS LOCKED UP THE INHERITOR OF THE NIDANA OF FARSIGHT IN **THE CAGE OF LAW.**
EVEN NOW, THAT DECREE CONTINUES.

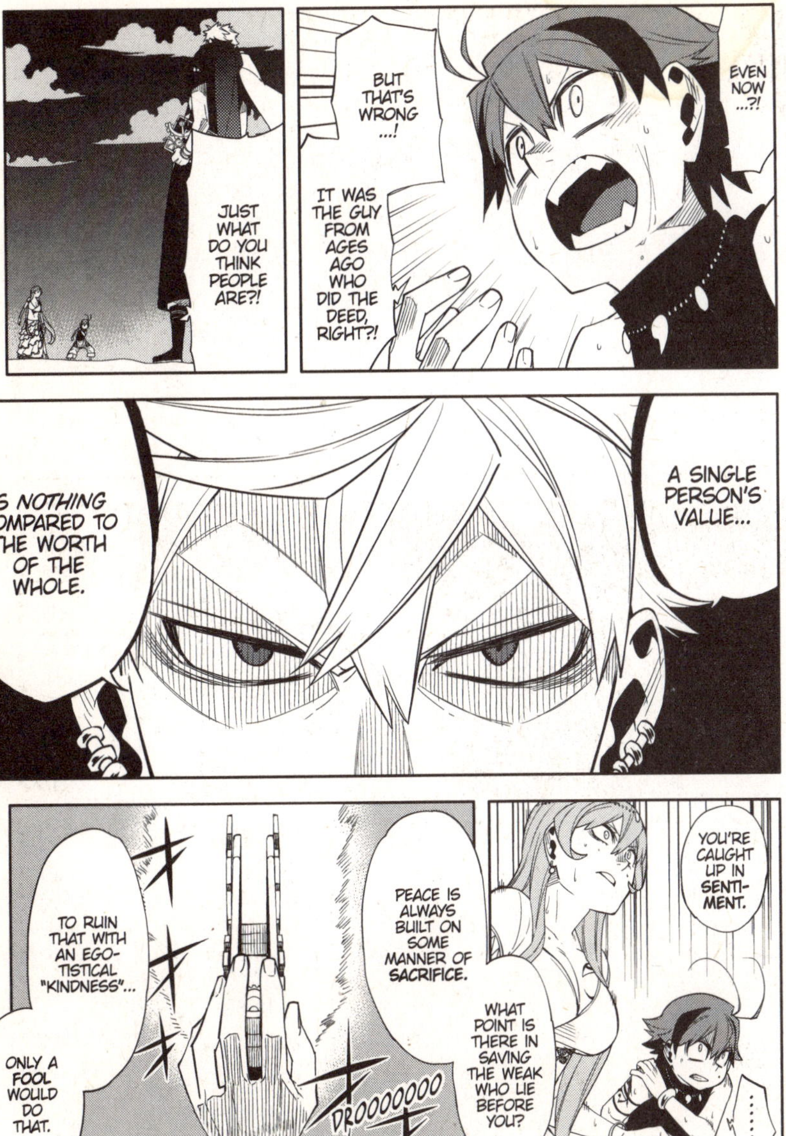
EVEN NOW ...?!
BUT THAT'S WRONG ...!
IT WAS THE GUY FROM AGES AGO WHO DID THE DEED, RIGHT?!
JUST WHAT DO YOU THINK PEOPLE ARE?!
A SINGLE PERSON'S VALUE...
IS *NOTHING* COMPARED TO THE WORTH OF THE WHOLE.
YOU'RE CAUGHT UP IN SENTI-MENT.
PEACE IS ALWAYS BUILT ON SOME MANNER OF **SACRIFICE.**
WHAT POINT IS THERE IN SAVING THE WEAK WHO LIE BEFORE YOU?
......!
TO RUIN THAT WITH AN EGO-TISTICAL "KINDNESS"...
DROOOOOOOO
ONLY A FOOL WOULD DO THAT.

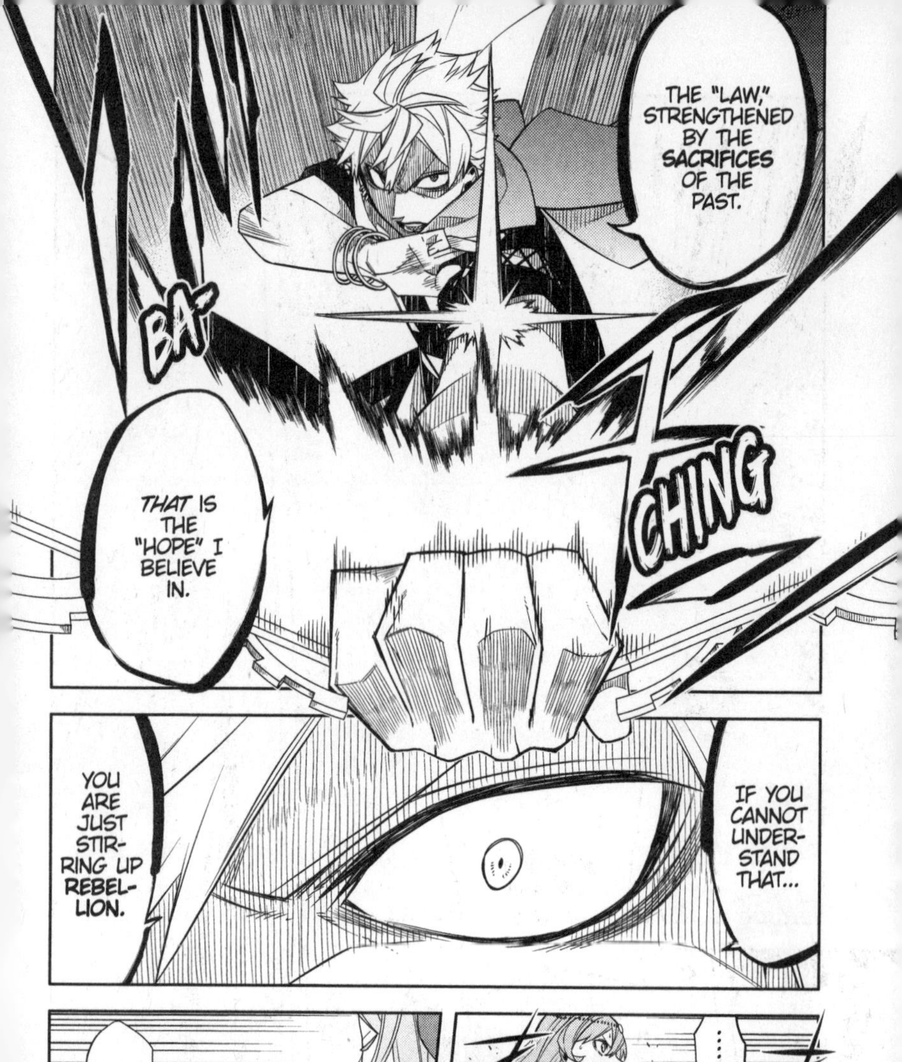
THE "LAW," STRENGTHENED BY THE SACRIFICES OF THE PAST.
BA-
CHING
THAT IS THE "HOPE" I BELIEVE IN.
IF YOU CANNOT UNDER-STAND THAT...
YOU ARE JUST STIR-RING UP REBEL-LION.
......!!
IF YOU'RE GONNA ATTACK, GO RIGHT AHEAD!
ADVAI ...!
RROOOO

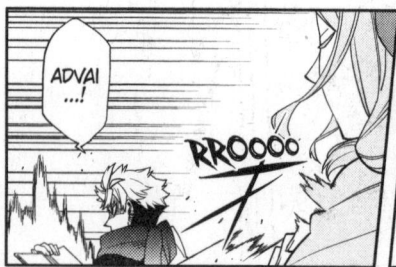

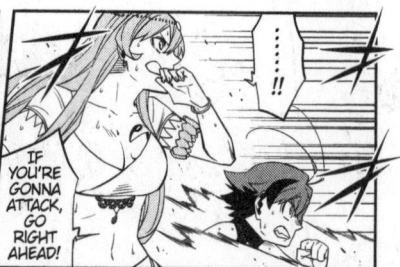

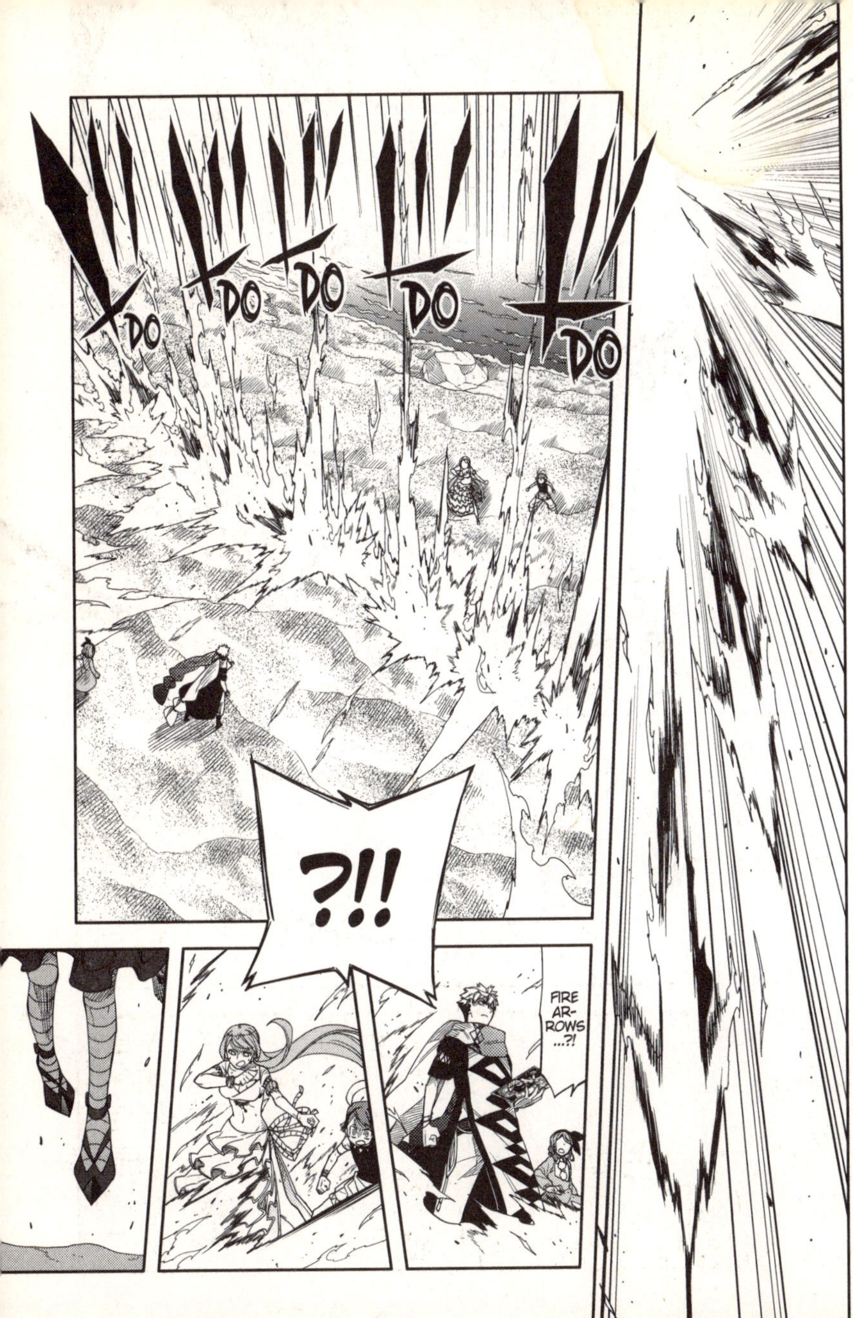
DO
DO
DO
DO
DO
?!!
FIRE ARROWS ...?!

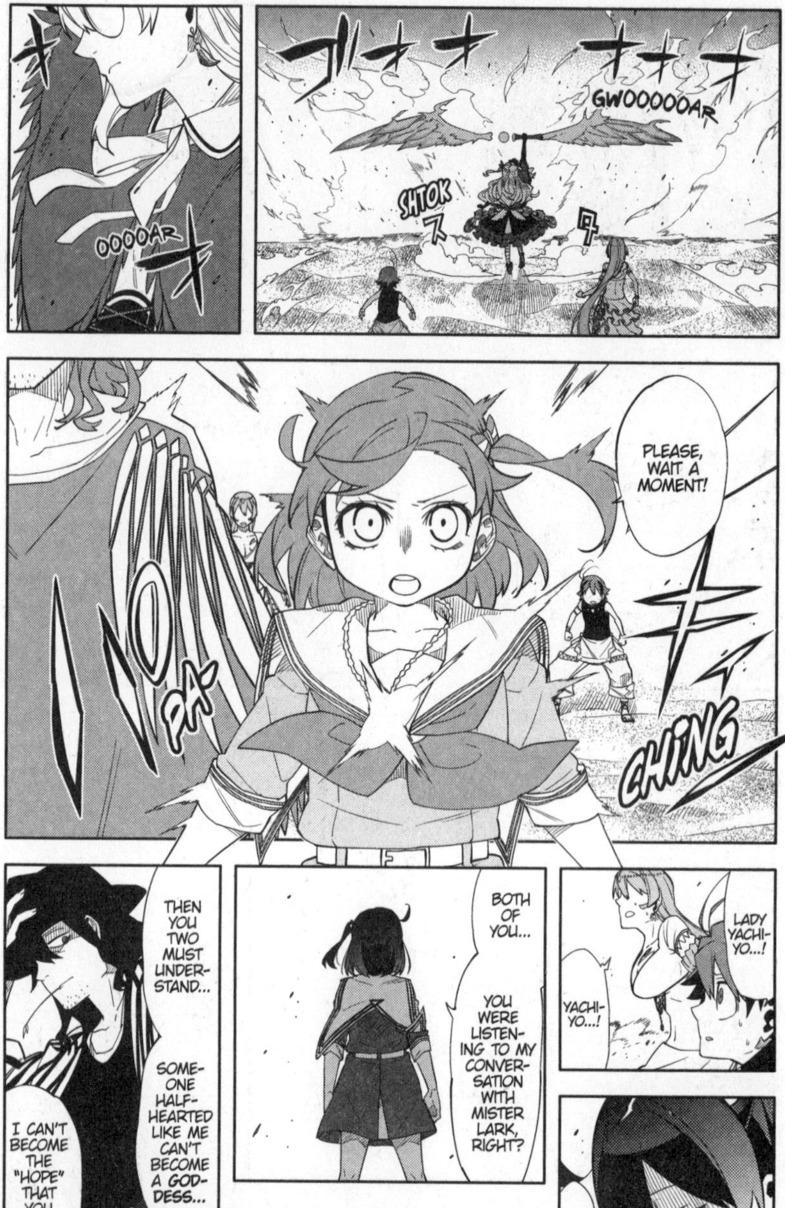
GWOOOOOOAR
SHTOK
OOOOAR
PLEASE, WAIT A MOMENT!
PA
CHING
LADY YACHI-YO...!
YACHI-YO...!
......
BOTH OF YOU...
YOU WERE LISTENING TO MY CONVERSATION WITH MISTER LARK, RIGHT?
THEN YOU TWO MUST UNDERSTAND...
SOMEONE HALF-HEARTED LIKE ME CAN'T BECOME A GODDESS...
I CAN'T BECOME THE "HOPE" THAT YOU WISH FOR...

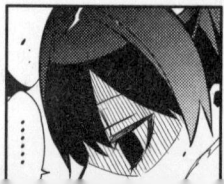

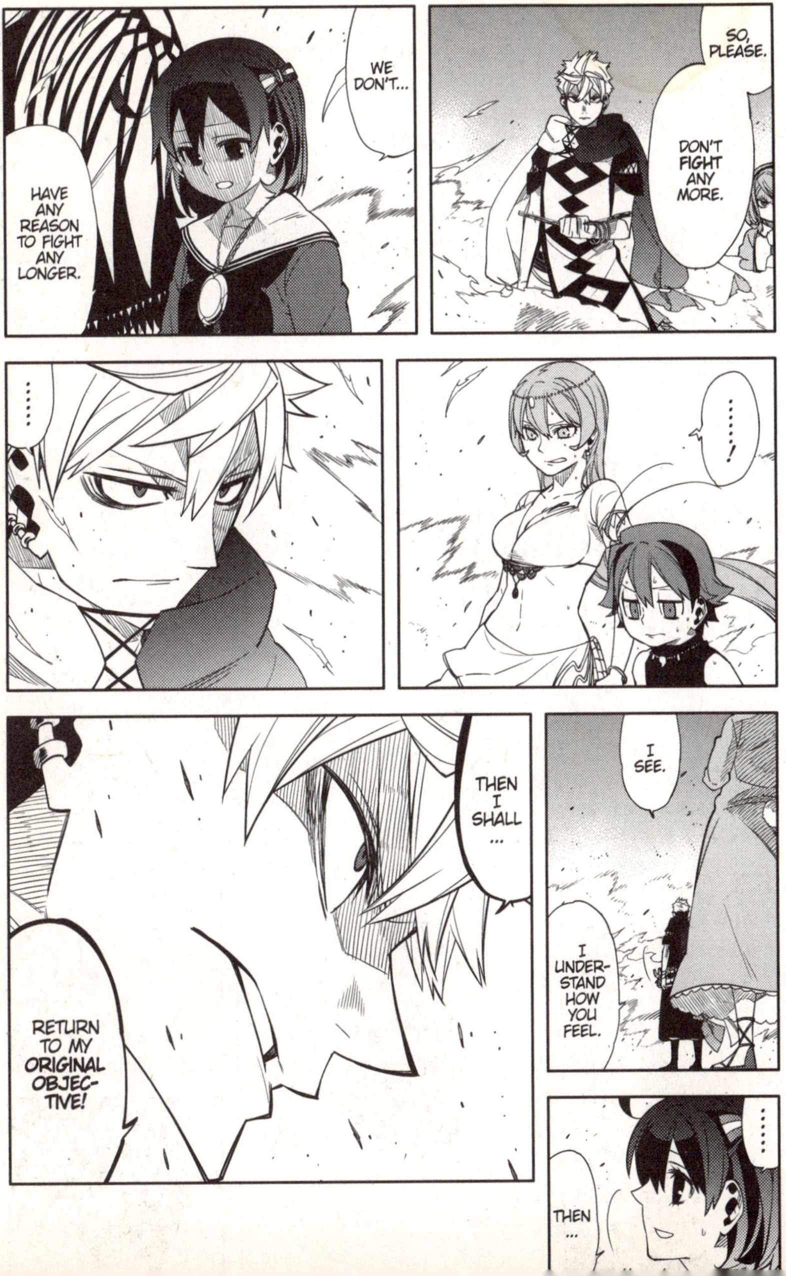
SO, PLEASE.
DON'T FIGHT ANY MORE.
WE DON'T...
HAVE ANY REASON TO FIGHT ANY LONGER.
......!
......
I SEE.
I UNDER-STAND HOW YOU FEEL.
......
THEN ...
THEN I SHALL ...
RETURN TO MY ORIGINAL OBJEC-TIVE!

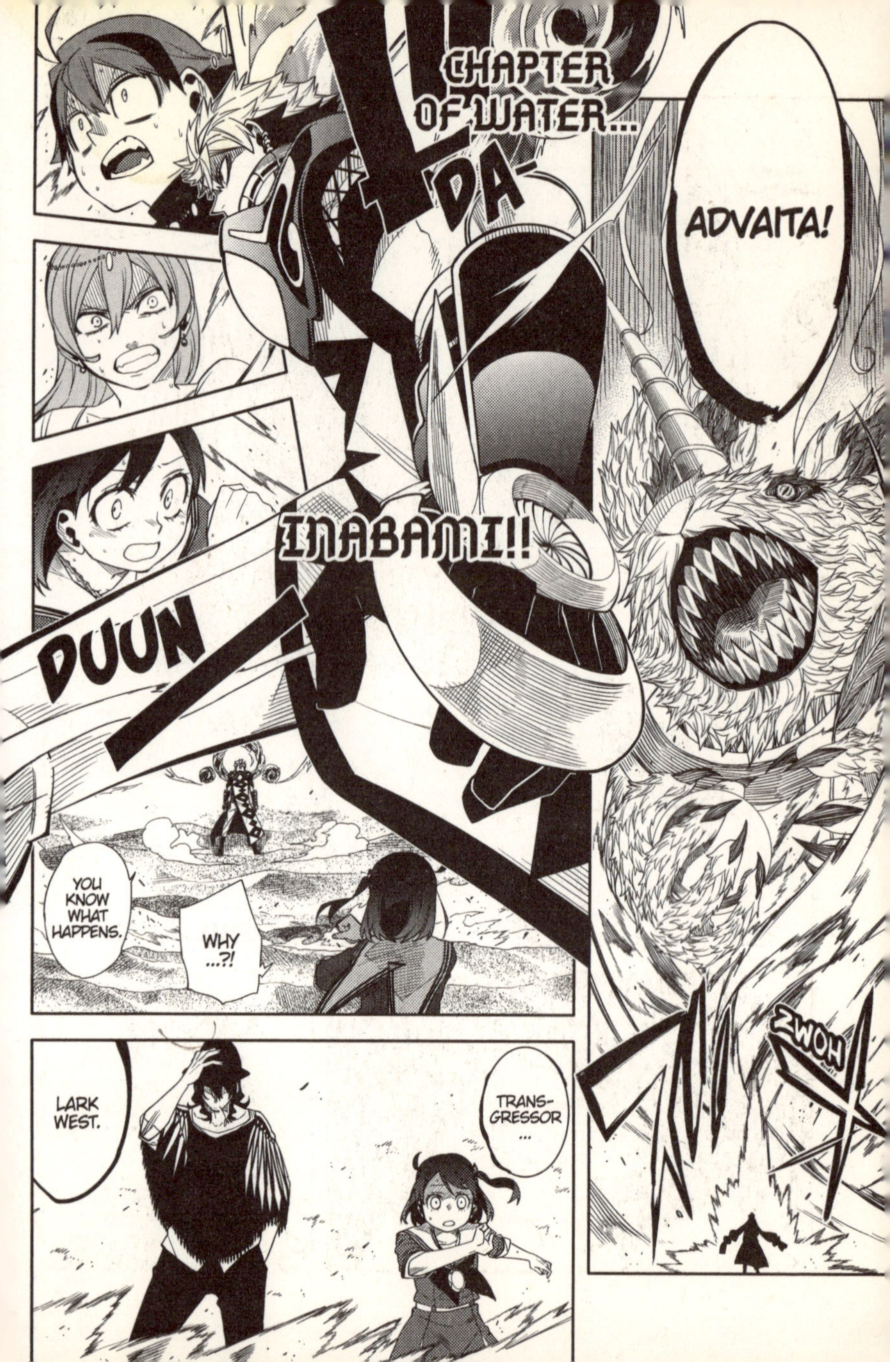
CHAPTER OF WATER... DA-
INABAMI!!
ADVAITA!
ZWOH
DUUN
WHY ...?!
YOU KNOW WHAT HAPPENS.
TRANS-GRESSOR ...
LARK WEST.

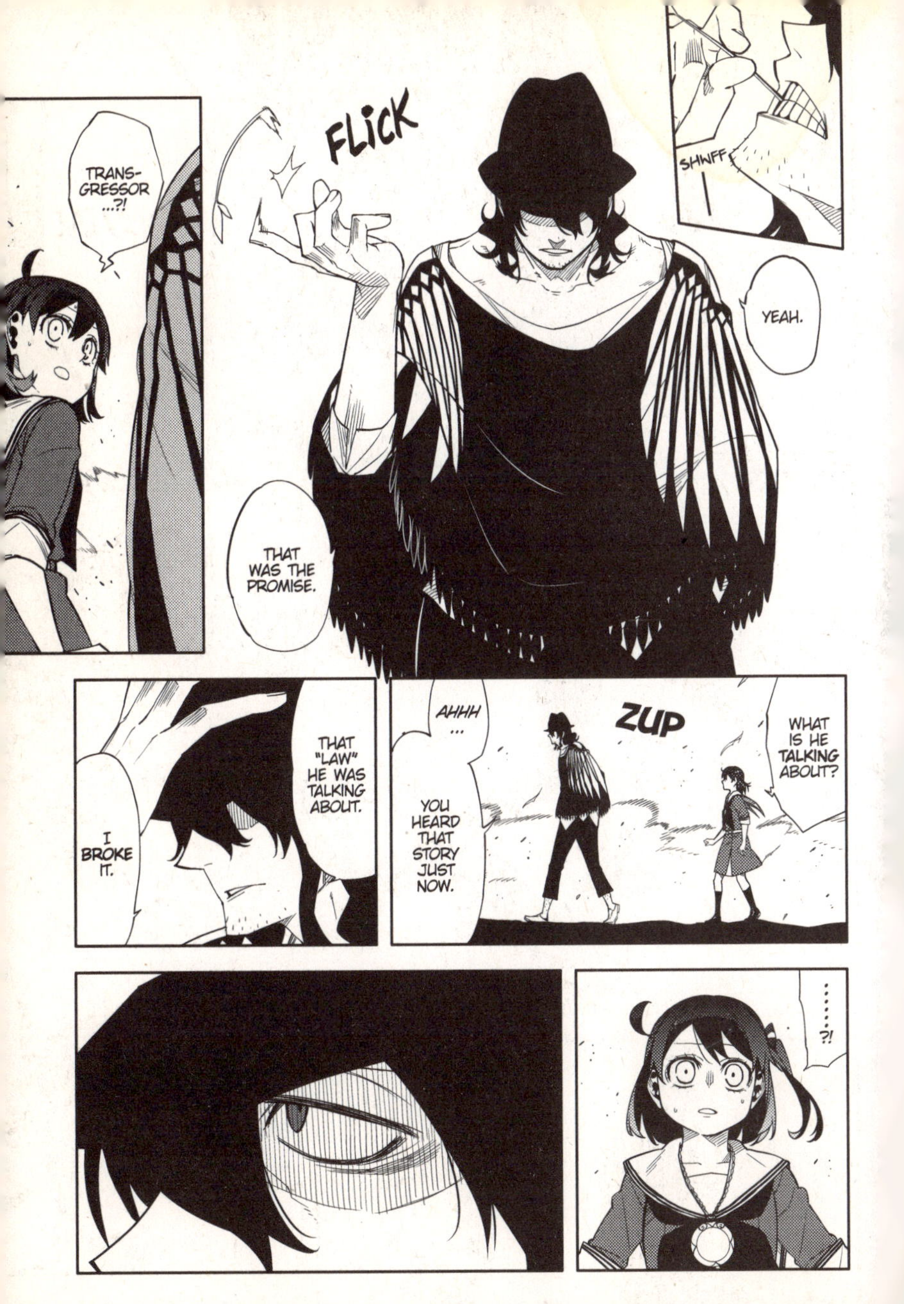
SHWFF
YEAH.
FLICK
THAT WAS THE PROMISE.
TRANS-GRESSOR ...?!
WHAT IS HE TALKING ABOUT?
ZUP
AHHH ...
YOU HEARD THAT STORY JUST NOW.
THAT "LAW" HE WAS TALKING ABOUT.
I BROKE IT.
.......?!

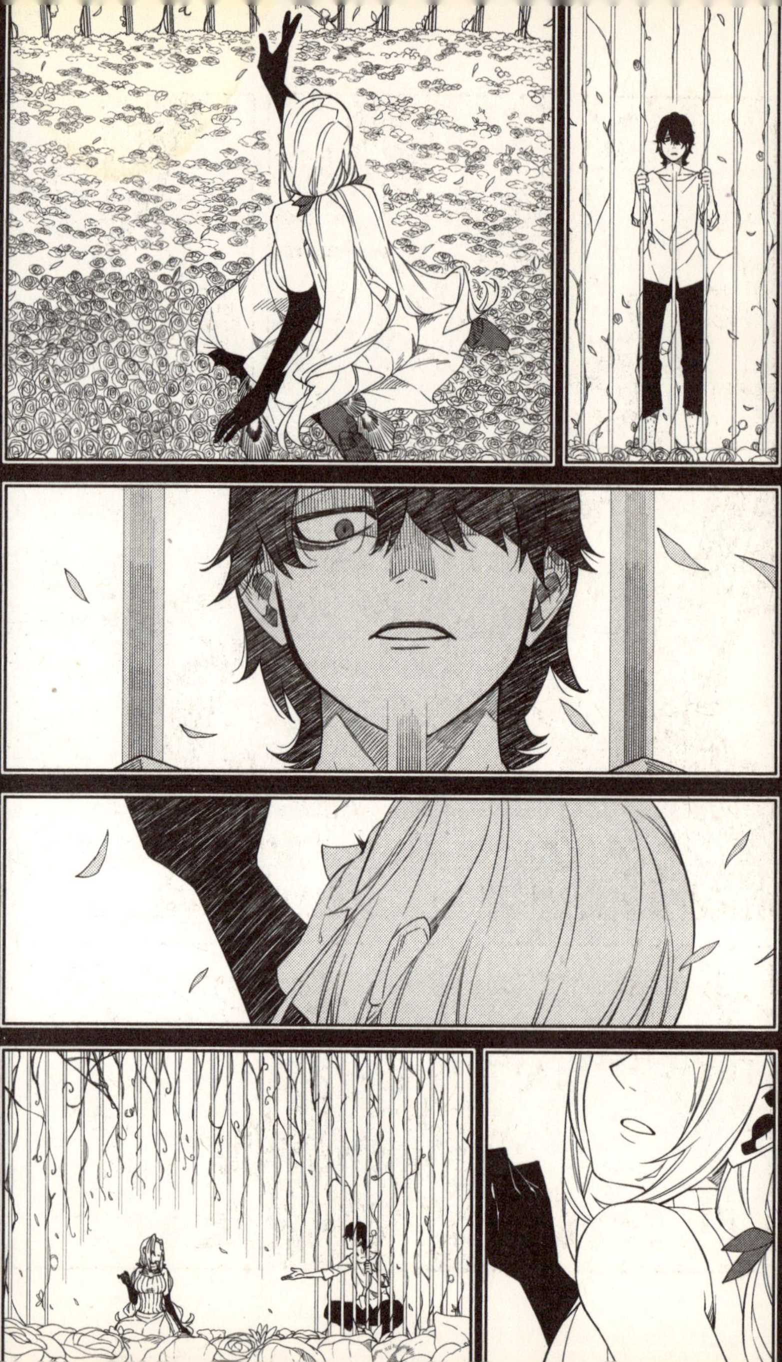

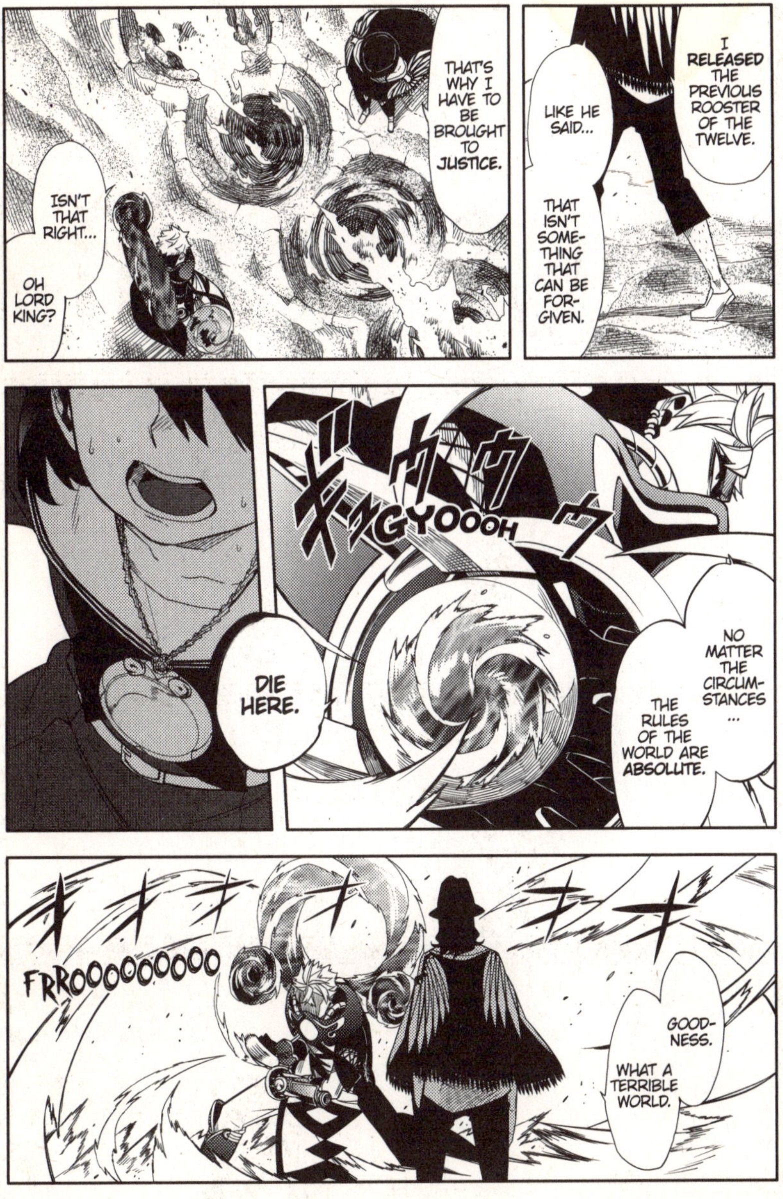
I RELEASED THE PREVIOUS ROOSTER OF THE TWELVE.
LIKE HE SAID...
THAT ISN'T SOMETHING THAT CAN BE FORGIVEN.
THAT'S WHY I HAVE TO BE BROUGHT TO JUSTICE.
ISN'T THAT RIGHT...
OH LORD KING?
GYOOOH
NO MATTER THE CIRCUMSTANCES...
THE RULES OF THE WORLD ARE ABSOLUTE.
DIE HERE.
FRROOOOOOOOOO
GOODNESS.
WHAT A TERRIBLE WORLD.

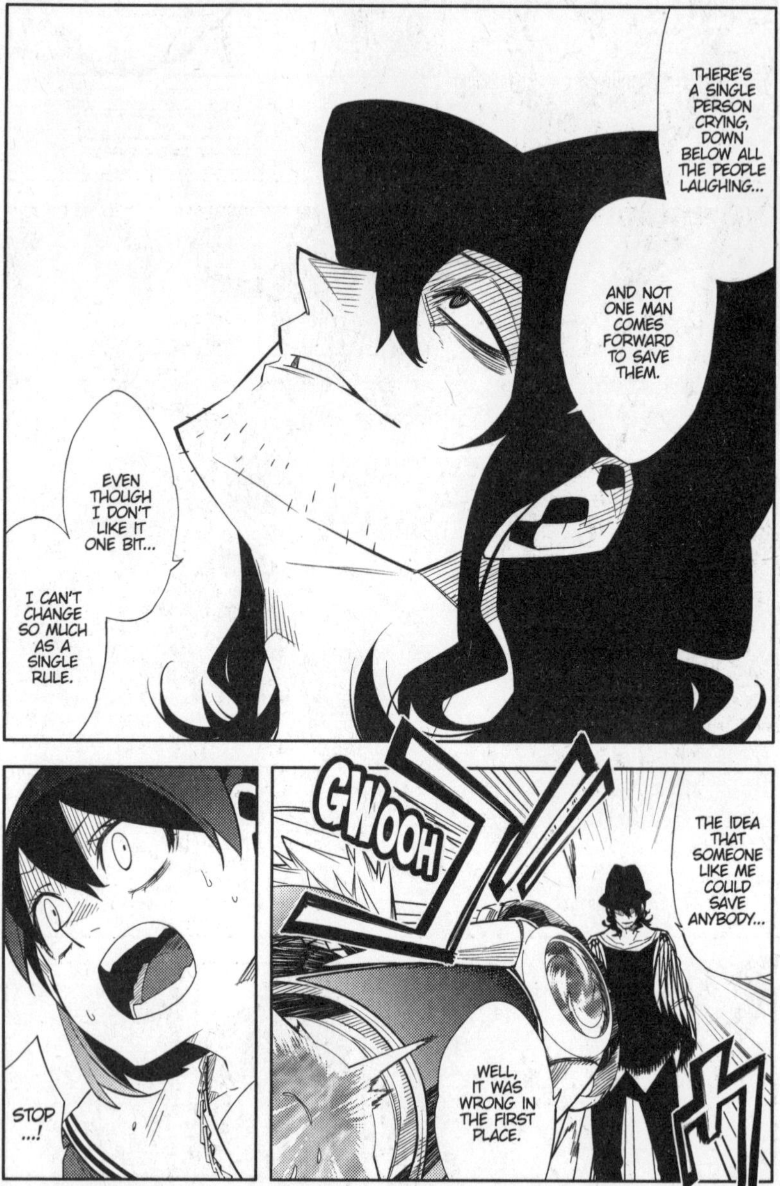
THERE'S A SINGLE PERSON CRYING, DOWN BELOW ALL THE PEOPLE LAUGHING...
AND NOT ONE MAN COMES FORWARD TO SAVE THEM.
EVEN THOUGH I DON'T LIKE IT ONE BIT...
I CAN'T CHANGE SO MUCH AS A SINGLE RULE.
GWOOH
THE IDEA THAT SOMEONE LIKE ME COULD SAVE ANYBODY...
WELL, IT WAS WRONG IN THE FIRST PLACE.
STOP ...!

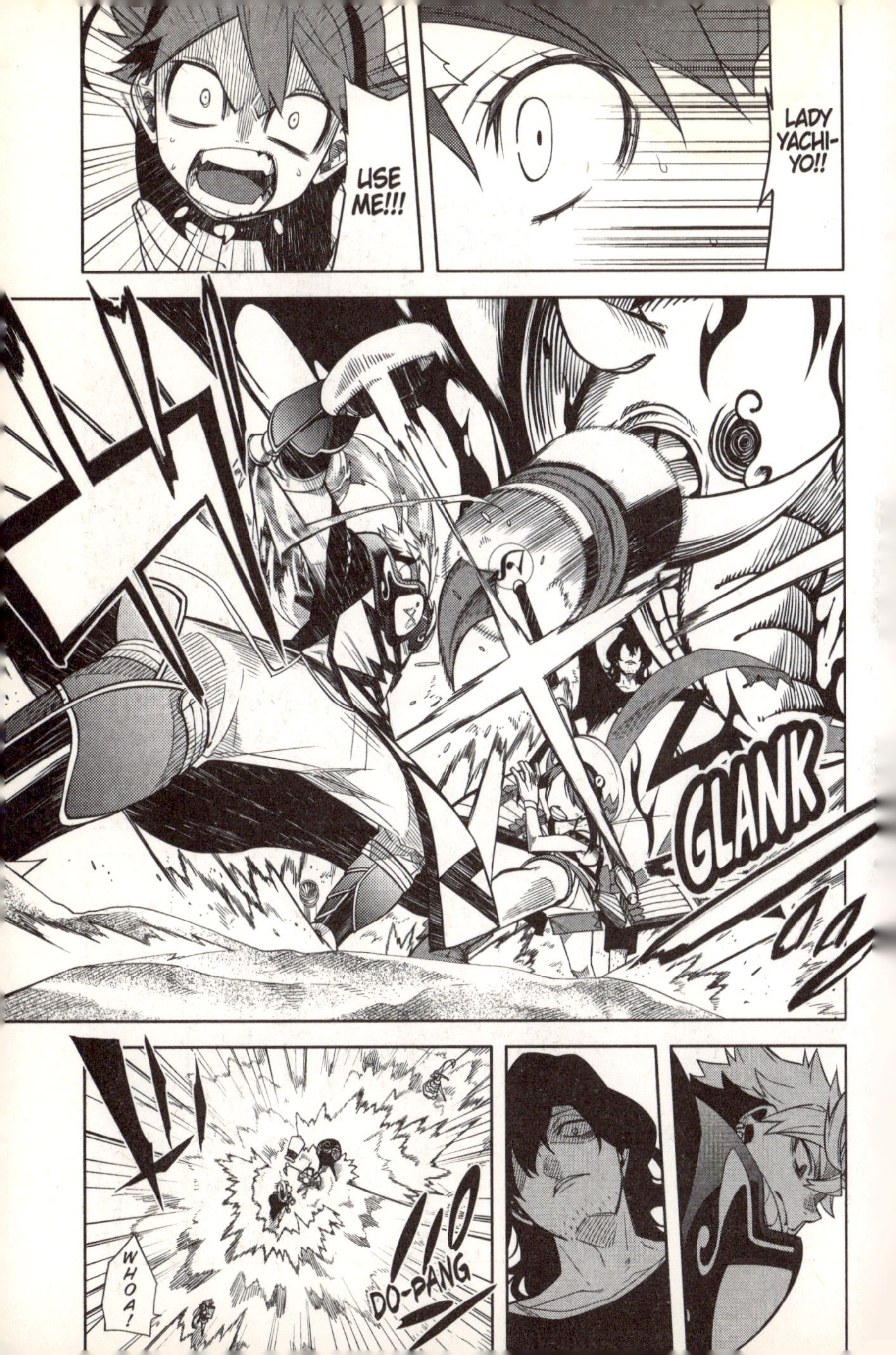
LADY YACHI-YO!!
USE ME!!!
GLANK
DO-PANG
WHOA!

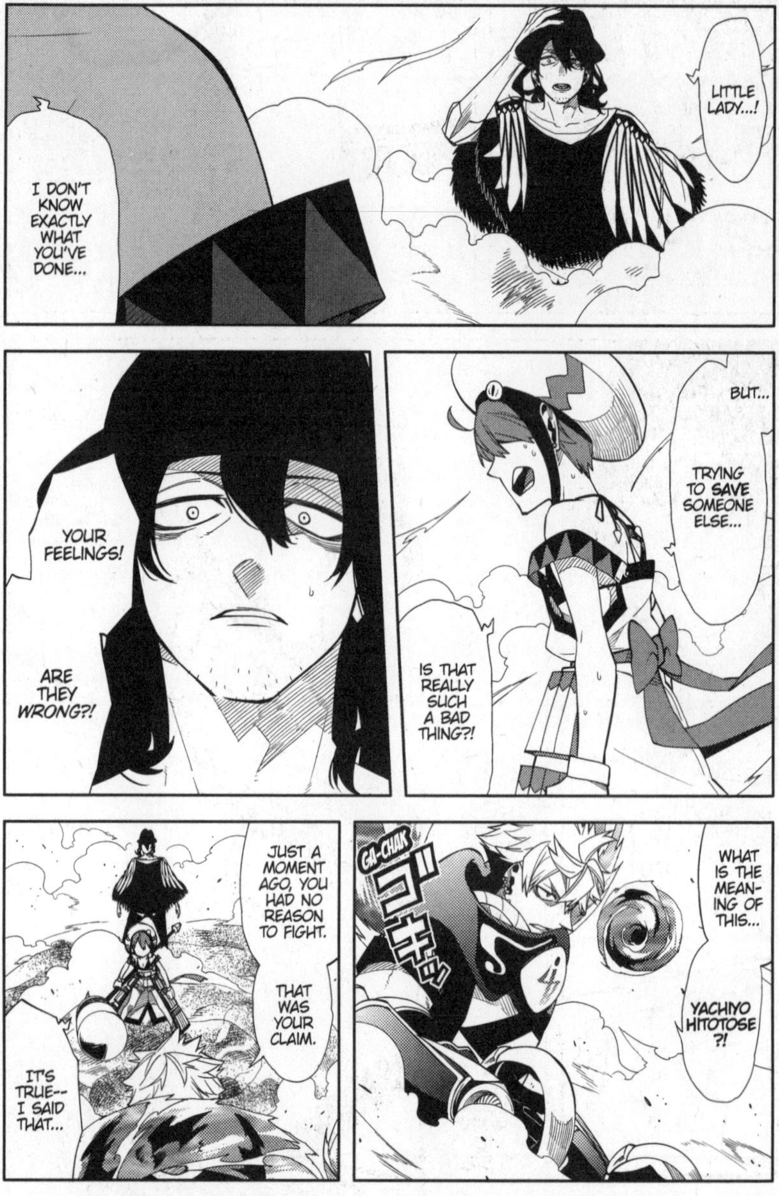
LITTLE LADY...!
I DON'T KNOW EXACTLY WHAT YOU'VE DONE...
BUT...
TRYING TO SAVE SOMEONE ELSE...
IS THAT REALLY SUCH A BAD THING?!
YOUR FEELINGS!
ARE THEY *WRONG*?!
WHAT IS THE MEANING OF THIS...
YACHIYO HITOTOSE?!
GA-CHAK
JUST A MOMENT AGO, YOU HAD NO REASON TO FIGHT.
THAT WAS YOUR CLAIM.
IT'S TRUE-- I SAID THAT...

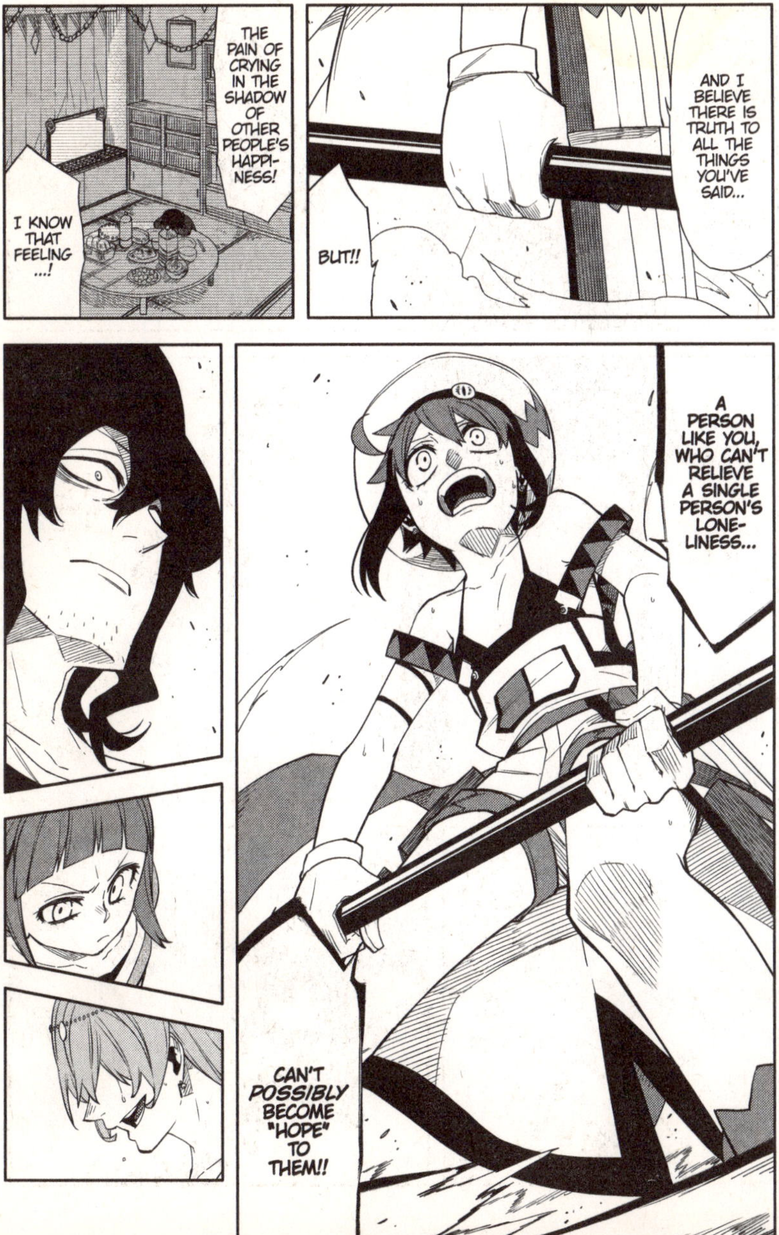
AND I BELIEVE THERE IS TRUTH TO ALL THE THINGS YOU'VE SAID...
BUT!!
THE PAIN OF CRYING IN THE SHADOW OF OTHER PEOPLE'S HAPPI-NESS!
I KNOW THAT FEELING ...!
A PERSON LIKE YOU, WHO CAN'T RELIEVE A SINGLE PERSON'S LONE-LINESS...
CAN'T *POSSIBLY* BECOME "HOPE" TO THEM!!

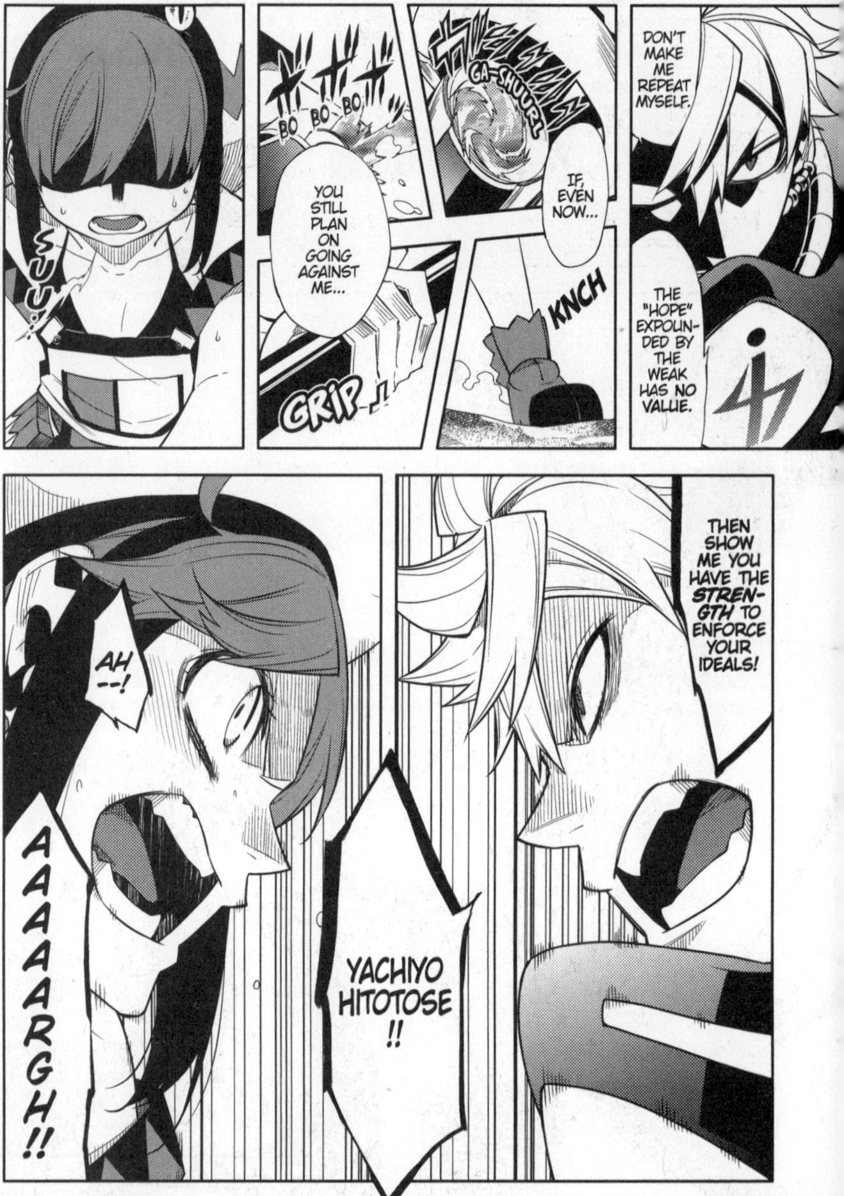

DON'T MAKE ME REPEAT MYSELF.
THE "HOPE" EXPOUNDED BY THE WEAK HAS NO VALUE.
GA-SHUURL
IF, EVEN NOW...
KNCH
BO BO BO
YOU STILL PLAN ON GOING AGAINST ME...
GRIP
SUUU
THEN SHOW ME YOU HAVE THE STRENGTH TO ENFORCE YOUR IDEALS!
YACHIYO HITOTOSE!!
AH--!
AAAAAARGH!!

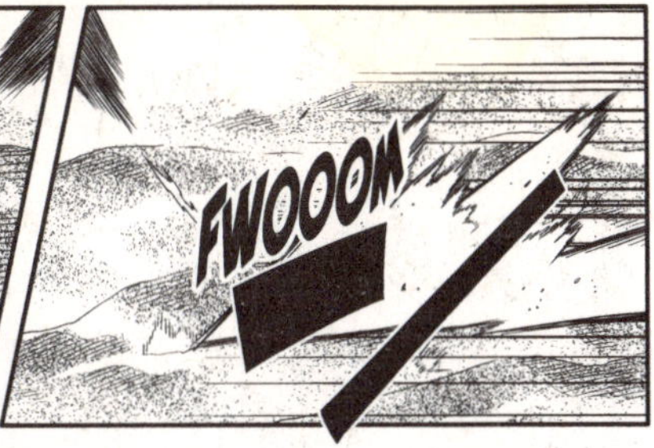
FWOOOM
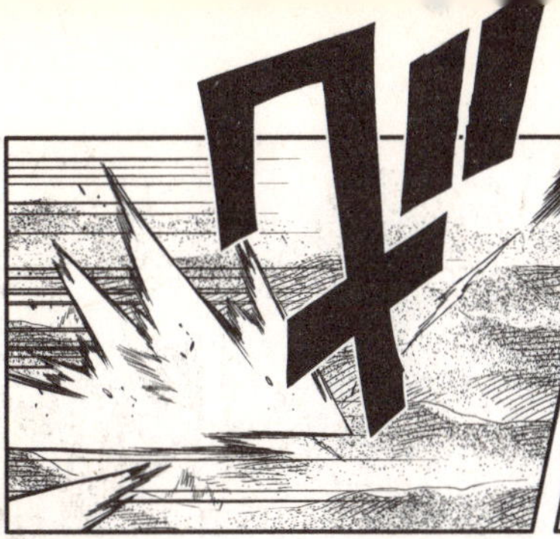
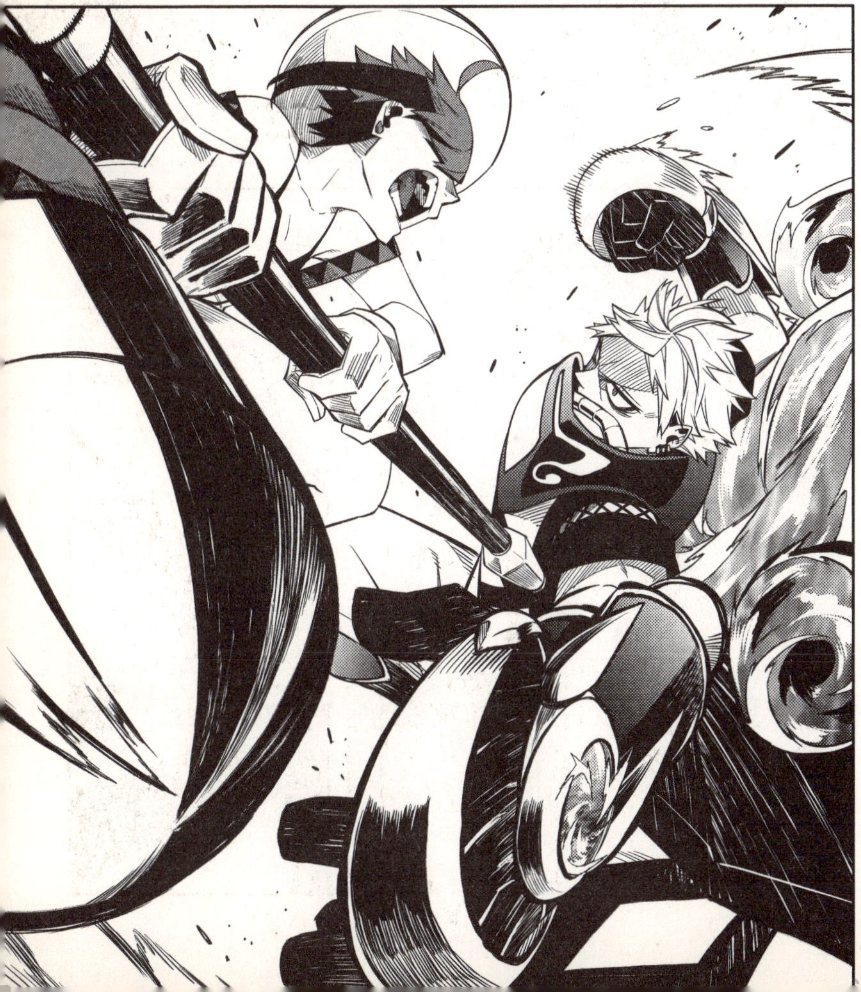

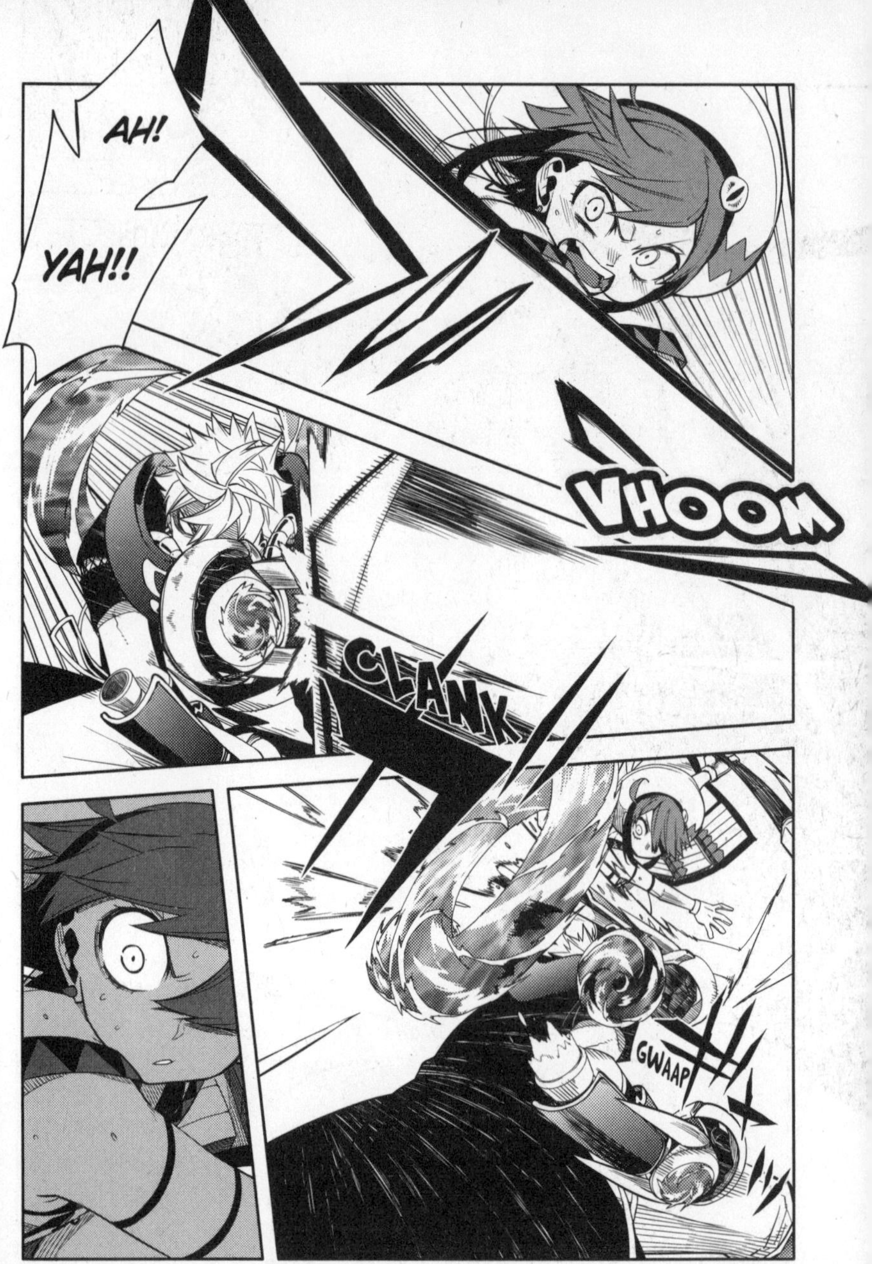
AH!
YAH!!
VHOOM
CLANK
GWAAP

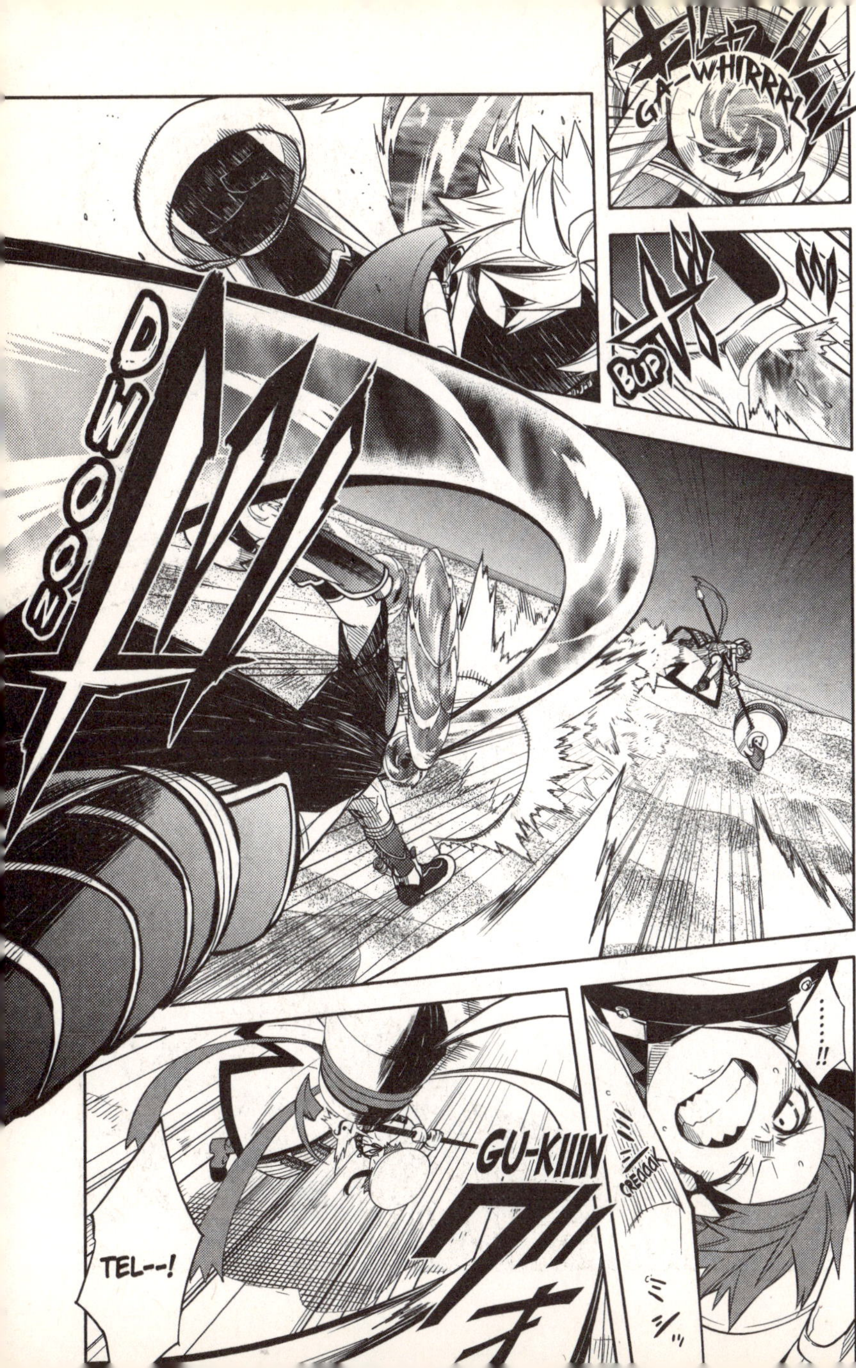
GA-WHIRRRL
BUP
DWOOON
......!!
CREAAAK
GU-KIIIN
TEL--!

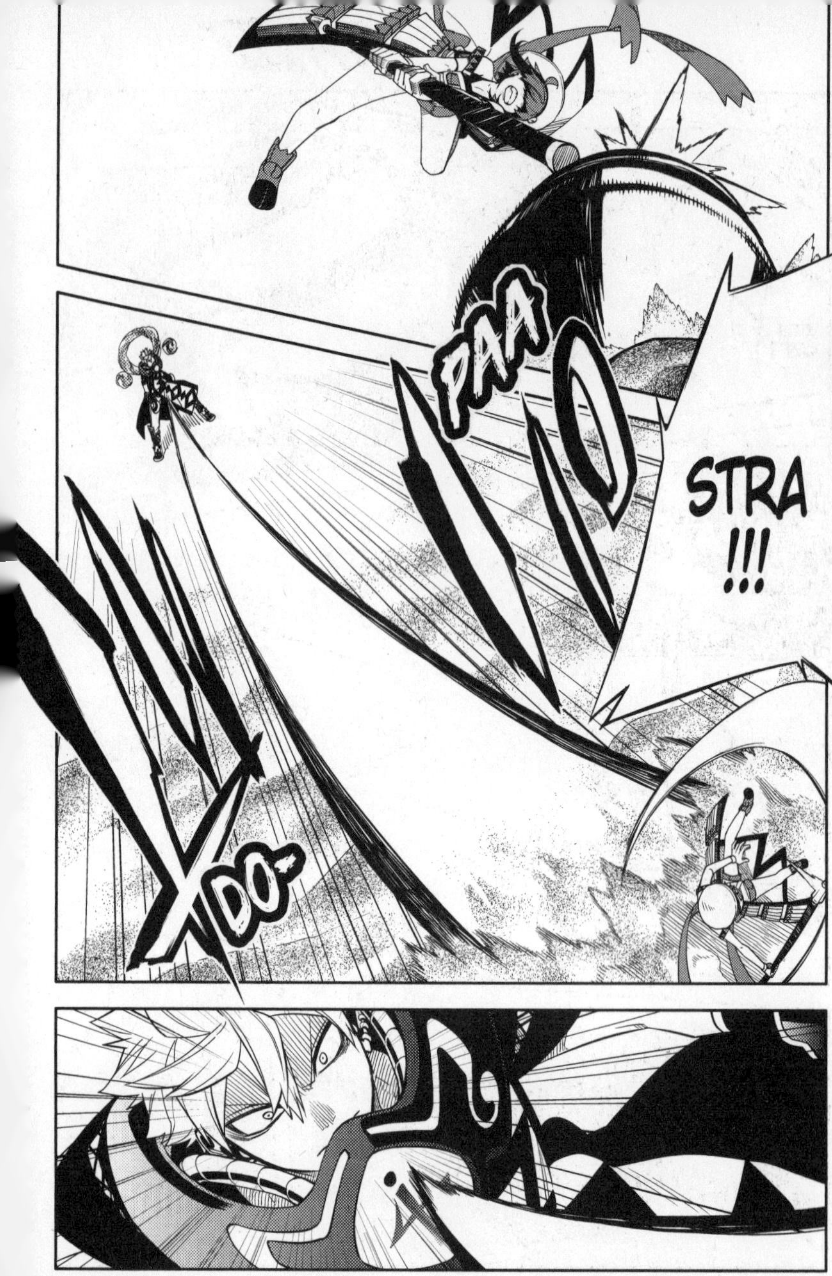
STRA !!!
PAA
DO-

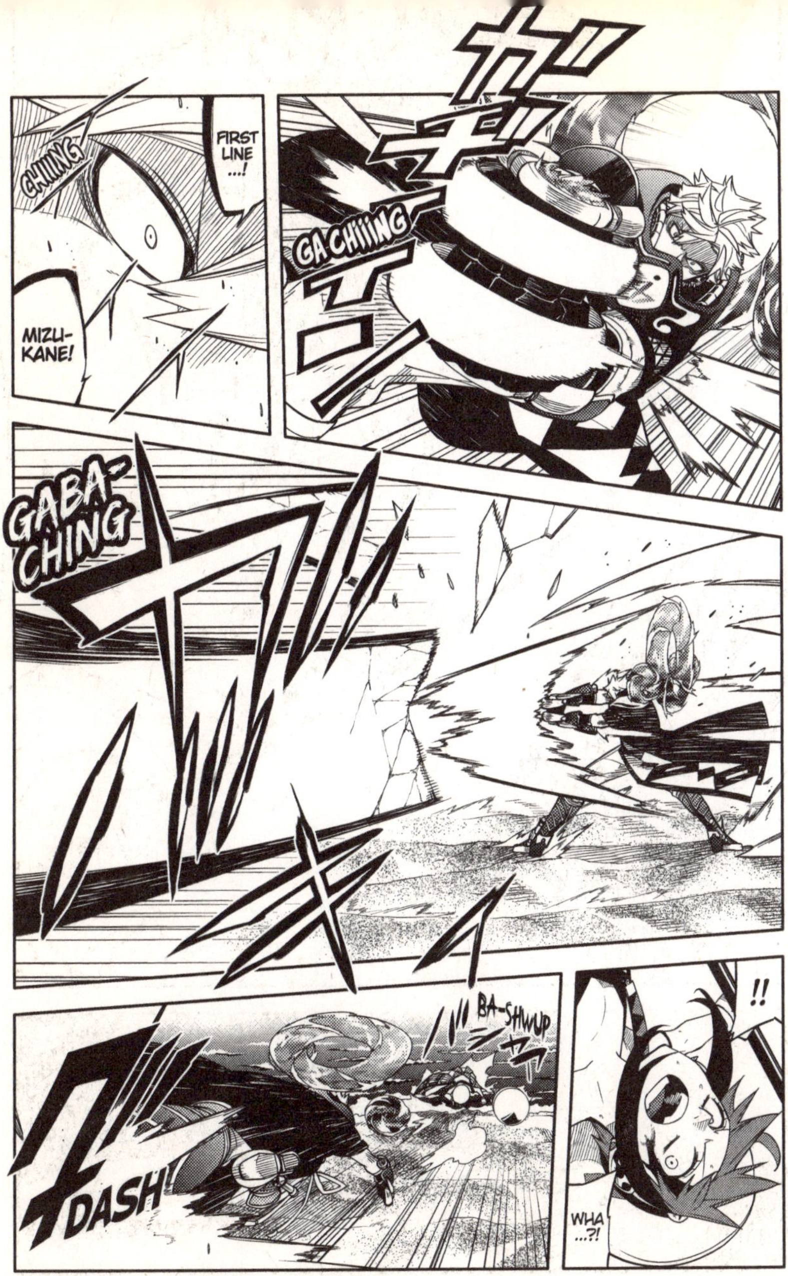
GA CHIIING
FIRST LINE ...!
CHIIING
MIZU-KANE!
GABA-CHING
!!
WHA ...?!
BA-SHWUP
DASH

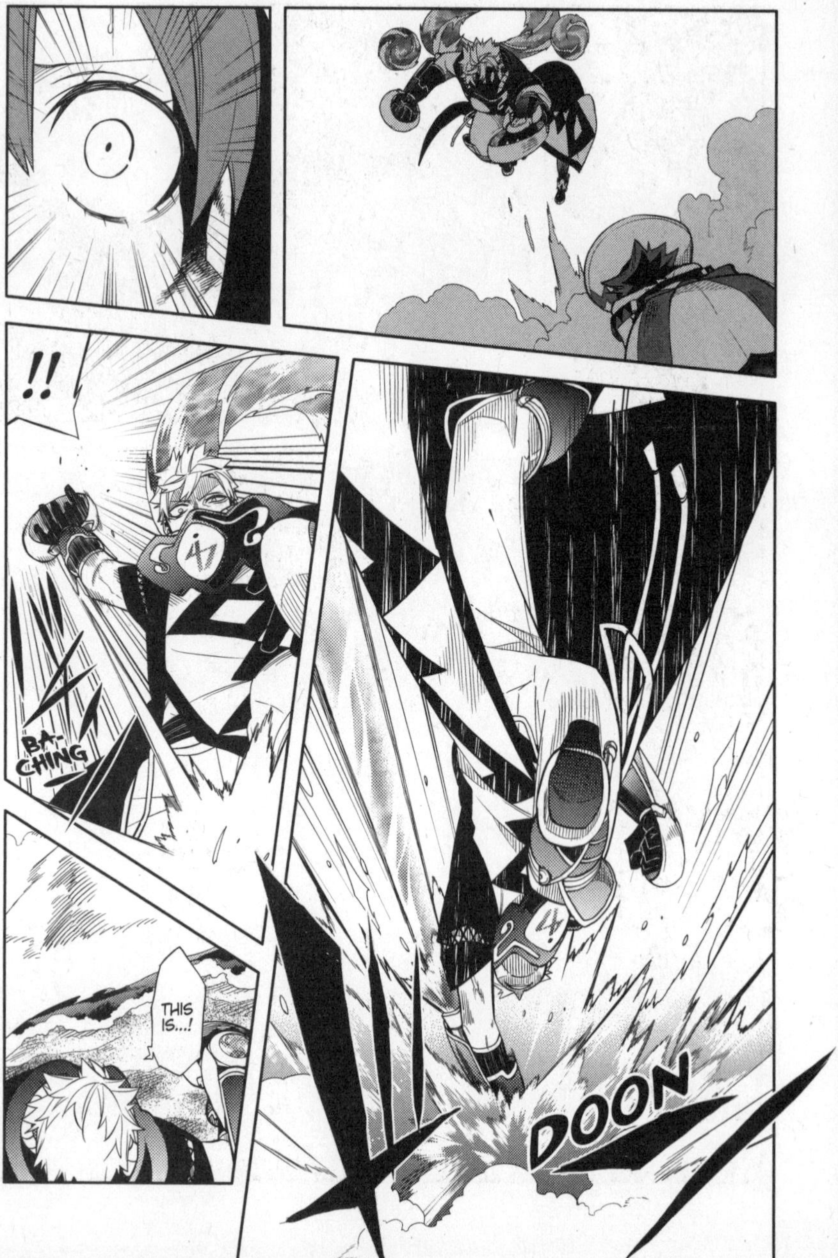
DOON
!!
BA-CHING
THIS IS...!

VWAAAM...
TRANS-LUCENT VERDANT BANDS ...
THAT DANCE IN MOON-LIGHT.
ZUAAA

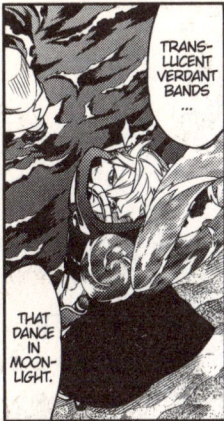

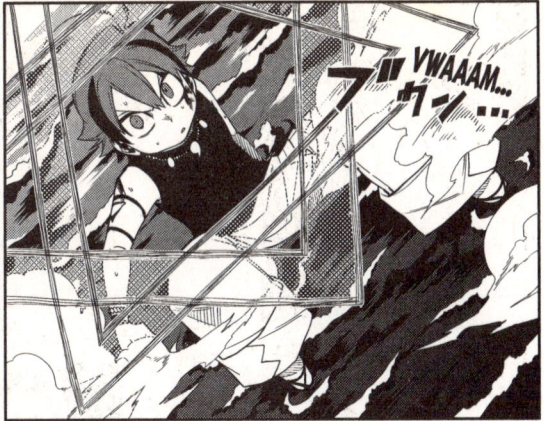

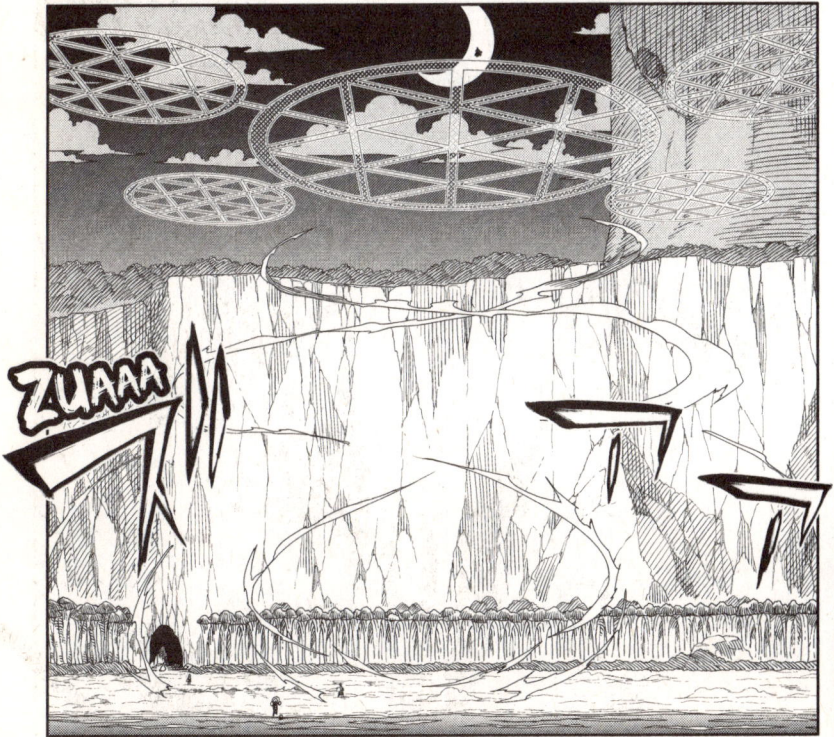

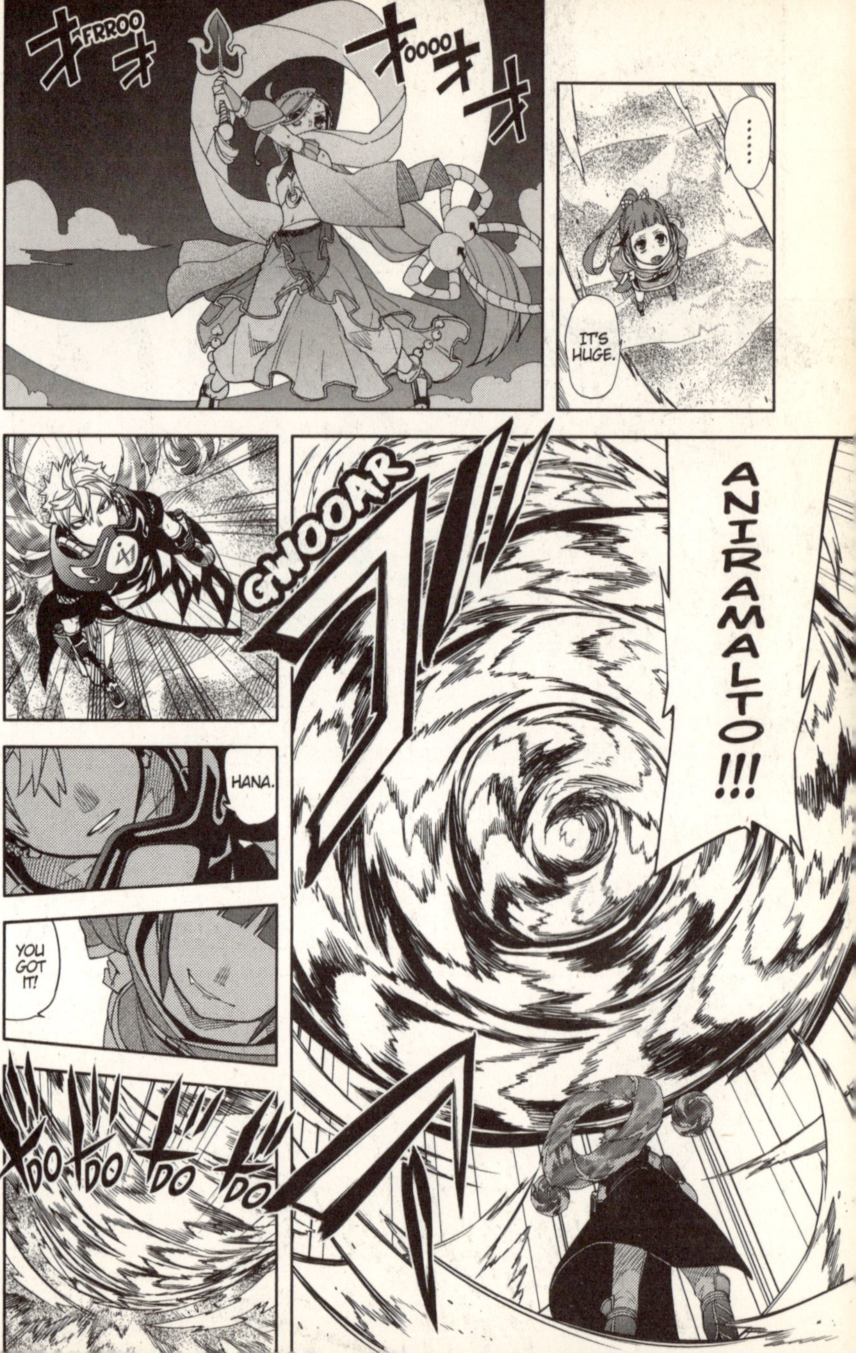
......
IT'S HUGE.
FRROO
OOOO
ANIRAMALTO!!!
GWOOAR
HANA.
YOU GOT IT!
DO DO DO DO

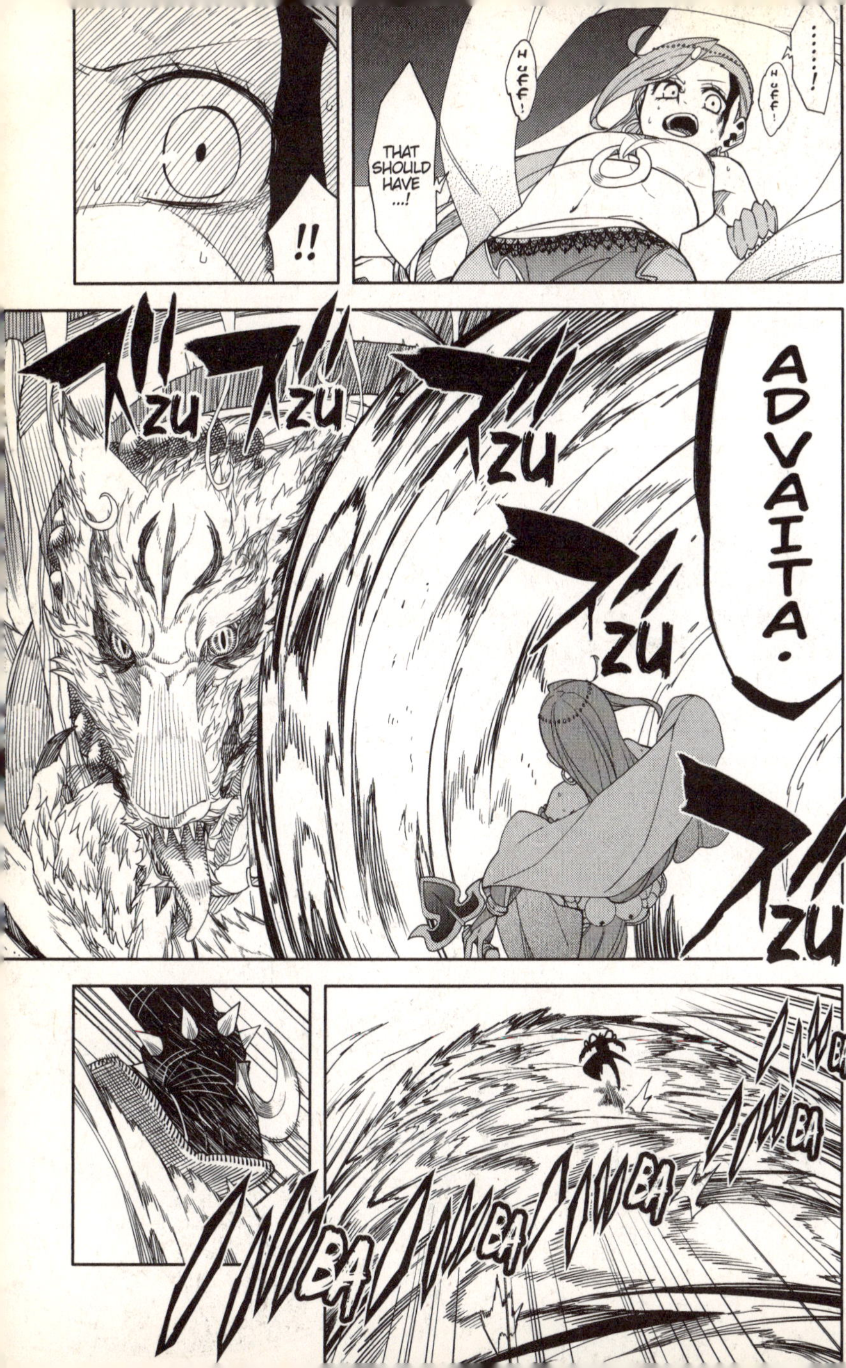
......!
HUFF!
HUFF!
THAT SHOULD HAVE ...!
!!
ADVAITA.
ZU
ZU
ZU
ZU
ZU
ZU
BA
BA
BA
BA
BA
BA

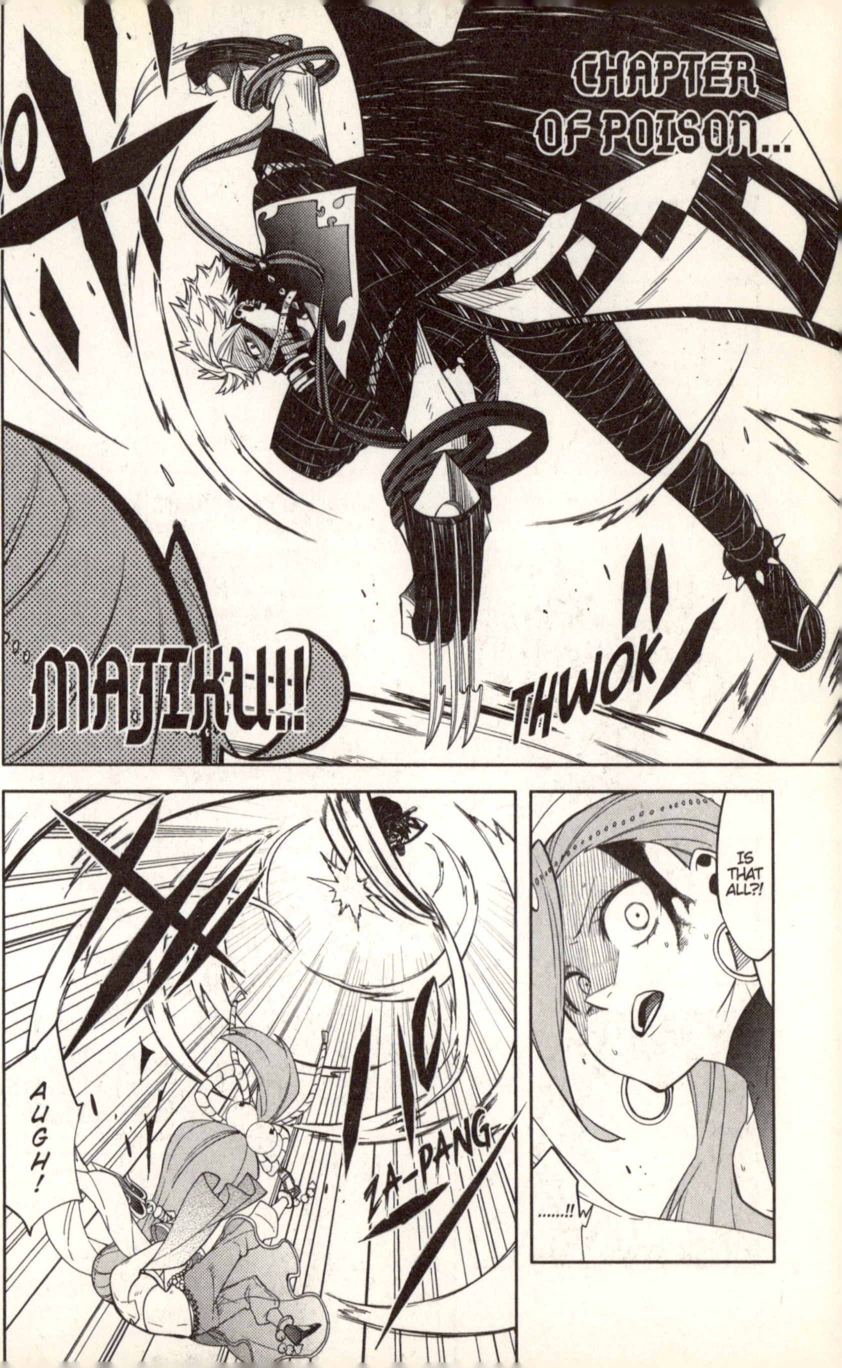
CHAPTER OF POISON...
BOX!!
THWOK!!
MAJIKU!!
IS THAT ALL?!
......!!
ZA-PANG
AUGH!

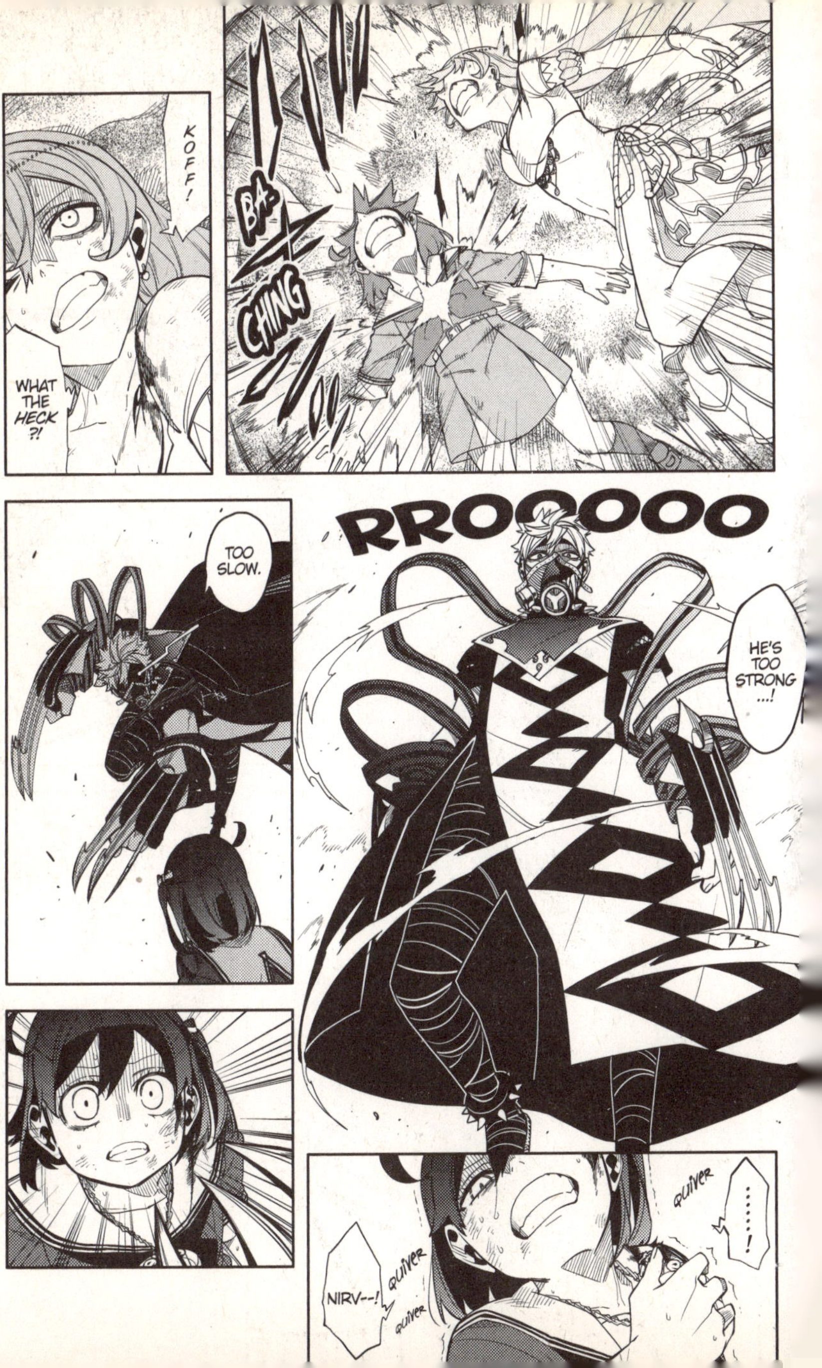
BA-CHING
KOFF!
WHAT THE HECK?!
RROOOOO
HE'S TOO STRONG...!
TOO SLOW.
QUIVER
......!
NIRV--!
QUIVER
QUIVER

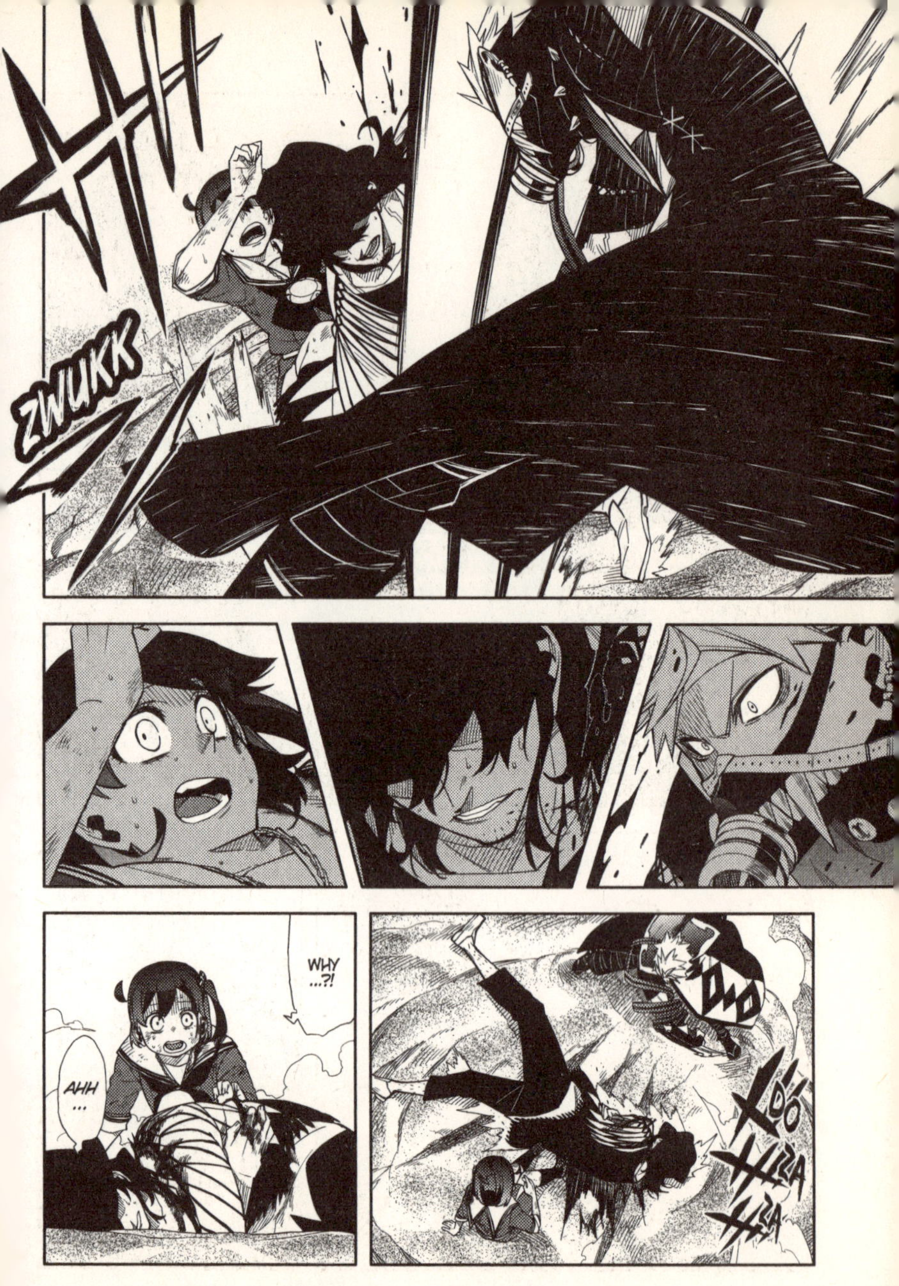
ZWUKK
DÓ ZA ZA
WHY ...?!
AHH ...

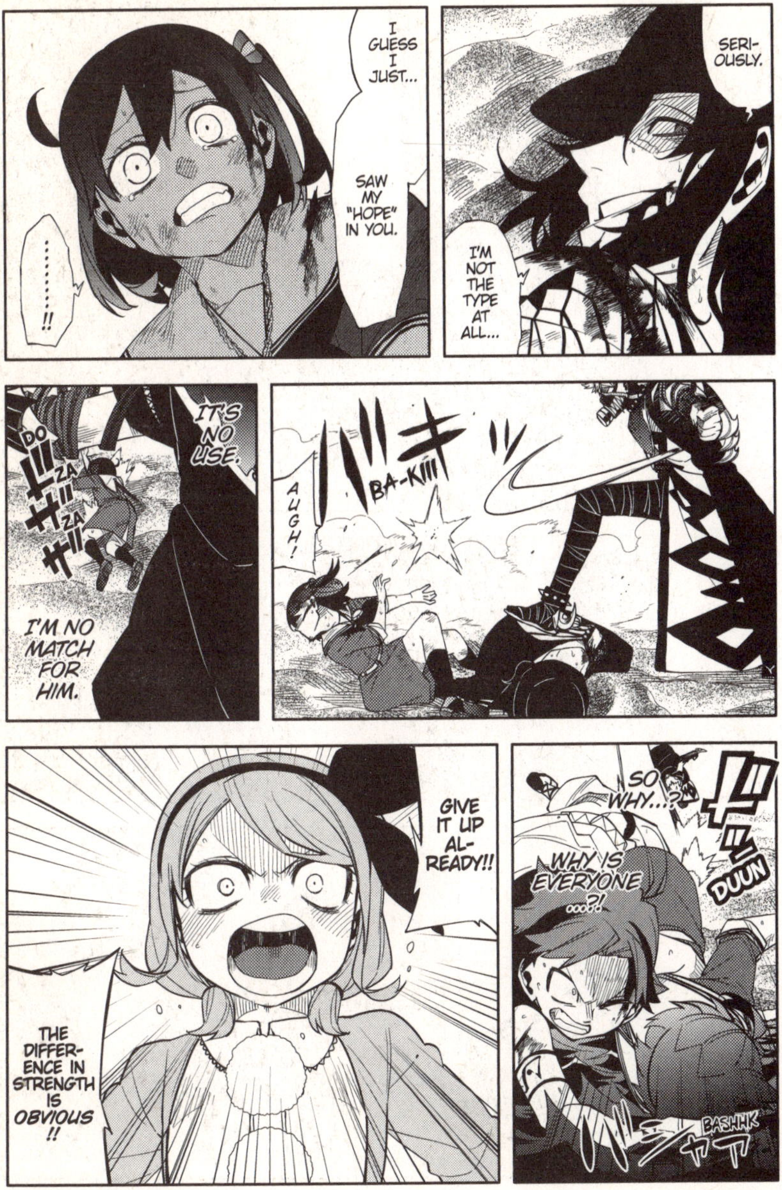
SERI-OUSLY.
I'M NOT THE TYPE AT ALL...
I GUESS I JUST...
SAW MY "HOPE" IN YOU.
.......!!
BA-KIII
AUGH!
IT'S NO USE.
DO
ZA
ZA
I'M NO MATCH FOR HIM.
SO WHY...?
WHY IS EVERYONE ...?!
DUUN
BASHHK
GIVE IT UP AL-READY!!
THE DIFFER-ENCE IN STRENGTH IS OBVIOUS!!

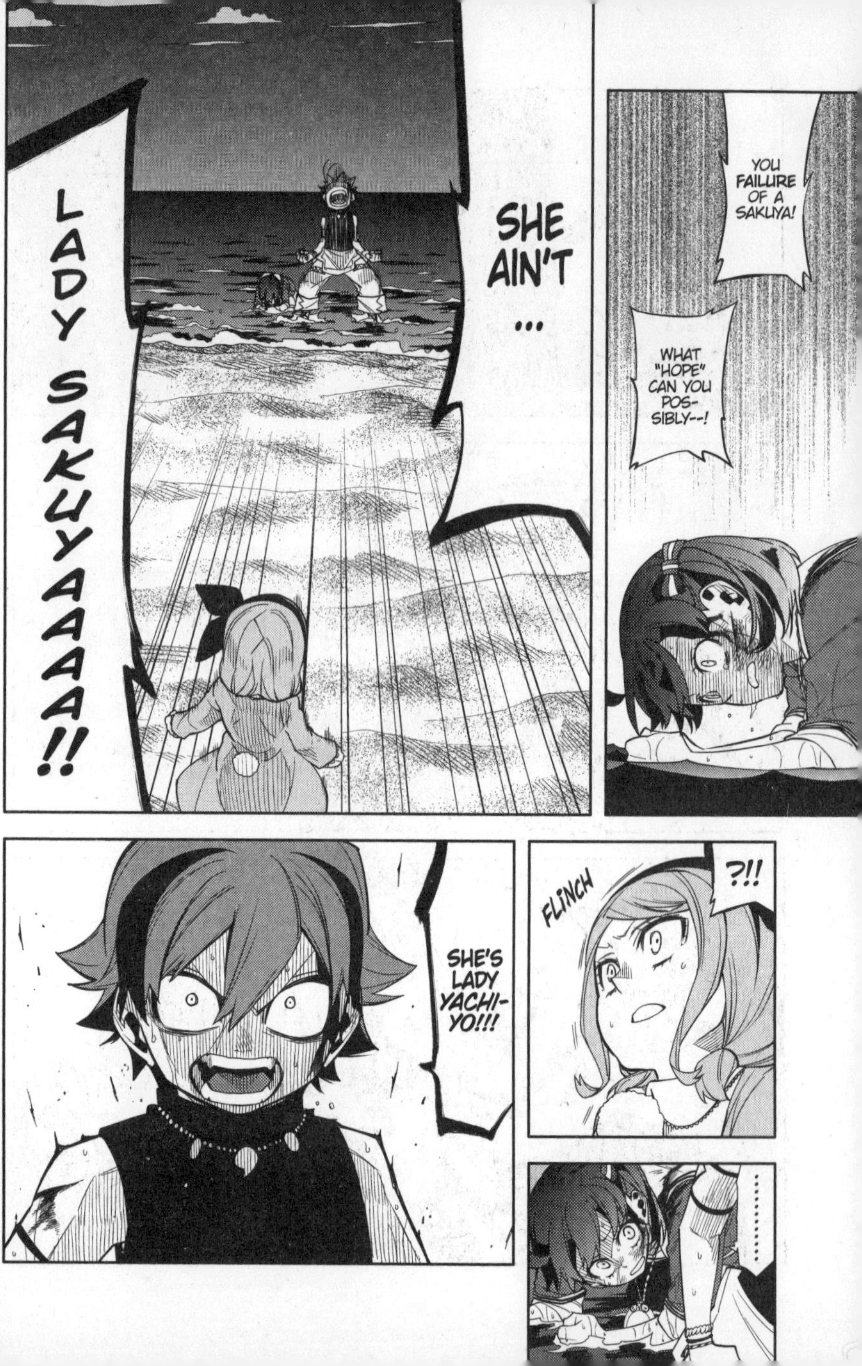
YOU FAILURE OF A SAKUYA!
WHAT "HOPE" CAN YOU POS-SIBLY--!
SHE AIN'T ...
LADY SAKUYAAAAAA!!
?!!
FLINCH
......
SHE'S LADY YACHI-YO!!!

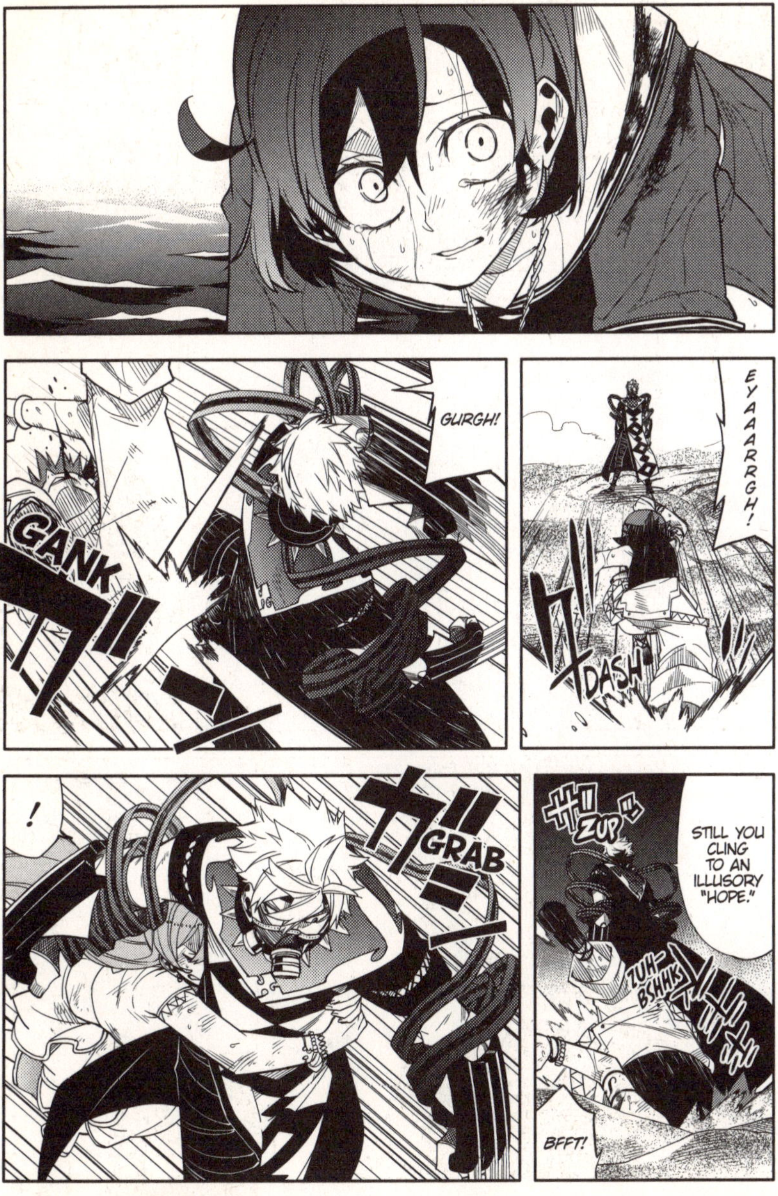
EYAAAARRGH!
DASH
GURGH!
GANK
STILL YOU CLING TO AN ILLUSORY "HOPE."
ZUP
ZUH-BSHHKS
BFFT!
GRAB
!

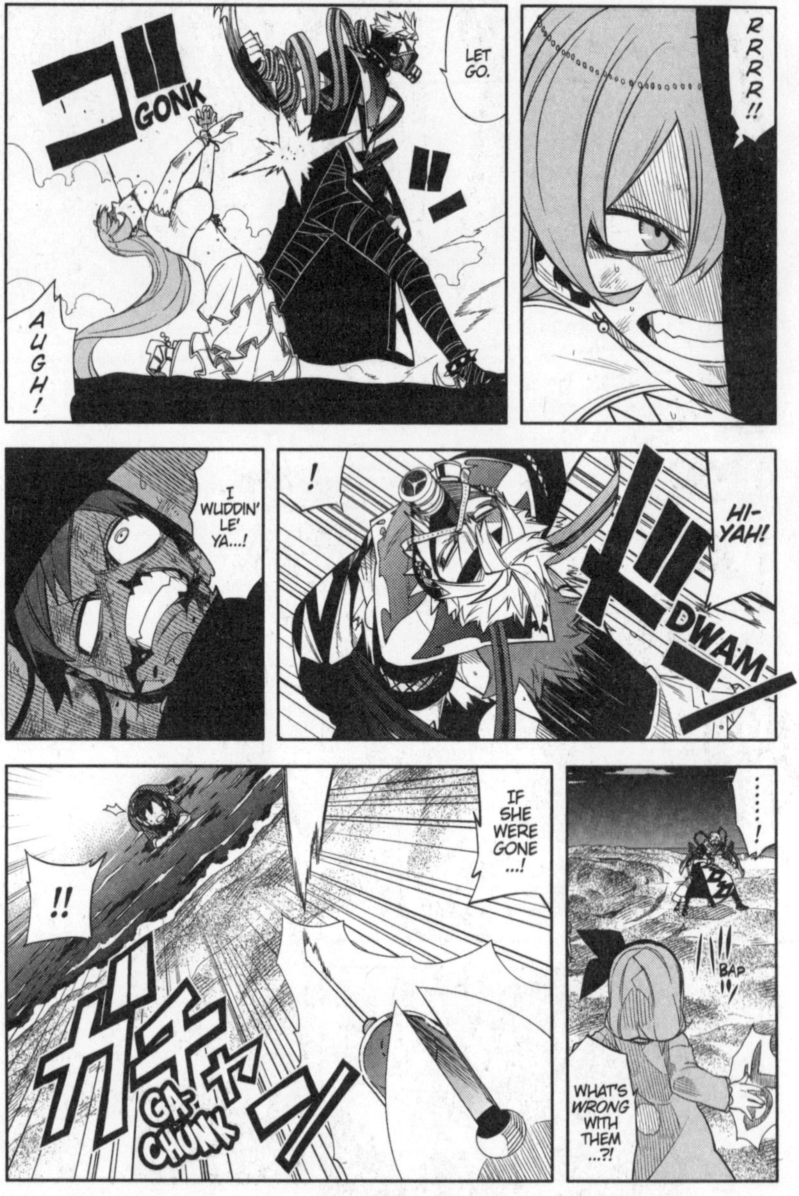
RRRR!!
LET GO.
GONK
AUGH!
HI-YAH!
!
DWAM
I WUDDIN' LE' YA...!
......!
BAP
WHAT'S WRONG WITH THEM ...?!
IF SHE WERE GONE ...!
!!
CA-CHUNK

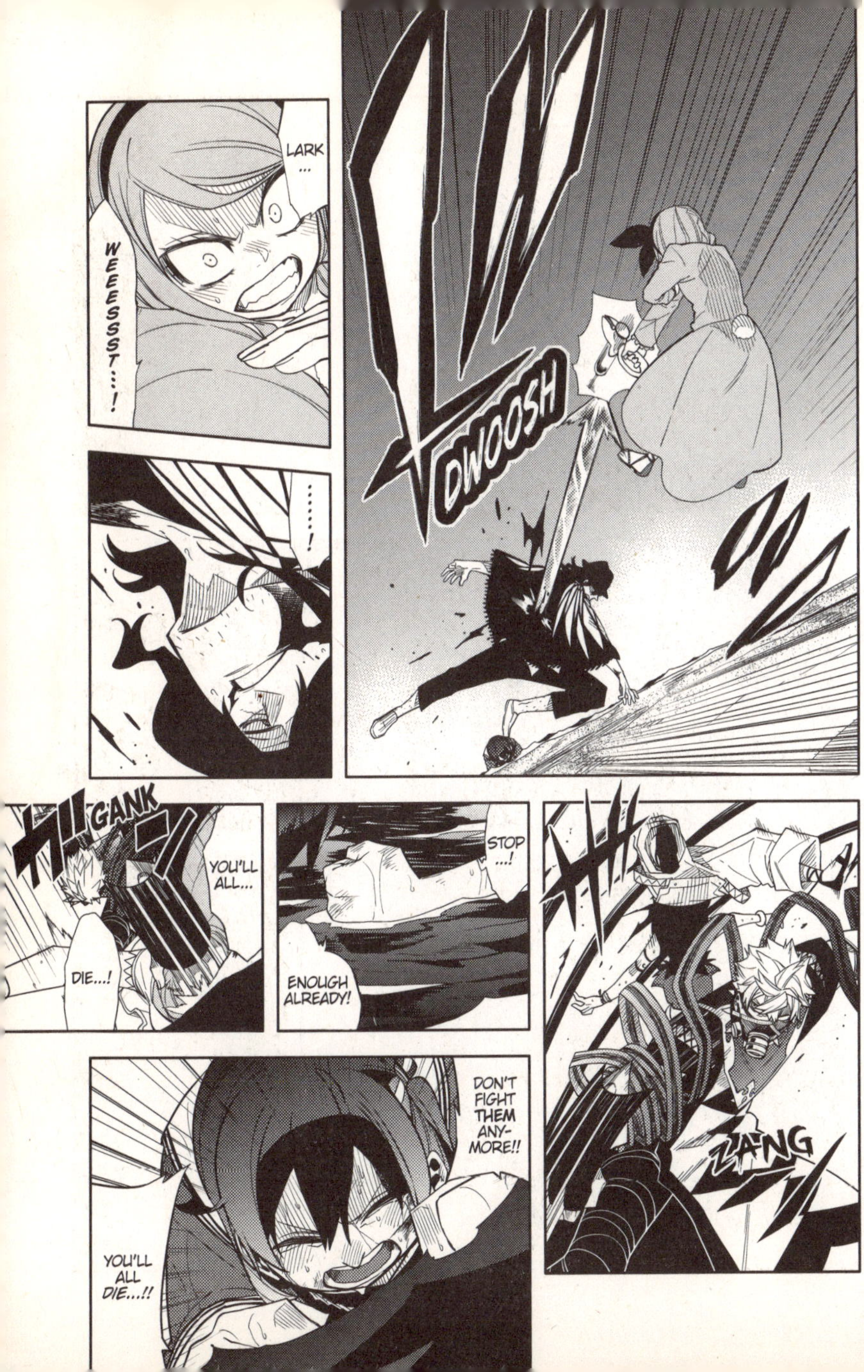
DWOOSH
LARK...
WEEESSST...!
......!
ZANG
STOP...!
ENOUGH ALREADY!
GANK
YOU'LL ALL...
DIE...!
DON'T FIGHT THEM ANYMORE!!
YOU'LL ALL DIE...!!

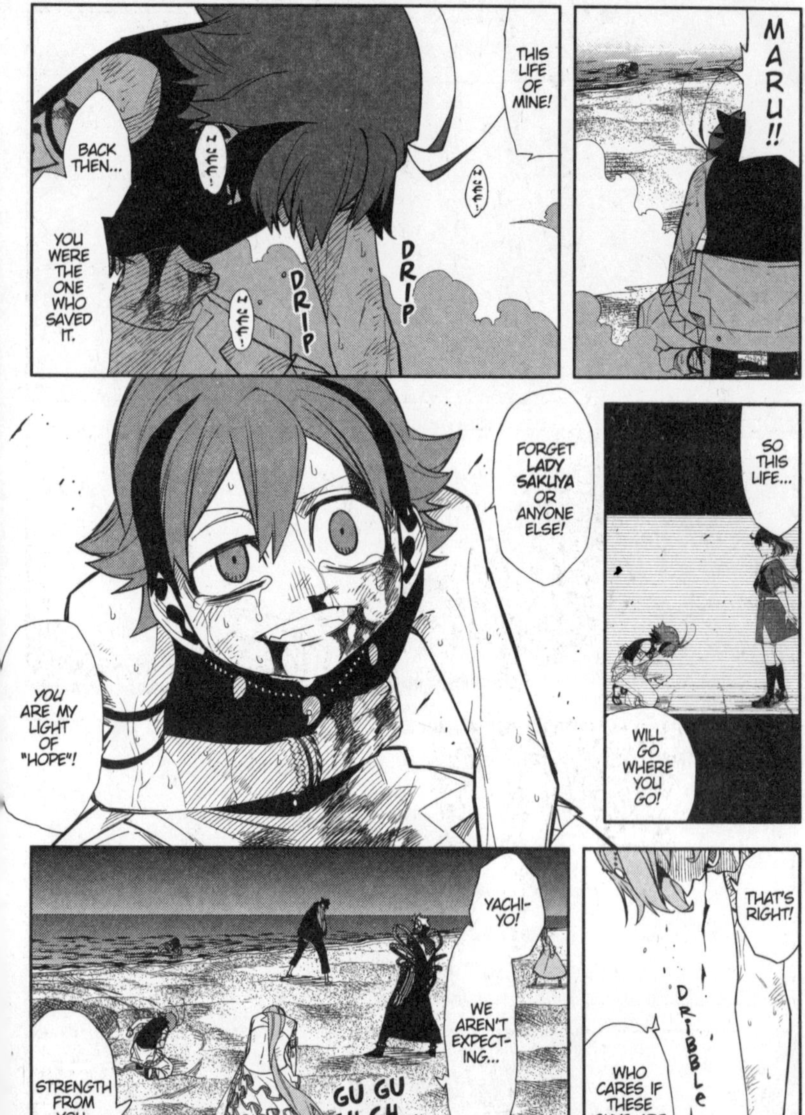
MARU!!
THIS LIFE OF MINE!
HUFF!
BACK THEN...
HUFF!
DRIP
DRIP
YOU WERE THE ONE WHO SAVED IT.
HUFF!
SO THIS LIFE...
WILL GO WHERE YOU GO!
FORGET LADY SAKUYA OR ANYONE ELSE!
YOU ARE MY LIGHT OF "HOPE"!
THAT'S RIGHT!
DRIBBLE
WHO CARES IF THESE GUYS ARE STRONG?!
YACHI-YO!
WE AREN'T EXPECT-ING...
GU GU GH GH...
STRENGTH FROM YOU.

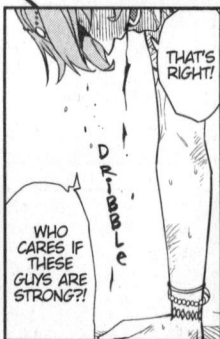

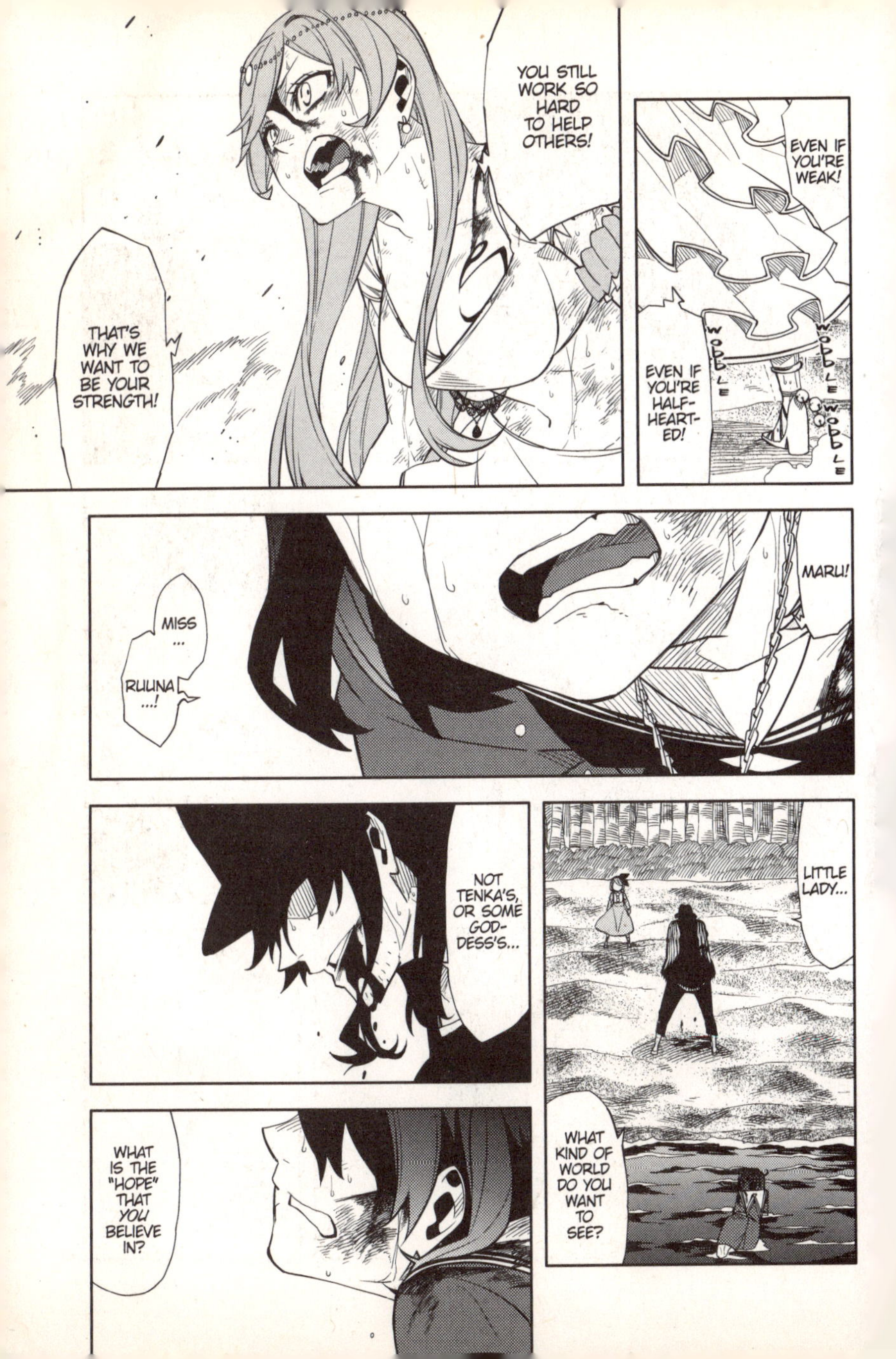
EVEN IF YOU'RE WEAK!
EVEN IF YOU'RE HALF-HEARTED!
WOBBLE
WOBBLE
WOBBLE
YOU STILL WORK SO HARD TO HELP OTHERS!
THAT'S WHY WE WANT TO BE YOUR STRENGTH!
MARU!
MISS ...
RUUNA ...!
LITTLE LADY...
WHAT KIND OF WORLD DO YOU WANT TO SEE?
NOT TENKA'S, OR SOME GOD-DESS'S...
WHAT IS THE "HOPE" THAT *YOU* BELIEVE IN?

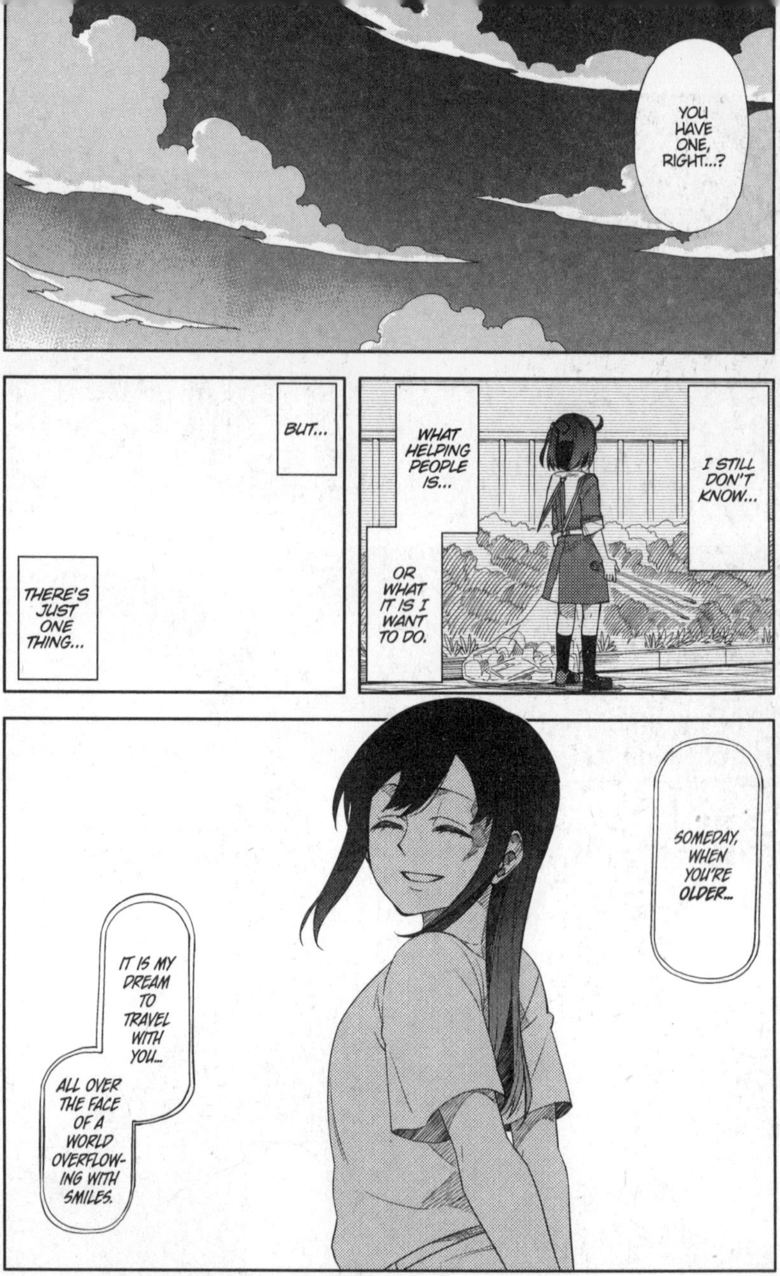
YOU HAVE ONE, RIGHT...?
I STILL DON'T KNOW...
WHAT HELPING PEOPLE IS...
OR WHAT IT IS I WANT TO DO.
BUT...
THERE'S JUST ONE THING...
SOMEDAY, WHEN YOU'RE OLDER...
IT IS MY DREAM TO TRAVEL WITH YOU...
ALL OVER THE FACE OF A WORLD OVERFLOW-ING WITH SMILES.

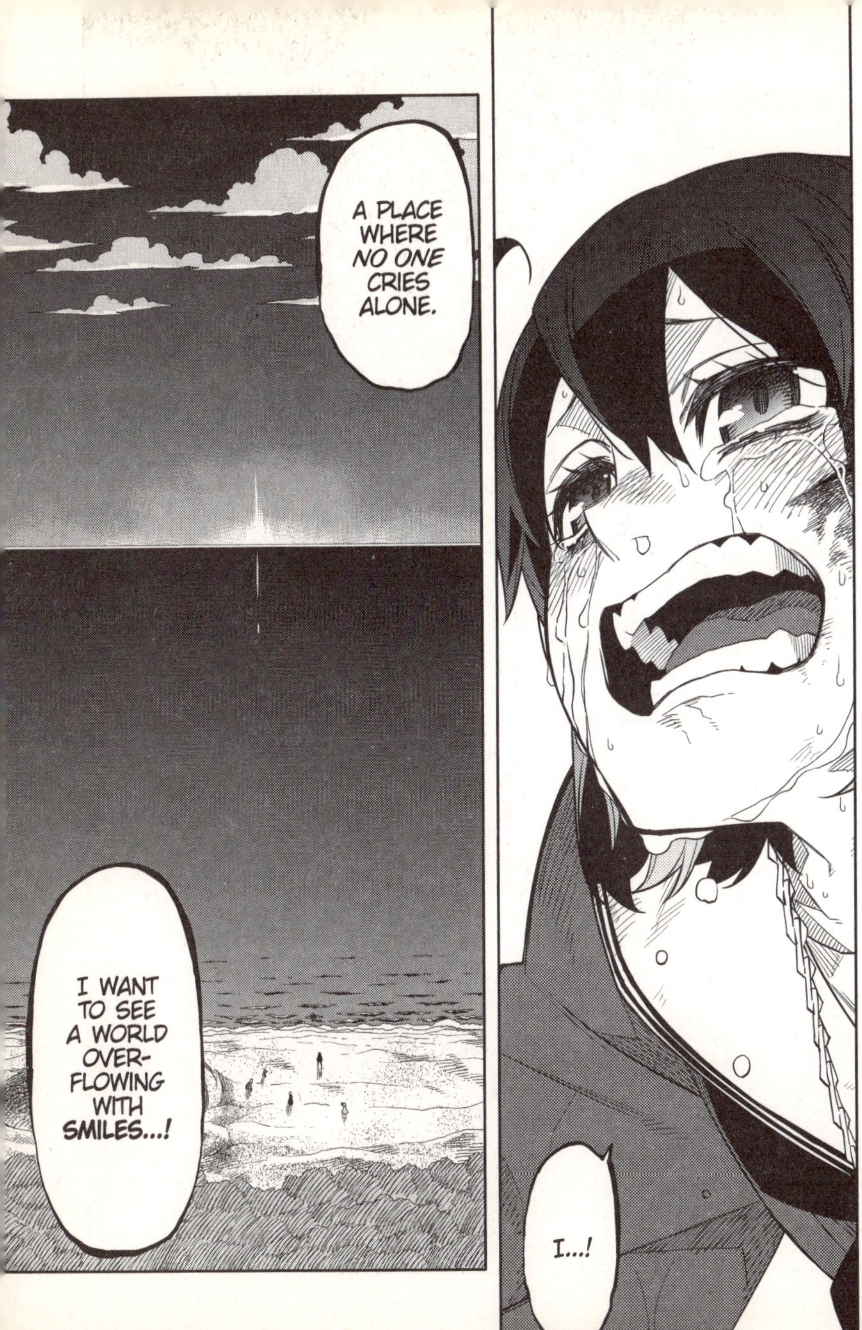
I...!
A PLACE WHERE NO ONE CRIES ALONE.
I WANT TO SEE A WORLD OVER-FLOWING WITH SMILES...!

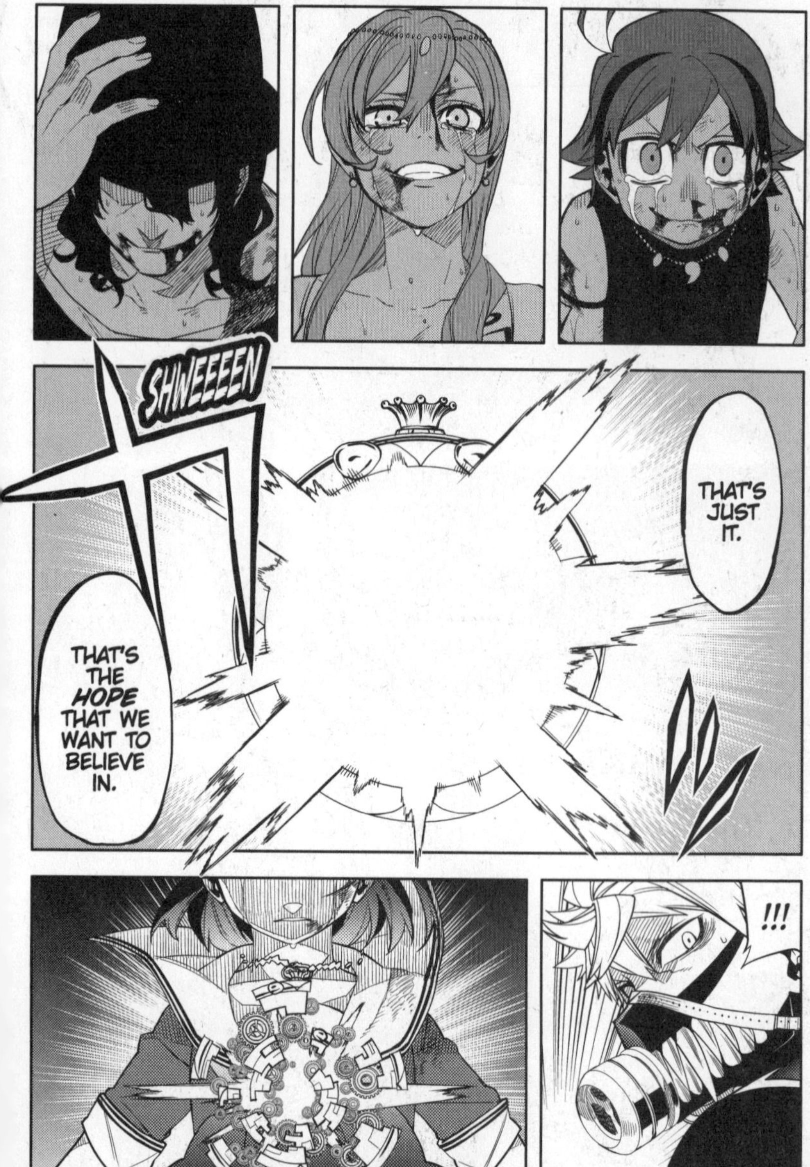
THAT'S JUST IT.
SHWEEEEN
THAT'S THE *HOPE* THAT WE WANT TO BELIEVE IN.
!!!

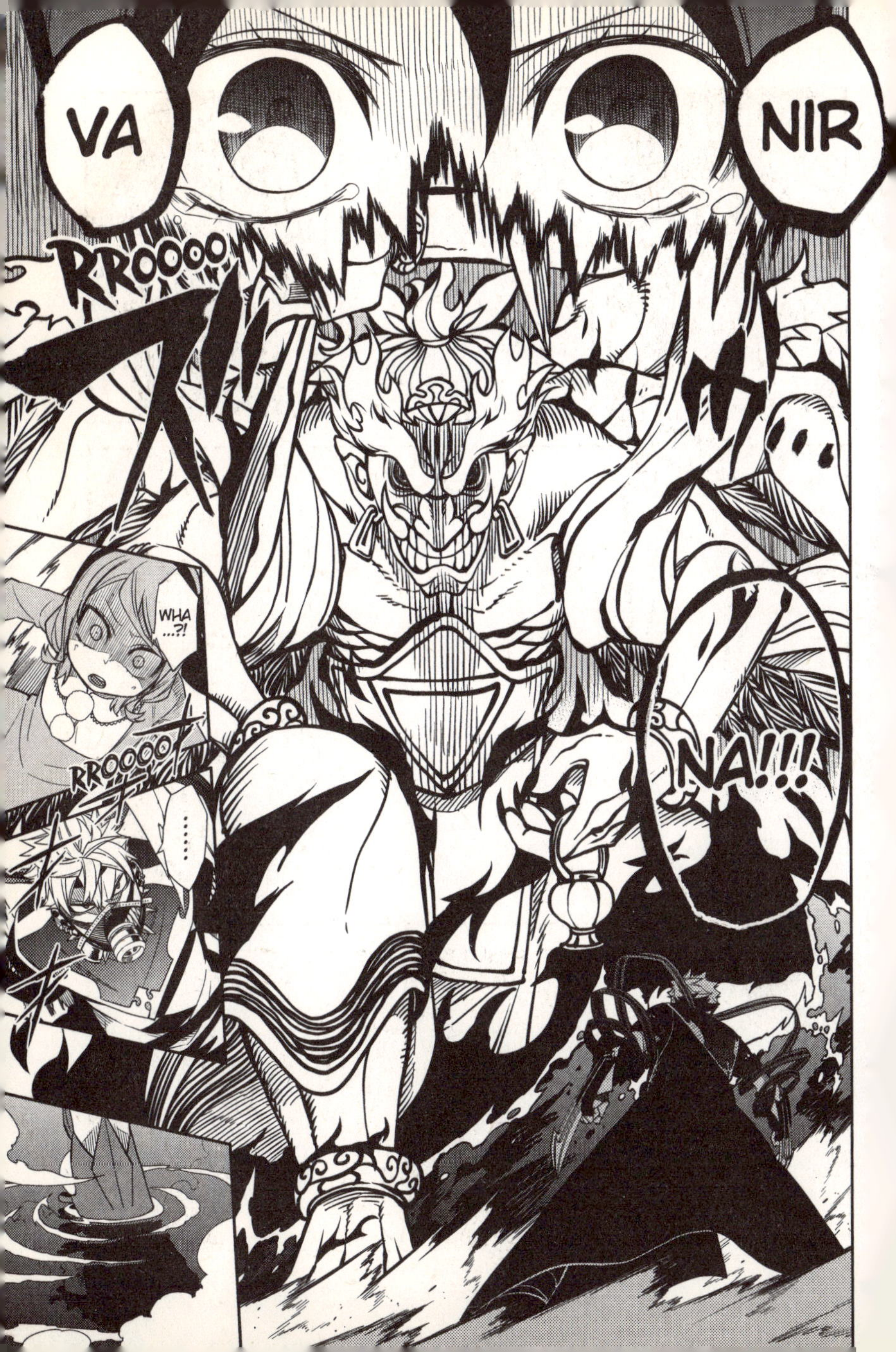
VA
NIR
RROOOO
NA!!!
WHA ...?!
RROOOO
......

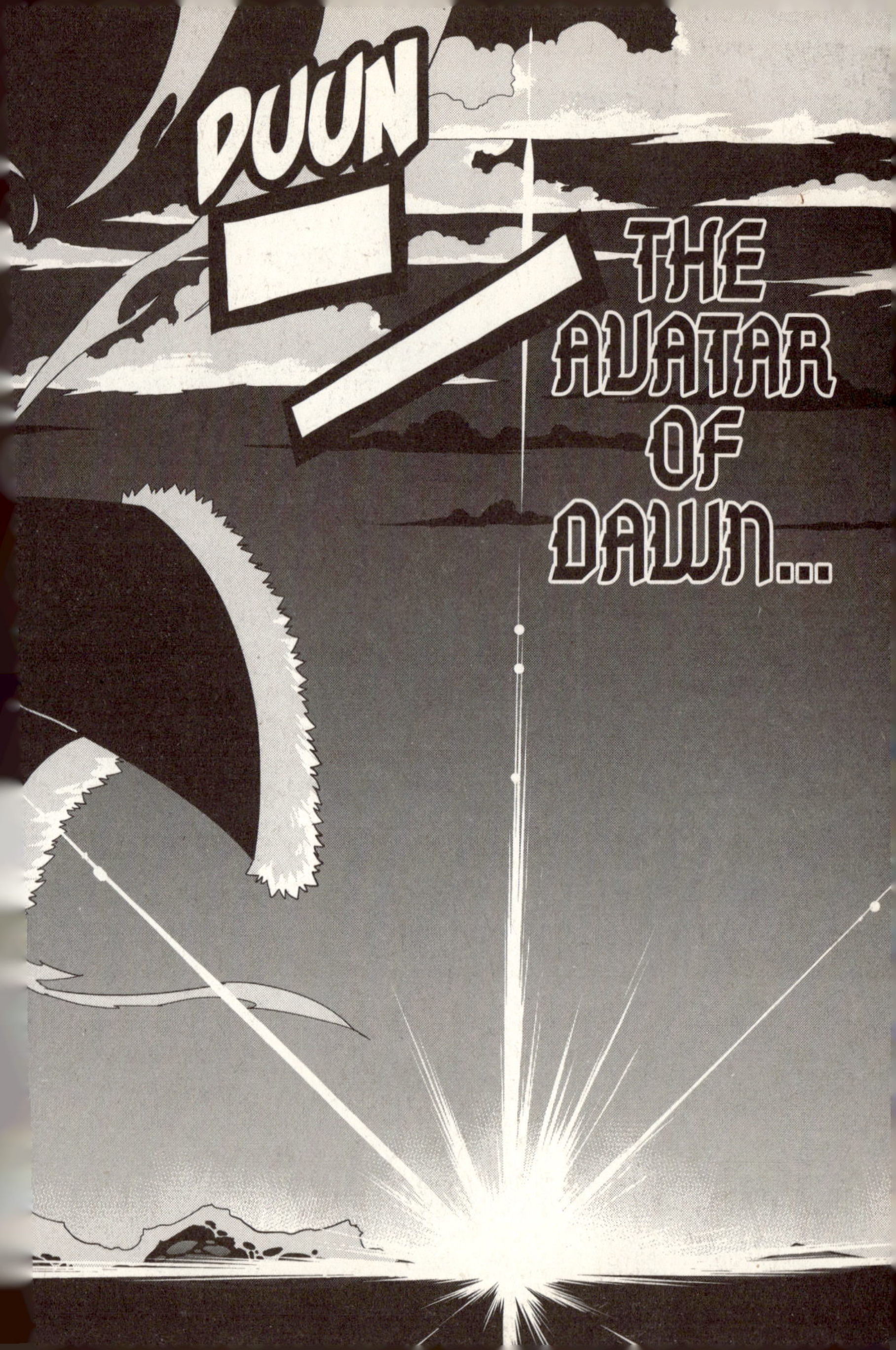
DUUN
THE AVATAR OF DAWN...

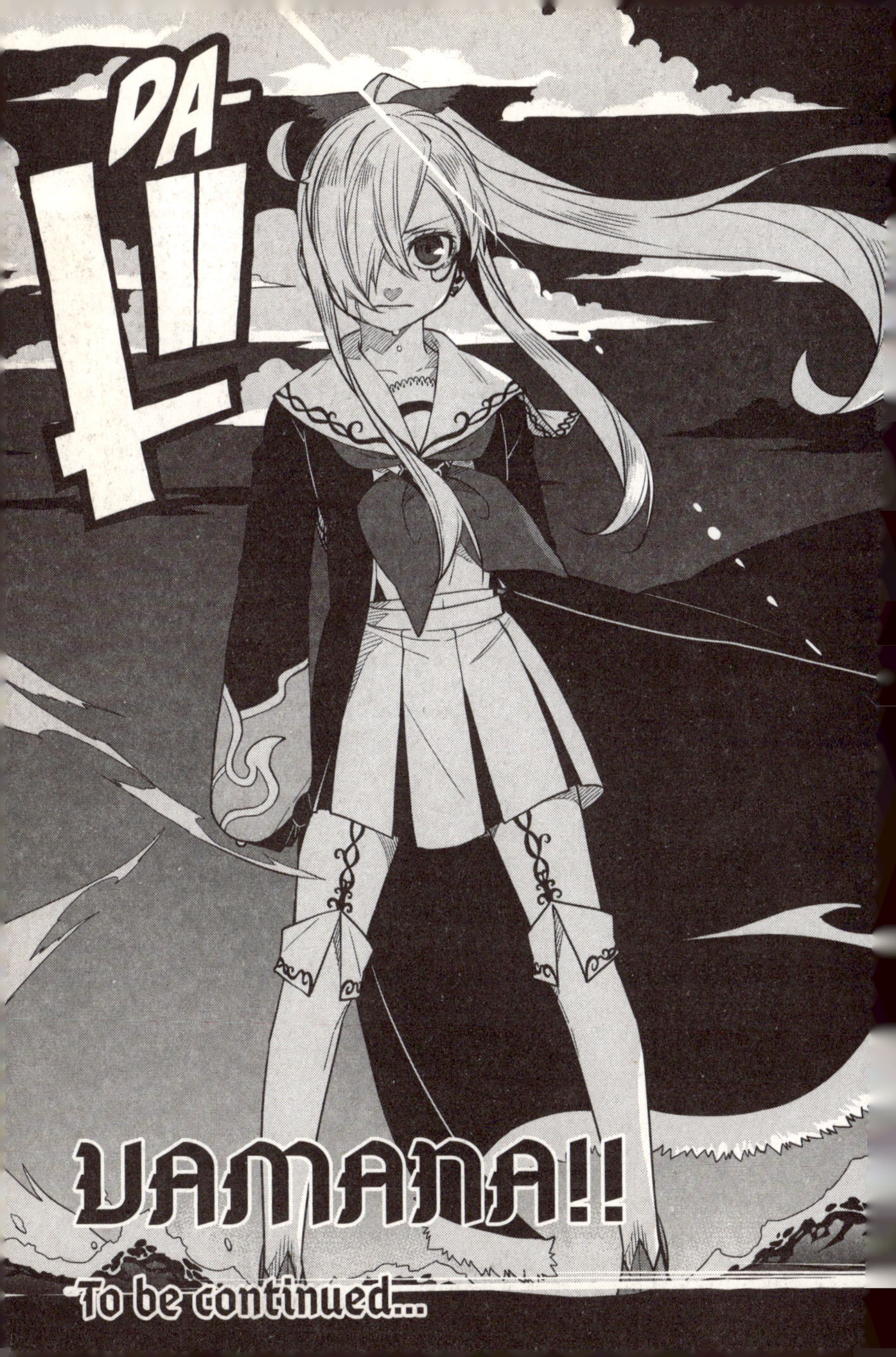
DA-
VAMANA!!
To be continued...

NIRVANA

ニルヴァーナ

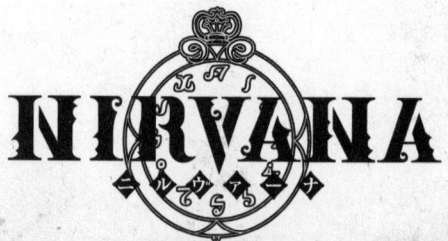

Afterword

ZOWLS

Thank you very much for picking up *NIRVANA* Volume 2. We were able to focus on the feelings of various characters by centering the story in this volume around Yachiyo's past. "What is the meaning of true friendship?" We continue to ponder that question every day as we face the creation of this story.

The kind of narrative we wanted to create for this serialization finally came together in these two volumes. Please look forward to seeing how Yachiyo and the others continue to stand against the many obstacles that stand in their path.

I hope that you continue supporting us in the next volume. See you next time!

NIRVANA
ニルヴァーナ

Travel Records

✡ Phalam

The primordial sea said to be the birthplace of myriad creatures during the Age of Deities. Supposedly, this ocean once covered half the world, but now its name is typically used only to describe the inland sea that connects the world's two great continents.

Abundant fish were once an integral aspect of commerce in the many countries surrounding Phalam. However, the appearance of the blau has led not only to a decline in the fishing industry, but also severely limited travel between the continents.

Fox Island of Phalam
-Maadarah Island-

An uninhabited island in the middle of Phalam. The swirling waters that surround the island make it difficult for boats to reach its shores.

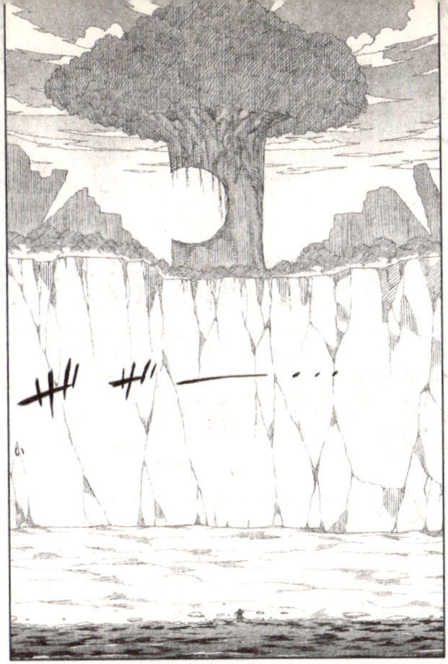
ザ ザ ー…

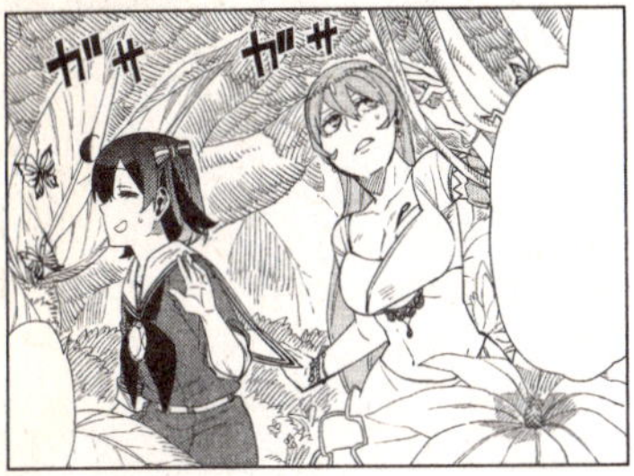
ガサ
ガサ

There are various ruins around the island that point to the prior existence of an old civilization. Due to the complete isolation of the island, a unique culture can apparently be found there.

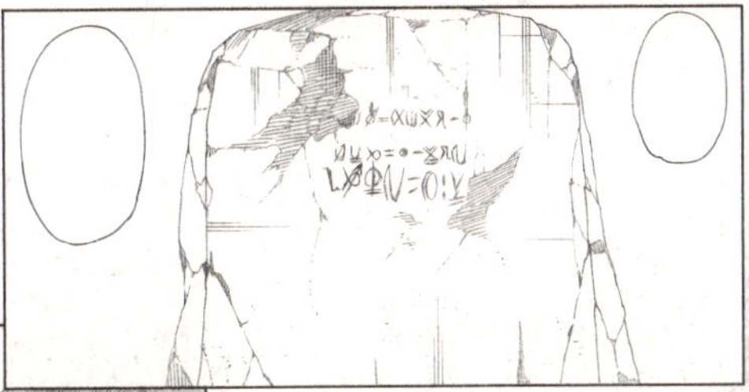

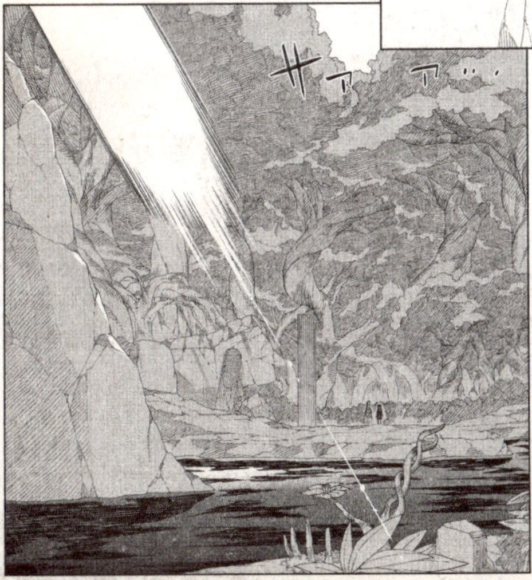
サァ ァ…

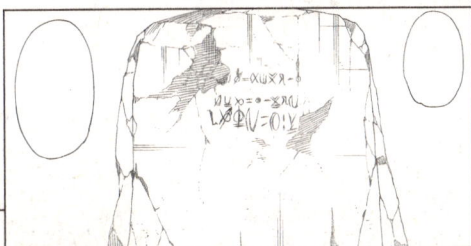

Within the lore surrounding Phalam, it is written: "Long ago, a highly advanced civilization flourished upon the island of Maadarah. Lady Sakuya used their technology to bring 'Atoma' into being." As if to prove the truth of these words, strange phenomena unexplainable by the science of Gulgraf sometimes manifest in Phalam's waters.

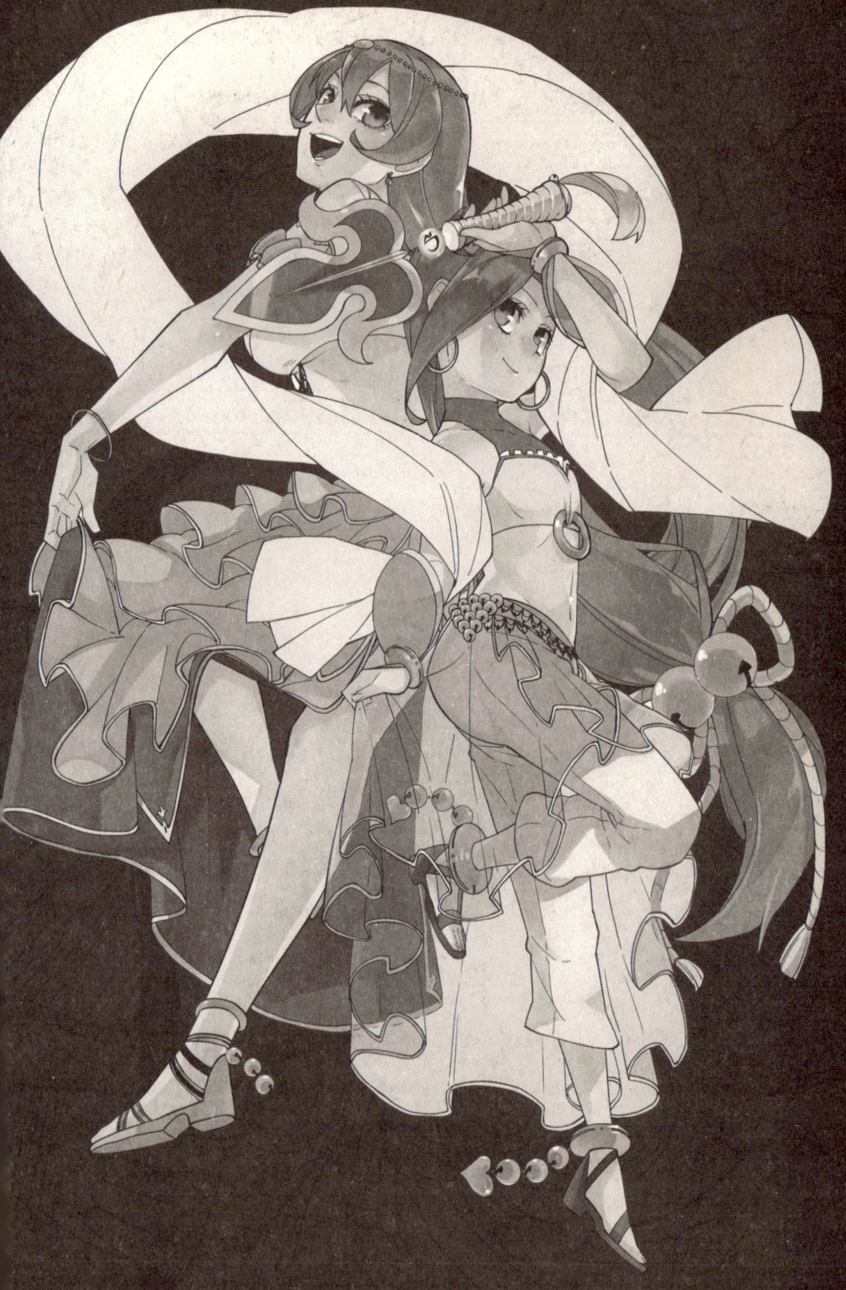

Next Volume

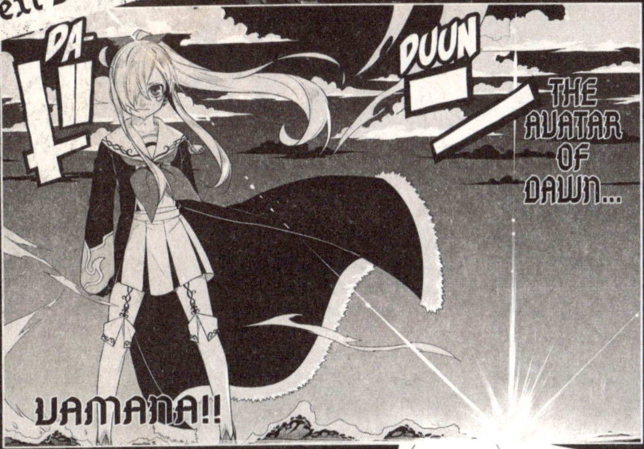

DA-
DUUN
THE AVATAR OF DAWN...
VAMANA!!

Through the strength of her friends, Yachiyo has obtained a new Avatar!! How will the battle with Tenka end...?!

In order to gain information about the goddess Sakuya, and to search for more of the Twelve, Yachiyo's group heads to the Country of Divination, Bodhi!!

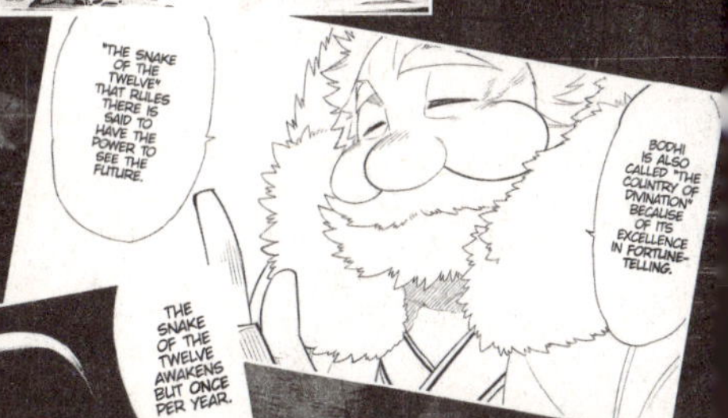

BODHI IS ALSO CALLED "THE COUNTRY OF DIVINATION" BECAUSE OF ITS EXCELLENCE IN FORTUNE-TELLING.
"THE SNAKE OF THE TWELVE" THAT RULES THERE IS SAID TO HAVE THE POWER TO SEE THE FUTURE.

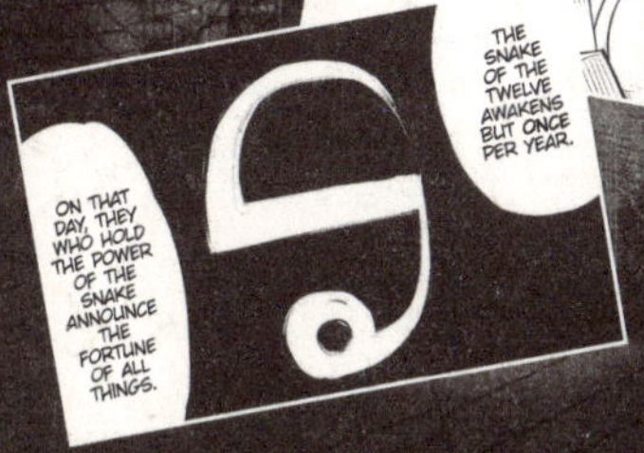

THE SNAKE OF THE TWELVE AWAKENS BUT ONCE PER YEAR.
ON THAT DAY, THEY WHO HOLD THE POWER OF THE SNAKE ANNOUNCE THE FORTUNE OF ALL THINGS.

NIRVANA
ニルヴァーナ

Volume 3 comic chronicling a new Heaven and Earth brings new developments!

NIRVANA

st ... VOLUME 2

COVER DESIGN
Nicky Lim

PROOFREADER
Danielle King
Brett Hallahan

ASSISTANT EDITOR
Jenn Grunigen

PRODUCTION ASSISTANT
CK Russell

PRODUCTION MANAGER
Lissa Pattillo

EDITOR-IN-CHIEF
Adam Arnold

PUBLISHER
Jason DeAngelis

... LACE

... KADOKAWA CORPORATION, Tokyo.

... with KADOKAWA CORPORATION, Tokyo.

Seven Seas books may be purchased in bulk for promotional, educational, or business use. Please contact your local bookseller or the Macmillan Corporate and Premium Sales Department at 1-800-221-7945, extension 5442, or by e-mail at MacmillanSpecialMarkets@macmillan.com.

Seven Seas and the Seven Seas logo are trademarks of Seven Seas Entertainment, LLC. All rights reserved.

ISBN: 978-1-626926-51-6

Printed in Canada

First Printing: March 2018

10 9 8 7 6 5 4 3 2 1

FOLLOW US ONLINE: **www.sevenseasentertainment.com**

READING DIRECTIONS

This book reads from *right to left*, Japanese style. If this is your first time reading manga, you start reading from the top right panel on each page and take it from there. If you get lost, just follow the numbered diagram here. It may seem backwards at first, but you'll get the hang of it! Have fun!!

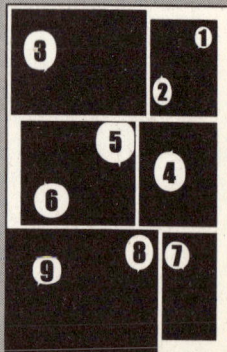